John Lothrop Motley

# The Life and Death of John of Barneveld, Advocate of Holland

with a view of the primary causes and movements of the thirty years' war - Vol. 1

John Lothrop Motley

**The Life and Death of John of Barneveld, Advocate of Holland**
*with a view of the primary causes and movements of the thirty years' war - Vol. 1*

ISBN/EAN: 9783337387730

Printed in Europe, USA, Canada, Australia, Japan

Cover: Foto ©Andreas Hilbeck / pixelio.de

More available books at **www.hansebooks.com**

VIEW OF THE VYVERBERG AT THE HAGUE.

# THE LIFE AND DEATH

OF

# JOHN OF BARNEVELD

ADVOCATE OF HOLLAND

WITH

*A VIEW OF THE PRIMARY CAUSES AND MOVEMENTS
OF THE THIRTY YEARS' WAR*

BY

## JOHN LOTHROP MOTLEY, D.C.L., LL.D.

CORRESPONDING MEMBER OF THE INSTITUTE OF FRANCE, ETC.

IN TWO VOLUMES—Vol. I

WITH ILLUSTRATIONS

NEW YORK
HARPER & BROTHERS, PUBLISHERS
FRANKLIN SQUARE

# PREFACE.

THESE volumes make a separate work in themselves. They form also the natural sequel to the other histories already published by the Author, as well as the necessary introduction to that concluding portion of his labours which he has always desired to lay before the public; a History of the Thirty Years' War.

For the two great wars which successively established the independence of Holland and the disintegration of Germany are in reality but one; a prolonged Tragedy of Eighty Years. The brief pause, which in the Netherlands was known as the Twelve Years' Truce with Spain, was precisely the epoch in which the elements were slowly and certainly gathering for the renewal over nearly the whole surface of civilized Europe of that immense conflict which for more than forty years had been raging within the narrow precincts of the Netherlands.

The causes and character of the two wars were essentially the same. There were many changes of persons and of scenery during a struggle which lasted for nearly three generations of mankind; yet a natural succession both of actors, motives, and events will be observed from the beginning to the close.

The designs of Charles V. to establish universal monarchy, which he had passionately followed for a lifetime through a series of colossal crimes against humanity and of private misdeeds against individuals, such as it has rarely been permitted to a single despot to perpetrate, had been baffled at last. Disappointed, broken, but even to our own generation never completely unveiled, the tyrant had withdrawn from the stage of human affairs, leaving his son to carry on the great conspiracy against Human Right, independence of nations, liberty of thought, and equality of religions, with the additional vigour which sprang from intensity of conviction.

For Philip possessed at least that superiority over his father that he was a sincere bigot. In the narrow and gloomy depths of his soul he had doubtless persuaded himself that it was necessary for the redemption of the human species that the empire of the world should be vested in his hands, that Protestantism in all its forms should be extirpated as a malignant disease, and that to behead, torture, burn alive, and bury alive all heretics who opposed the decree of himself and the Holy Church was the highest virtue by which he could merit Heaven.

The father would have permitted Protestantism if Protestantism would have submitted to universal monarchy. There would have been small difficulty in the early part of his reign in effecting a compromise between Rome and Augsburg, had the gigantic secular ambition of Charles not preferred to weaken the Church and to convert conscientious religious reform into political mutiny ; a crime against him who claimed the sovereignty of Christendom.

The materials for the true history of that reign lie in the Archives of Spain, Austria, Rome, Venice, and the Netherlands, and in many other places. When out of them one day a complete and authentic narrative shall have been constructed, it will be seen how completely the policy of Charles foreshadowed and necessitated that of Philip, how logically, under the successors of Philip, the Austrian dream of universal empire ended in the shattering, in the minute subdivision, and the reduction to a long impotence of that Germanic Empire which had really belonged to Charles.

Unfortunately the great Republic which, notwithstanding the aid of England on the one side and of France on the other, had withstood almost single-handed the onslaughts of Spain, now allowed the demon of religious hatred to enter into its body at the first epoch of peace, although it had successfully exorcised the evil spirit during the long and terrible war.

There can be no doubt whatever that the discords within the interior of the Dutch Republic during the period of the Truce, and their tragic catastrophe, had weakened her purpose and partially paralysed her arm. When the noble Commonwealth went forward to the renewed and general conflict which succeeded the concentrated one in which it had been the chief actor, the effect of those misspent twelve years became apparent.

Indeed the real continuity of the war was scarcely broken by the fitful armistice. The death of John of Cleve, an event almost simultaneous with the conclusion of the Truce, seemed to those gifted with political vision the necessary precursor of a new and more general war.

The secret correspondence of Barneveld shows the almost prophetic accuracy with which he indicated the course of events and the approach of an almost universal conflict, while that tragedy was still in the future, and was to be enacted after he had been laid in his bloody grave. No man then living was so accustomed as he was to sweep the political horizon, and to estimate the signs and portents of the times. No statesman was left in Europe during the epoch of the Twelve Years' Truce to compare with him in experience, breadth of vision, political tact, or administrative sagacity.

Imbued with the grand traditions and familiar with the great personages of a most heroic epoch ; the trusted friend or respected counsellor of William the Silent, Henry IV., Elizabeth, and the sages and soldiers on whom they leaned; having been employed during an already long lifetime in the administration of greatest affairs, he stood alone after the deaths of Henry of France and the second Cecil, and the retirement of Sully, among the natural leaders of mankind.

To the England of Elizabeth, of Walsingham, Raleigh, and the Cecils, had succeeded the Great Britain of James, with his Carrs and Carletons, Nauntons, Lakes, and Winwoods. France, widowed of Henry and waiting for Richelieu, lay in the clutches of Concini's, Epernons, and Bouillons, bound hand and foot to Spain. Germany, falling from Rudolph to Matthias, saw Styrian Ferdinand in the background ready to shatter the fabric of a hundred years of attempted Reformation. In the Republic of the Netherlands were the great soldier and the only remaining statesman of the age. At a moment when the breathing space had been agreed upon before the conflict should be renewed, on a wider field than ever, between Spanish-Austrian world-empire and independence of the nations; between the ancient and only Church and the spirit of religious Equality; between popular Right and royal and sacerdotal Despotism; it would have been desirable that the soldier and the statesman should stand side by side, and that the fortunate Confederacy, gifted with two such champions and placed by its own achievements at the very head of the great party of resistance, should be true to herself.

These volumes contain a slight and rapid sketch of Barneveld's career up to the point at which the Twelve Years' Truce with Spain was signed in the year 1609. In previous works the Author has attempted to assign the great Advocate's place as part and parcel of history during the continuance of the War for Independence. During the period of the Truce he will be found the central figure. The history of Europe, especially of the Netherlands, Britain, France, and Germany, cannot be thoroughly appreciated without a knowledge of the designs, the labours, and the fate of Barneveld.

The materials for estimating his character and judging his judges lie in the national archives of the land of which he was so long the foremost citizen. But they have not long been accessible. The letters, state papers, and other documents remain unprinted, and have rarely been read. M. van Deventer has published three most interesting volumes of the Advocate's correspondence, but they reach only to the beginning of 1609. He has suspended his labours exactly at the moment when these volumes begin. I have carefully studied however nearly the whole of that correspondence, besides a mass of other papers. The labour is not light, for the handwriting of the great Advocate is perhaps the worst that ever existed, and the papers, although kept in the admirable order which distinguishes the Archives of the Hague, have passed through many hands at former epochs before reaching their natural destination in the treasure-house of the nation. Especially the documents connected with the famous trial were for a long time hidden from mortal view, for Barneveld's judges had bound themselves by oath to bury the proceedings out of sight. And the concealment lasted for centuries. Very recently a small portion of those papers has been published by the Historical Society of Utrecht. The "Verhooren," or Interrogatories of the Judges, and the replies of Barneveld, have thus been laid before the reading public of Holland, while within the last two years the distinguished and learned historian, Professor Fruin, has edited the "Verhooren" of Hugo Grotius.

But papers like these, important as they are, make but

a slender portion of the material out of which a judgment concerning these grave events can be constructed. I do not therefore offer an apology for the somewhat copious extracts which I have translated and given in these volumes from the correspondence of Barneveld and from other manuscripts of great value—most of them in the Royal Archives of Holland and Belgium — which are unknown to the public.

I have avoided as much as possible any dealings with the theological controversies so closely connected with the events which I have attempted to describe. This work aims at being a political study. The subject is full of lessons, examples, and warnings for the inhabitants of all free states. Especially now that the republican system of government is undergoing a series of experiments with more or less success in one hemisphere—while in our own land it is consolidated, powerful, and unchallenged—will the conflicts between the spirits of national centralization and of provincial sovereignty, and the struggle between the church, the sword, and the magistracy for supremacy in a free commonwealth, as revealed in the first considerable republic of modern history, be found suggestive of deep reflection.

Those who look in this work for a history of the Synod of Dordtrecht will look in vain. The Author has neither wish nor power to grapple with the mysteries and passions which at that epoch possessed so many souls. The Assembly marks a political period. Its political aspects have been anxiously examined, but beyond the ecclesiastical threshold there has been no attempt to penetrate.

It was necessary for my purpose to describe in some detail the relations of Henry IV. with the Dutch Republic during the last and most pregnant year of his life, which makes the first of the present history. These relations are of European importance, and the materials for appreciating them are of unexpected richness, in the Dutch and Belgian Archives.

Especially the secret correspondence, now at the Hague, of that very able diplomatist Francis Aerssens with Barneveld during the years 1609, 1610, and 1611, together with many papers at Brussels, are full of vital importance.

They throw much light both on the vast designs which filled the brain of Henry at this fatal epoch and on his extraordinary infatuation for the young Princess of Condé by which they were traversed, and which was productive of such widespread political and tragical results. This episode forms a necessary portion of my theme, and has therefore been set forth from original sources.

I am under renewed obligations to my friend M. Gachard, the eminent publicist and archivist of Belgium, for his constant and friendly offices to me (which I have so often experienced before), while studying the documents under his charge relating to this epoch ; especially the secret correspondence of Archduke Albert with Philip III. and his ministers, and with Pecquius, the Archduke's agent at Paris.

It is also a great pleasure to acknowledge the unceasing courtesy and zealous aid rendered me during my renewed studies in the Archives at the Hague—lasting through nearly two years—by the Chief Archivist, M. van den Berg, and the gentlemen connected with that institution, especially M. de Jonghe and M. Hingman, without whose aid it would have been difficult for me to decipher and to procure copies of the almost illegible holographs of Barneveld.

I must also thank M. van Deventer for communicating copies of some curious manuscripts relating to my subject, some from private archives in Holland, and others from those of Simancas.

A single word only remains to be said in regard to the name of the statesman whose career I have undertaken to describe.

His proper appellation and that by which he has always been known in his own country is Oldenbarneveld, but in his lifetime and always in history from that time to this he has been called Barneveld in English as well as French, and this transformation, as it were, of the name has become so settled a matter that after some hesitation it has been adopted in the present work.

The Author would take this opportunity of expressing his gratitude for the indulgence with which his former attempts to illustrate an important period of European history have been received by the public, and his anxious hope that the present volumes may be thought worthy of attention. They are the result at least of severe and conscientious labour at the original sources of history, but the subject is so complicated and difficult that it may well be feared that the ability to depict and unravel is unequal to the earnestness with which the attempt has been made.

London, 1873.

# CONTENTS OF VOL. I.

## CHAPTER I.



## CHAPTER II.



## CHAPTER III.

## CHAPTER IV.



## CHAPTER V.



## CHAPTER VI.

## CHAPTER VII.



## CHAPTER VIII.



## CHAPTER IX.



## CHAPTER X.

# LIST OF ILLUSTRATIONS.

## VOL. I.



## VOL. II.

# THE LIFE AND DEATH

## OF

# JOHN OF BARNEVELD.

## CHAPTER I.

John of Barneveld the Founder of the Commonwealth of the United
Provinces—Maurice of Orange Stadholder, but Servant to the States-
General—The Union of Utrecht maintained—Barneveld makes a Compromise between Civil Functionaries and Church Officials—Embassies
to France, England, and to Venice—the Appointment of Arminius to be
Professor of Theology at Leyden creates Dissension—The Catholic League
opposed by the Great Protestant Union—Death of the Duke of Cleve
and Struggle for his Succession—The Elector of Brandenburg and
Palatine of Neuburg hold the Duchies at Barneveld's Advice against the
Emperor, though having Rival Claims themselves—Negotiations with
the King of France—He becomes the Ally of the States-General to
Protect the Possessory Princes, and prepares for war.

I propose to retrace the history of a great statesman's
career. That statesman's name, but for the dark and tragic
scenes with which it was ultimately associated, might after
the lapse of two centuries and a half have faded into comparative oblivion, so impersonal and shadowy his presence
would have seemed upon the great European theatre where
he was so long a chief actor, and where his efforts and his
achievements were foremost among those productive of long
enduring and widespread results.

There is no doubt whatever that John of Barneveld,
Advocate and Seal Keeper of the little province of Holland
during forty years of as troubled and fertile an epoch as any
in human history, was second to none of his contemporary
statesmen. Yet the singular constitution and historical

position of the republic whose destinies he guided and the peculiar and abnormal office which he held combined to cast a veil over his individuality. The ever teeming brain, the restless almost omnipresent hand, the fertile pen, the eloquent and ready tongue, were seen, heard, and obeyed by the great European public, by the monarchs, statesmen, and warriors of the time, at many critical moments of history, but it was not John of Barneveld that spoke to the world. Those "high and puissant Lords my masters the States-General" personified the young but already majestic republic. Dignified, draped, and concealed by that overshadowing title the informing and master spirit performed its never ending task.

Those who study the enormous masses of original papers in the archives of the country will be amazed to find how the penmanship, most difficult to decipher, of the Advocate meets them at every turn. Letters to monarchs, generals, ambassadors, resolutions of councils, of sovereign assemblies, of trading corporations, of great Indian companies, legal and historical disquisitions of great depth and length on questions agitating Europe, constitutional arguments, drafts of treaties among the leading powers of the world, instructions to great commissions, plans for European campaigns, vast combinations covering the world, alliances of empire, scientific expeditions and discoveries—papers such as these, covered now with the satirical dust of centuries, written in the small, crabbed, exasperating characters which make Barneveld's handwriting almost cryptographic, were once, when fairly engrossed and sealed with the great seal of the haughty burgher-aristocracy, the documents which occupied the close attention of the cabinets of Christendom.

It is not unfrequent to find four or five important despatches compressed almost in miniature upon one sheet of gigantic foolscap. It is also curious to find each one of these rough drafts conscientiously beginning in the statesman's own hand with the elaborate phrases of compliment belonging to the epoch such as "Noble, strenuous, severe, highly honourable, very learned, very discreet, and very wise masters," and ending with "May the Lord God Almighty eternally preserve you and hold you in His holy keeping in this world and for ever"—decorations which one might have thought it safe to leave to be filled in by the secretary or copying clerk.

Thus there have been few men at any period whose lives have been more closely identical than his with a national history. There have been few great men in any history whose names have become less familiar to the world, and lived less in the mouths of posterity. Yet there can be no doubt that if William the Silent was the founder of the independence of the United Provinces Barneveld was the founder of the Commonwealth itself. He had never the opportunity, perhaps he might have never had the capacity, to make such prodigious sacrifices in the cause of country as the great prince had done. But he had served his country strenuously from youth to old age with an abiding sense of duty, a steadiness of purpose, a broad vision, a firm grasp, and an opulence of resource such as not one of his compatriots could even pretend to rival.

Had that country of which he was so long the first citizen maintained until our own day the same proportionate position among the empires of Christendom as it held in the seventeenth century, the name of John of Barneveld would have perhaps been as familiar to all men as it is at this moment to nearly every inhabitant of the Netherlands. Even now political passion is almost as ready to flame forth either in ardent affection or enthusiastic hatred as if two centuries and a half had not elapsed since his death. His name is so typical of a party, a polity, and a faith, so indelibly associated with a great historical cataclysm, as to render it difficult even for the grave, the conscientious, the learned, the patriotic of his own compatriots to speak of him with absolute impartiality.

A foreigner who loves and admires all that is great and noble in the history of that famous republic and can have no hereditary bias as to its ecclesiastical or political theories may at least attempt the task with comparative coldness, although conscious of inability to do thorough justice to a most complex subject.

In former publications devoted to Netherland history I have endeavoured to trace the course of events of which the life and works of the Advocate were a vital ingredient down to the period when Spain after more than forty years of hard fighting virtually acknowledged the independence of the Republic and concluded with her a truce of twelve years.

That convention was signed in the spring of 1609. The ten ensuing years in Europe were comparatively tranquil, but April 9, they were scarcely to be numbered among the full 1609. and fruitful sheaves of a pacific epoch. It was a pause, a breathing spell during which the sulphurous clouds which had made the atmosphere of Christendom poisonous for nearly half a century had sullenly rolled away, while at every point of the horizon they were seen massing themselves anew in portentous and ever accumulating strength. At any moment the faint and sickly sunshine in which poor exhausted Humanity was essaying a feeble twitter of hope as it plumed itself for a peaceful flight might be again obscured. To us of a remote posterity the momentary division of epochs seems hardly discernible. So rapidly did that fight of Demons which we call the Thirty Years' War tread on the heels of the forty years' struggle for Dutch Independence which had just been suspended that we are accustomed to think and speak of the Eighty Years' War as one pure, perfect, sanguinary whole.

And indeed the Tragedy which was soon to sweep solemnly across Europe was foreshadowed in the first fitful years of peace. The throb of the elementary forces already shook the soil of Christendom. The fantastic but most significant conflict in the territories of the dead Duke of Cleve reflected the distant and gigantic war as in a mirage. It will be necessary to direct the reader's attention at the proper moment to that episode, for it was one in which the beneficent sagacity of Barneveld was conspicuously exerted in the cause of peace and conservation. Meantime it is not agreeable to reflect that this brief period of nominal and armed peace which the Republic had conquered after nearly two generations of warfare was employed by her in tearing her own flesh. The heroic sword which had achieved such triumphs in the cause of freedom could have been better employed than in an attempt at political suicide.

In a picture of the last decade of Barneveld's eventful life his personality may come more distinctly forward perhaps than in previous epochs. It will however be difficult to disentangle a single thread from the great historical tapestry of the Republic and of Europe in which his life and achievements are interwoven. He was a public man in the fullest sense of the word, and without his presence and influence the record of Holland, France, Spain, Britain, and Germany might have been essentially modified.

The Republic was so integral a part of that system which divided Europe into two great hostile camps according to creeds rather than frontiers that the history of its foremost citizen touches at every point the general history of Christendom.

The great peculiarity of the Dutch constitution at this epoch was that no principle was absolutely settled. In throwing off a foreign tyranny and successfully vindicating national independence the burghers and nobles had not had leisure to lay down any organic law. Nor had the day for profound investigation of the political or social contract arrived. Men dealt almost exclusively with facts, and when the facts arranged themselves illogically and incoherently the mischief was grave and difficult to remedy. It is not a trifling inconvenience for an organized commonwealth to be in doubt as to where, in whom, and of what nature is its sovereignty. Yet this was precisely the condition of the United Netherlands. To the external world so dazzling were the reputation and the achievements of their great captain that he was looked upon by many as the legitimate chief of the state and doubtless friendly monarchs would have cordially welcomed him into their brotherhood.

During the war he had been surrounded by almost royal state. Two hundred officers lived daily at his table. Great nobles and scions of sovereign houses were his pupils or satellites. The splendour of military despotism and the awe inspired by his unquestioned supremacy in what was deemed the greatest of all sciences invested the person of Maurice of Nassau with a grandeur which many a crowned potentate might envy. His ample appointments united with the spoils of war provided him with almost royal revenues, even before the death of his elder brother Philip William had placed in his hands the principality and wealthy possessions of Orange. Hating contradiction, arbitrary by instinct and by military habit, impatient of criticism, and having long acknowledged no master in the chief business of state, he found himself at the conclusion of the truce with his great occupation gone, and, although generously provided for by the treasury of the Republic, yet with an income proportionately limited.

Politics and theology were fields in which he had hardly served an apprenticeship, and it was possible that when he should step forward as a master in those complicated and difficult pursuits, soon to absorb the attention of the Commonwealth and the world, it might appear that war was not the only science that required serious preliminary studies.

Meantime he found himself not a king, not the master of a nominal republic, but the servant of the States-General, and the limited stadholder of five out of seven separate provinces.

And the States-General were virtually John of Barneveld. Could antagonism be more sharply defined?   Jealousy, that potent principle which controls the regular movements and accounts for the aberrations of humanity in widest spheres as well as narrowest circles far more generally and conclusively than philosophers or historians have been willing to admit, began forthwith to manifest its subtle and irresistible influence.

And there were not to be wanting acute and dangerous schemers who saw their profit in augmenting its intensity.

The Seven Provinces, when the truce of twelve years had been signed, were neither exhausted nor impoverished.   Yet they had just emerged from a forty years' conflict such as no people in human history had ever waged against a foreign tyranny.   They had need to repose and recruit, but they stood among the foremost great powers of the day.   It is not easy in imagination to thrust back the present leading empires of the earth into the contracted spheres of their not remote past.   But to feel how a little confederacy of seven provinces loosely tied together by an ill-defined treaty could hold so prominent and often so controlling a place in the European system of the seventeenth century, we must remember that there was then no Germany, no Russia, no Italy, no United States of America, scarcely even a Great Britain in the sense which belongs to that mighty empire now.

France, Spain, England, the Pope, and the Emperor were

the leading powers with which the Netherlands were daily called on to solve great problems and try conclusions ; the study of political international equilibrium, now rapidly and perhaps fortunately becoming one of the lost arts, being then the most indispensable duty of kings and statesmen.

Spain and France, which had long since achieved for themselves the political union of many independent kingdoms and states into which they had been divided were the most considerable powers and of necessity rivals.  Spain, or rather the House of Austria divided into its two great branches, still pursued its persistent and by no means fantastic dream of universal monarchy.  Both Spain and France could dispose of somewhat larger resources absolutely, although not relatively, than the Seven Provinces, while at least trebling them in population.  The yearly revenue of Spain after deduction of its pledged resources was perhaps equal to a million sterling, and that of France with the same reservation was about as much.  England had hardly been able to levy and make up a yearly income of more than £600,000 or £700,000 at the end of Elizabeth's reign or in the first years of James, while the Netherlands had often proved themselves capable of furnishing annually ten or twelve millions of florins, which would be the equivalent of nearly a million sterling.[1]

The yearly revenues of the whole monarchy of the Imperial house of Habsburg can scarcely be stated at a higher figure than £350,000.[2]

Thus the political game—for it was a game—was by no means a desperate one for the Netherlands, nor the resources

---

[1] The best sources for these statistics, imperfect as they are, will be found in the 'Relazioni' of the Venetian envoys, Molin, Foscarini, Contarini, Correr, and others.  See the published collections of Barozzi and Berchat, Venice, 1863.

[2] Gindely, 158.

of the various players so unequally distributed as at first sight it might appear.

The emancipation of the Provinces from the grasp of Spain and the establishment by them of a commonwealth, for that epoch a very free one, and which contained within itself the germs of a larger liberty, religious, political, and commercial, than had yet been known, was already one of the most considerable results of the Reformation. The probability of its continued and independent existence was hardly believed in by potentate or statesman outside its own borders, and had not been very long a decided article of faith even within them. The knotty problem of an acknowledgment of that existence, the admission of the new-born state into the family of nations, and a temporary peace guaranteed by two great powers, had at last been solved mainly by the genius of Barneveld working amid many disadvantages and against great obstructions. The truce had been made, and it now needed all the skill, coolness, and courage of a practical and original statesman to conduct the affairs of the Confederacy. The troubled epoch of peace was even now heaving with warlike emotions, and was hardly less stormy than the war which had just been suspended.

The Republic was like a raft loosely strung together, floating almost on a level of the ocean, and often half submerged, but freighted with inestimable treasures for itself and the world. It needed an unsleeping eye and a powerful brain to conduct her over the quicksands and through the whirlpools of an unmapped and intricate course.

The sovereignty of the country so far as its nature could be satisfactorily analysed seemed to be scattered through, and inherent in each one of, the multitudinous boards of magistracy—close corporations, self-elected—by which every city was governed. Nothing could be more preposterous. Practically, however, those boards were represented by deputies in each of the seven provincial assemblies, and these again sent councillors from among their number to the general assembly which was that of their High Mightinesses the Lords States-General.[1]

The Province of Holland, being richer and more powerful than all its six sisters combined, was not unwilling to impose a supremacy which on the whole was practically conceded by the rest. Thus the Union of Utrecht established in 1579 was maintained for want of anything better as the foundation of the Commonwealth.

The Advocate and Keeper of the Great Seal of that province was therefore virtually prime minister, president, attorney-general, finance minister, and minister of foreign affairs of the whole republic. This was Barneveld's position. He took the lead in the deliberations both of the States of Holland and the States-General, moved resolutions, advocated great measures of state, gave heed to their execution, collected the votes, summed up the proceedings, corresponded with and instructed ambassadors, received and negotiated with foreign ministers, besides directing and holding in his hands the various threads of the home policy and the rapidly growing colonial system of the Republic.

All this work Barneveld had been doing for thirty years.

The Reformation was by no means assured even in the

---

[1] Such a constitution, rudimentary and almost chaotic, would have been impossible on a large territorial scale. Nothing but the exiguity of the domain prevented its polity from falling into imbecility instead of manifesting that extraordinary vigour which astonished the world. The secret of its force lay in the democratic principle, the sentiment of national independence and popular freedom of movement which underlay these petty municipal sovereignties. They were indeed so numerous that, while claiming to be oligarchies, they made up a kind of irregular democracy. Had such a constitution been copied instead of avoided by the fathers of our own republic the consequences would have probably been disastrous. Disintegration of the commonwealth at an early day, and possibly the birth of a hundred rival states, with different religions, laws, and even languages— such might have been the phenomena exhibited on what is now the soil of the United States.

lands where it had at first made the most essential progress. But the existence of the new commonwealth depended on the success of that great movement which had called it into being. Losing ground in France, fluctuating in England, Protestantism was apparently more triumphant in vast territories where the ancient Church was one day to recover its mastery. Of the population of Bohemia, there were perhaps ten Protestants to one Papist,[1] while in the United Netherlands at least one-third of the people were still attached to the Catholic faith.

The great religious struggle in Bohemia and other dominions of the Habsburg family was fast leading to a war of which no man could even imagine the horrors or foresee the vast extent. The Catholic League and the Protestant Union were slowly arranging Europe into two mighty confederacies. They were to give employment year after year to millions of mercenary freebooters who were to practise murder, pillage, and every imaginable and unimaginable outrage as the most legitimate industry that could occupy mankind. The Holy Empire which so ingeniously combined the worst characteristics of despotism and republicanism kept all Germany and half Europe in the turmoil of a perpetual presidential election. A theatre where trivial personages and graceless actors performed a tragi-comedy of mingled folly, intrigue, and crime, and where earnestness and vigour were destined to be constantly baffled, now offered the principal stage for the entertainment and excitement of Christendom.

There was but one king in Europe, Henry the Béarnese. The men who sat on the thrones in Madrid, Vienna, London, would have lived and died unknown but for the crowns they wore, and while there were plenty of bustling politicians here and there in Christendom, there were not many statesmen.

---

[1] Gindely.

Among them there was no stronger man than John of
Barneveld, and no man had harder or more complicated
work to do.

Born in Amersfoort in 1547, of the ancient and knightly
house of Oldenbarneveldt, of patrician blood through all
his ancestors both male and female, he was not the heir
to large possessions, and was a diligent student and hard-
working man from youth upward. He was not wont to
boast of his pedigree until in later life, being assailed by
vilest slander, all his kindred nearest or most remote being
charged with every possible and unmentionable crime, and
himself stigmatized as sprung from the lowest kennels of
humanity—as if thereby his private character and public
services could be more legitimately blackened—he was
stung into exhibiting to the world the purity and antiquity
of his escutcheon, and a roll of respectably placed, well
estated, and authentically noble, if not at all illustrious,
forefathers in his country's records of the previous centuries.

Without an ancestor at his back he might have valued
himself still more highly on the commanding place he held
in the world by right divine of intellect, but as the father
of lies seemed to have kept his creatures so busy with the
Barneveld genealogy, it was not amiss for the statesman
once for all to make the truth known.

His studies in the universities of Holland, France, Italy,
and Germany had been profound. At an early age he was
one of the first civilians of the time. His manhood being
almost contemporary with the great war of freedom, he had
served as a volunteer and at his own expense through
several campaigns, having nearly lost his life in the disastrous attempt to relieve the siege of Haarlem, and having
been so disabled by sickness and exposure at the heroic
leaguer of Leyden as to have been deprived of the joy of
witnessing its triumphant conclusion.

Successfully practising his profession afterwards before the tribunals of Holland, he had been·called at the comparatively early age of twenty-nine to the important post of Chief Pensionary of Rotterdam. So long as 1576. William the Silent lived, that great prince was all in all to his country, and Barneveld was proud and happy to be among the most trusted and assiduous of his counsellors.

When the assassination of William seemed for an instant to strike the Republic with paralysis, Barneveld was foremost among the statesmen of Holland to spring forward and help to inspire it with renewed energy.

The almost completed negotiations for conferring the sovereignty, not of the Confederacy, but of the Province of Holland, upon the Prince had been abruptly brought to an end by his death. To confer that sovereign countship on his son Maurice, then a lad of eighteen and a student at Leyden, would have seemed to many at so terrible a crisis an act of madness, although Barneveld had been willing to suggest and promote the scheme. The confederates under his guidance soon hastened however to lay the sovereignty, and if not the sovereignty, the protectorship, of all the provinces at the feet first of England and then of France.

Barneveld was at the head of the embassy, and indeed was the indispensable head of all important embassies to each of those two countries throughout all this portion of his career. Both monarchs refused, almost spurned, the offered crown in which was involved a war with the greatest power in the world, with no compensating dignity or benefit, as it was thought, beside.

Then Elizabeth, although declining the sovereignty, promised assistance and sent the Earl of Leicester as governor-general at the head of a contingent of English troops. Precisely to prevent the consolidation thus threatened of the Provinces into one union, a measure which had been attempted more than once in the Burgundian epoch, and always successfully resisted by the spirit of provincial separatism, Barneveld now proposed and carried the appointment of Maurice of Nassau to the stadholdership of Holland. This was done against great opposition and amid fierce debate. Soon afterwards Barneveld was vehemently urged by the nobles and regents of the cities of Holland to accept the post of Advocate of that province. After repeatedly declining the arduous and most responsible office, he was at last induced to accept it. He did it under the remark-

1586.

able condition that in case any negotiation should be undertaken for the purpose of bringing back the Province of Holland under the dominion of the King of Spain, he should be considered as from that moment relieved from the service.[1]

His brother Elias Barneveld succeeded him as Pensionary of Rotterdam, and thenceforth the career of the Advocate is identical with the history of the Netherlands. Although a native of Utrecht, he was competent to exercise such functions in Holland, a special and ancient convention between those two provinces allowing the citizens of either to enjoy legal and civic rights in both. Gradually, without intrigue or inordinate ambition, but from force of circumstances and the commanding power of the man, the native authority stamped upon his forehead, he became the political head of the Confederacy. He created and maintained a system of public credit absolutely marvellous in the circumstances, by means of which an otherwise impossible struggle was carried to a victorious end.

When the stadholderate of the provinces of Gelderland, Utrecht, and Overyssel became vacant, it was again Barneveld's potent influence and sincere attachment to the House of Nassau that procured the election of Maurice to those

<hr>

[1] 'Waaragtige Historie,' ed. 1670, p. 23.

posts. Thus within six years after his father's death the youthful soldier who had already given proof of his surpassing military genius had become governor, commander-in-chief, and high admiral, of five of the seven provinces constituting the Confederacy.

At about the same period the great question of Church and State, which Barneveld had always felt to be among the vital problems of the age, and on which his opinions were most decided, came up for partial solution. It would have been too much to expect the opinion of any statesman to be so much in advance of his time as to favor religious equality. Toleration of various creeds, including the Roman Catholic, so far as abstinence from inquisition into consciences and private parlours could be called toleration, was secured, and that was a considerable step in advance of the practice of the sixteenth century. Burning, hanging, and burying alive of culprits guilty of another creed than the dominant one had become obsolete. But there was an established creed—the Reformed religion, founded on the Netherland Confession and the Heidelberg Catechism. And there was one established principle then considered throughout Europe the grand result of the Reformation; "*Cujus regio ejus religio;*" which was in reality as impudent an invasion of human right as any heaven-born dogma of Infallibility. The sovereign of a country, having appropriated the revenues of the ancient church, prescribed his own creed to his subjects. In the royal conscience were included the million consciences of his subjects. The inevitable result in a country like the Netherlands, without a personal sovereign, was a struggle between the new church and the civil government for mastery. And at this period, and always in Barneveld's opinion, the question of dogma was subordinate to that of church government. That there should be no authority over the King had been settled in England.

Henry VIII., Elizabeth, and afterwards James, having become popes in their own realm, had no great hostility to, but rather an affection for, ancient dogma and splendid ceremonial. But in the Seven Provinces, even as in France, Germany, and Switzerland, the reform where it had been effected at all had been more thorough, and there was little left of Popish pomp or aristocratic hierarchy. Nothing could be severer than the simplicity of the Reformed Church, nothing more imperious than its dogma, nothing more infallible than its creed. It was the true religion, and there was none other. But to whom belonged the ecclesiastical edifices, the splendid old minsters in the cities—raised by the people's confiding piety and the purchased remission of their sins in a bygone age—and the humbler but beautiful parish churches in every town and village? To the State, said Barneveld, speaking for government; to the community represented by the states of the provinces, the magistracies of the cities and municipalities. To the Church itself, the one true church represented by its elders, and deacons, and preachers, was the reply.

And to whom belonged the right of prescribing laws and ordinances of public worship, of appointing preachers, church servants, schoolmasters, sextons? To the Holy Ghost inspiring the Class and the Synod, said the Church.

To the civil authority, said the magistrates, by which the churches are maintained, and the salaries of the ecclesiastics paid. The states of Holland are as sovereign as the kings of England or Denmark, the electors of Saxony or Brandenburg, the magistrates of Zürich or Basel or other Swiss cantons. "*Cujus regio ejus religio.*"

In 1590 there was a compromise under the guidance of Barneveld. It was agreed that an appointing board should be established composed of civil functionaries and church officials in equal numbers. Thus should the interests of religion and of education be maintained.

The compromise was successful enough during the war. External pressure kept down theological passion, and there were as yet few symptoms of schism in the dominant church. But there was to come a time when the struggle between church and government was to break forth with an intensity and to rage to an extent which no man at that moment could imagine.

Towards the end of the century Henry IV. made peace with Spain. It was a trying moment for the Provinces. Barneveld was again sent forth on an embassy to the King. The cardinal point in his policy, as it had ever been in that of William the Silent, was to maintain close friendship with France, whoever might be its ruler. An alliance between that kingdom and Spain would be instantaneous ruin to the Republic. With the French and English sovereigns united with the Provinces, the cause of the Reformation might triumph, the Spanish world-empire be annihilated, national independence secured.

Henry assured the Ambassador that the treaty of Vervins was indispensable, but that he would never desert his old allies. In proof of this, although he had just bound himself to Spain to give no assistance to the Provinces, open or secret, he would furnish them with thirteen hundred thousand crowns, payable at intervals during four years. He was under great obligations to his good friends the States, he said, and nothing in the treaty forbade him to pay his debts.

It was at this period too that Barneveld was employed by the King to attend to certain legal and other private business for which he professed himself too poor at the moment to compensate him. There seems to have been nothing in the usages of the time or country to make the transaction, innocent in itself, in any degree disreputable. The King promised at some future day, when he should be more in funds, to pay him a liberal fee. Barneveld, who a dozen years afterwards received 20,000 florins for his labour, professed that he would much rather have had one thousand at the time.

Thence the Advocate, accompanied by his colleague, Justinus de Nassau, proceeded to England, where they had many stormy interviews with Elizabeth. The Queen swore with many an oath that she too would make peace with Philip, recommended the Provinces to do the same thing with submission to their ancient tyrant, and claimed from the States immediate payment of one million sterling in satisfaction of their old debts to her. It would have been as easy for them at that moment to pay a thousand million. It was at last agreed that the sum of the debt should be fixed at £800,000, and that the cautionary towns should be held in Elizabeth's hands by English troops until all the debt should be discharged. Thus England for a long time afterwards continued to regard itself as in a measure the sovereign and proprietor of the Confederacy, and Barneveld then and there formed the resolve to relieve the country of the incubus, and to recover those cautionary towns and fortresses at the earliest possible moment. So long as foreign soldiers commanded by military governors existed on the soil of the Netherlands, they could hardly account themselves independent. Besides, there was the perpetual and horrid nightmare, that by a sudden pacification between Spain and England those important cities, keys to the country's defence, might be handed over to their ancient tyrant.

Elizabeth had been pacified at last, however, by the eloquence of the Ambassador. "I will assist you even if you were up to the neck in water," she said. "Jusque là," she added, pointing to her chin.

Five years later Barneveld, for the fifth time at the head of a great embassy, was sent to England to congratulate James on his accession. It was then and there that he took measure of the monarch with whom he was destined to have many dealings, and who was to exert so baleful an influence on his career. At last came the time when it was felt that peace between Spain and her revolted provinces might be made. The conservation of their ancient laws, privileges, and charters, the independence of the States, and included therein the freedom to establish the Reformed religion, had been secured by forty years of fighting.

The honour of Spain was saved by a conjunction. She agreed to treat with her old dependencies "*as*" with states over which she had no pretensions. Through virtue of an "*as*," a truce after two years' negotiation, perpetually traversed and secretly countermined by the military party under the influence of Maurice, was carried by the determination of Barneveld. The great objects of the war had been secured. The country was weary of nearly half a century of bloodshed. It was time to remember that there could be such a condition as Peace.

The treaty was signed, ratifications exchanged, and the usual presents of considerable sums of money to the negotiators made. Barneveld earnestly protested against carrying out the custom on this occasion, and urged that those presents should be given for the public use. He was overruled by those who were more desirous of receiving their reward than he was, and he accordingly, in common with the other diplomatists, accepted the gifts.[1]

The various details of these negotiations have been related by the author in other volumes, to which the present one is intended as a sequel. It has been thought necessary merely

[1] 'Waaragt. Hist.' 103.

to recall very briefly a few salient passages in the career of the Advocate up to the period when the present history really opens.

Their bearing upon subsequent events will easily be observed. The truce was the work of Barneveld. It was detested by Maurice and by Maurice's partisans.

" I fear that our enemies and evil reports are the cause of many of our difficulties," said the Advocate to the States' envoy in Paris, in 1606.[1] " You are to pay no heed to private advices. Believe and make others believe that more than one half the inhabitants of the cities and in the open country are inclined to peace. And I believe, in case of continuing adversities, that the other half will not remain constant, principally because the Provinces are robbed of all traffic, prosperity, and navigation, through the actions of France and England. I have always thought it for the advantage of his Majesty to sustain us in such wise as would make us useful in his service. As to his remaining permanently at peace with Spain, that would seem quite out of the question."

The King had long kept, according to treaty, a couple of French regiments in the States' service, and furnished, or was bound to furnish, a certain yearly sum for their support. But the expenses of the campaigning had been rapidly increasing and the results as swiftly dwindling. The Advocate now explained that, " without loss both of important places and of reputation," the States could not help spending every month that they took the field 200,000 florins over and above the regular contributions, and some months a great deal more.[2] This sum, he said, in nine months, would more than eat up the whole subsidy of the King. If they were to be in the field by March or beginning of April, they would require from him an extraordinary

<hr>

[1] Barneveld to F. Aerssens, 18 Jan. 1606. (Hague Arch. MS.)     [2] Ibid.

sum of 200,000 crowns, and as much more in June or July.

Eighteen months *later*, when the magnificent naval victory of Heemskerk in the Bay of Gibraltar[1] had just made a startling interlude to the languishing negotiations for peace, the Advocate again warned the French King of the difficulty in which the Republic still laboured of carrying on the mighty struggle alone. Spain was the common enemy of all. No peace or hope was possible for the leading powers as long as Spain was perpetually encamped in the very heart of Western Europe. The Netherlands were not fighting their own battle merely, but that of freedom and independence against the all-encroaching world-power. And their means to carry on the conflict were dwindling, while at the same time there was a favourable opportunity for cropping some fruit from their previous labours and sacrifices.

" We are led to doubt," he wrote once more to the envoy in France,[2] " whether the King's full powers will come from Spain. This defeat is hard for the Spaniards to digest. Meantime our burdens are quite above our capacity, as you will understand by the enclosed statement, which is made out with much exactness to show what is absolutely necessary for a vigorous defence on land and a respectable position at sea to keep things from entire confusion. The Provinces could raise means for the half of this estimate. But it is a great difference when the means differ one half from the expenses. The sovereignst and most assured remedy would be the one so often demanded, often projected, and sometimes almost prepared for execution, namely that our neighbour kings, princes, and republics should earnestly take the matter in hand and drive the Spaniards and their adherents out of the Netherlands and over the mountains. Their own

---

[1] See 'History of the United Netherlands,' iv. ch. xlvii.
[2] Barneveld to F. Aerssens, 2 June 1607. (Hague Archives MS.)

dignity and security ought not to permit such great bodies of troops of both belligerents permanently massed in the Netherlands. Still less ought they to allow these Provinces to fall into the hands of the Spaniards, whence they could with so much more power and convenience make war upon all kings, princes, and republics. This must be prevented by one means or another. It ought to be enough for every one that we have been between thirty and forty years a firm bulwark against Spanish ambition. Our constancy and patience ought to be strengthened by counsel and by deed in order that we may exist; a Christian sympathy and a small assistance not being sufficient. Believe and cause to be believed that the present condition of our affairs requires more aid in counsel and money than ever before, and that nothing could be better bestowed than to further this end.

"Messieurs Jeannin, Buzenval, and de Russy have been all here these twelve days. We have firm hopes that other kings, princes, and republics will not stay upon formalities, but will also visit the patients here in order to administer sovereign remedies.

"Lend no ear to any flying reports. We say with the wise men over there, '*Metuo Danaos et dona ferentes.*' We know our antagonists well, and trust their hearts no more than before, '*sed ultra posse non est esse.*' To accept more burthens than we can pay for will breed military mutiny; to tax the community above its strength will cause popular tumults, especially in *rebus adversis*, of which the beginnings were seen last year, and without a powerful army the enemy is not to be withstood. I have received your letters to the 17th May. My advice is to trust to his[1] upright proceedings and with patience to overcome all things. Thus shall the detractors and calumniators best be confounded. Assure

---

[1] The King's probably.

his Majesty and his ministers that I will do my utmost to avert our ruin and his Majesty's disservice."

The treaty was made, and from that time forth the antagonism between the eminent statesman and the great military chieftain became inevitable. The importance of the one seemed likely to increase day by day. The occupation of the other for a time was over.

During the war Maurice had been, with exception of Henry IV., the most considerable personage in Europe. He was surrounded with that visible atmosphere of power the poison of which it is so difficult to resist, and through the golden haze of which a mortal seems to dilate for the vulgar eye into the supernatural. The attention of Christendom was perpetually fixed upon him. Nothing like his sieges, his encampments, his military discipline, his scientific campaigning had been seen before in modern Europe. The youthful aristocracy from all countries thronged to his camp to learn the game of war, for he had restored by diligent study of the ancients much that was noble in that pursuit, and had elevated into an art that which had long since degenerated into a system of butchery, marauding, and rapine. And he had fought with signal success and unquestionable heroism the most important and most brilliant pitched battle of the age. He was a central figure of the current history of Europe. Pagan nations looked up to him as one of the leading sovereigns of Christendom. The Emperor of Japan addressed him as his brother monarch, assured him that his subjects trading to that distant empire should be welcomed and protected, and expressed himself ashamed that so great a prince, whose name and fame had spread through the world, should send his subjects to visit a country so distant and unknown, and offer its emperor a friendship which he was unconscious of deserving.[1]

[1] Van Meteren, 651; de la Pise, 752.

He had been a commander of armies and a chief among men since he came to man's estate, and he was now in the very vigour of life, in his forty-second year. Of Imperial descent and closely connected by blood or alliance with many of the most illustrious of reigning houses, the acknowledged master of the most royal and noble of all sciences, he was of the stuff of which kings were made, and belonged by what was then accounted right divine to the family of kings. His father's death had alone prevented his elevation to the throne of Holland, and such possession of half the sovereignty of the United Netherlands would probably have expanded into dominion over all the seven with a not fantastic possibility of uniting the ten still obedient provinces into a single realm. Such a kingdom would have been more populous and far wealthier than contemporary Great Britain and Ireland. Maurice, then a student at Leyden, was too young at that crisis, and his powers too undeveloped to justify any serious attempt to place him in his father's place.

The Netherlands drifted into a confederacy of aristocratic republics, not because they had planned a republic, but because they could not get a king, foreign or native. The documents regarding the offer of the sovereign countship to William remained in the possession of Maurice, and a few years before the peace there had been a private meeting of leading personages, of which Barneveld was the promoter and chief spokesman, to take into consideration the propriety and possibility of conferring that sovereignty upon the son which had virtually belonged to the father. The obstacles were deemed so numerous, and especially the scheme seemed so fraught with danger to Maurice, that it was reluctantly abandoned by his best friends, among whom unquestionably was the Advocate.

There was no reason whatever why the now successful and mature soldier, to whom the country was under such vast obligations, should not aspire to the sovereignty. The Provinces had not pledged themselves to republicanism, but rather to monarchy, and the crown, although secretly coveted by Henry IV., could by no possibility now be conferred on any other man than Maurice. It was no impeachment on his character that he should nourish thoughts in which there was nothing criminal.

But the peace negotiations had opened a chasm. It was obvious enough that Barneveld having now so long exercised great powers, and become as it were the chief magistrate of an important commonwealth, would not be so friendly as formerly to its conversion into a monarchy and to the elevation of the great soldier to its throne. The Advocate had even been sounded, cautiously and secretly, so men believed, by the Princess-Dowager, Louise de Coligny, widow of William the Silent, as to the feasibility of procuring the sovereignty for Maurice. She had done this at the instigation of Maurice, who had expressed his belief that the favourable influence of the Advocate would make success certain and who had represented to her that, as he was himself resolved never to marry, the inheritance after his death would fall to her son Frederick Henry. The Princess, who was of a most amiable disposition, adored her son. Devoted to the House of Nassau and a great admirer of its chief, she had a long interview with Barneveld, in which she urged the scheme upon his attention without in all probability revealing that she had come to him at the solicitation of Maurice.

The Advocate spoke to her with frankness and out of the depths of his heart. He professed an ardent attachment to her family, a profound reverence for the virtues, sacrifices, and achievements of her lamented husband, and a warm desire to do everything to further the interests of the son who had proved himself so worthy of his parentage.

But he proved to her that Maurice, in seeking the sovereignty, was seeking his ruin. The Hollanders, he said, liked to be persuaded and not forced. Having triumphantly shaken off the yoke of a powerful king, they would scarcely consent now to accept the rule of any personal sovereign. The desire to save themselves from the claws of Spain had led them formerly to offer the dominion over them to various potentates. Now that they had achieved peace and independence and were delivered from the fears of Spanish ferocity and French intrigue, they shuddered at the dangers from royal hands out of which they had at last escaped. He believed that they would be capable of tearing in pieces any one who might make the desired proposition. After all, he urged, Maurice was a hundred times more fortunate as he was than if he should succeed in desires so opposed to his own good. This splendour of sovereignty was a false glare which would lead him to a precipice. He had now the power of a sovereign without the envy which ever followed it. Having essentially such power, he ought, like his father, to despise an empty name, which would only make him hated. For it was well known that William the Silent had only yielded to much solicitation, agreeing to accept that which then seemed desirable for the country's good but to him was more than indifferent.

Maurice was captain-general and admiral-general of five provinces. He appointed to governments and to all military office. He had a share of appointment to the magistracies. He had the same advantages and the same authority as had been enjoyed in the Netherlands by the ancient sovereign counts, by the dukes of Burgundy, by Emperor Charles V. himself.

Every one now was in favour of increasing his pensions, his salaries, his material splendour. Should he succeed in seizing the sovereignty, men would envy him even to the ribbands of his pages' and his lackeys' shoes. He turned to the annals of Holland and showed the Princess that there had hardly been a sovereign count against whom his subjects had not revolted, marching generally into the very court-yard of the palace at the Hague in order to take his life.

Convinced by this reasoning, Louise de Coligny had at once changed her mind, and subsequently besought her step-son to give up a project sure to be fatal to his welfare, his peace of mind, and the good of the country. Maurice listened to her coldly, gave little heed to the Advocate's logic, and hated him in his heart from that day forth.

The Princess remained loyal to Barneveld to the last.[1]

Thus the foundation was laid of that terrible enmity which, inflamed by theological passion, was to convert the period of peace into a hell, to rend the Provinces asunder when they had most need of repose, and to lead to tragical results for ever to be deplored. Already in 1607 Francis Aerssens had said that the two had become so embroiled and things had gone so far that one or the other would have to leave the country.[2] He permitted also the ridiculous statement to be made in his house at Paris, that Henry IV. believed the Advocate to have become Spanish, and had declared that Prince Maurice would do well to have him put into a sack and thrown into the sea.[3]

His life had been regularly divided into two halves, the campaigning season and the period of winter quarters. In the one his business and his talk was of camps, marches, sieges, and battles only. In the other he was devoted to his stud, to tennis, to mathematical and mechanical inventions,

---

[1] 'Mémoires de Messire Louis Au-béry, Seigneur du Maurier,' 1680, pp. 183, *sqq.* The story rests en-tirely on the testimony of du Mau-rier, son of the French ambassa-dor so long resident at the Hague, who often recounted it secretly, in all its details, to his family. It has so great intrinsic probability and is sus-tained as to its general bearings by so much of collateral circumstance that I do not hesitate to accept it as substantially accurate.

[2] Vreede, 'Inleiding tot eene Gesch. d. Nederl. Diplomatie,' i. 150.

[3] Ibid. p. 151.

and to chess, of which he was passionately fond, and which he did not play at all well. A Gascon captain serving in the States' army was his habitual antagonist in that game, and, although the stakes were but a crown a game, derived a steady income out of his gains, which were more than equal to his pay. The Prince was sulky when he lost, sitting, when the candles were burned out and bed-time had arrived, with his hat pulled over his brows, without bidding his guest good night, and leaving him to find his way out as he best could ; and, on the contrary, radiant with delight when successful, calling for valets to light the departing captain through the corridor, and accompanying him to the door of the apartment himself. That warrior was accordingly too shrewd not to allow his great adversary as fair a share of triumph as was consistent with maintaining the frugal income on which he reckoned.

He had small love for the pleasures of the table, but was promiscuous and unlicensed in his amours. He was methodical in his household arrangements, and rather stingy than liberal in money matters. He personally read all his letters, accounts, despatches, and other documents trivial or important, but wrote few letters with his own hand, so that, unlike his illustrious father's correspondence, there is little that is characteristic to be found in his own. He was plain but not shabby in attire, and was always dressed in exactly the same style, wearing doublet and hose of brown woollen, a silk under vest, a short cloak lined with velvet, a little plaited ruff on his neck, and very loose boots. He ridiculed the smart French officers who, to show their fine legs, were wont to wear such tight boots as made them perspire to get into them, and maintained, in precept and practice, that a man should be able to jump into his boots and mount and ride at a moment's notice. The only ornaments he indulged in, except, of course, on state occasions, were a golden hilt to his famous sword, and a rope of diamonds tied around his felt hat.

He was now in the full flower of his strength and his fame, in his forty-second year, and of a noble and martial presence. The face, although unquestionably handsome, offered a sharp contrast within itself; the upper half all intellect, the lower quite sensual. Fair hair growing thin, but hardly tinged with grey, a bright, cheerful, and thoughtful forehead, large hazel eyes within a singularly large orbit of brow ; a straight, thin, slightly aquiline, well-cut nose— such features were at open variance with the broad, thick-lipped, sensual mouth, the heavy pendant jowl, the sparse beard on the glistening cheek, and the moleskin-like moustachio and chin tuft. Still, upon the whole, it was a face and figure which gave the world assurance of a man and a commander of men. Power and intelligence were stamped upon him from his birth.

Barneveld was tall and majestic of presence, with large quadrangular face, austere, blue eyes looking authority and command, a vast forehead, and a grizzled beard. Of fluent and convincing eloquence with tongue and pen, having the power of saying much in few words, he cared much more for the substance than the graces of speech or composition. This tendency was not ill exemplified in a note of his written on a sheet of questions addressed to him by a States' ambassador about to start on an important mission, but a novice in his business, the answers to which questions were to serve for his diplomatic instructions.[1]

"Item and principally," wrote the Envoy, "to request of M. de Barneveld a formulary or copy of the best, soundest, wisest, and best couched despatches done by several pre-

---

[1] Boetzelaer van Langerne,"V'machstucken ende poincten by my ingestelt ende by den adv. Oldenbarnevelt geappostilleert tot myner onderrichtinge ende instructie voor myn vertrek naer Vrankryck." (Hague Archives MS.)

ceding ambassadors in order to regulate myself accordingly for the greater service of the Province and for my uttermost reputation."

The Advocate's answer, scrawled in his nearly illegible hand, was—

" Unnecessary.  The truth in shortest about matters of importance shall be taken for good style."

With great love of power, which he was conscious of exerting with ease to himself and for the good of the public, he had little personal vanity, and not the smallest ambition of authorship.  Many volumes might be collected out of the vast accumulation of his writings now mouldering and forgotten in archives.  Had the language in which they are written become a world's language, they would be worthy of attentive study, as containing noble illustrations of the history and politics of his age, with theories and sentiments often far in advance of his age.  But he cared not for style. " The truth in shortest about matters of importance " was enough for him ; but the world in general, and especially the world of posterity, cares much for style.  The vehicle is often prized more than the freight.  The name of Barneveld is fast fading out of men's memory.  The fame of his pupil and companion in fortune and misfortune, Hugo Grotius, is ever green.  But Grotius was essentially an author rather than a statesman : he wrote for the world and posterity with all the love, pride, and charm of the devotee of literature, and he composed his noblest works in a language which is ever living because it is dead.  Some of his writings, epoch-making when they first appeared, are text-books still familiar in every cultivated household on earth.  Yet Barneveld was vastly his superior in practical statesmanship, in law, in the science of government, and above all in force of character, while certainly not his equal in theology, nor making any pretensions to poetry.  Although a ripe scholar, he rarely wrote in Latin, and not often in French. His ambition was to do his work thoroughly according to his view of duty, and to ask God's blessing upon it without craving overmuch the applause of men.

Such were the two men, the soldier and the statesman. Would the Republic, fortunate enough to possess two such magnificent and widely contrasted capacities, be wise enough to keep them in its service, each supplementing the other, and the two combining in a perfect whole?

Or was the great law of the Discords of the World, as potent as that other principle of Universal Harmony and planetary motion which an illustrious contemporary—that Würtemberg astronomer, once a soldier of the fierce Alva, now the half-starved astrologer of the brain-sick Rudolph—was at that moment discovering, after "God had waited six thousand years for him to do it," to prevail for the misery of the Republic and shame of Europe? Time was to show.

The new state had forced itself into the family of sovereignties somewhat to the displeasure of most of the Lord's anointed. Rebellious and republican, it necessarily excited the jealousy of long-established and hereditary governments.

The King of Spain had not formally acknowledged the independence of the United Provinces. He had treated with them as free, and there was supposed to be much virtue in the conjunction. But their sovereign independence was virtually recognized by the world. Great nations had entered into public and diplomatic relations and conventions with them, and their agents at foreign courts were now dignified with the rank and title of ambassadors.

The Spanish king had likewise refused to them the concession of the right of navigation and commerce in the East Indies, but it was a matter of notoriety that the absence of the word India, suppressed as it was in the treaty, implied an immense triumph on the part of the States, and that their flourishing and daily increasing commerce in the farthest East and the imperial establishments already rising there were cause of envy and jealousy not to Spain alone, but to friendly powers.

Yet the government of Great Britain affected to regard them as something less than a sovereign state. Although Elizabeth had refused the sovereignty once proffered to her, although James had united with Henry IV. in guaranteeing the treaty just concluded between the States and Spain, that monarch had the wonderful conception that the Republic was in some sort a province of his own, because he still held the cautionary towns in pledge for the loans granted by his predecessor. His agents at Constantinople were instructed to represent the new state as unworthy to accredit its envoys as those of an independent power. The Provinces were represented as a collection of audacious rebels, a piratical scum of the sea.[1]   But the Sultan knew his interests better than to incur the enmity of this rising maritime power. The Dutch envoy declaring that he would sooner throw himself into the Bosphorus than remain to be treated with less consideration than that accorded to the ministers of all great powers, the remonstrances of envious colleagues were hushed, and Haga was received with all due honours.

Even at the court of the best friend of the Republic, the French king, men looked coldly at the upstart commonwealth. Francis Aerssens, the keen and accomplished minister of the States, resident in Paris for many years, was received as ambassador after the truce with all the ceremonial befitting the highest rank in the diplomatic service ; yet Henry could not yet persuade himself to look upon the power accrediting him as a thoroughly organized commonwealth.

The English ambassador asked the King if he meant to

_______
[1] Van Rees and Brill.

continue his aid and assistance to the States during the truce.　"Yes," answered Henry.

"And a few years beyond it?"

"No.　I do not wish to offend the King of Spain from mere gaiety of heart."

"But they are free," replied the Ambassador; "the King of Spain could have no cause for offence."

"They are free," said the King, "but not sovereign." "Judge then," wrote Aerssens to Barneveld, "how we shall be with the King of Spain at the end of our term when our best friends make this distinction among themselves to our disadvantage.　They insist on making a difference between liberty and sovereignty; considering liberty as a mean term between servitude and sovereignty."[1]

"You would do well," continued the Dutch ambassador, "to use the word 'sovereignty' on all occasions instead of 'liberty.' "[2]　The hint was significant and the advice sound.

The haughty republic of Venice, too, with its "golden Book" and its pedigree of a thousand years, looked askance at the republic of yesterday rising like herself out of lagunes and sand banks, and affecting to place herself side by side with emperors, kings, and the lion of St. Mark. But the all-accomplished council of that most serene commonwealth had far too much insight and too wide experience in political combinations to make the blunder of yielding to this aristocratic sentiment.

The natural enemy of the Pope, of Spain, of Austria, must of necessity be the friend of Venice, and it was soon thought highly desirable to intimate half officially that a legation from the States-General to the Queen of the

---

[1] Aerssens to Barneveld, 14 Jan. 1609. (National Archives at the Hague MS.)
[2] Ibid.

Adriatic, announcing the conclusion of the Twelve Years' Truce, would be extremely well received.

The hint was given by the Venetian ambassador at Paris to Francis Aerssens, who instantly recommended van der Myle, son-in-law of Barneveld, as a proper personage to be entrusted with this important mission. At this moment an open breach had almost occurred between Spain and Venice, and the Spanish ambassador at Paris, Don Pedro de Toledo, naturally very irate with Holland, Venice, and even with France, was vehement in his demonstrations. The arrogant Spaniard had for some time been employed in an attempt to negotiate a double marriage between the Dauphin and the eldest daughter of Phllip III., and between the eldest son of that king and the Princess Elizabeth of France. An indispensable but secret condition of this negotiation was the absolute renunciation by France of its alliance and friendly relations with the United Provinces. The project was in truth a hostile measure aimed directly at the life of the Republic. Henry held firm however, and Don Pedro was about to depart malcontent, his mission having totally failed. He chanced, when going to his audience of leavetaking, after the arrival of his successor, Don Iuigo de Cardenas, to meet the Venetian ambassador, Antonio Foscarini. An altercation took place between them, during which the Spaniard poured out his wrath so vehemently, calling his colleague with neat alliteration "a poltroon, a pantaloon, and a pig," that Henry heard him.[1]

What Signor Antonio replied has not been preserved, but it is stated that he was first to seek a reconciliation, not liking, he said, Spanish assassinations.[2]

Meantime the double marriage project was for a season at

[1] Aerssens to Barneveld, 9 Feb. 1609. (Hague Archives MS.)
[2] Ibid. ". . . qui ce nonobstant a cerché l'accord le premier, d'autant, dit-il, que les assassinats des Espagnols ne lui plaisent pas."

least suspended, and the alliance between the two republics went forwards. Van der Myle, appointed ambassador to Venice, soon afterwards arrived in Paris, where he made a very favourable impression, and was highly lauded by Aerssens in his daily correspondence with Barneveld. No portentous shadow of future and fatal discord between those statesmen fell upon the cheerful scene. Before the year closed, he arrived at his post, and was received with great distinction, despite the obstacles thrown in his way by Spain and other powers; the ambassador of France itself, de Champigny, having privately urged that he ought to be placed on the same footing with the envoys of Savoy and of Florence.

Van der Myle at starting committed the trifling fault of styling the States-General "most illustrious" (*illustrissimi*) instead of "most serene," the title by which Venice designated herself.

The fault was at once remedied, however, Priuli the Doge seating the Dutch ambassador on his right hand at his solemn reception, and giving directions that van der Myle should be addressed as Excellency, his post being assigned him directly after his seniors, the ambassadors of Pope, Emperor, and kings.[1] The same precedence was settled in Paris, while Aerssens, who did not consider himself placed in a position of greater usefulness by his formal installation as ambassador, received private intimation from Henry, with whom he was on terms of great confidence and intimacy, that he should have private access to the King as frequently and as informally as before.[2] The theory that the ambassador, representing the personality of his sovereign, may visit the monarch to whom he is accredited, without ceremony and at

[1] Aerssens to Barneveld, 23 April 1609, 13 June 1609, 6 Sept. 1609, 30 Nov. 1609, 16 Dec. 1609. (Hague Arch. MSS.) Same to van der Myle, 17 Dec. 1609. (Ibid. MS.)
[2] Ibid.

his own convenience, was as rarely carried into practice in the sixteenth century as in the nineteenth, while on the other hand Aerssens, as the private and confidential agent of a friendly but not publicly recognized commonwealth, had been for many years in almost daily personal communication with the King.

It is also important to note that the modern fallacy according to which republics being impersonal should not be represented by ambassadors had not appeared in that important epoch in diplomatic history. On the contrary, the two great republics of the age, Holland and Venice, vindicated for themselves, with as much dignity and reason as success, their right to the highest diplomatic honours.

The distinction was substantial not shadowy ; those haughty commonwealths not considering it advantageous or decorous that their representatives should for want of proper official designations be ranked on great ceremonial occasions with the ministers of petty Italian principalities or of the three hundred infinitesimal sovereignties of Germany.

It was the advice of the French king especially, who knew politics and the world as well as any man, that the envoys of the Republic which he befriended and which stood now on the threshold of its official and national existence, should assert themselves at every court with the self-reliance and courtesy becoming the functionaries of a great power. That those ministers were second to the representatives of no other European state in capacity and accomplishment was a fact well known to all who had dealings with them, for the States required in their diplomatic representatives knowledge of history and international law, modern languages, and the classics, as well as familiarity with political customs and social courtesies ; the breeding of gentlemen in short and the accomplishments of scholars. It is both a literary enjoyment and a means of historical and political instruction to read after the lapse of centuries their reports and despatches. They worthily compare as works of art with those diplomatic masterpieces the letters and 'Relazioni' of the Venetian ambassadors; and it is well known that the earlier and some of the most important treatises on public and international law ever written are from the pens of Hollanders, who indeed may be said to have invented that science.

The Republic having thus steadily shouldered its way into the family of nations was soon called upon to perform a prominent part in the world's affairs. More than in our own epoch there was a close political commingling of such independent states as held sympathetic views on the great questions agitating Europe. The policy of isolation so wisely and successfully carried out by our own trans-Atlantic commonwealth was impossible for the Dutch republic, born as it was of a great religious schism, and with its narrow territory wedged between the chief political organizations of Christendom. Moreover the same jealousy on the part of established powers which threw so many obstacles in its path to recognized sovereignty existed in the highest degree between its two sponsors and allies, France and England, in regard to their respective relations to the new state.

"If ever there was an obliged people," said Henry's secretary of state, Villeroy, to Aerssens, "then it is you Netherlanders to his Majesty. He has converted your war into peace, and has never abandoned you. It is for you now to show your affection and gratitude." [1]

In the time of Elizabeth, and now in that of her successor, there was scarcely a day in which the envoys of the

<hr>

[1] Aerssens to Barneveld.   (MS.)

States were not reminded of the immense load of favour from England under which they tottered, and of the greater sincerity and value of English friendship over that of France.

Sully often spoke to Aerssens on the subject in even stronger language, deeming himself the chief protector and guardian angel of the Republic, to whom they were bound by ties of eternal gratitude. " But if the States," he said, " should think of caressing the King of England more than him, or even of treating him on an equality with his Majesty, Henry would be very much affronted. He did not mean that they should neglect the friendship of the King of Britain, but that they should cultivate it after and in subordination to his own, for they might be sure that James held all things indifferent, their ruin or their conservation, while his Majesty had always manifested the contrary both by his counsels and by the constant furnishing of supplies." [1]

Henry of France and Navarre—soldier, statesman, wit, above all a man and every inch a king—brimful of human vices, foibles, and humours, and endowed with those high qualities of genius which enabled him to mould events and men by his unscrupulous and audacious determination to conform to the spirit of his times which no man better understood than himself, had ever been in such close relations with the Netherlands as to seem in some sort their sovereign.

James Stuart, emerging from the school of Buchanan and the atmosphere of Calvinism in which he had been bred, now reigned in those more sunny and liberal regions where Elizabeth so long had ruled. Finding himself at once, after years of theological study, face to face with a foreign commonwealth and a momentous epoch, in which politics were

[1] Aerssens to Barneveld. (Hague Archives MS.)

so commingled with divinity as to offer daily the most puzzling problems, the royal pedant hugged himself at beholding so conspicuous a field for his talents.

To turn a throne into a pulpit, and amaze mankind with his learning, was an ambition most sweet to gratify. The Calvinist of Scotland now proclaimed his deadly hatred of Puritans in England and Holland, and denounced the Netherlanders as a pack of rebels whom it always pleased him to irritate, and over whom he too claimed, through the possession of the cautionary towns, a kind of sovereignty. Instinctively feeling that in the rough and unlovely husk of Puritanism was enclosed the germ of a wider human liberty than then existed, he was determined to give battle to it with his tongue, his pen, with everything but his sword.

Doubtless the States had received most invaluable assistance from both France and England, but the sovereigns of those countries were too apt to forget that it was their own battles, as well as those of the Hollanders, that had been fought in Flanders and Brabant. But for the alliance and subsidies of the faithful States, Henry would not so soon have ascended the throne of his ancestors, while it was matter of history that the Spanish government had for years been steadily endeavouring to subjugate England not so much for the value of the conquest in itself as for a stepping-stone to the recovery of the revolted Netherlands.

For the dividing line of nations or at least of national alliances was a frontier not of language but of faith. Germany was but a geographical expression. The union of Protestantism, subscribed by a large proportion of its three hundred and seven sovereigns, ran zigzag through the country, a majority probably of the people at that moment being opposed to the Roman Church.[1]

[1] Gindely, anno 1609.

It has often been considered amazing that Protestantism having accomplished so much should have fallen backwards so soon, and yielded almost undisputed sway in vast regions to the long dominant church. But in truth there is nothing surprising about it. Catholicism was and remained a unit, while its opponents were eventually broken up into hundreds of warring and politically impotent organizations. Religious faith became distorted into a weapon for selfish and greedy territorial aggrandizement in the hands of Protestant princes. *" Cujus regio ejus religio"* was the taunt hurled in the face of the imploring Calvinists of France and the Low Countries by the arrogant Lutherans of Germany. Such a sword smote the principle of religious freedom and mutual toleration into the dust, and rendered them comparatively weak in the conflict with the ancient and splendidly organized church.

The Huguenots of France, notwithstanding the protection grudgingly afforded them by their former chieftain, were dejected and discomfited by his apostasy, and Henry, placed in a fearfully false position, was an object of suspicion to both friends and foes. In England it is difficult to say whether a Jesuit or a Puritan was accounted the more noxious animal by the dominant party.

In the United Provinces perhaps one half the population was either openly or secretly attached to the ancient church, while among the Protestant portion a dire and tragic convulsion was about to break forth, which for a time at least was to render Remonstrants and Contra-Remonstrants more fiercely opposed to each other than to Papists.

The doctrine of predestination in its sternest and strictest sense had long been the prevailing one in the Reformed Church of the revolted Netherlands, as in those of Scotland, France, Geneva, and the Palatinate. No doubt up to the period of the truce a majority had acquiesced in that dogma and its results, although there had always been many preachers to advocate publicly a milder creed. It was not until the appointment of Jacob Arminius to the professorship of theology at Leyden, in the place of Francis Junius, in the year 1603, that a danger of schism in the Church seemed impending. Then rose the great Gomarus in his wrath, and with all the powers of splendid eloquence, profound learning, and the intense bigotry of conviction, denounced the horrible heresy. Conferences between the two before the Court of Holland, theological tournaments between six champions on a side, gallantly led by their respective chieftains, followed, with the usual result of confirming both parties in the conviction that to each alone belonged exclusively the truth.

The original influence of Arminius had however been so great that when the preachers of Holland had been severally called on by a synod to sign the Heidelberg Catechism, many of them refused. Here was open heresy and revolt. It was time for the true church to vindicate its authority. The great war with Spain had been made, so it was urged and honestly believed, not against the Inquisition, not to prevent Netherlanders from being burned and buried alive by the old true church, not in defence of ancient charters, constitutions, and privileges—the precious result of centuries of popular resistance to despotic force—not to maintain an amount of civil liberty and local self-government larger in extent than any then existing in the world, not to assert equality of religion for all men, but simply to establish the true religion, the one church, the only possible creed ; the creed and church of Calvin.

It is perfectly certain that the living fire which glowed in the veins of those hot gospellers had added intense enthusiasm to the war spirit throughout that immense struggle. It is quite possible that without that enthusiasm the war might not have been carried on to its successful end. But it is equally certain that Catholics, Lutherans, Baptists, and devotees of many other creeds, had taken part in the conflict in defence both of hearth and altar, and that without that aid the independence of the Provinces would never have been secured.

Yet before the war was ended the arrogance of the Reformed priesthood had begun to dig a chasm. Men who with William the Silent and Barneveld had indulged in the vision of religious equality as a possible result of so much fighting against the Holy Inquisition were perhaps to be disappointed.

Preachers under the influence of the gentle Arminius having dared to refuse signing the Creed were to be dealt with. It was time to pass from censure to action.

1606.

Heresy must be trampled down. The churches called for a national synod, and they did this as by divine right. " My Lords the States-General must observe," they said, " that this assembly now demanded is not a human institution but an ordinance of the Holy Ghost in its community, not depending upon any man's authority, but proceeding from God to the community." They complained that the true church was allowed to act only through the civil government, and was thus placed at a disadvantage compared even with Catholics and other sects, whose proceedings were winked at. " Thus the true church suffered from its apparent and public freedom, and hostile sects gained by secret connivance." [1]

A crisis was fast approaching. The one church claimed infallibility and superiority to the civil power. The Holy Ghost was placed in direct, ostentatious opposition to My Lords the States-General. It was for Netherlanders to

---

[1] Continuation of Arend's ' Vad. Hist.' by van Rees and Dr. Brill, iii. p. 420.

decide whether, after having shaken off the Holy Inquisition, and subjected the old true church to the public authority, they were now to submit to the imperious claims of the new true church.

There were hundreds of links connecting the Church with the State.  In that day a divorce between the two was hardly possible or conceivable.  The system of Congregationalism so successfully put into practice soon afterwards in the wilderness of New England, and to which so much of American freedom political as well as religious is due, was not easy to adopt in an old country like the Netherlands.  Splendid churches and cathedrals, the legal possession of which would be contended for by rival sects, could scarcely be replaced by temporary structures of lath and plaster, or by humble back parlours of mechanics' shops.  There were questions of property of complicated nature.  Not only the states and the communities claimed in rivalry the ownership of church property, but many private families could show ancient advowsons and other claims to present or to patronize, derived from imperial or ducal charters.

So long as there could be liberty of opinion within the Church upon points not necessarily vital, open schism could be avoided, by which the cause of Protestantism throughout Europe must be weakened, while at the same time subordination of the priesthood to the civil authority would be maintained.  But if the Holy Ghost, through the assembled clergy, were to dictate an iron formulary to which all must conform, to make laws for church government which every citizen must obey, and to appoint preachers and schoolmasters from whom alone old and young could receive illumination and instruction religious or lay, a theocracy would be established which no enlightened statesman could tolerate.

The States-General agreed to the synod, but imposed a

condition that there should be a revision of Creed and Catechism.  This was thundered down with one blast.
1606.  The condition implied a possibility that the vile
heresy of Arminius might be correct.  An unconditional synod
was demanded.  The Heidelberg Creed and Netherland Catechism were sacred, infallible, not to be touched.  The answer
of the government, through the mouth of Barneveld, was
that " to My Lords the States-General as the foster-fathers
and protectors of the churches every right belonged."

Thus far the States-General under the leadership of the
Advocate were unanimous.  The victory remained with
State against Church.  But very soon after the truce had
been established, and men had liberty to devote themselves
to peaceful pursuits, the ecclesiastical trumpet again sounded
far and wide, and contending priests and laymen rushed madly
to the fray.  The Remonstrance and Contra-Remonstrance,
and the appointment of Conrad Vorstius, a more abominable
heretic than Arminius, to the vacant chair of Arminius—a
step which drove Gomarus and the Gomarites to frenzy,
although Gomarus and Vorstius remained private and intimate friends to the last—are matters briefly to be mentioned on a later page.

Thus to the four chief actors in the politico-religious
drama, soon to be enacted as an interlude to an eighty
years' war, were assigned parts at first sight inconsistent
with their private convictions.  The King of France, who
had often abjured his religion, and was now the best of
Catholics, was denounced ferociously in every Catholic
pulpit in Christendom as secretly an apostate again, and
the open protector of heretics and rebels.[1]  But the cheerful
Henry troubled himself less than he perhaps had cause to
do with these thunderblasts.  Besides, as we shall soon see, he
had other objects political and personal to sway his opinions.

---

[1] Van Meteren, fo. 645.

James the ex-Calvinist, crypto-Arminian, pseudo-Papist, and avowed Puritan hater, was girding on his armour to annihilate Arminians and to defend and protect Puritans in Holland, while swearing that in England he would pepper them and harry them and hang them and that he would even like to bury them alive.

Barneveld, who turned his eyes, as much as in such an inflammatory age it was possible, from subtle points of theology, and relied on his great-grandfather's motto of humility, *"Nil scire tutissima fides"* was perhaps nearer to the dogma of the dominant Reformed Church than he knew, although always the consistent and strenuous champion of the civil authority over Church as well as State.

Maurice was no theologian. He was a steady church-goer, and his favorite divine, the preacher at his court chapel, was none other than Uytenbogaert. The very man who was instantly to be the champion of the Arminians, the author of the Remonstrance, the counsellor and comrade of Barneveld and Grotius, was now sneered at by the Goma-rites as the "Court Trumpeter." The preacher was not destined to change his opinions. Perhaps the Prince might alter. But Maurice then paid no heed to the great point at issue, about which all the Netherlanders were to take each other by the throat—absolute predestination. He knew that the Advocate had refused to listen to his stepmother's suggestion as to his obtaining the sovereignty. "He knew nothing of predestination," he was wont to say, "whether it was green, or whether it was blue. He only knew that his pipe and the Advocate's were not likely to make music together." This much of predestination he did know, that if the Advocate and his friends were to come to open conflict with the Prince of Orange-Nassau, the conqueror of Nieuw-poort, it was predestined to go hard with the Advocate and his friends.

The theological quibble did not interest him much, and he was apt to blunder about it.

" Well, preacher," said he one day to Albert Huttenus, who had come to him to intercede for a deserter condemned to be hanged, "are you one of those Arminians who believe that one child is born to salvation and another to damnation ?"

Huttenus, amazed to the utmost at the extraordinary question, replied, " Your Excellency will be graciously pleased to observe that this is not the opinion of those whom one calls by the hateful name of Arminians, but the opinion of their adversaries."

" Well, preacher," rejoined Maurice, "don't you think I know better ? " And turning to Count Lewis William, Stadholder of Friesland, who was present, standing by the hearth with his hand on a copper ring of the chimneypiece, he cried,

" Which is right, cousin, the preacher or I ? "

" No, cousin," answered Count Lewis, " you are in the wrong." [1]

Thus to the Catholic League organized throughout Europe in solid and consistent phalanx was opposed the Great Protestant Union, ardent and enthusiastic in detail, but undisciplined, disobedient, and inharmonious as a whole.

The great principle, not of religious toleration, which is a phrase of insult, but of religious equality, which is the natural right of mankind, was to be evolved after a lapse of

[1] The anecdote rests on the authority of the annotator to the 2nd edition of Brandt's ' Hist. v. d. Rechtspleging.' (1710) p. 179. He derived it, he says, from the MS. note of a man well known to him, venerable and trustworthy, who had heard it more than once from the mouth of Dr. Huttenus himself.

Of course it may be disputed by violent partisans who deem such stories criminal or discreditable to a plain soldier. It seems characteristic enough, and the evidence is sufficient for such a trifle.

additional centuries out of the elemental conflict which had already lasted so long.  Still later was the total divorce of State and Church to be achieved as the final consummation of the great revolution.  Meantime it was almost inevitable that the privileged and richly endowed church, with ecclesiastical armies and arsenals vastly superior to anything which its antagonist could improvise, should more than hold its own.

At the outset of the epoch which now occupies our attention, Europe was in a state of exhaustion and longing for repose.  Spain had submitted to the humiliation of a treaty of truce with its rebellious subjects which was substantially a recognition of their independence.  Nothing could be more deplorable than the internal condition of the country which claimed to be mistress of the world and still aspired to universal monarchy.

It had made peace because it could no longer furnish funds for the war.  The French ambassador, Barante, returning from Madrid, informed his sovereign that he had often seen officers in the army prostrating themselves on their knees in the streets before their sovereign as he went to mass, and imploring him for payment of their salaries, or at least an alms to keep them from starving, and always imploring in vain.[1]

The King, who was less than a cipher, had neither capacity to feel emotion, nor intelligence to comprehend the most insignificant affair of state.  Moreover the means were wanting to him even had he been disposed to grant assistance.  The terrible Duke of Lerma was still his inexorable lord and master, and the secretary of that powerful personage, who kept an open shop for the sale of offices of state both high and low, took care that all the proceeds

---

[1] Aerssens to Barneveld, 30 Jan. 1609.  (MS.)

should flow into the coffers of the Duke and his own lap instead of the royal exchequer.

In France both king and people declared themselves disgusted with war. Sully disapproved of the treaty just concluded between Spain and the Netherlands, feeling sure that the captious and equivocal clauses contained in it would be interpreted to the disadvantage of the Republic and of the Reformed religion whenever Spain felt herself strong enough to make the attempt. He was especially anxious that the States should make no concessions in regard to the exercise of the Catholic worship within their territory, believing that by so doing they would compromise their political independence besides endangering the cause of Protestantism everywhere. A great pressure was put upon Sully that moment by the King to change his religion.

"You will all be inevitably ruined if you make concessions in this regard," said he to Aerssens. "Take example by me. I should be utterly undone if I had listened to any overture on this subject." [1]

Nevertheless it was the opinion of the astute and caustic envoy that the Duke would be forced to yield at last. The Pope was making great efforts to gain him, and thus to bring about the extirpation of Protestantism in France. And the King, at that time much under the influence of the Jesuits, had almost set his heart on the conversion. Aerssens insinuated that Sully was dreading a minute examination into the affairs of his administration of the finances—a groundless calumny—and would be thus forced to comply. Other enemies suggested that nothing would effect this much desired apostasy but the office of Constable of France, which it was certain would never be bestowed on him. [2]

---

[1] Aerssens to Barneveld, 9 Feb. and 27 March 1609. (Hague Archives MS.)
[2] Ibid.

At any rate it was very certain that Henry at this period was bent on peace.

"Make your account," said Aerssens to Barneveld, as the time for signing the truce drew nigh, "on this indubitable foundation that the King is determined against war, whatever pretences he may make. His bellicose demeanour has been assumed only to help forward our treaty, which he would never have favoured, and ought never to have favoured, if he had not been too much in love with peace. This is a very important secret if we manage it discreetly, and a very dangerous one if our enemies discover it."[1]

Sully would have much preferred that the States should stand out for a peace rather than for a truce, and believed it might have been obtained if the King had not begun the matter so feebly, and if he had let it be understood that he would join his arms to those of the Provinces in case of rupture.

He warned the States very strenuously that the Pope and the King of Spain, and a host of enemies open and covert, were doing their best to injure them at the French court. They would find little hindrance in this course if the Republic did not show its teeth, and especially if it did not stiffly oppose all encroachments of the Roman religion, without even showing any deference to the King in this regard, who was much importuned on the subject.

He advised the States to improve the interval of truce by restoring order to their finances and so arranging their affairs that on the resumption of hostilities, if come they must, their friends might be encouraged to help them, by the exhibition of thorough vigour on their part.[2]

[1] Aerssens to Barneveld, 27 March 1609.  (MS.)
[2] Ibid.

France then, although utterly indisposed for war at that moment, was thoroughly to be relied on as a friend and in case of need an ally, so long as it was governed by its present policy. There was but one king left in Europe since the death of Elizabeth of England.

But Henry was now on the abhorred threshold of old age which he obstinately refused to cross.

There is something almost pathetic, in spite of the censure which much of his private life at this period provokes, in the isolation which now seemed his lot.

Deceived and hated by his wife and his mistresses, who were conspiring with each other and with his ministers, not only against his policy but against his life; with a vile Italian adventurer, dishonouring his household, entirely dominating the queen, counteracting the royal measures, secretly corresponding, by assumed authority, with Spain, in direct violation of the King's instructions to his ambassadors, and gorging himself with wealth and offices at the expense of everything respectable in France; surrounded by a pack of malignant and greedy nobles, who begrudged him his fame, his authority, his independence; without a home, and almost without a friend, the Most Christian King in these latter days led hardly as merry a life as when fighting years long for his crown, at the head of his Gascon chivalry, the beloved chieftain of Huguenots.[1]

Of the triumvirate then constituting his council, Villeroy, Sillery, and Sully, the two first were ancient Leaguers, and more devoted at heart to Philip of Spain than to Henry of France and Navarre.

Both silent, laborious, plodding, plotting functionaries, thriftily gathering riches; skilled in routine and adepts at

[1] See especially 'Mémoires de Sully,' ed. Paris, 1747, vols. vii. and viii. *passim*, and Michelet's remarkable volume, 'Henry IV. et Richelieu.'

intrigue ; steady self-seekers, and faithful to office in which their lives had passed, they might be relied on at any emergency to take part against their master, if to ruin would prove more profitable than to serve him.

There was one man who was truer to Henry than Henry had been to himself. The haughty, defiant, austere grandee, brave soldier, sagacious statesman, thrifty financier, against whom the poisoned arrows of religious hatred, envious ambition, and petty court intrigue were daily directed, who watched grimly over the exchequer confided to him, which was daily growing fuller in despite of the cormorants who trembled at his frown ; hard worker, good hater, conscientious politician, who filled his own coffers without dishonesty, and those of the state without tyranny; unsociable, arrogant, pious, very avaricious, and inordinately vain, Maximilian de Béthune, Duke of Sully, loved and respected Henry as no man or woman loved and respected him. In truth, there was but one living being for whom the Duke had greater reverence and affection than for the King, and that was the Duke of Sully himself.

At this moment he considered himself, as indeed he was, in full possession of his sovereign's confidence. But he was alone in this conviction. Those about the court, men like Epernon and his creatures, believed the great financier on the brink of perdition. Henry, always the loosest of talkers even in regard to his best friends, had declared, on some temporary vexation in regard to the affair between Aiguillon and Balagny, that he would deal with the Duke as with the late Marshal de Biron, and make him smaller than he had ever made him great:[1] goading him on this occasion with importunities, almost amounting to commands, that both he and his son should forthwith change their religion or expect instant ruin. The blow was so severe that Sully shut him-

---

[1] Aerssens to Barneveld, 9 Feb. 1609.  (MS.)

self up, refused to see anyone, and talked of retiring for good
to his estates.[1]   But he knew, and Henry knew, how indispensable he was, and the anger of the master was as short-
lived as the despair of the minister.

There was no living statesman for whom Henry had a more
sincere respect than for the Advocate of Holland.  " His
Majesty admires and greatly extols your wisdom, which he
judges necessary for the preservation of our State; deeming
you one of the rare and sage counsellors of the age." [2]   It is
true that this admiration was in part attributed to the singular coincidence of Barneveld's views of policy with the King's
own.  Sully, on his part, was a severe critic of that policy.
He believed that better terms might have been exacted from
Spain in the late negotiations, and strongly objected to the
cavilling and equivocal language of the treaty.  Rude in
pen as in speech, he expressed his mind very freely in his
conversation and correspondence with Henry in regard to
leading personages and great affairs, and made no secret of
his opinions to the States' ambassador.

He showed his letters in which he had informed the King
that he ought never to have sanctioned the truce without
better securities than existed, and that the States would never
have moved in any matter without him.  It would have
been better to throw himself into a severe war than to see
the Republic perish.  He further expressed the conviction
that Henry ought to have such authority over the Netherlands that they would embrace blindly whatever counsel he
chose to give them, even if they saw in it their inevitable
ruin ; and this not so much from remembrance of assistance
rendered by him, but from the necessity in which they
should always feel of depending totally upon him.

" You may judge, therefore," concluded Aerssens, " as to

<hr>

[1] Aerssens to Barneveld, 9 Feb. 1609.   (MS.)
[2] Same to same, 27 March 1609.   (MS.)

how much we can build on such foundations as these.  I have been amazed at these frank communications, for in those letters he spares neither My Lords the States, nor his Excellency Prince Maurice, nor yourself; giving his judgment of each of you with far too much freedom and without sufficient knowledge." [1]

Thus the alliance between the Netherlands and France, notwithstanding occasional traces of caprice and flaws of personal jealousy, was on the whole sincere, for it was founded on the surest foundation of international friendship, the self-interest of each.  Henry, although boasting of having bought Paris with a mass, knew as well as his worst enemy that in that bargain he had never purchased the confidence of the ancient church, on whose bosom he had flung himself with so much dramatic pomp.  His noble position, as champion of religious toleration, was not only unappreciated in an age in which each church and every sect arrogated to itself a monopoly of the truth, but it was one in which he did not himself sincerely believe.

After all, he was still the chieftain of the Protestant Union, and, although Eldest Son of the Church, was the bitter antagonist of the League and the sworn foe to the House of Austria.  He was walking through pitfalls with a crowd of invisible but relentless foes dogging his every footstep.  In his household or without were daily visions of dagger and bowl, and he felt himself marching to his doom.  How could the man on whom the heretic and rebellious Hollanders and the Protestant princes of Germany relied as on their saviour escape the unutterable wrath and the patient vengeance of a power that never forgave ?

In England the jealousy of the Republic and of France as co-guardian and protector of the Republic was even greater than in France.  Though placed by circumstances

---

[1] Aerssen's letter last cited.  (MS.)

in the position of ally to the Netherlands and enemy to Spain, James hated the Netherlands and adored Spain. His first thought on escaping the general destruction to which the Gunpowder Plot was to have involved himself and family and all the principal personages of the realm seems to have been to exculpate Spain from participation in the crime. His next was to deliver a sermon to Parliament, exonerating the Catholics and going out of his way to stigmatize the Puritans as entertaining doctrines which should be punished with fire. As the Puritans had certainly not been accused of complicity with Guy Fawkes or Garnet, this portion of the discourse was at least superfluous. But James loathed nothing so much as a Puritan. A Catholic at heart, he would have been the warmest ally of the League had he only been permitted to be Pope of Great Britain. He hated and feared a Jesuit, not for his religious doctrines, for with these he sympathized, but for his political creed. He liked not that either Roman Pontiff or British Presbyterian should abridge his heaven-born prerogative. The doctrine of Papal superiority to temporal sovereigns was as odious to him as Puritan rebellion to the hierarchy of which he was the chief. Moreover, in his hostility to both Papists and Presbyterians, there was much of professional rivalry. Having been deprived by the accident of birth of his true position as theological professor, he lost no opportunity of turning his throne into a pulpit and his sceptre into a controversial pen.

Henry of France, who rarely concealed his contempt for Master Jacques, as he called him, said to the English ambassador, on receiving from him one of the King's books, and being asked what he thought of it—" It is not the business of us kings to write, but to fight. Everybody should mind his own business, but it is the vice of most men to wish to appear learned in matters of which they are ignorant." [1]

<hr>

[1] Aerssens to Barneveld, 24 June 1609. (Hague Archives MS.)

The flatterers of James found their account in pandering to his sacerdotal and royal vanity. "I have always believed," said the Lord Chancellor, after hearing the King argue with and browbeat a Presbyterian deputation, "that the high-priesthood and royalty ought to be united, but I never witnessed the actual junction till now, after hearing the learned discourse of your Majesty." Archbishop Whitgift, grovelling still lower, declared his conviction that James, in the observations he had deigned to make, had been directly inspired by the Holy Ghost.[1]

Nothing could be more illogical and incoherent with each other than his theological and political opinions. He imagined himself a defender of the Protestant faith, while hating Holland and fawning on the House of Austria.

In England he favoured Arminianism, because the Anglican Church recognized for its head the temporal chief of the State. In Holland he vehemently denounced the Arminians, indecently persecuting their preachers and statesmen, who were contending for exactly the same principle—the supremacy of State over Church. He sentenced Bartholomew Legate to be burned alive in Smithfield as a blasphemous heretic, and did his best to compel the States of Holland to take the life of Professor Vorstius of Leyden. He persecuted the Presbyterians in England as furiously as he defended them in Holland. He drove Bradford and Carver into the New England wilderness, and applauded Gomarus and Walaeus and the other famous leaders of the Presbyterian party in the Netherlands with all his soul and strength.

He united with the French king in negotiations for Netherland independence, while denouncing the Provinces as guilty of criminal rebellion against their lawful sovereign.

"He pretends," said Jeannin, "to assist in bringing about the peace, and nevertheless does his best openly to prevent it."

---

[1] Rapin, 'Hist. d'Angleterre' (la Haye, 1725), t. vii. 14.

Richardot declared that the firmness of the King of Spain proceeded entirely from reliance on the promise of James that there should be no acknowledgment in the treaty of the liberty of the States. Henry wrote to Jeannin that he knew very well "what that —— was capable of, but that he should not be kept awake by anything he could do."[1]

As a king he spent his reign—so much of it as could be spared from gourmandizing, drunkenness, dalliance with handsome minions of his own sex, and theological pursuits —in rescuing the Crown from dependence on Parliament ; in straining to the utmost the royal prerogative ; in substituting proclamations for statutes ; in doing everything in his power, in short, to smooth the path for his successor to the scaffold. As father of a family he consecrated many years of his life to the wondrous delusion of the Spanish marriages.

The Gunpowder Plot seemed to have inspired him with an insane desire for that alliance, and few things in history are more amazing than the persistency with which he pursued the scheme, until the pursuit became not only ridiculous, but impossible.

With such a man, frivolous, pedantic, conceited, and licentious, the earnest statesmen of Holland were forced into close alliance. It is pathetic to see men like Barneveld and Hugo Grotius obliged, on great occasions of state, to use the language of respect and affection to one by whom they were hated, and whom they thoroughly despised.

But turning away from France, it was in vain for them to look for kings or men either among friends or foes. In Germany religious dissensions were gradually ripening into open war, and it would be difficult to imagine a more hopelessly incompetent ruler than the man who was nominally chief of the Holy Roman Realm. Yet the distracted Ru-

[1] Rapin, vii. 59, 60.

dolph was quite as much an emperor as the chaos over which he was supposed to preside was an empire. Perhaps the very worst polity ever devised by human perverseness was the system under which the great German race was then writhing and groaning. A mad world with a lunatic to govern it; a democracy of many princes, little and big, fighting amongst each other, and falling into daily changing combinations as some masterly or mischievous hand whirled the kaleidoscope; drinking Rhenish by hogsheads, and beer by the tun; robbing churches, dictating creeds to their subjects, and breaking all the commandments themselves; a people at the bottom dimly striving towards religious freedom and political life out of abject social, ecclesiastical, and political serfdom, and perhaps even then dumbly feeling within its veins, with that prophetic instinct which never abandons great races, a far distant and magnificent Future of national unity and Imperial splendour, the very reverse of the confusion which was then the hideous Present; an Imperial family at top with many heads and slender brains; a band of brothers and cousins wrangling, intriguing, tripping up each others' heels, and unlucky Rudolph, in his Hradschin, looking out of window over the peerless Prague, spread out in its beauteous landscape of hill and dale, darkling forest, dizzy cliffs, and rushing river, at his feet, feebly cursing the unhappy city for its ingratitude to an invisible and impotent sovereign; his excellent brother Matthias meanwhile marauding through the realms and taking one crown after another from his poor bald head.

It would be difficult to depict anything more precisely what an emperor in those portentous times should not be. He collected works of art of many kinds—pictures, statues, gems. He passed his days in his galleries contemplating in solitary grandeur these treasures, or in his stables, admiring a numerous stud of horses which he never drove or rode. Ambassadors and ministers of state disguised themselves as grooms and stable-boys to obtain accidental glimpses of a sovereign who rarely granted audiences. His nights were passed in star-gazing with Tycho de Brahe, or with that illustrious Suabian whose name is one of the great lights and treasures of the world. But it was not to study the laws of planetary motion nor to fathom mysteries of divine harmony that the monarch stood with Kepler in the observatory. The influence of countless worlds upon the destiny of one who, by capricious accident, if accident ever exists in history, had been entrusted with the destiny of so large a portion of one little world ; the horoscope, not of the Universe, but of himself ; such were the limited purposes with which the Kaiser looked upon the constellations.

For the Catholic Rudolph had received the Protestant Kepler, driven from Tübingen because Lutheran doctors, knowing from Holy Writ that the sun had stood still in Ajalon, had denounced his theory of planetary motion. His mother had just escaped being burned as a witch, and the world owes a debt of gratitude to the Emperor for protecting the astrologer, when enlightened theologians might, perhaps, have hanged the astronomer.[1]

A red-faced, heavy-jowled, bald-headed, somewhat goggle-eyed old gentleman, Rudolph did his best to lead the life of a hermit, and escape the cares of royalty. Timid by temperament, yet liable to fits of uncontrollable anger, he broke his furniture to pieces when irritated, and threw dishes that displeased him in his butler's face, but left affairs of state mainly to his valet, who earned many a penny by selling the Imperial signature.

He had just signed the famous "Majestätsbrief," by 1609. which he granted vast privileges to the Protestants of Bohemia, and had bitten the pen to pieces in a paroxysm

[1] Wolfgang Menzel, 'Geschichte der Deutschen,' B. iii. 188.

of anger, after dimly comprehending the extent of the concessions which he had made.

There were hundreds of sovereign states over all of
which floated the shadowy and impalpable authority of an
Imperial crown scarcely fixed on the head of any one of the
rival brethren and cousins ; there was a confederation of
Protestants, with the keen-sighted and ambitious Christian
of Anhalt acting as its chief, and dreaming of the Bohemian
crown ; there was the just-born Catholic League, with the
calm, far-seeing, and egotistical rather than self-seeking
Maximilian at its head ; each combination extending over
the whole country, stamped with imbecility of action from its
birth, and perverted and hampered by inevitable jealousies.
In addition to all these furrows ploughed by the very genius
of discord throughout the unhappy land was the wild and
secret intrigue with which Leopold, Archduke and Bishop,
dreaming also of the crown of Wenzel, was about to tear its
surface as deeply as he dared.[1]

Thus constituted were the leading powers of Europe in the
earlier part of 1609—the year in which a peaceful period
seemed to have begun. To those who saw the entangled
interests of individuals, and the conflict of theological
dogmas and religious and political intrigue which furnished
so much material out of which wide-reaching schemes of
personal ambition could be spun, it must have been obvious
that the interval of truce was necessarily but a brief interlude between two tragedies.

It seemed the very mockery of Fate that, almost at the
very instant when after two years' painful negotiation a truce
had been made, the signal for universal discord should be
sounded. One day in the early summer of 1609, Henry
IV. came to the Royal Arsenal, the residence of Sully,
accompanied by Zamet and another of his intimate com-

[1] Anton Gindely, ‘Rudolf II. und seine Zeit,’ Band ii. 35–60, &c.

panions. He asked for the Duke and was told that he was busy in his study. "Of course," said the King, turning to his followers, " I dare say you expected to be told that he was out shooting, or with the ladies, or at the barber's. But who works like Sully? Tell him," he said, "to come to the balcony in his garden, where he and I are not accustomed to be silent."

As soon as Sully appeared, the King observed : "Well; here the Duke of Cleve is dead, and has left everybody his heir." [1]

It was true enough, and the inheritance was of vital importance to the world.

It was an apple of discord thrown directly between the two rival camps into which Christendom was divided. The Duchies of Cleve, Berg, and Jülich, and the Counties and Lordships of Mark, Ravensberg, and Ravenstein, formed a triangle, political and geographical, closely wedged between Catholicism and Protestantism, and between France, the United Provinces, Belgium, and Germany. Should it fall into Catholic hands, the Netherlands were lost, trampled upon in every corner, hedged in on all sides, with the House of Austria governing the Rhine, the Meuse, and the Scheldt. It was vital to them to exclude the Empire from the great historic river which seemed destined to form the perpetual frontier of jealous powers and rival creeds.

Should it fall into heretic hands, the States were vastly strengthened, the Archduke Albert isolated and cut off from the protection of Spain and of the Empire. France, although Catholic, was the ally of Holland and the secret but well known enemy of the House of Austria. It was inevitable that the king of that country, the only living statesman that wore a crown, should be appealed to by all

<hr>

[1] 'Mémoires de Sully,' vii. 306, 307.

parties and should find himself in the proud but dangerous position of arbiter of Europe.

In this emergency he relied upon himself and on two men besides, Maximilian de Béthune and John of Barneveld.

The conference between the King and Sully and between both and Francis Aerssens, ambassador of the States, were of almost daily occurrence. The minute details given in the adroit diplomatist's correspondence indicate at every stage the extreme deference paid by Henry to the opinion of Holland's Advocate and the confidence reposed by him in the resources and the courage of the Republic.

All the world was claiming the heritage of the duchies. It was only strange that an event which could not be long deferred and the consequences of which were soon to be so grave, the death of the Duke of Cleve, should at last burst like a bomb-shell on the council tables of the sovereigns and statesmen of Europe. That mischievous madman John William died childless in the spring of 1609. His sister Sibylla, an ancient and malignant spinster, had governed him and his possessions except in his lucid intervals. The mass of the population over which he ruled being Protestant, while the reigning family and the chief nobles were of the ancient faith, it was natural that the Catholic party under the lead of Maximilian of Bavaria should deem it all-important that there should be direct issue to that family. Otherwise the inheritance on his death would probably pass to Protestant princes.[1]

The first wife provided for him was a beautiful princess, Jacobea of Baden. The Pope blessed the nuptials, and sent the bride a golden rose, but the union was sterile and unhappy. The Duke, who was in the habit of careering through his palace in full armour, slashing at and wounding anyone

<hr>

[1] W. Menzel, iii. 203, 204.

that came in his way, was at last locked up. The hapless Jacobea, accused by Sibylla of witchcraft and other crimes possible and impossible, was thrown into prison. Two years long the devilish malignity of the sister-in-law was exercised upon her victim, who, as it is related, was not allowed natural sleep during all that period, being at every hour awakened by command of Sibylla. At last the Duchess was strangled in prison.[1] A new wife was at once provided for the lunatic, Antonia of Lorraine. The two remained childless, and Sibylla at the age of forty-nine took to herself a husband, the Margrave of Burgau, of the House of Austria, the humble birth of whose mother, however, did not allow him the rank of Archduke. Her efforts thus to provide Catholic heirs to the rich domains of Cleve proved as fruitless as her previous attempts.[2]

And now Duke John William had died, and the representatives of his three dead sisters, and the living Sibylla were left to fight for the duchies.

It would be both cruel and superfluous to inflict on the reader a historical statement of the manner in which these six small provinces were to be united into a single state. It would be an equally sterile task to retrace the legal arguments by which the various parties prepared themselves to vindicate their claims, each pretender more triumphantly than the other. The naked facts alone retain vital interest, and of these facts the prominent one was the assertion of the Emperor that the duchies, constituting a fief masculine, could descend to none of the pretenders, but were at his disposal as sovereign of Germany.

On the other hand nearly all the important princes of that country sent their agents into the duchies to look after the interests real or imaginary which they claimed,

---

[1] W. Menzel, iii. 203, 204.        [2] Ibid.

There were but four candidates who in reality could be considered serious ones.

Mary Eleanor, eldest sister of the Duke, had been married in the lifetime of their father to Albert Frederic of Brandenburg, Duke of Prussia. To the children of this marriage was reserved the succession of the whole property in case of the masculine line becoming extinct. Two years afterwards the second sister, Anne, was married to Duke Philip Lewis, Count-Palatine of Neuburg; the children of which marriage stood next in succession to those of the eldest sister, should that become extinguished. Four years later the third sister, Magdalen, espoused the Duke John, Count-Palatine of Deux-Ponts; who, like Neuburg, made resignation of rights of succession in favour of the descendants of the Brandenburg marriage.[1] The marriage of the youngest sister, Sibylla, with the Margrave of Burgau has been already mentioned. It does not appear that her brother, whose lunatic condition hardly permitted him to assure her the dowry which had been the price of renunciation in the case of her three elder sisters, had obtained that renunciation from her.

The claims of the childless Sibylla as well as those of the Deux-Ponts branch were not destined to be taken into serious consideration.

The real competitors were the Emperor on the one side and the Elector of Brandenburg and the Count-Palatine of Neuburg on the other.

It is not necessary to my purpose to say a single word as to the legal and historical rights of the controversy. Volumes upon volumes of forgotten lore might be consulted, and they would afford exactly as much refreshing nutriment as would the heaps of erudition hardly ten years old, and yet as antiquated as the title-deeds of the Pharaohs, concerning the claims to the Duchies of Schleswig-

---

[1] 'Mémoires de Sully,' vii. 312, sqq.

Holstein.  The fortunate house of Brandenburg may have been right or wrong in both disputes.  It is certain that it did not lack a more potent factor in settling the political problems of the world in the one case any more than in the other.

But on the occasion with which we are occupied it was not on the might of his own right hand that the Elector of Brandenburg relied.  Moreover, he was dilatory in appealing to the two great powers on whose friendship he must depend for the establishment of his claims : the United Republic and the King of France.  James of England was on the whole inclined to believe in the rights of Brandenburg.  His ambassador, however, with more prophetic vision than perhaps the King ever dreamt of, expressed a fear lest Brandenburg should grow too great and one day come to the Imperial crown.[1]

The States openly favoured the Elector.  Henry was at first disposed towards Neuburg, but at his request Barneveld furnished a paper on the subject, by which the King seems to have been entirely converted to the pretensions of Brandenburg.[2]

But the solution of the question had but little to do with the legal claim of any man.  It was instinctively felt throughout Christendom that the great duel between the ancient church and the spirit of the Reformation was now to be renewed upon that narrow, debateable spot.

The Emperor at once proclaimed his right to arbitrate on the succession and to hold the territory until decision should be made ; that is to say, till the Greek Kalends.  His familiar and most tricksy spirit, Bishop-Archduke Leopold,

---

[1] " Il craint la puissance de Brandebourg s'il parvient à cette succession d'autant plus qu'à la longueur il pourroit venir à l'Empire."—Aerssens to Barneveld, 13 June 1609.  (Hague Archives MS.)

[2] Same to same, 13 May 1609 ; and see several letters of Aerssens to Barneveld, in May 1609.  (Hague Archives MS.)

played at once on his fears and his resentments against the ever encroaching, ever menacing, Protestantism of Germany, with which he had just sealed a compact so bitterly detested.

That bold and bustling prelate, brother of the Queen of Spain and of Ferdinand of Styria, took post from Prague in the middle of July. Accompanied by a certain canon of the Church and disguised as his servant, July 1609. he arrived after a rapid journey before the gates of Jülich, chief city and fortress of the duchies. The governor of the place, Nestelraed, inclined like most of the functionaries throughout the duchies to the Catholic cause, was delighted to recognize under the livery of the lackey the cousin and representative of the Emperor. Leopold, who had brought but five men with him, had conquered his capital at a blow. For while thus comfortably established as temporary governor of the duchies he designed through the fears or folly of Rudolph to become their sovereign lord. Strengthened by such an acquisition and reckoning on continued assistance in men and money from Spain and the Catholic League, he meant to sweep back to the rescue of the perishing Rudolph, smite the Protestants of Bohemia, and achieve his appointment to the crown of that kingdom.[1]

The Spanish ambassador at Prague had furnished him with a handsome sum of money for the expenses of his journey and preliminary enterprise. It should go hard but funds should be forthcoming to support him throughout this audacious scheme. The champion of the Church, the sovereign prince of important provinces, the possession of which ensured conclusive triumph to the House of Austria and to Rome—who should oppose him in his path to Empire? Certainly not the moody Rudolph, the slippery and unstable Matthias, the fanatic and Jesuit-ridden Ferdinand.

---

[1] A. Gindely, 'Rudolf II.' ii. 35, *seqq.*

"Leopold in Jülich," said Henry's agent in Germany, "is a ferret in a rabbit warren." [1]

But early in the spring and before the arrival of Leopold, the two pretenders, John Sigismund, Elector of Brandenburg, and Philip Lewis, Palatine of Neuburg, had made an arrangement. By the earnest advice of Barneveld in the name of the States-General and as the result of a general council of many Protestant princes of Germany, it had been settled that those two should together provisionally hold and administer the duchies until the principal affair could be amicably settled.[2]

May 1609.

The possessory princes were accordingly established in Düsseldorf with the consent of the provincial estates, in which place those bodies were wont to assemble.

Here then was Spain in the person of Leopold quietly perched in the chief citadel of the country, while Protestantism in the shape of the possessory princes stood menacingly in the capital.

Hardly was the ink dry on the treaty which had suspended for twelve years the great religious war of forty years, not yet had the ratifications been exchanged, but the trumpet was again sounding, and the hostile forces were once more face to face.

Leopold, knowing where his great danger lay, sent a friendly message to the States-General, expressing the hope that they would submit to his arrangements until the Imperial decision should be made.[3]

The States, through the pen and brain of Barneveld, replied that they had already recognized the rights of the possessory princes, and were surprised that the Bishop-Archduke should oppose them. They expressed the hope that, when better informed, he would see the validity of the

<hr>

[1] 'Mémoires de Sully,' vii. 331.
[2] Van Rees and Brill, iii. d. ii. stukk, 406, *sqq.*          [3] Ibid.

Treaty of Dortmund.  " My Lords the States-General," said the Advocate, " will protect the princes against violence and actual disturbances, and are assured that the neighbouring kings and princes will do the same.  They trust that his Imperial Highness will not allow matters to proceed to extremities." [1]

This was language not to be mistaken.  It was plain that the Republic did not intend the Emperor to decide a question of life and death to herself, nor to permit Spain, exhausted by warfare, to achieve this annihilating triumph by a petty intrigue.

While in reality the clue to what seemed to the outside world a labyrinthine maze of tangled interests and passions was firmly held in the hand of Barneveld, it was not to him nor to My Lords the States-General that the various parties to the impending conflict applied in the first resort.

Mankind were not yet sufficiently used to this young republic, intruding herself among the family of kings, to defer at once to an authority which they could not but feel.

Moreover, Henry of France was universally looked to both by friends and foes as the probable arbiter or chief champion in the great debate.  He had originally been inclined to favour Neuberg, chiefly, so Aerssens thought, on account of his political weakness.  The States-General on the other hand were firmly disposed for Brandenburg from the first, not only as a strenuous supporter of the Reformation and an ancient ally of their own always interested in their safety, but because the establishment of the Elector on the Rhine would roll back the Empire beyond that river.  As Aerssens expressed it, they would have the Empire for a frontier, and have no longer reason to fear the Rhine. [2]

The King, after the representations of the States, saw good

---

[1] See Barneveld's Memoir to van der Myle.  (Hague Archives MS.)
[2] Aerssens to Barneveld, 23 April

1609.  Same to same, 27 April and 13 May.  (Hague Archives MS.)

ground to change his opinion and, becoming convinced that
the Palatine had long been coquetting with the Austrian
party, soon made no secret of his preference for Brandenburg. Subsequently Neuburg and Brandenburg fell into
a violent quarrel notwithstanding an arrangement that the
Palatine should marry the daughter of the Elector. In the
heat of discussion Brandenburg on one occasion is said to have
given his intended son-in-law a box on the ear,[1] an argument
*ad hominem* which seems to have had the effect of sending
the Palatine into the bosom of the ancient church and
causing him to rely thenceforth upon the assistance of the
League. Meantime, however, the *Condominium* settled by
the Treaty of Dortmund continued in force; the third
brother of Brandenburg and the eldest son of Neuburg
sharing possession and authority at Düsseldorf until a final
decision could be made.

A flock of diplomatists, professional or volunteers, openly
accredited or secret, were now flying busily about through the
troubled atmosphere, indicating the coming storm in which
they revelled. The keen-sighted, subtle, but dangerously intriguing ambassador of the Republic, Francis Aerssens, had
his hundred eyes at all the keyholes in Paris, that centre of
ceaseless combination and conspiracy, and was besides in
almost daily confidential intercourse with the King. Most
patiently and minutely he kept the Advocate informed,
almost from hour to hour, of every web that was spun, every
conversation public or whispered in which important affairs
were treated anywhere and by anybody. He was all-sufficient
as a spy and intelligencer, although not entirely trustworthy
as a counsellor. Still no man on the whole could scan the
present or forecast the future more accurately than he was
able to do from his advantageous position and his long
experience of affairs.

<hr>

[1] W. Menzel, iii. 205.

There was much general jealousy between the States and the despotic king, who loved to be called the father of the Republic and to treat the Hollanders as his deeply obliged and very ungrateful and miserly little children.[1]  The India trade was a sore subject, Henry having throughout the negotiations sought to force or wheedle the States into renouncing that commerce at the command of Spain, because he wished to help himself to it afterwards, and being now in the habit of secretly receiving Isaac Le Maire and other Dutch leaders in that lucrative monopoly, who lay disguised in Paris and in the house of Zamet—but not concealed from Aerssens, who pledged himself to break the neck of their enterprise—and were planning with the King a French East India Company in opposition to that of the Netherlands.[2]

On the whole, however, despite these commercial intrigues which Barneveld through the aid of Aerssens was enabled to baffle, there was much cordiality and honest friendship between the two countries.  Henry, far from concealing his political affection for the Republic, was desirous of receiving a special embassy of congratulation and gratitude from the States on conclusion of the truce ; not being satisfied with the warm expressions of respect and attachment conveyed through the ordinary diplomatic channel.

" He wishes," wrote Aerssens to the Advocate, "a public demonstration in order to show on a theatre to all Christendom the regard and deference of My Lords the States for his Majesty."  The Ambassador suggested that Cornelis van der Myle, son-in-law of Barneveld, soon to be named first envoy for Holland to the Venetian republic, might be selected as chief of such special embassy.[3]

---

[1] Report of the Special Ambassadors to France; an important MS. in the Archives of the Hague, to be cited freely hereafter.

[2] See the MS. correspondence of Aerssens with Barneveld, years 1609 and 1610, *passim*.

[3] Aerssens to Barneveld, 23 April 1609.  Same to same, 21 May, 1609. (MSS.)

" Without the instructions you gave me," wrote Aerssens, " Neuburg might have gained his cause in this court. Brandenburg is doing himself much injury by not soliciting the King."

" Much deference will be paid to your judgment," added the envoy, " if you see fit to send it to his Majesty."

Meantime, although the agent of Neuburg was busily dinning in Henry's ears the claims of the Palatine, and even urging old promises which, as he pretended, had been made, thanks to Barneveld, he took little by his importunity, notwithstanding that in the opinion both of Barneveld and Villeroy his claim *stricti juris* was the best. But it was policy and religious interests, not the strict letter of the law, that were likely to prevail. Henry, while loudly asserting that he would oppose any usurpation on the part of the Emperor or any one else against the *Condominium*, privately renewed to the States assurances of his intention to support ultimately the claims of Brandenburg, and notified them to hold the two regiments of French infantry, which by convention they still kept at his expense in their service, to be ready at a moment's warning for the great enterprise which he was already planning. " You would do well perhaps," wrote Aerssens to Barneveld, " to set forth the various interests in regard to this succession, and of the different relations of the claimants towards our commonwealth ; but in such sort nevertheless and so dexterously that the King may be able to understand your desires, and on the other hand may see the respect you bear him in appearing to defer to his choice." [1]

Neuburg, having always neglected the States and made advances to Archduke Albert, and being openly preferred over Brandenburg by the Austrians, who had however no intention of eventually tolerating either, could make but small headway

---

[1] MS. letter of Aerssens before cited, 13 May 1609.

at court, notwithstanding Henry's indignation that Brandenburg had not yet made the slightest demand upon him for assistance.[1]

The Elector had keenly solicited the aid of the States, who were bound to him by ancient contract on this subject, but had manifested wonderful indifference or suspicion in regard to France. "These nonchalant Germans," said Henry on more than one occasion, "do nothing but sleep or drink." [2]

It was supposed that the memory of Metz might haunt the imagination of the Elector. That priceless citadel, fraudulently extorted by Henry II. as a forfeit for assistance to the Elector of Saxony three quarters of a century before, gave solemn warning to Brandenburg of what might be exacted by a greater Henry, should success be due to his protection. It was also thought that he had too many dangers about him at home, the Poles especially, much stirred up by emissaries from Rome, making many troublesome demonstrations against the Duchy of Prussia.[3]

It was nearly midsummer before a certain Baron Donals arrived as emissary of the Elector. He brought with him many documents in support of the Branden- June 24, burg claims, and was charged with excuses for the 1609. dilatoriness of his master.[4] Much stress was laid of course on the renunciation made by Neuburg at the time of his marriage, and Henry was urged to grant his protection to the Elector in his good rights. But thus far there were few signs of any vigorous resolution for active measures in an affair which could scarcely fail to lead to war.

"I believe," said Henry to the States' ambassador, "that the

<hr>

[1] Aerssens to Duplessis-Mornay, 15 May 1609. (MS.)

[2] ". . . je suis encore assez verd, m'a dit S. M^te, pour mener une armée en Clèves. J'en aurai bon marché, mais les Allemands ne font que dormir ou boire. Ils en auroient le profit et me departeront la peine : touttefois je ne souffrirai pas l'accroissement de ceux d'Autriche," &c.—Aerssens to Barneveld, 26 July 1609. (MS.)

[3] Same to same, 24 June 1609. (MS.)

[4] Ibid.

right of Brandenburg is indubitable, and it is better for you and for me that he should be the man rather than Neuburg, who has always sought assistance from the House of Austria. But he is too lazy in demanding possession. It is the fault of the doctors by whom he is guided. This delay works in favour of the Emperor, whose course however is less governed by any determination of his own than by the irresolution of the princes." [1]

Then changing the conversation, Henry asked the Ambassador whether the daughter of de Maldere, a leading statesman of Zealand, was married or of age to be married, and if she was rich ; adding that they must make a match between her and Barneveld's second son, then a young gentleman in the King's service, and very much liked by him. [2]

Two months later a regularly accredited envoy, Belin by name, arrived from the Elector. His instructions were general. He was to thank the King for his declarations in favour of the possessory princes, and against all usurpation on the part of the Spanish party. Should the religious cord be touched, he was to give assurances that no change would be made in this regard. He was charged with loads of fine presents in yellow amber, such as ewers, basins, tables, cups, chessboards, for the King and Queen, the Dauphin, the Chancellor, Villeroy, Sully, Bouillon, and other eminent personages. [3] Beyond the distribution of these works of art and the exchange of a few diplomatic commonplaces, nothing serious in the way of warlike business was transacted, and Henry was a few weeks later much amused by receiving a letter from the possessory princes coolly thrown into the post-office, and addressed like an ordinary letter to a private person, in which he was requested to advance them a loan

<hr>

[1] Aerssens to Barneveld, 24 June 1609. (MS.)        [2] Ibid.
[3] Same to same, 27 Aug. 1609. (MS.)

of 400,000 crowns.[1]  There was a great laugh at court at a demand made like a bill of exchange at sight upon his Majesty as if he had been a banker, especially as there happened to be no funds of the drawers in his hands.[2]  It was thought that a proper regard for the King's quality and the amount of the sum demanded required that the letter should be brought at least by an express messenger, and Henry was both diverted and indignant at these proceedings, at the months' long delay before the princes had thought proper to make application for his protection, and then for this cool demand for alms on a large scale as a proper beginning of their enterprise.

Such was the languid and extremely nonchalant manner in which the early preparations for a conflict which seemed likely to set Europe in a blaze, and of which possibly few living men might witness the termination, were set on foot by those most interested in the immediate question.

Chessboards in yellow amber and a post-office order for 400,000 crowns could not go far in settling the question of the duchies in which the great problem dividing Christendom as by an abyss was involved.

Meantime, while such were the diplomatic beginnings of the possessory princes, the League was leaving no stone unturned to awaken Henry to a sense of his true duty to the Church of which he was Eldest Son.

Don Pedro de Toledo's mission in regard to the Spanish marriages had failed because Henry had spurned the condition which was unequivocally attached to them on the part of Spain, the king's renunciation of his alliance with the Dutch Republic, which then seemed an equivalent to its ruin.  But the treaty of truce and half-independence had been signed at last by the States and their ancient master, and the English and French negotiators had taken their

Aerssens to Barneveld, 18 Sept. 1609.  (MS.)          [2] Ibid.

departure, each receiving as a present for concluding the convention 20,000 livres from the Archdukes, and 30,000 from the States-General.[1]  Henry, returning one summer's morning from the chase and holding the Count of Soissons by one hand and Ambassador Aerssens by the other, told them he had just received letters from Spain by which he learned that people were marvellously rejoiced at the conclusion of the truce.  Many had regretted that its conditions were so disadvantageous and so little honourable to the grandeur and dignity of Spain, but to these it was replied that there were strong reasons why Spain should consent to peace on these terms rather than not have it at all. During the twelve years to come the King could repair his disasters and accumulate mountains of money in order to finish the war by the subjugation of the Provinces by force of gold.[2]

Soissons here interrupted the King by saying that the States on their part would finish it by force of iron.

Aerssens, like an accomplished courtier, replied they would finish it by means of his Majesty's friendship.

The King continued by observing that the clear-sighted in Spain laughed at these rodomontades, knowing well that it was pure exhaustion that had compelled the King to such extremities.  "I leave you to judge," said Henry, " whether he is likely to have any courage at forty-five years of age, having none now at thirty-two.  Princes show what they have in them of generosity and valour at the age of twenty-five or never."  He said that orders had been sent from Spain to disband all troops in the obedient Netherlands except Spaniards and Italians, telling the Archdukes that they must raise the money out of the country to content them.  They must pay for a war made for their benefit, said Philip.  As for him he would not furnish one maravedi.[3]

<hr>

[1] Aerssens to Duplessis-Mornay, 7 July 1609.  (Archives MS.)
[2] Aerssens to Barneveld, 28 May 1609.  (MS.)          [3] Ibid.

Aerssens asked if the Archdukes would disband their troops so long as the affair of Cleve remained unsettled. "You are very lucky," replied the King, "that Europe is governed by such princes as you wot of. The King of Spain thinks of nothing but tranquillity. The Archdukes will never move except on compulsion. The Emperor, whom every one is so much afraid of in this matter, is in such plight that one of these days, and before long, he will be stripped of all his possessions. I have news that the Bohemians are ready to expel him."[1]

It was true enough that Rudolph hardly seemed a formidable personage. The Utraquists and Bohemian Brothers, making up nearly the whole population of the country, were just extorting religious liberty from their unlucky master in his very palace and at the point of the knife. The envoy of Matthias was in Paris demanding recognition of his master as King of Hungary, and Henry did not suspect the wonderful schemes of Leopold, the ferret in the rabbit warren of the duchies, to come to the succour of his cousin and to get himself appointed his successor and guardian.

Nevertheless, the Emperor's name had been used to protest solemnly against the entrance into Düsseldorf of the Margrave Ernest of Brandenburg and Palatine Wolfgang William of Neuburg, representatives respectively of their brother and father.

The induction was nevertheless solemnly made by the Elector-Palatine and the Landgrave of Hesse, and joint possession solemnly taken by Brandenburg and Neuburg in the teeth of the protest, and expressly in order to cut short the dilatory schemes and the artifices of the Imperial court.

Henry at once sent a corps of observation consisting of 1500 cavalry to the Luxemburg frontier by way of Toul, Mezières, Verdun, and Metz, to guard against movements by

[1] Aerssens to Barneveld, 28 May 1609. (MS.)

the disbanded troops of the Archdukes, and against any active demonstration against the possessory princes on the part of the Emperor.[1]

The *Condominium* was formally established, and Henry stood before the world as its protector threatening any power that should attempt usurpation. He sent his agent Vidomacq to the Landgrave of Hesse with instructions to do his utmost to confirm the princes of the Union in organized resistance to the schemes of Spain, and to prevent any interference with the *Condominium*.

He wrote letters to the Archdukes and to the Elector of Cologne, sternly notifying them that he would permit no assault upon the princes, and meant to protect them in their rights. He sent one of his most experienced diplomatists, de Boississe, formerly ambassador in England, to reside for a year or more in the duchies as special representative of France, and directed him on his way thither to consult especially with Barneveld and the States-General as to the proper means of carrying out their joint policy either by diplomacy or, if need should be, by their united arms.[2]

Troops began at once to move towards the frontier to counteract the plans of the Emperor's council and the secret levies made by Duchess Sibylla's husband, the Margrave of Burgau. The King himself was perpetually at Monceaux watching the movements of his cavalry towards the Luxemburg frontier, and determined to protect the princes in their possession until some definite decision as to the sovereignty of the duchies should be made.

Meantime great pressure was put upon him by the opposite party. The Pope did his best through the Nuncius at Paris directly, and through agents at Prague, Brussels, and

<hr>

[1] Aerssens to Barneveld, 29 June 1609. (MS.)
[2] Same to same, 9 July 1609. (MS.)

Madrid indirectly, to awaken the King to a sense of the enormity of his conduct.

Being a Catholic prince, it was urged, he had no right to assist heretics. It was an action entirely contrary to his duty as a Christian and of his reputation as Eldest Son of the Church. Even if the right were on the side of the princes, his Majesty would do better to strip them of it and to clothe himself with it than to suffer the Catholic faith and religion to receive such notable detriment in an affair likely to have such important consequences.[1]

Such was some of the advice given by the Pontiff. The suggestions were subtle, for they were directed to Henry's self-interest both as champion of the ancient church and as a possible sovereign of the very territories in dispute. They were also likely, and were artfully so intended, to excite suspicion of Henry's designs in the breasts of the Protestants generally and of the possessory princes especially. Allusions indeed to the rectification of the French border in Henry II.'s time at the expense of Lorraine were very frequent. They probably accounted for much of the apparent supineness and want of respect for the King of which he complained every day and with so much bitterness.

The Pope's insinuations, however, failed to alarm him, for he had made up his mind as to the great business of what might remain to him of life; to humble the House of Austria and in doing so to uphold the Dutch Republic on which he relied for his most efficient support. The situation was a false one viewed from the traditional maxims which governed Europe. How could the Eldest Son of the Church and the chief of an unlimited monarchy make common cause with heretics and republicans against Spain and

---

[1] " . . . et quand bien le droict servit de leur côté, S. M<sup>té</sup> les en devroit plustot despouiller pour s'en vestir elle-mesmo sans souffrir que la religion et foy catholique reçoive une si notable bresche," &c.—Aerssens to Barneveld, 8 Aug. 1609. (MS.)

Rome? That the position was as dangerous as it was illogical, there could be but little doubt. But there was a similarity of opinion between the King and the political chief of the Republic on the great principle which was to illume the distant future but which had hardly then dawned upon the present; the principle of religious equality. As he protected Protestants in France so he meant to protect Catholics in the duchies. Apostate as he was from the Reformed Church as he had already been from the Catholic, he had at least risen above the paltry and insolent maxim of the princely Protestantism of Germany: "*Cujus regio ejus religio.*"

While refusing to tremble before the wrath of Rome or to incline his ear to its honeyed suggestions, he sent Cardinal Joyeuse with a special mission to explain to the Pope that while the interests of France would not permit him to allow the Spaniard's obtaining possession of provinces so near to her, he should take care that the Church received no detriment and that he should insist as a price of the succour he intended for the possessory princes that they should give ample guarantees for the liberty of Catholic worship.[1]

There was no doubt in the mind either of Henry or of Barneveld that the secret blows attempted by Spain at the princes were in reality aimed at the Republic and at himself as her ally.

While the Nuncius was making these exhortations in Paris, his colleague from Spain was authorized to propound a scheme of settlement which did not seem deficient in humour. At any rate Henry was much diverted with the suggestion, which was nothing less than that the decision as to the succession to the duchies should be left to a board of arbitration consisting of the King of Spain, the Emperor,

---

[1] Aerssens' letter, 8 Aug. 1609, last cited.

and the King of France.[1]  As Henry would thus be painfully placed by himself in a hopeless minority, the only result of the scheme would be to compel him to sanction a decision sure to be directly the reverse of his own resolve. He was hardly such a schoolboy in politics as to listen to the proposal except to laugh at it.

Meantime arrived from Jülich, without much parade, a quiet but somewhat pompous gentleman named Teynagel.[2] He had formerly belonged to the Reformed religion, but finding it more to his taste or advantage to become privy councillor of the Emperor, he had returned to the ancient church.  He was one of the five who had accompanied the Archduke Leopold to Jülich.

That prompt undertaking having thus far succeeded so well, the warlike bishop had now despatched Teynagel on a roving diplomatic mission.  Ostensibly he came to persuade Henry that, by the usages and laws of the Empire, fiefs left vacant for want of heirs male were at the disposal of the Emperor.  He expressed the hope therefore of obtaining the King's approval of Leopold's position in Jülich as temporary vicegerent of his sovereign and cousin.  The real motive of his mission, however, was privately to ascertain whether Henry was really ready to go to war for the protection of the possessory princes, and then to proceed to Spain.[3] It required an astute politician, however, to sound all the shoals, quicksands, and miseries through which the French government was then steering, and to comprehend with accuracy the somewhat varying humours of the monarch and the secret schemes of the ministers who immediately surrounded him.

People at court laughed at Teynagel and his mission, and Henry treated him as a crackbrained adventurer.[4]  He

---

[1] Aerssens to Barneveld, 27 July 1609.  (MS.)
[2] Same to same, 8 Aug. 1609. (MS.)
[3] Letter of Aerssens before cited.
[4] Aerssens to Barneveld, 16 Aug. 1609.  (MS.)

announced himself as envoy of the Emperor, although he had instructions from Leopold only. He had interviews with the Chancellor and with Villeroy, and told them that Rudolf claimed the right of judge between the various pretenders to the duchies. The King would not be pleased, he observed, if the King of Great Britain should constitute himself arbiter among claimants that might make their appearance for the crown of France ; but Henry had set himself up as umpire without being asked by any one to act in that capacity among the princes of Germany. The Emperor, on the contrary, had been appealed to by the Duke of Nevers, the Elector of Saxony, the Margrave of Burgau, and other liege subjects of the Imperial crown as a matter of course and of right. This policy of the King, if persisted in, said Teynagel, must lead to war. Henry might begin such a war, but he would be obliged to bequeath it to the Dauphin. He should remember that France had always been unlucky when waging war with the Empire and with the house of Austria.[1]

The Chancellor and Villeroy, although in their hearts not much in love with Henry's course, answered the emissary with arrogance equal to his own that their king could finish the war as well as begin it, that he confided in his strength and the justice of his cause, and that he knew very well and esteemed very little the combined forces of Spain and the Empire. They added that France was bound by the treaty of Vervins to protect the princes, but they offered no proof of that rather startling proposition.

Meantime Teynagel was busy in demonstrating that the princes of Germany were in reality much more afraid of Henry than of the Emperor. His military movements and deep designs excited more suspicion throughout that country and all Europe than the quiet journey of Leopold and five friends by post to Jülich.[2]

<hr>

[1] Aerssens to Barneveld, 16 Aug. 1600. (MS.)        [2] Ibid.

He had come provided with copies of the King's private letters to the princes, and seemed fully instructed as to his most secret thoughts. For this convenient information he was supposed to be indebted to the revelations of Father Cotton, who was then in disgrace ; having been detected in transmitting to the General of Jesuits Henry's most sacred confidences and confessions as to his political designs.[1]

Fortified with this private intelligence, and having been advised by Father Cotton to carry matters with a high hand in order to inspire the French court with a wholesome awe, he talked boldly about the legitimate functions of the Emperor. To interfere with them, he assured the ministers, would lead to a long and bloody war, as neither the King nor the Archduke Albert would permit the Emperor to be trampled upon.

Peter Pecquius, the crafty and experienced agent of the Archduke at Paris, gave the bouncing envoy more judicious advice, however, than that of the Jesuit, assuring him that he would spoil his whole case should he attempt to hold such language to the King.

He was admitted to an audience of Henry at Monceaux, but found him prepared to show his teeth as Aerssens had predicted. He treated Teynagel as a mere madcap and adventurer who had no right to be received as a public minister at all, and cut short his rodomontades by assuring him that his mind was fully made up to protect the possessory princes. Jeannin was present at the interview, although, as Aerssens well observed, the King required no pedagogue on such an occasion.[2] Teynagel soon afterwards departed malcontent to Spain, having taken little by his abnormal legation to Henry, and being destined to find at the court of Philip as urgent demands on that monarch for assistance to

<hr>

[1] Aerssens to Barneveld, 24 May and 8 and 16 Aug. 1609. (MS.)
[2] Letters of Aerssens, 8 and 16 Aug. last cited.

the League as he was to make for Leopold and the House of Austria.[1]

For the League, hardly yet thoroughly organized under the leadership of Maximilian of Bavaria, was rather a Catholic corrival than cordial ally of the Imperial house. It was universally suspected that Henry meant to destroy and discrown the Habsburgs, and it lay not in the schemes of Maximilian to suffer the whole Catholic policy to be bound to the fortunes of that one family.

Whether or not Henry meant to commit the anachronism and blunder of reproducing the part of Charlemagne might be doubtful. The supposed design of Maximilian to renew the glories of the House of Wittelsbach was equally vague. It is certain, however, that a belief in such ambitious schemes on the part of both had been insinuated into the cars of Rudolf, and had sunk deeply into his unsettled mind.[2]

Scarcely had Teynagel departed than the ancient President Richardot appeared upon the scene. "The mischievous old monkey," as he had irreverently been characterized during the Truce negotiations, "who showed his tail the higher he climbed," was now trembling at the thought that all the good work he had been so laboriously accomplishing during the past two years should be annihilated. The Archdukes, his masters, being sincerely bent on peace, had deputed him to Henry, who, as they believed, was determined to rekindle war. As frequently happens in such cases, they were prepared to smooth over the rough and almost impassable path to a cordial understanding by comfortable and cheap commonplaces concerning the blessings of peace, and to offer friendly compromises by which they might secure the prizes of war without the troubles and dangers of making it.

[1] Letters of Aerssens, 8 and 16 Aug. last cited. Compare A. Gindely, 'Rudolf II.' ii. 40, *sqq.*  [2] Ibid. 30, 42.

They had been solemnly notified by Henry that he would go to war rather than permit the House of Austria to acquire the succession to the duchies.[1]  They now sent Richardot to say that neither the Archdukes nor the King of Spain would interfere in the matter, and that they hoped the King of France would not prevent the Emperor from exercising his rightful functions of judge.

Henry, who knew that Don Baltasar de Cuñiga, Spanish ambassador at the Imperial court, had furnished Leopold, the Emperor's cousin, with 50,000 crowns to defray his first expenses in the Jülich expedition, considered that the veteran politician had come to perform a school boy's task.  He was more than ever convinced by this mission of Richardot that the Spaniards had organized the whole scheme, and he was likely only to smile at any propositions the President might make.

At the beginning of his interview, in which the King was quite alone, Richardot asked if he would agree to maintain neutrality like the King of Spain and the Archdukes, and allow the princes to settle their business with the Emperor.[2]

"No," said the King.

He then asked if Henry would assist them in their wrong.

"No," said the King.

He then asked if the King thought that the princes had justice on their side, and whether, if the contrary were shown, he would change his policy?

Henry replied that the Emperor could not be both judge and party in the suit and that the King of Spain was plotting to usurp the provinces through the instrumentality of his brother-in-law Leopold and under the name of the Emperor.  He would not suffer it, he said.

---

[1] Aerssens to Barneveld, 10 Aug. 1609. (MS.)  Same to same, 22 Aug. 1609. (MS.) Same to Digart, 10 Aug. 1609.  (MS.)

[2] Same to Barneveld, 2 Sept. 1609. (MS.)

"Then there will be a general war," replied Richardot, "since you are determined to assist these princes."

"Be it so," said the King.

"You are right," said the President, "for you are a great and puissant monarch, having all the advantages that could be desired, and in case of rupture I fear that all this immense power will be poured out over us who are but little princes."

"Cause Leopold to retire then and leave the princes in their right," was the reply. "You will then have nothing to fear. Are you not very unhappy to live under those poor weak archdukes? Don't you foresee that as soon as they die you will lose all the little you have acquired in the obedient Netherlands during the last fifty years?"[1]

The President had nothing to reply to this save that he had never approved of Leopold's expedition, and that when Spaniards make mistakes they always had recourse to their servants to repair their faults. He had accepted this mission inconsiderately, he said, inspired by a hope to conjure the rising storms mingled with fears as to the result which were now justified. He regretted having come, he said.

The King shrugged his shoulders.

Richardot then suggested that Leopold might be recognized in Jülich, and the princes at Düsseldorf, or that all parties might retire until the Emperor should give his decision.

All these combinations were flatly refused by the King, who swore that no one of the House of Austria should ever perch in any part of those provinces. If Leopold did not withdraw at once, war was inevitable.

He declared that he would break up everything and dare everything, whether the possessory princes formally applied

---

[1] Aerssens to Barneveld, 2 Sept. 1609. (MS.)

to him or not. He would not see his friends oppressed nor allow the Spaniard by this usurpation to put his foot on the throat of the States-General, for it was against them that this whole scheme was directed.

To the President's complaints that the States-General had been moving troops in Gelderland, Henry replied at once that it was done by his command, and that they were his troops.

With this answer Richardot was fain to retire crestfallen, mortified, and unhappy. He expressed repentance and astonishment at the result, and protested that those peoples were happy whose princes understood affairs. His princes were good, he said, but did not give themselves the trouble to learn their business.[1]

Richardot then took his departure from Paris, and very soon afterwards from the world. He died at Arras early in September, as many thought of chagrin at the ill success of his mission, while others ascribed it to a surfeit of melons and peaches.[2]

" *Senectus etiam morbus est*," said Aerssens with Seneca.

Henry said he could not sufficiently wonder at these last proceedings at his court, of a man he had deemed capable and sagacious, but who had been committing an irreparable blunder. He had never known two such impertinent ambassadors as Don Pedro de Toledo and Richardot on this occasion.[3] The one had been entirely ignorant of the object of his mission; the other had shown a vain presumption in thinking he could drive him from his fixed purpose by a flood of words. He had accordingly answered him on the spot without consulting his council, at which poor Richardot had been much amazed.[4]

---

[1] Aerssens to Barneveld, 2 Sept. 1609. (MS.)
[2] Same to same, 14 Sept. 1609. (MS.)
[3] Same to same, 2 Sept. 1609. (MS.)
[4] Ibid.

And now another envoy appeared upon the scene, an ambassador coming directly from the Emperor. Count Hohenzollern, a young man, wild, fierce, and arrogant, scarcely twenty-three years of age, arrived in Paris on the 7th of September, with a train of forty horsemen.[1]

De Colly, agent of the Elector-Palatine, had received an outline of his instructions, which the Prince of Anhalt had obtained at Prague. He informed Henry that Hohenzollern would address him thus : " You are a king. You would not like that the Emperor should aid your subjects in rebellion. He did not do this in the time of the League, although often solicited to do so. You should not now sustain the princes in disobeying the Imperial decree. Kings should unite in maintaining the authority and majesty of each other." He would then in the Emperor's name urge the claims of the House of Saxony to the duchies.[2]

Henry was much pleased with this opportune communication by de Colly of the private instructions to the Emperor's envoy, by which he was enabled to meet the wild and fierce young man with an arrogance at least equal to his own.

The interview was a stormy one. The King was alone in the gallery of the Louvre, not choosing that his words and gestures should be observed.[3] The Envoy spoke much in the sense which de Colly had indicated ; making a long argument in favour of the Emperor's exclusive right of arbitration, and assuring the King that the Emperor was resolved on war if interference between himself and his subjects was persisted in. He loudly pronounced the proceedings of the possessory princes to be utterly illegal, and contrary to all precedent. The Emperor would maintain his authority at

---

[1] "Fier et hagard,"—Ibid. Aerssens always calls this envoy " Hohenzollern;" Dr. Gindely calls him " Zollern."

[2] Aerssens to Barneveld, 18 Sept. 1600. (MS.)

[3] Ibid.

all hazards, and one spark of war would set everything in a blaze within the Empire and without.

Henry replied sternly but in general terms, and referred him for a final answer to his council.

" What will you do," asked the Envoy, categorically, at a subsequent interview about a month later, " to protect the princes in case the Emperor constrains them to leave the provinces which they have unjustly occupied ? "[1]

" There is none but God to compel me to say more than I choose to say," replied the King.  " It is enough for you to know that I will never abandon my friends in a just cause.  The Emperor can do much for the general peace. He is not to lend his name to cover this usurpation."

And so the concluding interview terminated in an exchange of threats rather than with any hope of accommodation.[2]

Hohenzollern used as high language to the ministers as to the monarch, and received payment in the same coin.  He rebuked their course not very adroitly as being contrary to the interests of Catholicism.  They were placing the provinces in the hands of Protestants, he urged.  It required no envoy from Prague to communicate this startling fact. Friends and foes, Villeroy and Jeannin, as well as Sully and Duplessis, knew well enough that Henry was not taking up arms for Rome.  "Sir ! do you look at the matter in that way ?" cried Sully, indignantly.  " The Huguenots are as good as the Catholics.  They fight like the devil ! "[3]

" The Emperor will never permit the princes to remain nor Leopold to withdraw," said the Envoy to Jeannin.

Jeannin replied that the King was always ready to listen

<hr>

[1] Aerssens to Barneveld, 18 Oct. 1609.  (MS.)

[2] Ibid.

[3] From a despatch of Colly, quoted by Gindely, ' Rudolf II.' B. ii. p. 39, note.  " Monsieur, la prenez vous par là ?  Ils ne valent pas moins pour cela, les Huguenots frappent comme le diable."

to reason, but there was no use in holding language of authority to him. It was money he would not accept.

"*Fiat justitia pereat mundus*," said the haggard Hohenzollern.

"Your world may perish," replied Jeannin, "but not ours. It is much better put together." [1]

A formal letter was then written by the King to the Emperor, in which Henry expressed his desire to maintain peace and fraternal relations, but notified him that if, under any pretext whatever, he should trouble the princes in their possession, he would sustain them with all his power, being bound thereto by treaties and by reasons of state. [2]

This letter was committed to the care of Hohenzollern, who forthwith departed, having received a present of 4000 crowns. [3] His fierce, haggard face thus vanishes for the present from our history.

The King had taken his ground, from which there was no receding. Envoys or agents of Emperor, Pope, King of Spain, Archduke at Brussels, and Archduke at Jülich, had failed to shake his settled purpose. Yet the road was far from smooth. He had thus far no ally but the States-General. He could not trust James of Great Britain. Boderic came back late in the summer from his mission to that monarch, reporting him as being favourably inclined to Brandenburg, but hoping for an amicable settlement in the duchies. [4] No suggestion being made even by the sagacious James as to the manner in which the ferret and rabbits were to come to a compromise, Henry inferred, if it came to fighting, that the English government would refuse assistance. James had asked Boderic in fact whether his sovereign and the States, being the parties chiefly interested, would be willing to fight it

----

[1] Aerssens to Barneveld, 7 Oct. 1609. (MS.)
[2] Same to same, 18 Oct. 1609. (MS.)
[3] Same to same, 27 Oct. 1609. (MS.)
[4] Same to same, 2 Sept. 1609. (MS.)

out without allies.  He had also sent Sir Ralph Winwood on a special mission to the Hague, to Düsseldorf, and with letters to the Emperor, in which he expressed confidence that Rudolph would approve the proceedings of the possessory princes.[1]  As he could scarcely do that while loudly claiming through his official envoy in Paris that the princes should instantly withdraw on pain of instant war, the value of the English suggestion of an amicable compromise might easily be deduced.

Great was the jealousy in France of this mission from England.  That the princes should ask the interference of James while neglecting, despising, or fearing Henry, excited Henry's wrath.  He was ready, and avowed his readiness, to put on armour at once in behalf of the princes, and to arbitrate on the destiny of Germany, but no one seemed ready to follow his standard.  No one asked him to arbitrate.  The Spanish faction wheedled and threatened by turns, in order to divert him from his purpose, while the Protestant party held aloof, and babbled of Charlemagne and of Henry II.

He said he did not mean to assist the princes by halves, but as became a King of France, and the princes expressed suspicion of him, talked of the example of Metz, and called the Emperor their very clement lord.[2]

It was not strange that Henry was indignant and jealous. He was holding the wolf by the ears, as he himself observed more than once.  The war could not long be delayed ; yet they in whose behalf it was to be waged treated him with a disrespect and flippancy almost amounting to scorn.

They tried to borrow money of him through the post, and neglected to send him an ambassador.  This was most decidedly putting the cart before the oxen, so Henry said, and so thought all his friends.  When they had blockaded the

[1] Aerssens to Barneveld, 6 Sept. 1609.  (MS.)
[2] Same to Duplessis-Mornay, 18 and 21 Oct. 1609.  (MS.)

road to Jülich, in order to cut off Leopold's supplies, they sent to request that the two French regiments in the States' service might be ordered to their assistance, Archduke Albert having threatened to open the passage by force of arms. "This is a fine stratagem," said Aerssens, "to fling the States-General headlong into the war, and, as it were, without knowing it."[1]

But the States-General, under the guidance of Barneveld, were not likely to be driven headlong by Brandenburg and Neuburg. They managed with caution, but with perfect courage, to move side by side with Henry, and to leave the initiative to him, while showing an unfaltering front to the enemy. That the princes were lost, Spain and the Emperor triumphant, unless Henry and the States should protect them with all their strength, was as plain as a mathematical demonstration.

Yet firm as were the attitude and the language of Henry, he was thought to be hoping to accomplish much by bluster. It was certain that the bold and unexpected stroke of Leopold had produced much effect upon his mind, and for a time those admitted to his intimacy saw, or thought they saw, a decided change in his demeanour.[2] To the world at large his language and his demonstrations were even more vehement than they had been at the outset of the controversy; but it was believed that there was now a disposition to substitute threats for action. The military movements set on foot were thought to be like the ringing of bells and firing of cannon to dissipate a thunderstorm.[3] Yet it was treason at court to doubt the certainty of war. The King ordered new suits of armour, bought splendid chargers,[4] and gave himself all the airs of a champion rushing to a tournament

---

[1] Aerssens to Vosbergen, 19 Oct. 1609. (MS.)
[2] Same to Barneveld, 29 July 1609.
(MS.)
[3] Same to same, 2 Aug. 1609. (MS.)
[4] Ibid.

as gaily as in the earliest days of his king-errantry. He spoke of his eager desire to break a lance with Spinola, and give a lesson to the young volunteer who had sprung into so splendid a military reputation, while he had been rusting, as he thought, in pacific indolence, and envying the laurels of the comparatively youthful Maurice. Yet those most likely to be well informed believed that nothing would come of all this fire and fury.

The critics were wrong. There was really no doubt of Henry's sincerity, but his isolation was terrible. There was none true to him at home but Sully. Abroad, the States-General alone were really friendly, so far as positive agreements existed. Above all, the intolerable tergiversations and suspicions of those most interested, the princes in possession, and their bickerings among themselves, hampered his movements.

Treason and malice in his cabinet and household, jealousy and fear abroad, were working upon and undermining him like a slow fever. His position was most pathetic, but his purpose was fixed.

James of England, who admired, envied, and hated Henry, was wont to moralize on his character and his general unpopularity, while engaged in negotiations with him. He complained that in the whole affair of the truce he had sought only his particular advantage. "This is not to be wondered at in one of his nature," said the King, "who only careth to provide for the felicities of his present life, without any respect for his life to come. Indeed, the consideration of his own age and the youth of his children, the doubt of their legitimation, the strength of competitioners, and the universal hatred borne unto him, makes him seek all means of security for preventing of all dangers." [1]

<hr>

[1] King to Cecil (probably in 1608). (MS. in the Cecil Archives at Hatfield.) See Appendix.

There were changes from day to day; hot and cold fits necessarily resulting from the situation. As a rule, no eminent general who has had much experience wishes to go into a new war inconsiderately and for the mere love of war. The impatience is often on the part of the non-combatants. Henry was no exception to the rule. He felt that the complications then existing, the religious, political, and dynastic elements arrayed against each other, were almost certain to be brought to a crisis and explosion by the incident of the duchies. He felt that the impending struggle was probably to be a desperate and a general one, but there was no inconsistency in hoping that the show of a vigorous and menacing attitude might suspend, defer, or entirely dissipate the impending storm.

The appearance of vacillation on his part from day to day was hardly deserving of the grave censure which it received, and was certainly in the interests of humanity.

His conferences with Sully were almost daily and marked by intense anxiety. He longed for Barneveld, and repeatedly urged that the Advocate, laying aside all other business, would come to Paris, that they might advise together thoroughly and face to face.[1] It was most important that the combination of alliances should be correctly arranged before hostilities began, and herein lay the precise difficulty. The princes applied formally and freely to the States-General for assistance. They applied to the King of Great Britain. The agents of the opposite party besieged Henry with entreaties, and, failing in those, with threats; going off afterwards to Spain, to the Archdukes, and to other Catholic powers in search of assistance.

The States-General professed their readiness to put an army of 15,000 foot and 3000 horse in the field for the

---

[1] Aerssens to Barneveld, 6 Oct. 1609 (MS.), and many other letters in the Archives.

spring campaign, so soon as they were assured of Henry's determination for a rupture.

"I am fresh enough still," said he to their ambassador, "to lead an army into Cleve.  I shall have a cheap bargain enough of the provinces.  But these Germans do nothing but eat and sleep.  They will get the profit and assign to me the trouble.  No matter, I will never suffer the aggrandizement of the House of Austria.  The States-General must disband no troops, but hold themselves in readiness." [1]

Secretary of State Villeroy held the same language, but it was easy to trace beneath his plausible exterior a secret determination to traverse the plans of his sovereign.  "The Cleve affair must lead to war," he said.  "The Spaniard, considering how necessary it is for him to have a prince there at his devotion, can never quietly suffer Brandenburg and Neuburg to establish themselves in those territories.  The support thus gained by the States-General would cause the loss of the Spanish Netherlands." [2]

This was the view of Henry, too, but the Secretary of State, secretly devoted to the cause of Spain, looked upon the impending war with much aversion.

"All that can come to his Majesty from war," he said, "is the glory of having protected the right.  Counterbalance this with the fatigue, the expense, and the peril of a great conflict, after our long repose, and you will find this to be buying glory too dearly." [3]

When a Frenchman talked of buying glory too dearly, it seemed probable that the particular kind of glory was not to his taste.

Henry had already ordered the officers, then in France, of the 4000 French infantry kept in the States' service at his expense to depart at once to Holland, and he privately

<hr>

[1] Aerssens to Barneveld, 29 July 1609.  (MS.)          [2] Ibid.
[3] Ibid.

announced his intention of moving to the frontier at the head of 30,000 men.[1]

Yet not only Villeroy, but the Chancellor and the Constable, while professing opposition to the designs of Austria and friendliness to those of Brandenburg and Neuburg, deprecated this precipitate plunge into war. " Those most interested," they said, " refuse to move ; fearing Austria, distrusting France. They leave us the burden and danger, and hope for the spoils themselves. We cannot play cat to their monkey. The King must hold himself in readiness to join in the game when the real players have shuffled and dealt the cards. It is no matter to us whether the Spaniard or Brandenburg or anyone else gets the duchies. The States-General require a friendly sovereign there, and ought to say how much they will do for that result." [2]

The Constable laughed at the whole business. Coming straight from the Louvre, he said " there would be no serious military movement, and that all those fine freaks would evaporate in air." [3]

But Sully never laughed. He was quietly preparing the ways and means for the war, and he did not intend, so far as he had influence, that France should content herself with freaks and let Spain win the game. Alone in the council he maintained that " France had gone too far to recede without sacrifice of reputation." " The King's word is engaged both within and without," he said. " Not to follow it with deeds would be dangerous to the kingdom. The Spaniard will think France afraid of war. We must strike a sudden blow, either to drive the enemy away or to crush him at once. There is no time for delay. The

<hr>

[1] Aerssens to Barneveld, 29 July 1609. (MS.)

[2] Ibid. ; also same to same, 28 Sept.

1609. (MS.) Aerssens to Duplessis-Mornay, 15 Nov. 1609. (MS.)

[3] Ibid.

Netherlands must prevent the aggrandizement of Austria or consent to their own ruin." [1]

Thus stood the game therefore. The brother of Brandenburg and son of Neuburg had taken possession of Düsseldorf.

The Emperor, informed of this, ordered them forthwith to decamp. He further summoned all pretenders to the duchies to appear before him, in person or by proxy, to make good their claims. They refused and appealed for advice and assistance to the States-General. Barneveld, aware of the intrigues of Spain, who disguised herself in the drapery of the Emperor, recommended that the Estates of Cleve, Jülich, Berg, Mark, Ravensberg, and Ravenstein, should be summoned in Düsseldorf. This was done and a resolution taken to resist any usurpation. [2]

The King of France wrote to the Elector of Cologne, who, by directions of Rome and by means of the Jesuits, had been active in the intrigue, that he would not permit the princes to be disturbed.

The Archduke Leopold suddenly jumped into the chief citadel of the country and published an edict of the Emperor. All the proceedings were thereby nullified as illegal and against the dignity of the realm and the princes proclaimed under ban.

A herald brought the edict and ban to the princes in full assembly. The princes tore it to pieces on the spot. [3] Nevertheless they were much frightened, and many members of the Estates took themselves off; others showing an inclination to follow.

The princes sent forthwith a deputation to the Hague to consult My Lords the States-General. The States-General sent an express messenger to Paris. Their ambassador

[1] Aerssens to Barneveld, 2 Aug. 1609. (MS.)
[2] Same to Duplessis-Mornay, 7 Aug. 1609. (MS.)   [3] Ibid.

there sent him back a week later, with notice of the King's determination to risk everything against everything to preserve the rights of the princes. It was added that Henry required to be solicited by them, in order not by volunteer succour to give cause for distrust as to his intentions.[1] The States-General were further apprised by the King that his interests and theirs were so considerable in the matter that they would probably be obliged to go into a brisk and open war, in order to prevent the Spaniard from establishing himself in the duchies. He advised them to notify the Archdukes in Brussels that they would regard the truce as broken if, under pretext of maintaining the Emperor's rights, they should molest the princes. He desired them further to send their forces at once to the frontier of Gelderland under Prince Maurice, without committing any overt act of hostility, but in order to show that both the King and the States were thoroughly in earnest.

· The King then sent to Archduke Albert, as well as to the Elector of Cologne, and despatched a special envoy to the King of Great Britain.

Immediately afterwards came communications from Barneveld to Henry, with complete adhesion to the King's plans. The States would move in exact harmony with him, neither before him nor after him, which was precisely what he wished. He complained bitterly to Aerssens, when he communicated the Advocate's despatches, of the slothful and timid course of the princes. He ascribed it to the arts of Leopold, who had written and inspired many letters against him insinuating that he was secretly in league and correspondence with the Emperor; that he was going to the duchies simply in the interest of the Catholics; that he was like Henry II. only seeking to extend the French frontier;

---

[1] Aerssens to Duplessis-Mornay, 7 Aug. 1600. (MS.)  Same to Digart,
10 Aug. 1609. (MS.)

and Leopold, by these intrigues and falsehoods, had succeeded in filling the princes with distrust, and they had taken umbrage at the advance of his cavalry.[1]

Henry professed himself incapable of self-seeking or ambition.  He meant to prevent the aggrandizement of Austria, and was impatient at the dilatoriness and distrust of the princes.

" All their enemies are rushing to the King of Spain.  Let them address themselves to the King of France," he said, " for it is we two that must play this game."

And when at last they did send an embassy, they prefaced it by a post letter demanding an instant loan, and with an intimation that they would rather have his money than his presence !    Sept. 11, 1609.

Was it surprising that the King's course should seem occasionally wavering when he found it so difficult to stir up such stagnant waters into honourable action?  Was it strange that the rude and stern Sully should sometimes lose his patience, knowing so much and suspecting more of the foul designs by which his master was encompassed, of the web of conspiracy against his throne, his life, and his honour, which was daily and hourly spinning ?

" We do nothing and you do nothing," he said one day to Aerssens.  " You are too soft, and we are too cowardly.  I believe that we shall spoil everything, after all.  I always suspect these sudden determinations of ours.  They are of bad augury.  We usually founder at last when we set off so fiercely at first.  There are words enough on every side, but there will be few deeds.  There is nothing to be got out of the King of Great Britain, and the King of Spain will end by securing these provinces for himself by a treaty."[2]

---

[1] Aerssens to Duplessis-Mornay, 7 Aug. 1609. (MS.)  Same to Digart, 10 Aug. 1609. (MS.)

[2] Same to Barneveld, 14 Nov. 1609. (MS.)

Sully knew better than this, but he did not care to let even the Dutch envoy know, as yet, the immense preparations he had been making for the coming campaign.

The envoys of the possessory princes, the Counts Solms, Colonel Pallandt, and Dr. Steyntgen, took their departure, after it had been arranged that final measures should be concerted at the general congress of the German Protestants to be held early in the ensuing year at Hall, in Suabia.

At that convention de Boississe would make himself heard on the part of France, and the representatives of the States-General, of Venice, and Savoy, would also be present.[1]

Meantime the secret conferences between Henry and his superintendent of finances and virtual prime minister were held almost every day. Scarcely an afternoon passed that the King did not make his appearance at the Arsenal, Sully's residence, and walk up and down the garden with him for hours, discussing the great project of which his brain was full. This great project was to crush for ever the power of the Austrian house; to drive Spain back into her own limits, putting an end to her projects for universal monarchy; and taking the Imperial crown from the House of Habsburg. By thus breaking up the mighty cousinship which, with the aid of Rome, overshadowed Germany and the two peninsulas, besides governing the greater part of both the Indies, he meant to bring France into the preponderant position over Christendom which he believed to be her due.

It was necessary, he thought, for the continued existence of the Dutch commonwealth that the opportunity should be taken once for all, now that a glorious captain commanded its armies and a statesman unrivalled for experience, insight, and patriotism controlled its politics and its diplomacy, to drive the Spaniard out of the Netherlands

[1] 'Mémoires de Sully,' vii. 337, *sqq.*

The Cleve question, properly and vigorously handled, presented exactly the long desired opportunity for carrying out these vast designs.

The plan of assault upon Spanish power was to be three-fold. The King himself at the head of 35,000 men, supported by Prince Maurice and the States' forces amounting to at least 14,000, would move to the Rhine and seize the duchies. The Duke de la Force would command the army of the Pyrences and act in concert with the Moors of Spain, who roused to frenzy by their expulsion from the kingdom could be relied on for a revolt or at least a most vigorous diversion.[1] Thirdly, a treaty with the Duke of Savoy by which Henry accorded his daughter to the Duke's eldest son, the Prince of Piedmont, a gift of 100,000 crowns, and a monthly pension during the war of 50,000 crowns a month, was secretly concluded.

Early in the spring the Duke was to take the field with at least 10,000 foot and 1200 horse, supported by a French army of 12,000 to 15,000 men under the experienced Marshal de Lesdiguières. These forces were to operate against the Duchy of Milan with the intention of driving the Spaniards out of that rich possession, which the Duke of Savoy claimed for himself, and of assuring to Henry the dictatorship of Italy. With the cordial alliance of Venice, and by playing off the mutual jealousies of the petty Italian princes, like Florence, Mantua, Montserrat, and others, against each other and against the Pope, it did not seem doubtful to Sully that the result would be easily accomplished. He distinctly urged the wish that the King should content himself with political influence, with the splendid position of holding all Italy dependent upon his will and guidance, but without annexing a particle of territory to his own crown

<hr>

[1] 'Mémoires de Sully,' t. vii. liv. xxvii. *passim.* Letters of Aerssens to Barneveld, 1609 and 1610 (MS.), *passim,* especially letter of 25 Dec. 1609.

It was Henry's intention, however, to help himself to the Duchy of Savoy, and to the magnificent city and port of Genoa [1] as a reward to himself for the assistance, matrimonial alliance, and aggrandizement which he was about to bestow upon Charles Emmanuel. Sully strenuously opposed these self-seeking views on the part of his sovereign, however, constantly placing before him the far nobler aim of controlling the destinies of Christendom, of curbing what tended to become omnipotent, of raising up and protecting that which had been abased, of holding the balance of empire with just and steady hand in preference to the more vulgar and commonplace ambition of annexing a province or two to the realms of France. [2]

It is true that these virtuous homilies, so often preached by him against territorial aggrandizement in one direction, did not prevent him from indulging in very extensive visions of it in another. But the dreams pointed to the east rather than to the south. It was Sully's policy to swallow a portion not of Italy but of Germany. He persuaded his master that the possessory princes, if placed by the help of France in the heritage which they claimed, would hardly be able to maintain themselves against the dangers which surrounded them except by a direct dependence upon France. In the end the position would become an impossible one, and it would be easy after the war was over to indemnify Brandenburg with money and with private property in the heart of France for example, and obtain the cession of those most coveted

---

[1] " . . . pour engager le duc de Savoie de rompre avec l'Espagne, on luy a accordé quasi tout ce qu'il a demandé—il semble que desormais on veut commencer à faire de la part du Roi n'estant pas raisonnable que le Roi face ceste grande dépense sans en espérer aucune utilité—et pourtant propose on de demander au Duc le duché de Savoje en contrechange du secours du Roi et de la cession de ses titres en outre la ville de Gennes avec plein pied en Italie ; je ne scais pas si on fera ces demandes au Duc comme il se dispute encore ; mais les faisant voilà notre dessin en Italie à vau l'eau. . . . On lève ici jusqu'à quarante mille fantassins sans conter les 6000 Suisses."—Aerssens to Barneveld, 20 Feb. 1610. (MS.)

[2] 'Mémoires de Sully,' *ubi sup.*

provinces between the Meuse and the Weser to the King. " What an advantage for France," whispered Sully, " to unite to its power so important a part of Germany. For it cannot be denied that by accepting the succour given by the King now those princes oblige themselves to ask for help in the future in order to preserve their new acquisition. Thus your Majesty will make them pay for it very dearly." [1]

Thus the very virtuous self-denial in regard to the Duke of Savoy did not prevent a secret but well developed ambition at the expense of the Elector of Brandenburg. For after all it was well enough known that the Elector was the really important and serious candidate. Henry knew full well that Neuburg was depending on the Austrians and the Catholics, and that the claims of Saxony were only put forward by the Emperor in order to confuse the princes and excite mutual distrust.

The King's conferences with the great financier were most confidential, and Sully was as secret as the grave. But Henry never could keep a secret even when it concerned his most important interests, and nothing would serve him but he must often babble of his great projects even to their minutest details in presence of courtiers and counsellors whom in his heart he knew to be devoted to Spain and in receipt of pensions from her king.[2] He would boast to them of the blows by which he meant to demolish Spain and the whole house of Austria, so that there should be no longer danger to be feared from that source to the tranquillity and happiness of Europe, and he would do this so openly and in presence of those who, as he knew, were perpetually setting traps for him and endeavouring to discover his deepest secrets as to make Sully's hair stand on end. The faithful minister would pluck his master by the cloak at times,[3] and

---

[1] 'Mémoires de Sully,' t. vii. p. 324.
[2] Ibid. p. 362.          [3] Ibid.

the King, with the adroitness which never forsook him when he chose to employ it, would contrive to extricate himself from a dilemma and pause at the brink of tremendous disclosures. But Sully could not be always at his side, nor were the Nuncius or Don Inigo de Cardenas or their confidential agents and spies always absent. Enough was known of the general plan, while as to the probability of its coming into immediate execution, perhaps the enemies of the King were often not more puzzled than his friends.

But what the Spanish ambassador did not know, nor the Nuncius, nor even the friendly Aerssens, was the vast amount of supplies which had been prepared for the coming conflict by the finance minister. Henry did not know it himself. "The war will turn on France as on a pivot," said Sully; "it remains to be seen if we have supplies and money enough. I will engage if the war is not to last more than three years and you require no more than 40,000 men at a time that I will show you munitions and ammunition and artillery and the like to such an extent that you will say, 'It is enough.'

"As to money ——"

"How much money have I got?" asked the King; "a dozen millions?"

"A little more than that," answered the Minister.

"Fourteen millions?"

"More still."

"Sixteen?" continued the King.

"More yet," said Sully.

And so the King went on adding two millions at each question until thirty millions were reached, and when the question as to this sum was likewise answered in the affirmative, he jumped from his chair, hugged his minister around the neck, and kissed him on both cheeks.

"I want no more than that," he cried.

Sully answered by assuring him that he had prepared a report showing a reserve of forty millions on which he might draw for his war expenses, without in the least degree infringing on the regular budget for ordinary expenses.[1]

The King was in a transport of delight, and would have been capable of telling the story on the spot to the Nuncius had he met him that afternoon, which fortunately did not occur.

But of all men in Europe after the faithful Sully, Henry most desired to see and confer daily and secretly with Barneveld. He insisted vehemently that, neglecting all other business, he should come forthwith to Paris at the head of the special embassy which it had been agreed that the States should send. No living statesman, he said, could compare to Holland's Advocate in sagacity, insight, breadth of view, knowledge of mankind and of great affairs, and none he knew was more sincerely attached to his person or felt more keenly the value of the French alliance.

With him he indeed communicated almost daily through the medium of Aerssens, who was in constant receipt of most elaborate instructions from Barneveld, but he wished to confer with him face to face, so that there would be no necessity of delay in sending back for instructions, limitations, and explanation. No man knew better than the King did that so far as foreign affairs were concerned the States-General were simply Barneveld.

On the 22nd January the States' ambassador had a long and secret interview with the King.[2] He informed him that the Prince of Anhalt had been assured by Barneveld that the possessory princes would be fully supported in their position by the States, and that the special deputies of

---

[1] 'Mémoires de Sully,' t. vii. pp. 340-342.

[2] Aerssens to Barneveld, 24 Jan. 1610. (MS.) Many citations will be given from this very remarkable despatch, which, so far as I know, has never been printed or even alluded to.

Archduke Albert, whose presence at the Hague made Henry uneasy, as he regarded them as perpetual spies, had been dismissed. Henry expressed his gratification. They are there, he said, entirely in the interest of Leopold, who has just received 500,000 crowns from the King of Spain, and is to have that sum annually, and they are only sent to watch all your proceedings in regard to Cleve.

The King then fervently pressed the Ambassador to urge Barneveld's coming to Paris with the least possible delay. He signified his delight with Barneveld's answer to Anhalt, who thus fortified would be able to do good service at the assembly at Hall. He had expected nothing else from Barneveld's sagacity, from his appreciation of the needs of Christendom, and from his affection for himself. He told the Ambassador that he was anxiously waiting for the Advocate in order to consult with him as to all the details of the war. The affair of Cleve, he said, was too special a cause. A more universal one was wanted. The King preferred to begin with Luxemburg, attacking Charlemont or Namur, while the States ought at the same time to besiege Venlo, with the intention afterwards of uniting with the King in laying siege to Maestricht.

He was strong enough, he said, against all the world, but he still preferred to invite all princes interested to join him in putting down the ambitious and growing power of Spain. Cleve was a plausible pretext, but the true cause, he said, should be found in the general safety of Christendom.

Boississe had been sent to the German princes to ascertain whether and to what extent they would assist the King. He supposed that once they found him engaged in actual warfare in Luxemburg, they would get rid of their jealousy and panic fears of him and his designs. He expected them to furnish at least as large a force as he would supply as a contingent.

For it was understood that Anhalt as generalissimo of the German forces would command a certain contingent of French troops, while the main army of the King would be led by himself in person.

Henry expressed the conviction that the King of Spain would be taken by surprise finding himself attacked in three places and by three armies at once, he believing that the King of France was entirely devoted to his pleasures and altogether too old for warlike pursuits, while the States, just emerging from the misery of their long and cruel conflict, would be surely unwilling to plunge headlong into a great and bloody war.[1]

Henry inferred this, he said, from observing the rude and brutal manner in which the soldiers in the Spanish Netherlands were now treated. It seemed, he said, as if the Archdukes thought they had no further need of them, or as if a stamp of the foot could raise new armies out of the earth. "My design," continued the King, "is the more likely to succeed as the King of Spain, being a mere gosling and a valet of the Duke of Lerma, will find himself stripped of all his resources and at his wits' end ;[2] unexpectedly embarrassed as he will be on the Italian side, where we shall be threatening to cut the jugular vein of his pretended universal monarchy."[3]

He intimated that there was no great cause for anxiety in regard to the Catholic League just formed at Würzburg. He doubted whether the King of Spain would join it, and he had learned that the Elector of Cologne was making very little progress in obtaining the Emperor's adhesion. As to this point the King had probably not yet thoroughly understood that the Bavarian League was intended to keep clear

---

[1] Aerssens to Barneveld, 24 Jan. 1610. (MS.)

[2] " . . . et pourra reussir ce dessein de S. M. plus facilement que le roi d'Espagne, n'étant qu'un oyson et valet du duc de Lerma, se trouve denué de tous moyens," &c.—Ibid.

[3] Ibid.

of the House of Habsburg, Maximilian not being willing to identify the success of German Catholicism with the fortunes of that family.

Henry expressed the opinion that the King of Spain, that is to say, his counsellors, meant to make use of the Emperor's name while securing all the profit, and that Rudolph quite understood their game, while Matthias was sure to make use of this opportunity, supported by the Protestants of Bohemia, Austria, and Moravia, to strip the Emperor of the last shred of Empire.

The King was anxious that the States should send a special embassy at once to the King of Great Britain. His ambassador, de la Boderie, gave little encouragement of assistance from that quarter, but it was at least desirable to secure his neutrality. " 'Tis a prince too much devoted to repose," said Henry, " to be likely to help in this war, but at least he must not be allowed to traverse our great designs. He will probably refuse the league offensive and defensive which I have proposed to him, but he must be got, if possible, to pledge himself to the defensive. I mean to assemble my army on the frontier, as if to move upon Jülich, and then suddenly sweep down on the Meuse, where, sustained by the States' army and that of the princes, I will strike my blows and finish my enterprise before our adversary has got wind of what is coming. We must embark James in the enterprise if we can, but at any rate we must take measures to prevent his spoiling it." [1]

Henry assured the Envoy that no one would know anything of the great undertaking but by its effect ; that no one could possibly talk about it with any knowledge except himself, Sully, Villeroy, Barneveld, and Aerssens. [2] With them alone he conferred confidentially, and he doubted not

[1] Aerssens to Barneveld, 24 Jan. 1610.  (MS.)
[2] Ibid.

that the States would embrace this opportunity to have done for ever with the Spaniards. He should take the field in person, he said, and with several powerful armies would sweep the enemy away from the Meuse, and after obtaining control of that river would quietly take possession of the sea-coast of Flanders, shut up Archduke Albert between the States and the French, who would thus join hands and unite their frontiers.

Again the King expressed his anxiety for Barneveld's coming, and directed the Ambassador to urge it, and to communicate to him the conversation which had just taken place. He much preferred, he said, a general war. He expressed doubts as to the Prince of Anhalt's capacity as chief in the Cleve expedition, and confessed that being jealous of his own reputation he did not like to commit his contingent of troops to the care of a stranger and one so new to his trade. The shame would fall on himself, not on Anhalt in case of any disaster. Therefore, to avoid all petty jealousies and inconveniences of that nature by which the enterprise might be ruined, it was best to make out of this small affair a great one, and the King signified his hope that the Advocate would take this view of the case and give him his support. He had plenty of grounds of war himself, and the States had as good cause of hostilities in the rupture of the truce by the usurpation attempted by Leopold with the assistance of Spain and in the name of the Emperor. He hoped, he said, that the States would receive no more deputations from Archduke Albert, but decide to settle everything at the point of the sword. The moment was propitious, and, if neglected, might never return. Marquis Spinola was about to make a journey to Spain on various matters of business. On his return, Henry said, he meant to make him prisoner as a hostage for the Prince of Condé, whom the Archdukes were harbouring and detaining  This

would be the pretext, he said, but the object would be to
deprive the Archdukes of any military chief, and thus to
throw them into utter confusion.  Count van den Berg
would never submit to the authority of Don Luis de Velasco,
nor Velasco to his, and not a man could come from Spain
or Italy, for the passages would all be controlled by
France.[1]

Fortunately for the King's reputation, Spinola's journey
was deferred, so that this notable plan for disposing of the
great captain fell to the ground.

Henry agreed to leave the two French regiments and
the two companies of cavalry in the States' service as usual,
but stipulated in certain contingencies for their use.

Passing to another matter concerning which there had
been so much jealousy on the part of the States, the formation of the French East India Company—to organize
which undertaking Le Roy and Isaac Le Maire of Amsterdam
had been living disguised in the house of Henry's famous
companion, the financier Zamet at Paris—the King said that
Barneveld ought not to envy him a participation in the great
profits of this business.[2]

Nothing would be done without consulting him after his
arrival in Paris.  He would discuss the matter privately
with him, he said, knowing that Barneveld was a great
personage, but however obstinate he might be, he felt sure
that he would always yield to reason.  On the other hand the
King expressed his willingness to submit to the Advocate's
opinions if they should seem the more just.[3]

On leaving the King the Ambassador had an interview

---

[1] Aerssens to Barneveld, 24 Jan.
1610.  (MS.)

[2] Same to same. 21 Dec. 1609 ; 2
Dec. 1609 ; 16 Dec. 1609 ; 24 Jan.
1610.  (MSS.)

[3] " . . . qu'il en disputera particu-
lièrement avec vous, sachant que vous
êtes un grand personnage, mais quelque opiniâtre que puissiez être, elle
sait que cederiez toujours, et en tout
à la raison, comme elle se soubmettra
aussi à la votre sy la lui présenteriez
plus forte."—Letter of Aerssens, 24
Jan. 1610.  (MS. before cited.)

with Sully, who again expressed his great anxiety for the arrival of Barneveld, and his hopes that he might come with unlimited powers, so that the great secret might not leak out through constant referring of matters back to the Provinces.

After rendering to the Advocate a detailed account of this remarkable conversation, Aerssens concluded with an intimation that perhaps his own opinion might be desired as to the meaning of all those movements developing themselves so suddenly and on so many sides.

"I will say," he observed, "exactly what the poet sings of the army of ants—

> 'Ili motus animorum atque haec certamina tanta
> Pulveris exigui jactu contacta quiescunt.'

If the Prince of Condé comes back, we shall be more plausible than ever. If he does not come back, perhaps the consideration of the future will sweep us onwards. All have their special views, and M. de Villeroy more warmly than all the rest." [1]

[1] Aerssens to Barneveld, 24 Jan. 1610.  (MS.)

# CHAPTER II.



" If the Prince of Condé comes back."   What had the Prince
of Condé, his comings and his goings, to do with this vast
enterprise ?

It is time to point to the golden thread of most fantastic
passion which runs throughout this dark and eventful
history.

One evening in the beginning of the year which had just
come to its close there was to be a splendid fancy ball at
the Louvre in the course of which several young ladies of
highest rank were to perform a dance in mythological
costume.

The King, on ill terms with the Queen, who harassed
him with scenes of affected jealousy, while engaged in
permanent plots with her paramour and master, the
Italian Concini, against his policy and his life ; on still
worse terms with his latest mistress in chief, the Marquise
de Verneuil, who hated him and revenged herself for enduring his caresses by making him the butt of her venomous
wit, had taken the festivities of a court in dudgeon where
he possessed hosts of enemies and flatterers but scarcely a
single friend.

He refused to attend any of the rehearsals of the ballet, but one day a group of Diana and her nymphs passed him in the great gallery of the palace.[1] One of the nymphs as she went by turned and aimed her gilded javelin at his heart. Henry looked and saw the most beautiful young creature, so he thought, that mortal eye had ever gazed upon, and according to his wont fell instantly over head and ears in love. He said afterwards that he felt himself pierced to the heart and was ready to faint away.[2]

The lady was just fifteen years of age. The King was turned of fifty-five. The disparity of age seemed to make the royal passion ridiculous. To Henry the situation seemed poetical and pathetic. After this first interview he never missed a single rehearsal. In the intervals he called perpetually for the services of the court poet Malherbe, who certainly contrived to perpetrate in his behalf some of the most detestable verses that even he had ever composed.

The nymph was Marguérite de Montmorency, daughter of the Constable of France, and destined one day to become the mother of the great Condé, hero of Rocroy. There can be no doubt that she was exquisitely beautiful. Fair-haired, with a complexion of dazzling purity, large expressive eyes, delicate but commanding features, she had a singular fascination of look and gesture, and a winning, almost childlike, simplicity of manner. Without feminine artifice or commonplace coquetry, she seemed to bewitch and subdue at a glance men of all ranks, ages, and pursuits; kings and cardinals, great generals, ambassadors and statesmen, as well as humbler mortals whether Spanish, Italian,

---

[1] Tallemant des Reaux (ed. 1854), i. 170. Bentivoglio, 'Relazione della Fuga di Francia d'Henrico di Borbone Principe de Condé' ('Opere,' Parigi, 1748), p. 153. Michelet, 'Hist. de la France au 17<sup>me</sup> Siècle: Henri IV et Richelieu,' pp. 161, 162.

[2] Tallemant des Reaux, i. 171.

French, or Flemish.[1]  The Constable, an ignorant man who, as the King averred, could neither write nor read, understood as well as more learned sages the manners and humours of the court.  He had destined his daughter for the young and brilliant Bassompierre, the most dazzling of all the cavaliers of the day.  The two were betrothed.

But the love-stricken Henry, then confined to his bed with the gout, sent for the chosen husband of the beautiful Margaret.[2]

" Bassompierre, my friend," said the aged king, as the youthful lover knelt before him at the bedside, " I have become not in love, but mad, out of my senses, furious for Mademoiselle de Montmorency.  If she should love you, I should hate you.  If she should love me, you would hate me. 'Tis better that this should not be the cause of breaking up our good intelligence, for I love you with affection and inclination.  I am resolved to marry her to my nephew the Prince of Condé, and to keep her near my family.  She will be the consolation and support of my old age into which I am now about to enter.  I shall give my nephew, who loves the chace a thousand times better than he does ladies, 100,000 livres a year, and I wish no other favour from her than her affection without making further pretensions." [3]

It was eight o'clock of a black winter's morning, and the tears as he spoke ran down the cheeks of the hero of Ivry and bedewed the face of the kneeling Bassompierre.[4]

The courtly lover sighed and—obeyed.  He renounced

---

[1] " Haveva la principessa di Condé alhora eedici anni xxx la sua bellezza corrispondera alla relazione che ne haveva portata inanzi la fama," says Cardinal Bentivoglio, who was Papal nuncio at Brussels during this period, and was himself much in love with the Princess, as she related long afterwards to Lenet at Chantilly (P. Lenet, ' Mémoires,' ed. Petitot, p.   ). " Era bianchissima, piena di gratia negli occhi e nel volto; piena di vezzi nel parlare ed in ogni suo gesto; tutta naturalmente si commendava per so medesima la sua bellezza perche non l' ajutava alcun donnesco artificio."— ' Rel. della Fuga.' 155.

[2] ' Mémoires de Bassompierre,' ed. Petitot, i. p. 387. 877.

[3] Ibid.

[4] Ibid. pp. 386–388.

the hand of the beautiful Margaret, and came daily to play at dice with the King at his bedside with one or two other companions.

And every day the Duchess of Angoulême, sister of the Constable, brought her fair niece to visit and converse with the royal invalid. But for the dark and tragic clouds which were gradually closing around that eventful and heroic existence there would be something almost comic in the spectacle of the sufferer making the palace and all France ring with the howlings of his grotesque passion for a child of fifteen as he lay helpless and crippled with the gout.

One day as the Duchess of Angoulême led her niece away from their morning visit to the King, Margaret as she passed by Bassompierre shrugged her shoulders with a scornful glance. Stung by this expression of contempt, the lover who had renounced her sprang from the dice table, buried his face in his hat, pretending that his nose was bleeding, and rushed frantically from the palace.[1]

Two days long he spent in solitude, unable to eat, drink, or sleep, abandoned to despair and bewailing his wretched fate, and it was long before he could recover sufficient equanimity to face his lost Margaret and resume his place at the King's dicing table. When he made his appearance, he was according to his own account so pale, changed, and emaciated that his friends could not recognise him.[2]

The marriage with Condé, first prince of the blood, took place early in the spring. The bride received magnificent presents, and the husband a pension of 100,000 livres a year. The attentions of the King became soon outrageous and the reigning scandal of the hour. Henry, discarding the grey jacket and simple cos-

March 10, 1609.

----

[1] 'Mémoires de Bassompierre,' ed Petitot, i. p. 389.
[2] Ibid.

tume on which he was wont to pride himself, paraded himself about in perfumed ruffs and glittering doublet, an ancient fop, very little heroic, and much ridiculed. The Princess made merry with the antics of her royal adorer, while her vanity at least, if not her affection, was really touched, and there was one great round of court festivities in her honour, at which the King and herself were ever the central figures. But Condé was not at all amused. Not liking the part assigned to him in the comedy thus skilfully arranged by his cousin king, never much enamoured of his bride, while highly appreciating the 100,000 livres of pension, he remonstrated violently with his wife, bitterly reproached the King, and made himself generally offensive. "The Prince is here," wrote Henry to Sully, "and is playing the very devil. You would be in a rage and be ashamed of the things he says of me. But at last I am losing patience, and am resolved to give him a bit of my mind." [1]  He wrote in the same terms to Montmorency. [2]  The Constable, whose conduct throughout the affair was odious and pitiable, promised to do his best to induce the Prince, instead of playing the devil, to listen to reason, as he and the Duchess of Angoulême understood reason.

Henry had even the ineffable folly to appeal to the Queen to use her influence with the refractory Condé. Mary de' Medici replied that there were already thirty go-betweens at work, and she had no idea of being the thirty-first. [3]

Condé, surrounded by a conspiracy against his honour and happiness, suddenly carried off his wife to the country, much to the amazement and rage of Henry.

In the autumn he entertained a hunting party at a seat of his, the Abbey of Verneuille, on the borders of Picardy.  De

<hr>

[1] 'Mém. de Sully,' vii. 247.
[2] Henrard, 'Henri IV et la Princesse de Condé,' Bruxelles, 1870, p. 27.
[3] Henrard, 30.

Traigny, governor of Amiens, invited the Prince, Princess, and the Dowager-Princess to a banquet at his château not far from the Abbey.  On their road thither they passed a group of huntsmen and grooms in the royal livery.  Among them was an aged lackey with a plaister over one eye, holding a couple of hounds in leash.  The Princess recognized at a glance under that ridiculous disguise the King.[1]

"What a madman!" she murmured as she passed him, "I will never forgive you;" but as she confessed many years afterwards, this act of gallantry did not displease her.[2]

In truth, even in mythological fable, Love has scarcely ever reduced demi-god or hero to more fantastic plight than was this travesty of the great Henry.  After dinner Madame de Traigny led her fair guest about the castle to show her the various points of view.  At one window she paused, saying that it commanded a particularly fine prospect.  The Princess looked from it across a courtyard, and saw at an opposite window an old gentleman holding his left hand tightly upon his heart to show that it was wounded, and blowing kisses to her with the other.  "My God ! it is the King himself," she cried to her hostess.  The princess with this exclamation rushed from the window, feeling or affecting much indignation, ordered horses to her carriage instantly, and overwhelmed Madame de Traigny with reproaches.  The King himself, hastening to the scene, was received with passionate invectives, and in vain attempted to assuage the Princess's wrath and induce her to remain.[3]

They left the château at once, both Prince and Princess. One night, not many weeks afterwards, the Duc de Sully, in the Arsenal at Paris, had just got into bed Nov. 30, at past eleven o'clock when he received a visit 1609. from Captain de Praslin, who walked straight into his bed-

---

[1]  'Mémoires de Pierre Lenet' (ed. Petitot). i. 140.  Tallemant des Reaux i. 172.                [2] Ibid.                [3] Ibid. 141.

chamber, informing him that the King instantly required his presence.

Sully remonstrated. He was obliged to rise at three the next morning, he said, enumerating pressing and most important work which Henry required to be completed with all possible haste. "The King said you would be very angry," replied Praslin; "but there is no help for it. Come you must, for the man you know of has gone out of the country, as you said he would, and has carried away the lady on the crupper behind him."

"Ho, ho," said the Duke, "I am wanted for that affair, am I?" And the two proceeded straightway to the Louvre, and were ushered, of all apartments in the world, into the Queen's bedchamber. Mary de' Medici had given birth only four days before to an infant, Henrietta Maria, future queen of Charles I. of England. The room was crowded with ministers and courtiers; Villeroy, the Chancellor, Bassompierre, and others, being stuck against the wall at small intervals like statues, dumb, motionless, scarcely daring to breathe. The King, with his hands behind him and his grey beard sunk on his breast, was pacing up and down the room in a paroxysm of rage and despair

"Well," said he, turning to Sully as he entered, "our man has gone off and carried everything with him. What do you say to that?"

The Duke beyond the boding "I told you so" phrase of consolation which he was entitled to use, having repeatedly warned his sovereign that precisely this catastrophe was impending, declined that night to offer advice. He insisted on sleeping on it. The manner in which the proceedings of the King at this juncture would be regarded by the Archdukes Albert and Isabella—for there could be no doubt that Condé had escaped to their territory—and by the King of Spain, in complicity with whom the step had unquestionably been taken—was of gravest political importance.[1]

Henry had heard the intelligence but an hour before. He was at cards in his cabinet with Bassompierre and others when d'Elbene entered and made a private communication to him.  " Bassompierre, my friend," whispered the King immediately in that courtier's ear, "I am lost.  This man has carried his wife off into a wood.  I don't know if it is to kill her or to take her out of France.  Take care of my money and keep up the game."[2]

Bassompierre followed the King shortly afterwards and brought him his money.  He said that he had never seen a man so desperate, so transported.

The matter was indeed one of deepest and universal import.  The reader has seen by the preceding narrative how absurd is the legend often believed in even to our own days that war was made by France upon the Archdukes and upon Spain to recover the Princess of Condé from captivity in Brussels.

From contemporary sources both printed and unpublished; from most confidential conversations and revelations, we have seen how broad, deliberate, and deeply considered were the warlike and political combinations in the King's ever restless brain.  But although the abduction of the new Helen by her own Menelaus was not the cause of the impending Iliad, there is no doubt whatever that the incident had much to do with the crisis, was the turning point in a great tragedy, and that but for the vehement passion of the King for this youthful princess events might have developed themselves on a far different scale from that which they were destined to assume.  For this reason a court intrigue, which history under other conditions might justly disdain,

----

[1] 'Mém. de Bassompierre,' i. 420, 421, &c.  'Mém. de Sully,' vii. 255, &c.
[2] Ibid.  Ibid.

assumes vast proportions and is taken quite away from the scandalous chronicle which rarely busies itself with grave affairs of state.

"The flight of Condé," wrote Aerssens, "is the catastrophe to the comedy which has been long enacting.   'Tis to be hoped that the sequel may not prove tragical." [1]

"The Prince," for simply by that title he was usually called to distinguish him from all other princes in France, was next of blood.   Had Henry no sons, he would have succeeded him on the throne.   It was a favourite scheme of the Spanish party to invalidate Henry's divorce from Margaret of Valois, and thus to cast doubts on the legitimacy of the Dauphin and the other children of Mary de' Medici.

The Prince in the hands of the Spanish government might prove a docile and most dangerous instrument to the internal repose of France not only after Henry's death but in his life-time.   Condé's character was frivolous, unstable, excitable, weak, easy to be played upon by designing politicians, and he had now the deepest cause for anger and for indulging in ambitious dreams.

He had been wont during this unhappy first year of his marriage to loudly accuse Henry of tyranny, and was now likely by public declaration to assign that as the motive of his flight.   Henry had protested in reply that he had never been guilty of tyranny but once in his life, and that was when he allowed this youth to take the name and title of Condé.[2]

For the Princess-Dowager his mother had lain for years in prison, under the terrible accusation of having murdered her husband, in complicity with her paramour, a Gascon page, named Belcastel.   The present prince had been born several months after his reputed father's death.   Henry, out of

<hr>

[1] Aerssens to Carew, 30 Nov. 1609.   (MS.)
[2] Sully, *ubi sup.*

good nature, or perhaps for less creditable reasons, had come to the rescue of the accused princess, and had caused the process to be stopped, further enquiry to be quashed, and the son to be recognized as legitimate Prince of Condé. The Dowager had subsequently done her best to further the King's suit to her son's wife, for which the Prince bitterly reproached her to her face, heaping on her epithets which she well deserved.[1]

Henry at once began to threaten a revival of the criminal suit, with a view of bastardizing him again, although the Dowager had acted on all occasions with great docility in Henry's interests.

The flight of the Prince and Princess was thus not only an incident of great importance to the internal politics of France, but had a direct and important bearing on the impending hostilities. Its intimate connection with the affairs of the Netherland commonwealth was obvious. It was probable that the fugitives would make their way towards the Archdukes' territory, and that afterwards their first point of destination would be Breda, of which Philip William of Orange, eldest brother of Prince Maurice, was the titular proprietor. Since the truce recently concluded the brothers, divided so entirely by politics and religion, could meet on fraternal and friendly terms, and Breda, although a city of the Commonwealth, received its feudal lord. The Princess of Orange was the sister of Condé. The morning after the flight the King, before daybreak, sent for the Dutch ambassador.[2] He directed him to despatch a courier forthwith to Barneveld, notifying him that the Prince had left the kingdom without the permission or knowledge of his sovereign, and stating the King's belief that he had fled to the territory of the Archdukes. If he should come to Breda or to any other place

[1] L'Estoile, 'Registres journaux sur le Règne de Henry IV' (ed. Petitot), vol. iii. 269.

[2] Aerssens to Barneveld, 30 Nov. 1609. (MS.)

within the jurisdiction of the States, they were requested to make sure of his person at once, and not to permit him to retire until further instructions should be received from the King. De Praslin, captain of the body-guards and lieutenant of Champagne, it was further mentioned, was to be sent immediately on secret mission concerning this affair to the States and to the Archdukes.

The King suspected Condé of crime, so the Advocate was to be informed. He believed him to be implicated in the conspiracy of Poitou ; the six who had been taken prisoners having confessed that they had thrice conferred with a prince at Paris, and that the motive of the plot was to free themselves and France from the tyranny of Henry IV. The King insisted peremptorily, despite of any objections from Aerssens, that the thing must be done and his instructions carried out to the letter. So much he expected of the States, and they should care no more for ulterior consequences, he said, than he had done for the wrath of Spain when he frankly undertook their cause. Condé was important only because his relative, and he declared that if the Prince should escape, having once entered the territory of the Republic, he should lay the blame on its government.

"If you proceed languidly in the affair," wrote Aerssens to Barneveld, " our affairs will suffer for ever." [1]

Nobody at court believed in the Poitou conspiracy, or that Condé had any knowledge of it. The reason of his flight was a mystery to none, but as it was immediately followed by an intrigue with Spain, it seemed ingenious to Henry to make use of a transparent pretext to conceal the ugliness of the whole affair.[2]

---

[1] Aerssens to Barneveld, 30 Nov. 1609. (MS.)

[2] " . . . et luy peut être se voudra couvrir de quelque aultre raison quy sera heureuse sy creue au dehors.  Je crains qu'on a fait crever l'apostume à la trop presser.  Vous scaviez trop bien ceste histoire sans qu'il soit besoin de vous en entretenir davantage."— Aerssens to Carew, before cited.

He hoped that the Prince would be arrested at Breda and
sent back by the States.  Villeroy said that if it was not
done, they would be guilty of black ingratitude.  It would
be an awkward undertaking, however, and the States
devoutly prayed that they might not be put to the test.
The crafty Aerssens suggested to Barneveld that if Condé
was not within their territory it would be well to assure the
King that, had he been there, he would have been delivered
up at once.  "By this means," said the Ambassador, "you
will give no cause of offence to the Prince, and will at the
same time satisfy the King.  It is important that he should
think that you depend immediately upon him.  If you see
that after his arrest they take severe measures against him,
you will have a thousand ways of parrying the blame which
posterity might throw upon you.  History teaches you
plenty of them." [1]

He added that neither Sully nor anyone else thought
much of the Poitou conspiracy.  Those implicated asserted
that they had intended to raise troops there to assist the
King in the Cleve expedition.  Some people said that Henry
had invented this plot against his throne and life.  The
Ambassador, in a spirit of prophecy, quoted the saying
of Domitian : "*Misera conditio imperantium quibus de con-
spiratione non creditur nisi occisis.*"

Meantime the fugitives continued their journey.  The
Prince was accompanied by one of his dependants, a rude
officer, de Rochefort, who carried the Princess on a pillion
behind him.  She had with her a lady-in-waiting named
du Certeau and a lady's maid named Philippote.  She had
no clothes but those on her back, not even a change of
linen.  Thus the young and delicate lady made the wintry
journey through the forests.  They crossed the frontier at

---

[1] Aerssens to Barneveld, 8 Dec. 1609.  (MS.)

Landrecies,[1] then in the Spanish Netherlands, intending to traverse the Archduke's territory in order to reach Breda, where Condé meant to leave his wife in charge of his sister, the Princess of Orange, and then to proceed to Brussels.

He wrote from the little inn at Landrecies to notify the Archduke of his project. He was subsequently informed that Albert would not prevent his passing through his territories, but should object to his making a fixed residence within them.[2] The Prince also wrote subsequently to the King of Spain and to the King of France.

To Henry he expressed his great regret at being obliged to leave the kingdom in order to save his honour and his life, but that he had no intention of being anything else than his very humble and faithful cousin, subject, and servant. He would do nothing against his service, he said, unless forced thereto, and he begged the King not to take it amiss if he refused to receive letters from any one whomsoever at court, saving only such letters as his Majesty himself might honour him by writing.[3]

---

[1] Bentivoglio, 'Rel. della Fuga,' 153, 154. Le Père G. Daniel, 'Histoire de France,' Paris, 1756, t. xii. p. 541, *sqq.* Magistrats de Landrecies à l'Archiduc Albert, 1 Dec. 1609.

I desire to express my obligations to the excellent work of Captain Paul Henrard, 'Henri IV et la Princesse de Condé,' Brussels, 1870, who has narrated this singular episode with succinctness and elegance, enriching his volumes with an appendix containing the diplomatic correspondence of Pecquius, so far as it relates to this subject, besides other previously unpublished documents. I have read much of the original manuscript of the Archdukes and of Pecquius, both for this and some subsequent epochs, in the Royal Archives at Brussels. My citations, however, of these letters are from M. Henrard's printed collection, as careful comparison with the originals has shown me their perfect accuracy.

Many of these papers, as well as additional ones from the Archives of Simancas, are likewise printed in the second volume of the instructive work of H. R. H. the Duc d'Aumale, 'Histoire des Princes de Condé pendant les XVI<sup>e</sup> et XVII<sup>e</sup> Siècles,' from which I have derived much information.

[2] " . . . mais qu'il pouvoit asseurer le dict Seigneur Roy que nous ne souffrirons qu'il face séjour et moins sa demeure fixe rière les pais de notre obéissance et que nous avions faict dire mesmo responce au dit Sieur de Praslain," &c. &c.—Archdukes to P. Pecquius, 4 Dec. 1609, in Henrard. Archdukes to Ortemberg, agent at Rome, same date.

[3] 'Mém. de Sully,' vii. 264, note 30. 'Mém. pour l'Hist. de France,' ann. 1610.

The result of this communication to the King was of course to enrage that monarch to the utmost, and his first impulse on finding that the Prince was out of his reach was to march to Brussels at once and take possession of him and the Princess by main force.  More moderate counsels prevailed for the moment however, and negotiations were attempted.

Praslin did not contrive to intercept the fugitives, but the States-General, under the advice of Barneveld, absolutely forbade their coming to Breda or entering any part of their jurisdiction.  The result of Condé's application to the King of Spain was an ultimate offer of assistance and asylum, through a special emissary, one Añover; for the politicians of Madrid were astute enough to see what a card the Prince might prove in their hands.

Henry instructed his ambassador in Spain[1] to use strong and threatening language in regard to the harbouring a rebel and a conspirator against the throne of France ; while on the other hand he expressed his satisfaction with the States for having prohibited the Prince from entering their territory.[2]  He would have preferred, he said, if they had allowed him entrance and forbidden his departure, but on the whole he was content.  It was thought in Paris that the Netherland government had acted with much adroitness in thus abstaining both from a violation of the law of nations and from giving offence to the King.

A valet of Condé was taken with some papers of the Prince about him, which proved a determination on his part never to return to France during the lifetime of Henry.[3]  They made no statement of the cause of his flight, except to intimate that it might be left to the judgment of every one, as it was unfortunately but too well known to all.

[1] ' Recueil des Lettres missives de Henri IV.' t. v.
[2] Aerssens to Barneveld, 16 Dec.
1609.  (Hagues Archives MS.)
[3] Same to same, 8 Dec. 1609.  (MS.)

Refused entrance into the Dutch territory, the Prince was obliged to renounce his project in regard to Breda, and brought his wife to Brussels. He gave Bentivoglio, the Papal nuncio, two letters to forward to Italy, one to the Pope, the other to his nephew, Cardinal Borghese. Encouraged by the advices which he had received from Spain, he justified his flight from France both by the danger to his honour and to his life, recommending both to the protection of his Holiness and his Eminence. Bentivoglio sent the letters, but while admitting the invincible reasons for his departure growing out of the King's pursuit of the Princess, he refused all credence to the pretended violence against Condé himself.[1] Condé informed de Praslin that he would not consent to return to France. Subsequently he imposed as conditions of return that the King should assign to him certain cities and strongholds in Guienne, of which province he was governor, far from Paris and very near the Spanish frontier; a measure dictated by Spain and which inflamed Henry's wrath almost to madness.[2] The King insisted on his instant return, placing himself and of course the Princess entirely in his hands and receiving a full pardon for this effort to save his honour.[3] The Prince and Princess of Orange came from Breda to Brussels to visit their brother and his wife. Here they established them in the Palace of Nassau, once the residence in his brilliant youth of William the Silent; a magnificent mansion, surrounded by park and garden, built on the brow of the almost precipitous hill, beneath which is spread out so picturesquely the antique and beautiful capital of Brabant.

The Archdukes received them with stately courtesy at their own palace. On their first ceremonious visit to the

---

[1] Bent. 'Rel. della Fuga,' 156.
[2] Ibid. Daniel, 'Hist. de France,' xii. 514, *sqq.*

[3] Bent. 'Rel. della Fuga,' 157. Aerssens to Barneveld. (H. Arch. MS.)

sovereigns of the land, the formal Archduke, coldest and chastest of mankind, scarcely lifted his eyes to gaze on the wondrous beauty of the Princess, yet assured her after he had led her through a portrait gallery of fair women that formerly these had been accounted beauties, but that henceforth it was impossible to speak of any beauty but her own.[1]

The great Spinola fell in love with her at once, sent for the illustrious Rubens from Antwerp to paint her portrait,[2] and offered Mademoiselle de Château Vert 10,000 crowns in gold if she would do her best to further his suit with her mistress.[3] The Genoese banker-soldier made love, war, and finance on a grand scale.[4] He gave a magnificent banquet and ball in her honour on Twelfth Night, and the festival was the wonder of the town. Nothing like it had been seen in Brussels for years. At six in the evening Spinola in splendid costume, accompanied by Don Luis Velasco, Count Ottavio Visconti, Count Bucquoy, with other nobles of lesser note, drove to the Nassau Palace to bring the Prince and Princess and their suite to the Marquis's mansion. Here a guard of honour of thirty musketeers was standing before the door, and they were conducted from their coaches by Spinola preceded by twenty-four torch-bearers up the grand staircase to a hall, where they were received by the Princesses of Mansfeld, Velasco, and other distinguished dames. Thence they were led through several apartments rich with tapestry and blazing with crystal and silver plate to a splendid saloon where was a silken canopy, under which the Princess of Condé and the Princess of Orange seated themselves, the Nuncius Bentivoglio to his delight being placed next the beautiful Margaret. After reposing for a little while they were led to the ball-room, brilliantly lighted

---

[1] Henrard, 47.    [2] Ibid. 56.
[3] Peequius to Archduke Albert, 3 March 1610, in Henrard.
[4] Henrard, p. 76.

with innumerable torches of perfumed wax and hung with tapestry of gold and silk, representing in fourteen embroidered designs the chief military exploits of Spinola. Here the banquet, a cold collation, was already spread on a table decked and lighted with regal splendour. As soon as the guests were seated, an admirable concert of instrumental music began. Spinola walked up and down providing for the comforts of his company, the Duke of Aumale stood behind the two princesses to entertain them with conversation, Don Luis Velasco served the Princess of Condé with plates, handed her the dishes, the wine, the napkins, while Bucquoy and Visconti in like manner waited upon the Princess of Orange; other nobles attending to the other ladies. Forty-eight pages in white, yellow, and red scarves brought and removed the dishes. The dinner, of courses innumerable, lasted two hours and a half, and the ladies, being thus fortified for the more serious business of the evening, were led to the tiring-rooms while the hall was made ready for dancing. The ball was opened by the Princess of Condé and Spinola, and lasted until two in the morning. As the apartment grew warm, two of the pages went about with long staves and broke all the windows until not a single pane of glass remained. The festival was estimated by the thrifty chronicler of Antwerp to have cost from 3000 to 4000 crowns. It was, he says, "an earthly paradise of which soon not a vapour remained." He added that he gave a detailed account of it "not because he took pleasure in such voluptuous pomp and extravagance, but that one might thus learn the vanity of the world."[1] These courtesies and assiduities on the part of the great "shop-keeper," as the Constable called him, had so much effect, if not on the Princess, at least on Condé himself, that he threatened to throw his wife out of window if she refused to

---

[1] Van Meteren, 'Ned. Hist.' b. xxxi. p. 687.

caress Spinola.[1]  These and similar accusations were made
by the father and aunt when attempting to bring about a
divorce of the Princess from her husband.[2]  The Nuncius
Bentivoglio, too, fell in love with her, devoting himself to
her service, and his facile and eloquent pen to chronicling
her story.  Even poor little Philip of Spain in the depths
of the Escurial heard of her charms,[3] and tried to imagine
himself in love with her by proxy.

Thenceforth there was a succession of brilliant festivals in
honour of the Princess.  The Spanish party was radiant with
triumph, the French maddened with rage.  Henry in Paris
was chafing like a lion at bay.  A petty sovereign whom he
could crush at one vigorous bound was protecting the lady
for whose love he was dying.  He had secured Condé's
exclusion from Holland, but here were the fugitives
splendidly established in Brussels ; the Princess surrounded
by most formidable suitors, the Prince encouraged in his
rebellious and dangerous schemes by the power which the
King most hated on earth, and whose eternal downfall he
had long since sworn to accomplish.

For the weak and frivolous Condé began to prattle publicly
of his deep projects of revenge.  Aided by Spanish money
and Spanish troops he would show one day who was the
real heir to the throne of France—the illegitimately born
Dauphin or himself.

The King sent for the first president of Parliament,
Harlay, and consulted with him as to the proper means of
reviving the suppressed process against the Dowager and
of publicly degrading Condé from his position of first prince
of the blood which he had been permitted to usurp.[4]  He
likewise procured a decree accusing him of high-treason and

<hr>

[1] Peequius to Archduke Albert, 3
March 1610, in Henrard.
[2] Ibid.
[3] Same to same, 31 March 1610,
in Henrard.
[4] Aerssens to Barneveld, 8 Dec.
1609.  (MS.)

ordering him to be punished at his Majesty's pleasure, to be prepared by the Parliament of Paris; going down to the court himself in his impatience and seating himself in every-day costume on the bench of judges to see that it was immediately proclaimed.[1]

Instead of at once attacking the Archdukes in force as he intended in the first ebullition of his wrath, he resolved to send de Boutteville-Montmorency, a relative of the Constable, on special and urgent mission to Brussels. He was to propose that Condé and his wife should return with the Prince and Princess of Orange to Breda, the King pledging himself that for three or four months nothing should be undertaken against him.[2] Here was a sudden change of determination fit to surprise the States-General, but the King's resolution veered and whirled about hourly in the tempests of his wrath and love.

That excellent old couple, the Constable and the Duchess of Angoulême, did their best to assist their sovereign in his fierce attempts to get their daughter and niece into his power.

The Constable procured a piteous letter to be written[3] to Archduke Albert, signed "Montmorency his mark," imploring him not to "suffer that his daughter, since the Prince refused to return to France, should leave Brussels to be a wanderer about the world following a young prince who had no fixed purpose in his mind.[4]

Archduke Albert, through his ambassador in Paris, Peter Pecquius, suggested the possibility of a reconciliation between Henry and his kinsman, and offered himself as intermediary. He enquired whether the King would find it

---

[1] 'Mém. de Sully,' vii. 270, note.

[2] Aerssens to Barneveld, 16 Dec. 1609. (MS.)

[3] Henry said that with his Chancellor (Sillery), who knew no Latin, and his Constable, who could neither write nor read, he could get through the most difficult affairs. 'Mémoires de Sully,' vii. 227, note 22.

[4] Montmorency to Archduke Albert, 16 Jan. 1610, in Henrard.

agreeable that he should ask for pardon in name of the Prince. Henry replied that he was willing that the Archduke should accord to Condé secure residence for the time within his dominions on three inexorable conditions :—Firstly, that the Prince should ask for pardon without any stipulations, the King refusing to listen to any treaty or to assign him towns or places of security as had been vaguely suggested, and holding it utterly unreasonable that a man sueing for pardon should, instead of deserved punishment, talk of terms and acquisitions ; secondly, that, if Condé should reject the proposition, Albert should immediately turn him out of his country, showing himself justly irritated at finding his advice disregarded ; thirdly, that, sending away the Prince, the Archduke should forthwith restore the Princess to her father the Constable and her aunt Angoulême, who had already made their petitions to Albert and Isabella for that end, to which the King now added his own most particular prayers.

If the Archduke should refuse consent to these three conditions, Henry begged that he would abstain from any farther attempt to effect a reconciliation and not suffer Condé to remain any longer within his territories.

Pecquius replied that he thought his master might agree to the two first propositions while demurring to the third, as it would probably not seem honourable to him to separate man and wife, and as it was doubtful whether the Princess would return of her own accord.[1]

The King, in reporting the substance of this conversation to Aerssens, intimated his conviction that they were only wishing in Brussels to gain time ; that they were waiting for letters from Spain, which they were expecting ever since the return of Condé's secretary from Milan, whither he

---

[1] Aerssens to Barneveld, 22 Dec. 1609. (MS.)  Same to Caron, 27 Dec. 1609. (MS.)

had been sent to confer with the Governor, Count Fuentes.[1] He said farther that he doubted whether the Princess would go to Breda, which he should now like, but which Condé would not now permit. This he imputed in part to the Princess of Orange, who had written a letter full of invectives against himself to the Dowager-Princess of Condé which she had at once sent to him. Henry expressed at the same time his great satisfaction with the States-General and with Barneveld in this affair, repeating his assurances that they were the truest and best friends he had.

The news of Condé's ceremonious visit to Leopold in Jülich could not fail to exasperate the King almost as much as the pompous manner in which he was subsequently received at Brussels; Spinola and the Spanish Ambassador going forth to meet him.[2]  At the same moment the secretary of Vaucelles, Henry's ambassador in Madrid, arrived in Paris, confirming the King's suspicions that Condé's flight had been concerted with Don Inigo de Cardenas, and was part of a general plot of Spain against the peace of the kingdom. The Duc d'Épernon, one of the most dangerous plotters at the court, and deep in the intimacy of the Queen and of all the secret adherents of the Spanish policy, had been sojourning a long time at Metz, under pretence of attending to his health, had sent his children to Spain, as hostages according to Henry's belief, had made himself master of the citadel, and was turning a deaf ear to all the commands of the King.[3]

The supporters of Condé in France were openly changing their note and proclaiming by the Prince's command that he had left the kingdom in order to preserve his quality of first prince of the blood, and that he meant to make good

---

[1] Aerssens to Caron, 27 Dec. 1609.  (MS.)
[2] Same to Barneveld, 29 Dec. 1609.  (MS.)     [3] Ibid.

his right of primogeniture against the Dauphin and all competitors.[1]

Such bold language and such open reliance on the support of Spain in disputing the primogeniture of the Dauphin were fast driving the most pacifically inclined in France into enthusiasm for the war.

The States, too, saw their opportunity more vividly every day. "What could we desire more," wrote Aerssens to Barneveld, "than open war between France and Spain? Posterity will for ever blame us if we reject this great occasion."[2]

Peter Pecquius, smoothest and sliest of diplomatists, did his best to make things comfortable, for there could be little doubt that his masters most sincerely deprecated war. On their heads would come the first blows, to their provinces would return the great desolation out of which they had hardly emerged. Still the Archduke, while racking his brains for the means of accommodation, refused, to his honour, to wink at any violation of the law of nations, gave a secret promise, in which the Infanta joined, that the Princess should not be allowed to leave Brussels without her husband's permission,[3] and resolutely declined separating the pair except with the full consent of both. In order to protect himself from the King's threats, he suggested sending Condé to some neutral place for six or eight months, to Prague, to Breda, or anywhere else; but Henry knew that Condé would never allow this unless he had the means by Spanish gold of bribing the garrison there, and so of holding the place in pretended neutrality, but in reality at the devotion of the King of Spain.[4]

Meantime Henry had despatched the Marquis de Cœuvres,

[1] Aerssens to van der Wareke, 6 Jan. 1610.  (MS.)
[2] Same to Barneveld, 6 Jan. 1610. (MS.)
[3] Bent. 'Rel. della Fuga,' 159.
[4] Aerssens to Barneveld, 24 Jan. 1610.  (MS.)

brother of the beautiful Gabrielle, Duchess de Beaufort, and one of the most audacious and unscrupulous of courtiers, on a special mission to Brussels.[1]   De Coeuvres saw Condé before presenting his credentials to the Archduke, and found him quite impracticable.   Acting under the advice of the Prince of Orange, he expressed his willingness to retire to some neutral city of Germany or Italy, drawing meanwhile from Henry a pension of 40,000 crowns a year.   But de Coeuvres firmly replied that the King would make no terms with his vassal nor allow Condé to prescribe conditions to him.   To leave him in Germany or Italy, he said, was to leave him in the dependence of Spain.   The King would not have this constant apprehension of her intrigues while living, nor leave such matter in dying for turbulence in his kingdom.   If it appeared that the Spaniards wished to make use of the Prince for such purposes, he would be beforehand with them, and show them how much more injury he could inflict on Spain than they on France.[2] Obviously committed to Spain, Condé replied to the entreaties of the emissary that if the King would give him half his kingdom he would not accept the offer nor return to France; at least before the 8th of February, by which date he expected advices from Spain.   He had given his word, he said, to lend his ear to no overtures before that time.[3]   He made use of many threats, and swore that he would throw himself entirely into the arms of the Spanish king if Henry would not accord him the terms which he had proposed.[4]

To do this was an impossibility.   To grant him places of security would, as the King said, be to plant a standard for all the malcontents of France to rally around.   Condé had

<hr>

[1] Bent. 'Rel. della Fuga,' 157, 158. Daniel, 'Hist. de France,' t. xii. 546, 547.

[3] Bent. 'Rel. della Fuga,' 158.

[2] Aerssens to Barneveld, 24 Jan. 1610.   (MS.)

[4] Peter Peronius to Archduke Albert, 4 Feb. 1610.   Hearard, 205.

evidently renounced all hopes of a reconciliation, however painfully his host the Archduke might intercede for it. He meant to go to Spain. Spinola was urging this daily and hourly, said Henry, for he had fallen in love with the Princess, who complained of all these persecutions in her letters to her father, and said that she would rather die than go to Spain.

The King's advices from de Coeuvres were however to the effect that the step would probably be taken, that the arrangements were making, and that Spinola had been shut up with Condé six hours long with nobody present but Rochefort and a certain counsellor of the Prince of Orange named Keeremans.[1]

Henry was taking measures to intercept them on their flight by land, but there was some thought of their proceeding to Spain by sea. He therefore requested the States to send two ships of war, swift sailers, well equipped, one to watch in the roads of St. Jean and the other on the English coast. These ships were to receive their instructions from Admiral de Vicq, who would be well informed of all the movements of the Prince and give warning to the captains of the Dutch vessels by a preconcerted signal. The King begged that Barneveld would do him this favour, if he loved him, and that none might have knowledge of it but the Advocate and Prince Maurice. The ships would be required for two or three months only, but should be equipped and sent forth as soon as possible.[2]

The States had no objection to performing this service, although it subsequently proved to be unnecessary, and they were quite ready at that moment to go openly into the war to settle the affairs of Cleve, and once for all to drive the Spaniards out of the Netherlands and beyond seas and

<hr>

[1] Letter of Aerssens, 24 Jan. 1610. (MS. before cited.) Aerssens to Barneveld, 31 Jan. 1610. (MS.)    [2] Letter of Aerssens, 24 Jan. 1610.

mountains. Yet strange to say, those most conversant with the state of affairs could not yet quite persuade themselves that matters were serious, and that the King's mind was fixed. Should Condé return, renounce his Spanish stratagems, and bring back the Princess to court, it was felt by the King's best and most confidential friends that all might grow languid again, the Spanish faction get the upper hand in the King's councils, and the States find themselves in a terrible embarrassment.[1]

On the other hand, the most prying and adroit of politicians were puzzled to read the signs of the times. Despite Henry's garrulity, or perhaps in consequence of it, the envoys of Spain, the Empire, and of Archduke Albert were ignorant whether peace were likely to be broken or not, in spite of rumours which filled the air. So well had the secrets been kept which the reader has seen discussed in confidential conversations—the record of which has always remained unpublished — between the King and those admitted to his intimacy that very late in the winter Pecquius, while sadly admitting 'to his masters that the King was likely to take part against the Emperor in the affair of the duchies, expressed the decided opinion that it would be limited to the secret sending of succour to Brandenburg and Neuburg as formerly to the United Provinces, but that he would never send troops into Cleve, or march thither himself.[2]

It is important, therefore, to follow closely the development of these political and amorous intrigues, for they furnish one of the most curious and instructive lessons of history ; there being not the slightest doubt that upon their issue chiefly depended the question of a great and general war.

---

[1] Aerssens to Duplessis-Mornay, 29 Jan. 1610.  (MS.)
[2] Pecquius to Archduke Albert, 10 Feb. 1610, in Henrard, 216.

Pecquius, not yet despairing that his master would effect a reconciliation between the King and Condé, proposed again that the Prince should be permitted to reside for a time in some place not within the jurisdiction of Spain or of the Archdukes, being allowed meantime to draw his annual pension of 100,000 livres. Henry ridiculed the idea of Condé's drawing money from him while occupying his time abroad with intrigues against his throne and his children's succession. He scoffed at the Envoy's pretences that Condé was not in receipt of money from Spain, as if a man so needy and in so embarrassing a position could live without money from some source ; and as if he were not aware, from his correspondents in Spain, that funds were both promised and furnished to the Prince.

He repeated his determination not to accord him pardon unless he returned to France, which he had no cause to leave, and, turning suddenly on Pecquius, demanded why, the subject of reconciliation having failed, the Archduke did not immediately fulfil his promise of turning Condé out of his dominions.[1]

Upon this Albert's minister drew back with the air of one amazed, asking how and when the Archduke had ever made such a promise.

" To the Marquis de Coeuvres," replied Henry.

Pecquius asked if his ears had not deceived him, and if the King had really said that de Coeuvres had made such a statement.

Henry repeated and confirmed the story.

Upon the Minister's reply that he had himself received no such intelligence from the Archduke, the King suddenly changed his tone, and said,

" No, I was mistaken—I was confused—the Marquis never wrote me this; but did you not say yourself that I might

<hr>

[1] Pecquius to Archduke Albert, 4 Feb. 1610, in Henrard.

be assured that there would be no difficulty about it if the Prince remained obstinate." [1]

Pecquius replied that he had made such a proposition to his masters by his Majesty's request ; but there had been no answer received, nor time for one, as the hope of reconciliation had not yet been renounced. He begged Henry to consider whether, without instructions from his master, he could have thus engaged his word.

" Well," said the King, " since you disavow it, I see very well that the Archduke has no wish to give me pleasure, and that these are nothing but tricks that you have been amusing me with all this time. Very good ; each of us will know what we have to do."

Pecquius considered that the King had tried to get him into a net, and to entrap him into the avowal of a promise which he had never made. Henry remained obstinate in his assertions, notwithstanding all the envoy's protestations. [2]

" A fine trick, indeed, and unworthy of a king, ' *Si dicere fas est,*' " he wrote to Secretary of State Praets. [3] " But the force of truth is such that he who spreads the snare always tumbles into the ditch himself."

Henry concluded the subject of Condé at this interview by saying that he could have his pardon on the conditions already named, and not otherwise.

He also made some complaints about Archduke Leopold, who, he said, notwithstanding his demonstrations of wishing a treaty of compromise, was taking towns by surprise which he could not hold, and was getting his troops massacred on credit.

Pecquius expressed the opinion that it would be better to leave the Germans to make their own arrangements among

<hr>

[1] Pecquius to Archduke Albert, 4 Feb. 1610, in Henrard.
[2] Ibid.
[3] Same to Praets, 4 Feb. 1610, in Henrard, 208, 209.

themselves, adding that neither his masters nor the King of Spain meant to mix themselves up in the matter.

"Let them mix themselves in it or keep out of it, as they like," said Henry, "I shall not fail to mix myself up in it."[1] The King was marvellously out of humour.

Before finishing the interview, he asked Pecquius whether Marquis Spinola was going to Spain very soon, as he had permission from his Majesty to do so, and as he had information that he would be on the road early in Lent.   The Minister replied that this would depend on the will of the Archduke, and upon various circumstances.   The answer seemed to displease the King, and Pecquius was puzzled to know why.[2]   He was not aware, of course, of Henry's project to kidnap the Marquis on the road, and keep him as a surety for Condé.

The Envoy saw Villeroy after the audience, who told him not to mind the King's ill-temper, but to bear it as patiently as he could.   His Majesty could not digest, he said, his infinite displeasure at the obstinacy of the Prince ; but they must nevertheless strive for a reconciliation.   The King was quick in words, but slow in deeds, as the Ambassador might have observed before, and they must all try to maintain peace, to which he would himself lend his best efforts.[3]

As the Secretary of State was thoroughly aware that the King was making vast preparations for war, and had given in his own adhesion to the project, it is refreshing to observe the candour with which he assured the representative of the adverse party of his determination that friendliest relations should be preserved.

It is still more refreshing to find Villeroy, the same afternoon, warmly uniting with Sully, Lesdiguières, and the Chancellor, in the decision that war should begin forthwith.[4]

---

[1] Pecquius to Archduke Albert, letter last cited.

[2] ". . . responce qui sembloit luy deplaire, je ne scay pourquoi."—

[2] Pecqnius to Praets, last cited.

[3] Ibid.

[4] Aerssens to Barneveld, 7 Feb. 1610.   (MS.)

For the King held a council at the Arsenal immediately after this interview with Pecquius, in which he had become convinced that Condé would never return. He took the Queen with him, and there was not a dissentient voice as to the necessity of beginning hostilities at once.[1]

Sully, however, was alone in urging that the main force of the attack should be in the north, upon the Rhine and Meuse. Villeroy and those who were secretly in the Spanish interest were for beginning it with the southern combination and against Milan. Sully believed the Duke of Savoy to be variable and attached in his heart to Spain, and he thought it contrary to the interests of France to permit an Italian prince to grow so great on her frontier. He therefore thoroughly disapproved the plan, and explained to the Dutch ambassador that all this urgency to carry on the war in the south came from hatred to the United Provinces, jealousy of their aggrandizement, detestation of the Reformed religion, and hope to engage Henry in a campaign which he could not carry on successfully. But he assured Aerssens that he had the means of counteracting these designs and of bringing on an invasion for obtaining possession of the Meuse. If the possessory princes found Henry making war in the Milanese only, they would feel themselves ruined, and might throw up the game. He begged that Barneveld would come on to Paris at once, as now or never was the moment to assure the Republic for all time.[2]

The King had acted with malicious adroitness in turning the tables upon the Prince and treating him as a rebel and

---

[1] Aerssens to Barneveld, 7 Feb. 1610. (MS.) Compare Pecquius to Archduke Albert, 10 Feb. 1610, Henrard, 215.

[2] Letter of Aerssens last cited. A comparison of the famous 'Économies royales,' or 'Memoirs of Sully,' compiled from recollection, and dictated to secretaries, and the letters of Aerssens, written at the moment and on the spot, shows in general extraordinary accuracy on the part of the great soldier and statesman, while at the same time exhibiting an occasional discrepancy and default of memory.

a traitor because, to save his own and his wife's honour, he had fled from a kingdom where he had but too good reason to suppose that neither was safe.  The Prince, with infinite want of tact, had played into the King's hands.  He had bragged of his connection with Spain and of his deep designs, and had shown to all the world that he was thenceforth but an instrument in the hands of the Spanish cabinet, while all the world knew the single reason for which he had fled.

The King, hopeless now of compelling the return of Condé, had become most anxious to separate him from his wife.  Already the subject of divorce between the two had been broached, and it being obvious that the Prince would immediately betake himself into the Spanish dominions, the King was determined that the Princess should not follow him thither.

He had the incredible effrontery and folly to request the Queen to address a letter to her at Brussels, urging her to return to France.  But Mary de' Medici assured her husband that she had no intention of becoming his assistant, using, to express her thought, the plainest and most vigorous word that the Italian language could supply.[1]  Henry had then recourse once more to the father and aunt.

That venerable couple being about to wait upon the Archduke's envoy, in compliance with the royal request, Pecquius, out of respect to their advanced age, went to the Constable's residence.  Here both the Duchess and Constable, with tears in their eyes, besought that diplomatist to do his utmost to prevent the Princess from the sad fate of any longer sharing her husband's fortunes.

The father protested that he would never have consented to her marriage, preferring infinitely that she should have espoused any honest gentleman with 2000 crowns a year

---

[1] Henrard, 102, citing Siri, 'Mém. rec.' partie x. p. 84.

than this first prince of the blood, with a character such as it had proved to be; but that he had not dared to disobey the King.[1]

He spoke of the indignities and cruelties to which she was subjected, said that Rochefort, whom Condé had employed to assist him in their flight from France, and on the crupper of whose horse the Princess had performed the journey, was constantly guilty of acts of rudeness and incivility towards her; that but a few days past he had fired off pistols in her apartment where she was sitting alone with the Princess of Orange, exclaiming that this was the way he would treat anyone who interfered with the commands of his master, Condé; that the Prince was incessantly railing at her for refusing to caress the Marquis of Spinola; and that, in short, he would rather she were safe in the palace of the Archduchess Isabella, even in the humblest position among her gentlewomen, than to know her vagabondizing miserably about the world with her husband.[2]

This, he said, was the greatest fear he had, and he would rather see her dead than condemned to such a fate.[3]

He trusted that the Archdukes were incapable of believing the stories that he and the Duchess of Angoulême were influenced in the appeals they made for the separation of the Prince and Princess by a desire to serve the purposes of the King.[4] These were fables put about by Condé. All that the Constable and his sister desired was that the Archduchess would receive the Princess kindly when she should throw herself at her feet, and not allow her to be torn away against her will. The Constable spoke with great gravity and simplicity, and with all the signs of genuine emotion, and Peter Pecquius was much moved. He assured the aged pair that he would do his best to comply with their wishes,

<hr>

[1] Pecquius to Archduke Albert, 10 Feb. 1610, in Henrard.
[2] Ibid.        [3] Ibid.        [4] Ibid.

and should immediately apprise the Archdukes of the interview which had just taken place. Most certainly they were entirely disposed to gratify the Constable and the Duchess as well as the Princess herself, whose virtues, qualities, and graces had inspired them with affection, but it must be remembered that the law both human and divine required wives to submit themselves to the commands of their husbands and to be the companions of their good and evil fortunes. Nevertheless, he hoped that the Lord would so conduct the affairs of the Prince of Condé that the Most Christian King and the Archdukes would all be satisfied.[1]

These pious and consolatory commonplaces on the part of Peter Pecquius deeply affected the Constable. He fell upon the Envoy's neck, embraced him repeatedly, and again wept plentifully.

[1] Pecquius to Archduke Albert, 10 Feb. 1610, in Henrard.

# CHAPTER III.



It was in the latter part of the Carnival, the Saturday
night preceding Shrove Tuesday, 1610.   The winter had been
Feb. 13, 1610.   a rigorous one in Brussels, and the snow lay in
drifts three feet deep in the streets.   Within and
about the splendid palace of Nassau there was much com-
motion.   Lights and flambeaux were glancing, loud voices,
martial music, discharge of pistols and even of artillery[1]
were heard together with the trampling of many feet, but
there was nothing much resembling the wild revelry or
cheerful mummery of that holiday season.   A throng of the
great nobles of Belgium with drawn swords and menacing
aspect were assembled in the chief apartments, a detachment of the Archduke's mounted body-guard was stationed
in the courtyard, and five hundred halberdiers of the burgher
guilds kept watch and ward about the palace.

The Prince of Condé, a square-built, athletic young man
of middle stature, with regular features, but a sulky expression, deepened at this moment into ferocity, was seen chasing
the secretary of the French resident minister out of the
courtyard, thwacking him lustily about the shoulders with
his drawn sword, and threatening to kill him or any other
Frenchman on the spot, should he show himself in that
palace.[2]   He was heard shouting rather than speaking, in

---

[1] Archduke Albert to Pecquius, 18 Feb. 1610, in Henrard.
[2] Ibid.

furious language against the King, against Coeuvres, against Berny, and bitterly bewailing his misfortunes, as if his wife were already in Paris instead of Brussels.[1]

Upstairs in her own apartment which she had kept for some days on pretext of illness sat the Princess Margaret, in company[2] of Madame de Berny, wife of the French minister, and of the Marquis de Coeuvres, Henry's special envoy, and a few other Frenchmen. She was passionately fond of dancing. The adoring cardinal described her as marvellously graceful and perfect in that accomplishment. She had begged her other adorer, the Marquis Spinola, "with sweetest words," that she might remain a few days longer in the Nassau Palace before removing to the Archduke's residence, and that the great general, according to the custom in France and Flanders, would be the one to present her with the violins. But Spinola, knowing the artifice concealed beneath these "sweetest words," had summoned up valour enough to resist her blandishments, and had refused a second entertainment.[3]

It was not, therefore, the disappointment at losing her ball that now made the Princess sad. She and her companions saw that there had been a catastrophe ; a plot discovered. There was bitter disappointment and deep dismay upon their faces. The plot had been an excellent one. De Coeuvres had arranged it all, especially instigated thereto by the father of the Princess acting in concurrence with the King.[4] That night when all was expected to be in accustomed quiet, the Princess, wrapped in her mantilla, was to have stolen down into the garden, accompanied only by her maid the adventurous and faithful Philipotte, to have gone through a breach which led through a garden wall to the city ramparts,[5] thence across the foss to the counterscarp, where

<hr>

[1] Bent. 'Rel. della Fuga,' 100.
[2] Ibid.
[3] Ibid.
[4] Daniel, xii. 547.
[5] Daniel, ubi sup.

a number of horsemen under trustworthy commanders were waiting. Mounting on the crupper behind one of the officers of the escort, she was then to fly to the frontier, relays of horses having been provided at every stage until she should reach Rocroy, the first pausing place within French territory;[1] a perilous adventure for the young and delicate Princess in a winter of almost unexampled severity.[2]

On the very morning of the day assigned for the adventure, despatches brought by special couriers from the Nuncius and the Spanish ambassador at Paris gave notice of the plot to the Archdukes and to Condé, although up to that moment none knew of it in Brussels. Albert, having been apprised that many Frenchmen had been arriving during the past few days, and swarming about the hostelries of the city and suburbs, was at once disposed to believe in the story. When Condé came to him, therefore, with confirmation from his own letters, and demanding a detachment of the body-guard in addition to the burgher militiamen already granted by the magistrates, he made no difficulty in granting the request.[3] It was as if there had been a threatened assault of the city, rather than the attempted elopement of a young lady escorted by a handful of cavaliers.

The courtyard of the Nassau Palace was filled with cavalry sent by the Archduke, while five hundred burgher guards sent by the magistrates were drawn up around the gate. The noise and uproar, gaining at every moment more mysterious meaning by the darkness of night, soon spread through the city. The whole population was awake, and swarming through the streets. Such a tumult had not for years been witnessed in Brussels, and the rumour flew

---

[1] Daniel, xii. 547. It is singular that this proposed first resting-place in the flight of the Princess should be the spot made so memorable afterwards by the victory of her son, the great Prince of Condé.

[2] L'Estoile, iii. 378.

[3] Archdukes to Pecquius, 13 Feb. 1610, in Henrard.

about and was generally believed that the King of France at the head of an army was at the gates of the city determined to carry off the Princess by force.[1]  But although the superfluous and very scandalous explosion might have been prevented, there could be no doubt that the stratagem had been defeated.

Nevertheless, the effrontery and ingenuity of de Coeuvres became now sublime.  Accompanied by his colleague, the resident minister, de Berny, who was sure not to betray the secret because he had never known it[2]—his wife alone having been in the confidence of the Princess—he proceeded straightway to the Archduke's palace, and, late in the night as it was, insisted on an audience.

Here putting on his boldest face when admitted to the presence, he complained loudly of the plot, of which he had just become aware, contrived by the Prince of Condé to carry off his wife to Spain against her will, by main force, and by assistance of Flemish nobles, archiducal body-guard, and burgher militia.

It was all a plot of Condé, he said, to palliate still more his flight from France.  Every one knew that the Princess could not fly back to Paris through the air.  To take her out of a house filled with people, to pierce or scale the walls of the city, to arrange her journey by ordinary means, and to protect the whole route by stations of cavalry, reaching from Brussels to the frontier, and to do all this in profound secrecy, was equally impossible.  Such a scheme had never been arranged nor even imagined, he said.  The true plotter was Condé, aided by ministers in Flanders hostile to France, and as the honour of the King and the reputation of the Princess had been injured by this scandal, the Ambassador loudly demanded a thorough investigation of the affair in order that vengeance might fall where it was due.[3]

<hr>

[1] Bent. 'Rel. della Fuga,' 161.          [2] Daniel. xii. 519.

[3] Bent. 161.

The prudent Albert was equal to the occasion. Not wishing to state the full knowledge which he possessed of de Coeuvres' agency and the King's complicity in the scheme of abduction to France, he reasoned calmly with the excited marquis, while his colleague looked and listened in dumb amazement, having previously been more vociferous and infinitely more sincere than his colleague in expressions of indignation.

The Archduke said that he had not thought the plot imputed to the King and his ambassador very probable. Nevertheless, the assertions of the Prince had been so positive as to make it impossible to refuse the guards requested by him. He trusted, however, that the truth would soon be known, and that it would leave no stain on the Princess, nor give any offence to the King.[1]

Surprised and indignant at the turn given to the adventure by the French envoys, he nevertheless took care to conceal these sentiments, to abstain from accusation, and calmly to inform them that the Princess next morning would be established under his own roof, and enjoy the protection of the Archduchess.

For it had been arranged several days before that Margaret should leave the palace of Nassau for that of Albert and Isabella on the 14th, and the abduction had been fixed for the night of the 13th precisely because the conspirators wished to profit by the confusion incident on a change of domicile.

The irrepressible de Coeuvres, even then hardly willing to give up the whole stratagem as lost, was at least determined to discover how and by whom the plot had been revealed. In a cemetery piled three feet deep with snow on the evening following that mid-winter's night which had been fixed for the Princess's flight, the unfortunate

_______________
[1] Bentivoglio, _ubi sup._

ambassador waited until a certain Vallobré, a gentleman of Spinola's, who was the go-between of the enamoured Genoese and the Princess, but whom de Coeuvres had gained over, came at last to meet him by appointment.[1]  When he arrived, it was only to inform him of the manner in which he had been baffled, to convince him that the game was up, and that nothing was left him but to retreat utterly foiled in his attempt, and to be stigmatized as a blockhead by his enraged sovereign.

Next day the Princess removed her residence to the palace of the Archdukes,[2] where she was treated with distinguished honour by Isabella, and installed ceremoniously in the most stately, the most virtuous, and the most dismal of courts.  Her father and aunt professed themselves as highly pleased with the result, and Pecquius wrote that " they were glad to know her safe from the importunities of the old fop who seemed as mad as if he had been stung by a tarantula." [3]

And how had the plot been revealed ?  Simply through the incorrigible garrulity of the King himself.  Apprised of the arrangement in all its details by the Constable,[4] who had first received the special couriers of de Coeuvres, he could not keep the secret to himself for a moment, and the person of all others in the world to whom he thought good to confide it was the Queen herself.[5]  She received the information with a smile, but straightway sent for the Nuncius Ubaldini, who at her desire instantly despatched a special courier to Spinola with full particulars of the time and mode of the proposed abduction.[6]

Nevertheless the ingenuous Henry, confiding in the capacity of his deeply offended queen to keep the secret which he had himself divulged, could scarcely contain

[1] Daniel, xii. 549.
[2] Archdukes to Pecquius, 15 Feb. 1610, in Henrard.
[3] Pecquius to Praets, 18 Feb. 1610, in Henrard.
[4] Daniel, xii. 547.
[5] Ibid. 518.
[6] Ibid.

himself for joy.  Off he went to Saint-Germain with a train of coaches, impatient to get the first news from de Coeuvres after the scheme should have been carried into effect, and intending to travel post towards Flanders to meet and welcome the Princess.

"Pleasant farce for Shrove Tuesday," wrote the secretary of Peequius, "is that which the Frenchmen have been arranging down there !  He in whose favour the abduction is to be made was seen going out the same day spangled and smart, contrary to his usual fashion, making a gambado towards Saint-Germain-en-Laye with four carriages and four to meet the nymph."[1]

Great was the King's wrath and mortification at this ridiculous exposure of his detestable scheme.  Vociferous were Villeroy's expressions of Henry's indignation at being supposed to have had any knowledge of or complicity in the affair.  "His Majesty cannot approve of the means one has taken to guard against a pretended plot for carrying off the Princess," said the Secretary of State; "a fear which was simulated by the Prince in order to defame the King."  He added that there was no reason to suspect the King, as he had never attempted anything of the sort in his life, and that the Archduke might have removed the Princess to his palace without sending an army to the hotel of the Prince of Orange, and causing such an alarm in the city, firing artillery on the rampart as if the town had been full of Frenchmen in arms, whereas one was ashamed next morning to find that there had been but fifteen in all.  "But it was all Marquis Spinola's fault," he said, "who wished to show himself off as a warrior."[2]

The King, having thus through the mouth of his secretary

---

[1] J. Simon to Praets, 20 Feb. 1610, in Henrard. Comp. Peequius to Archduke Albert, 18 Feb. 1610.

[2] Peequius to Archduke Albert, 18 Feb. 1610, in Henrard.  Same to same, 23 Feb. 1610.  Same to Praets, same date.

of state warmly protested against his supposed implication in the attempted abduction, began as furiously to rail at de Coeuvres for its failure ; telling the Duc de Vendôme[1] that his uncle was an idiot,[2] and writing that unlucky envoy most abusive letters for blundering in the scheme which had been so well concerted between them.  Then he sent for Malherbe, who straightway perpetrated more poems to express the King's despair, in which Henry was made to liken himself to a skeleton with a dried skin, and likewise to a violet turned up by the ploughshare and left to wither.[3]

He kept up through Madame de Berny a correspondence with " his beautiful angel," as he called the Princess, whom he chose to consider a prisoner and a victim ; while she, wearied to death with the frigid monotony and sepulchral gaieties of the archiducal court, which she openly called her dungeon,[4] diverted herself with the freaks and fantasies of her royal adorer, called him in very ill-spelled letters " her chevalier, her heart, her all the world," [5] and frequently wrote to beg him, at the suggestion of the intriguing Château Vert, to devise some means of rescuing her from prison.[6]

The Constable and Duchess meanwhile affected to be sufficiently satisfied with the state of things.  Condé, however, received a letter from the King, formally summoning him to return to France, and, in case of refusal, declaring him guilty of high-treason for leaving the kingdom without the leave and against the express commands of the King. To this letter brought to him by de Coeuvres, the Prince

---

[1] Son of Henry IV. by Gabrielle, Duchesse de Beaufort, sister of de Coeuvres.

[2] Pecquius to Praets, 1 March 1610, in Henrard.

[3] 'Œuvres de François de Malherbe' (ed. 1723), t. i. 146.

    " Aussi suis je un squelette
        Et la violette
     Qu'un froid hors de saison

     Ou le soc a touchée
      De ma peau séchée
    Est la comparaison."

[4] Bent. 'Rel. della Fuga,' 168. Pecquius to Archduke Albert, 19 March 1610.

[5] Tallemant des Reaux, i. 180.

[6] Archdukes to Pecquius, 9 March 1610, in Henrard.

replied by a paper, drawn up and served by a notary of Brussels, to the effect that he had left France to save his life and honour; that he was ready to return when guarantees were given him for the security of both. He would live and die, he said, faithful to the King. But when the King, departing from the paths of justice, proceeded through those of violence against him, he maintained that every such act against his person was null and invalid.[1] Henry had even the incredible meanness and folly to request the Queen to write to the Archdukes, begging that the Princess might be restored to assist at her coronation. Mary de' Medici vigorously replied once more that, "although obliged to wink at the King's amours, she declined to be his procuress."[2] Condé then went off to Milan very soon after the scene at the Nassau Palace and the removal of the Princess to the care of the Archdukes. He was very angry with his wife, from whom he expressed a determination to be divorced, and furious with the King, the validity of whose second marriage and the legitimacy of whose children he proposed with Spanish help to dispute.

The Constable was in favour of the divorce, or pretended to be so, and caused importunate letters to be written, which he signed, to both Albert and Isabella, begging that his daughter might be restored to him to be the staff of his old age, and likewise to be present at the Queen's coronation.[3] The Archdukes, however, resolutely refused to permit her to leave their protection without Condé's consent, or until after a divorce had been effected, notwithstanding that the father and aunt demanded it.[4] The Constable and Duchess

---

[1] Bent. 102. See also Aerssens' notes; also Henrard.

[2] Peequius to the Archdukes, 27 March 1610, in Henrard.

[3] Constable de Montmorency to Archduke Albert; same to the Infanta Isabella, 18 March and 20 April 1610, in Henrard. Henry IV. to Archduke Albert and to the Infanta, 19 April 1610, in Henrard.

[4] Archdukes to Peequius, 22 Feb. 1610, in Henrard.

however, acquiesced in the decision, and expressed immense gratitude to Isabella.

" The father and aunt have been talking to Pecquius," said Henry very dismally ; " but they give me much pain.  They are even colder than the season, but my fire thaws them as soon as I approach.

" P. S.—I am so pining away in my anguish that I am nothing but skin and bones.  Nothing gives me pleasure.  I fly from company, and if in order to comply with the law of nations I go into some assembly or other, instead of enlivening, it nearly kills me." [1]

And the King took to his bed.  Whether from gout, fever, or the pangs of disappointed love, he became seriously ill. Furious with every one, with Condé, the Constable, de Coeuvres, the Queen, Spinola, with the Prince of Orange,[2] whose councillor Keeremans had been encouraging Condé in his rebellion and in going to Spain with Spinola, he was now resolved that the war should go on.  Aerssens, cautious of saying too much on paper of this very delicate affair, always intimated to Barneveld that, if the Princess could be restored, peace was still possible, and that by moving an inch ahead of the King in the Cleve matter the States at the last moment might be left in the lurch.  He distinctly told the Advocate, on his expressing a hope that Henry might consent to the Prince's residence in some neutral place until a reconciliation could be effected, that the pinch of the matter was not there, and that van der Myle, who knew all about it, could easily explain it.[3]

Alluding to the project of reviving the process against the Dowager, and of divorcing the Prince and Princess, he said these steps would do much harm, as they would too

<hr>

[1] ' Lettres missives de Henri IV,' vii. 831.

[2] Aerssens to Prince of Orange, 26 Feb. 1610 ; same to Keeremans, same date.  (Hague Archives MS.)

[3] Same to Barneveld, 20 Feb. 1610 (MS.)

much justify the true cause of the retreat of the Prince, who was not believed when he merely talked of his right of primogeniture. "The matter weighs upon us very heavily," he said, "but the trouble is that we don't search for the true remedies. The matter is so delicate that I don't dare to discuss it to the very bottom." [1]

The Ambassador had a long interview with the King as he lay in his bed feverish and excited. He was more impatient than ever for the arrival of the States' special embassy, reluctantly acquiesced in the reasons assigned for the delay, but trusted that it would arrive soon with Barneveld at the head, and with Count Lewis William as a member for "the sword part of it."

He railed at the Prince of Orange, not believing that Keeremans would have dared to do what he had done but with the orders of his master. He said that the King of Spain would supply Condé with money and with everything he wanted, knowing that he could make use of him to trouble his kingdom. It was strange, he thought, that Philip should venture to these extremities with his affairs in such condition, and when he had so much need of repose. He recalled all his ancient grievances against Spain, his rights to the Kingdom of Navarre and the County of St. Pol violated; the conspiracy of Biron, the intrigues of Bouillon, the plots of the Count of Auvergne and the Marchioness of Verneuil, the treason of Meragne, the corruption of L'Hoste, and an infinity of other plots of the King and his ministers; of deep injuries to him and to the public repose, not to be tolerated by a mighty king like himself, with a grey beard. He would be revenged, he said, for this last blow, and so for all the rest. He would not leave a troublesome war on the hands of his young son. The occasion was favourable. It was just to defend the oppressed princes with the promptly

<hr>

[1] Aerssens to Barneveld, 7 Feb. 1610. (MS.)

accorded assistance of the States-General. The King of Great Britain was favourable. The Duke of Savoy was pledged. It was better to begin the war in his green old age than to wait the pleasure and opportunity of the King of Spain.

All this he said while racked with fever, and dismissed the Envoy at last, after a long interview, with these words : "Mr. Ambassador—I have always spoken roundly and frankly to you, and you will one day be my witness that I have done all that I could to draw the Prince out of the plight into which he has put himself. But he is struggling for the succession to this crown under instructions from the Spaniards, to whom he has entirely pledged himself. He has already received 6000 crowns for his equipment. I know that you and my other friends will work for the conservation of this monarchy, and will never abandon me in my designs to weaken the power of Spain. Pray God for my health." [1]

The King kept his bed a few days afterwards, but soon recovered. Villeroy sent word to Barneveld in answer to his suggestions of reconciliation that it was too late, that Condé was entirely desperate and Spanish. The crown of France was at stake, he said, and the Prince was promising himself miracles and mountains with the aid of Spain, loudly declaring the marriage of Mary de' Medici illegal, and himself heir to the throne. The Secretary of State professed himself as impatient as his master for the arrival of the embassy ; the States being the best friends France ever had and the only allies to make the war succeed.

Jeannin, who was now never called to the council, said that the war was not for Germany but for Condé, and that Henry could carry it on for eight years. He too was most anxious for Barneveld's arrival, and was of his opinion that

<hr>

[1] Letter of Aerssens, 20 Feb. 1610, before cited.  (MS.)

it would have been better for Condé to be persuaded to remain at Breda and be supported by his brother-in-law, the Prince of Orange. The impetuosity of the King had however swept everything before it, and Condé had been driven to declare himself Spanish and a pretender to the crown. There was no issue now but war.[1]

Boderie, the King's envoy in Great Britain, wrote that James would be willing to make a defensive league for the affairs of Cleve and Jülich only, which was the slenderest amount of assistance; but Henry always suspected Master Jacques of intentions to baulk him if possible and traverse his designs. But the die was cast. Spinola had carried off Condé in triumph; the Princess was pining in her gilt cage in Brussels, and demanding a divorce for desertion and cruel treatment; the King considered himself as having done as much as honour allowed him to effect a reconciliation, and it was obvious that, as the States' ambassador said, he could no longer retire from the war without shame, which would be the greatest danger of all.[2]

"The tragedy is ready to begin," said Aerssens. "They are only waiting now for the arrival of our ambassadors."[3]

On the 9th March the King before going to Fontainebleau for a few days summoned that envoy to the Louvre.[4] Impatient at a slight delay in his arrival, Henry came down into the courtyard as he was arriving and asked eagerly if Barneveld was coming to Paris. Aerssens replied that the Advocate had been hastening as much as possible the departure of the special embassy, but that the condition of affairs at home was such as not to permit him to leave the country at that moment. Van der Myle, who would be one

----

[1] Aerssens to Barneveld, 2 March 1610. (MS.)

[2] Ibid. Same to Digart, 1 March 1610. (MS.)

[3] Ibid.

[4] Same to Barneveld, 9 March 1610. (MS.)

of the ambassadors, would more fully explain this by word of mouth.

The King manifested infinite annoyance and disappointment that Barneveld was not to make part of the embassy.[1] "He says that he reposes such singular confidence in your authority in the state, experience in affairs, and affection for himself," wrote Aerssens, "that he might treat with you in detail and with open heart of all his designs. He fears now that the ambassadors will be limited in their powers and instructions, and unable to reply at once on the articles which at different times have been proposed to me for our enterprise. Thus much valuable time will be wasted in sending backwards and forwards."

The King also expressed great anxiety to consult with Count Lewis William in regard to military details, but his chief sorrow was in regard to the Advocate. "He acquiesced only with deep displeasure and regret in your reasons," said the Ambassador, "and says that he can hope for nothing firm now that you refuse to come."[2]

Villeroy intimated that Barneveld did not come for fear of exciting the jealousy of the English.[3]

---

[1] " S. M. m'a témoigné d'estre infinement marry que vous ne seriez pas du nombre des ambassadeurs," &c.—Letter of Aerssens last cited.
[2] Ibid.
[3] Ibid.

# CHAPTER IV.

Difficult Position of Barneveld — Insurrection at Utrecht subdued by the
States' Army—Special Embassies to England and France—Anger of the
King with Spain and the Archdukes — Arrangements of Henry for the
coming War — Position of Spain — Anxiety of the King for the Presence
of Barneveld in Paris — Arrival of the Dutch Commissioners in France
and their brilliant Reception — Their Interview with the King and his
Ministers — Negotiations — Delicate Position of the Dutch Government
— India Trade — Simon Danzer, the Corsair — Conversations of Henry
with the Dutch Commissioners — Letter of the King to Archduke Albert
— Preparations for the Queen's Coronation and of Henry to open the
Campaign in person—Perplexities of Henry—Forebodings and Warnings
—The Murder accomplished—Terrible Change in France — Triumph of
Concini and of Spain — Downfall of Sully — Disputes of the Grandees
among themselves — Special Mission of Condolence from the Republic —
Conference on the great Enterprise — Departure of van der Myle from
Paris.

THERE were reasons enough why the Advocate could not
go to Paris at this juncture. It was absurd in Henry to
suppose it possible. Everything rested on Barneveld's
shoulders. During the year which had just passed he had
drawn almost every paper, every instruction in regard to the
peace negotiations, with his own hand, had assisted at every
conference, guided and mastered the whole course of a most
difficult and intricate negotiation, in which he had not only
been obliged to make allowance for the humbled pride and
baffled ambition of the ancient foe of the Netherlands, but
to steer clear of the innumerable jealousies, susceptibilities,
cavillings, and insolences of their patronizing friends.

It was his brain that worked, his tongue that spoke, his
restless pen that never paused. His was not one of those
easy posts, not unknown in the modern administration of

great affairs, where the subordinate furnishes the intellect, the industry, the experience, while the bland superior, gratifying the world with his sign-manual, appropriates the applause. So long as he lived and worked, the States-General and the States of Holland were like a cunningly contrived machine, which seemed to be alive because one invisible but mighty mind vitalized the whole.

And there had been enough to do. It was not until midsummer of 1609 that the ratifications of the Treaty of Truce, one of the great triumphs in the history of diplomacy, had been exchanged, and scarcely had this period been put to the eternal clang of arms when the death of a lunatic threw the world once more into confusion. It was obvious to Barneveld that the issue of the Cleve-Jülich affair, and of the tremendous religious fermentation in Bohemia, Moravia, and Austria, must sooner or later lead to an immense war. It was inevitable that it would devolve upon the States to sustain their great though vacillating, their generous though encroaching, their sincere though most irritating, ally. And yet, thoroughly as Barneveld had mastered all the complications and perplexities of the religious and political question, carefully as he had calculated the value of the opposing forces which were shaking Christendom, deeply as he had studied the characters of Matthias and Rudolph, of Charles of Denmark and Ferdinand of Graz, of Anhalt and Maximilian, of Brandenburg and Neuburg, of James and Philip, of Paul V. and Charles Emmanuel, of Sully and Villeroy, of Salisbury and Bacon, of Lerma and Infantado ; adroitly as he could measure, weigh, and analyse all these elements in the great problem which was forcing itself on the attention of Europe—there was one factor with which it was difficult for this austere republican, this cold, unsusceptible statesman, to deal : the intense and imperious passion of a greybeard for a woman of sixteen.

For out of the cauldron where the miscellaneous elements of universal war were bubbling rose perpetually the fantastic image of Margaret Montmorency: the fatal beauty at whose caprice the heroic sword of Ivry and Cahors was now up-lifted and now sheathed.

Aerssens was baffled, and reported the humours of the court where he resided as changing from hour to hour. To the last he reported that all the mighty preparations then nearly completed "might evaporate in smoke" if the Princess of Condé should come back. Every ambassador in Paris was baffled. Peter Pecquius was as much in the dark as Don Inigo de Cardenas, as Ubaldini or Edmonds. No one save Sully, Aerssens, Barneveld, and the King knew the exten-sive arrangements and profound combinations which had been made for the war. Yet not Sully, Aerssens, Barneveld, or the King, knew whether or not the war would really be made.

Barneveld had to deal with this perplexing question day by day. His correspondence with his ambassador at Henry's court was enormous, and we have seen that the Ambassador was with the King almost daily; sleeping or waking; at dinner or the chase; in the cabinet or the courtyard.

But the Advocate was also obliged to carry in his arms, as it were, the brood of snarling, bickering, cross-grained German princes, to supply them with money, with arms, with counsel, with brains; to keep them awake when they went to sleep, to steady them in their track, to teach them to go alone. He had the congress at Hall in Suabia to super-vise and direct; he had to see that the ambassadors of the new republic, upon which they in reality were already half dependent and chafing at their dependence, were treated with the consideration due to the proud position which the Commonwealth had gained. Questions of etiquette were at that moment questions of vitality. He instructed his ambassadors to leave the congress on the spot if they were ranked after the envoys of princes who were only feudatories of the Emperor. The Dutch ambassadors, "recognising and relying upon no superiors but God and their sword," placed themselves according to seniority with the representatives of proudest kings.[1]

He had to extemporize a system of free international communication with all the powers of the earth—with the Turk at Constantinople, with the Czar of Muscovy; with the potentates of the Baltic, with both the Indies. The routine of a long established and well organized foreign office in a time-honoured state running in grooves; with well-balanced springs and well oiled wheels, may be a luxury of civilization; but it was a more arduous task to transact the greatest affairs of a state springing suddenly into recognized existence and mainly dependent for its primary construction and practical working on the hand of one man.

Worse than all, he had to deal on the most dangerous and delicate topics of state with a prince who trembled at danger and was incapable of delicacy; to show respect for a character that was despicable, to lean on a royal word falser than water, to inhale almost daily the effluvia from a court compared to which the harem of Henry was a temple of vestals. The spectacle of the slobbering James among his Kars and Hays and Villiers's and other minions is one at which history covers her eyes and is dumb; but the republican envoys, with instructions from a Barneveld, were obliged to face him daily, concealing their disgust, and bowing reverentially before him as one of the arbiters of their destinies and the Solomon of his epoch.

A special embassy was sent early in the year to England to convey the solemn thanks of the Republic to the King for his assistance in the truce negotiations, and to treat of

[1] Aerssens to Barneveld, 9 Feb. 1610. (MS.)

the important matters then pressing on the attention of both powers. Contemporaneously was to be despatched the embassy for which Henry was waiting so impatiently at Paris.

Certainly the Advocate had enough with this and other 'important business already mentioned to detain him at his post. Moreover the first year of peace had opened disastrously in the Netherlands. Tremendous tempests such as had rarely been recorded even in that land of storms had raged all the winter. The waters everywhere had burst their dykes, and inundations, which threatened to engulph the whole country, and which had caused enormous loss of property and even of life, were alarming the most courageous.[1] It was difficult in many districts to collect the taxes for the every-day expenses of the community, and yet the Advocate knew that the Republic would soon be forced to renew the war on a prodigious scale.

Still more to embarrass the action of the government and perplex its statesmen, an alarming and dangerous insurrection broke out in Utrecht.

In that ancient seat of the hard-fighting, imperious, and opulent sovereign archbishops of the ancient church an important portion of the population had remained Catholic. Another portion complained of the abolition of various privileges which they had formerly enjoyed ; among others that of a monopoly of beer-brewing for the province. All the population, as is the case with all populations in all countries and all epochs, complained of excessive taxation.

A clever politician, Dirk Kanter by name, a gentleman by birth, a scholar and philosopher by pursuit and education, and a demagogue by profession, saw an opportunity of taking an advantage of this state of things. More than twenty years before he had been burgomaster of the city, and had

---

[1] See reports of embassies hereafter to be cited.

much enjoyed himself in that position. He was tired of the
learned leisure to which the ingratitude of his fellow-citizens
had condemned him. He seems to have been of easy virtue
in the matter of religion, a Catholic, an Arminian, an ultra-
orthodox Contra-Remonstrant by turns. He now persuaded
a number of determined partisans that the time had come
for securing a church for the public worship of the ancient
faith, and at the same time for restoring the beer brewery,
reducing the taxes, recovering lost privileges, and many
other good things. Beneath the whole scheme lay a deep
design to effect the secession of the city and with it of the
opulent and important province of Utrecht from the Union.
Kanter had been heard openly to avow that after all the
Netherlands had flourished under the benign sway of the
House of Burgundy, and that the time would soon come for
returning to that enviable condition.

By a concerted assault the city hall was taken possession
of by main force, the magistracy was overpowered, Feb. 9,<br>1610.
and a new board of senators and common council-
men appointed, Kanter and a devoted friend of his, Heldingen by name, being elected burgomasters.[1]

The States-Provincial of Utrecht, alarmed at these proceedings in the city, appealed for protection against violence
to the States-General under the 3rd Article of the Union,
the fundamental pact which bore the name of Utrecht itself.
Prince Maurice proceeded to the city at the head of a
detachment of troops to quell the tumults. Kanter and his
friends were plausible enough to persuade him of the
legality and propriety of the revolution which they had
effected, and to procure his formal confirmation of the new
magistracy. Intending to turn his military genius and the
splendour of his name to account, they contrived to keep him
for a time at least in an amiable enthralment, and induced him

[1] Wagenaar, x. 25-32. Brill, Continuation of Arend, iii. d. ii. stuk, 420, 577.

to contemplate in their interest the possibility of renouncing the oath which subjected him to the authority of the States of Utrecht. But the far-seeing eye of Barneveld could not be blind to the danger which at this crisis beset the Stadholder and the whole republic. The Prince was induced to return to the Hague, but the city continued by armed revolt to maintain the new magistracy. They proceeded to reduce the taxes, and in other respects to carry out the measures on the promise of which they had come into power. Especially the Catholic party sustained Kanter and his friends, and promised themselves from him and from his influence over Prince Maurice to obtain a power of which they had long been deprived.

The States-General now held an assembly at Woerden, and summoned the malcontents of Utrecht to bring before that body a statement of their grievances. This was done, but there was no satisfactory arrangement possible, and the deputation returned to Utrecht, the States-General to the Hague. The States-Provincial of Utrecht urged more strongly than ever upon the assembly of the Union to save the city from the hands of a reckless and revolutionary government. The States-General resolved accordingly to interfere by force. A considerable body of troops was ordered to march at once upon Utrecht and besiege the city. Maurice, in his capacity of captain-general and stadholder of the province, was summoned to take charge of the army. He was indisposed to do so, and pleaded sickness. The States, determined that the name of Nassau should not be used as an encouragement to disobedience and rebellion, then directed the brother of Maurice, Frederic Henry, youngest son of William the Silent, to assume the command. Maurice insisted that his brother was too young, and that it was unjust to allow so grave a responsibility to fall upon his shoulders. The States, not particularly pleased with the Prince's attitude at this alarming juncture, and made anxious by the glamour which seemed to possess him since his conferences with the revolutionary party at Utrecht, determined not to yield.

The army marched forth and laid siege to the city, Prince Frederic Henry at its head. He was sternly instructed by the States-General, under whose orders he acted, to take possession of the city at all hazards. He was to insist on placing there a garrison of 2000 foot and 300 horse, and to permit not another armed man within the walls. The members of the council of state and of the States of Utrecht accompanied the army. For a moment the party in power was disposed to resist the forces of the Union. Dick Kanter and his friends were resolute enough; the Catholic priests turned out among the rest with their spades and worked on the entrenchments. The impossibility of hold- April 6, ing the city against the overwhelming power of 1610. the States was soon obvious, and the next day the gates were opened, and easy terms were granted. The new magistracy was set aside, the old board that had May 6, been deposed by the rebels reinstated. The revo- 1610. lution and the counter-revolution were alike bloodless, and it was determined that the various grievances of which the discontented party had complained should be referred to the States-General, to Prince Maurice, to the council of state, and to the ambassadors of France and England. Amnesty was likewise decreed on submission.[1]

The restored government was Arminian in its inclinations, the revolutionary one was singularly compounded both of Catholic and of ultra-orthodox elements. Quiet was on the whole restored, but the resources of the city were crippled. The event occurring exactly at the crisis of the Cleve and Jülich expedition angered the King of France.

[1] Wagenaar, Brill, *ubi sup.*

"The trouble of Utrecht," wrote Aerssens to Barneveld,[1] "has been turned to account here marvellously, the Archdukes and Spaniards boasting that many more revolts like this may be at once expected. I have explained to his Majesty, who has been very much alarmed about it, both its source and the hopes that it will be appeased by the prudence of his Excellency Prince Maurice and the deputies of the States. The King desires that everything should be pacified as soon as possible, so that there may be no embarrassment to the course of public affairs. But he fears, he tells me, that this may create some new jealousy between Prince Maurice and yourself. I don't comprehend what he means, although he held this language to me very expressly and without reserve. I could only answer that you were living on the best of terms together in perfect amity and intelligence. If you know if this talk of his has any other root, please to enlighten me, that I may put a stop to false reports, for I know nothing of affairs except what you tell me."

King James, on the other hand, thoroughly approved the promptness of the States-General in suppressing the tumult.

Nothing very serious of a like nature occurred in Utrecht until the end of the year, when a determined and secret conspiracy was discovered, having for its object to overpower the garrison and get bodily possession of Colonel John Ogle, the military commander of the town. At the bottom of the movement were the indefatigable Dirk Kanter and his friend Heldingen. The attempt was easily suppressed, and the two were banished from the town. Kanter died subsequently

---

[1] Aerssens to Barneveld, 9 March 1610.  (MS.)

[2] A little later Henry expressed great disapprobation of the proceedings of the States against Utrecht, saying that such imprudence might upset the Commonwealth if pains were not taken to prevent the siege. He blamed his ambassadors for not preventing it, and asked Aerssens if there were not time enough to send some one "pour faire le holà."— Same to same, 5 April, 1610.  (MS.)

in North Holland, in the odour of ultra-orthodoxy. Four of the conspirators—a post-master, two shoemakers, and a sexton, who had bound themselves by oath to take the lives of two eminent Arminian[1] preachers, besides other desperate deeds—were condemned to death, but pardoned on the scaffold. Thus ended the first revolution at Utrecht.[2]

Its effect did not cease, however, with the tumults which were its original manifestations. This earliest insurrection in organized shape against the central authority of the States-General; this violent though abortive effort to dissolve the Union and to nullify its laws; this painful necessity for the first time imposed upon the federal government to take up arms against misguided citizens of the Republic, in order to save itself from disintegration and national death, were destined to be followed by far graver convulsions on the self-same spot. Religious differences and religious hatreds were to mingle their poison with antagonistic political theories and personal ambitions, and to develop on a wide scale the danger ever lurking in a constitution whose fundamental law was unstable, ill defined, and liable to contradictory interpretations. For the present it need only be noticed that the States-General, guided by Barneveld, most vigorously suppressed the local revolt and the incipient secession, while Prince Maurice, the right arm of the executive, the stadholder of the province, and the representative of the military power of the Commonwealth, was languid in the exertion of that power, inclined to listen to the specious arguments of the Utrecht rebels, and accused at least of tampering with the fell spirit which the Advocate was resolute to destroy. Yet there was no suspicion of treason,

---

[1] One of whom was Taurinus, author of a famous pamphlet, to which allusion will be made later

[2] Wagenaar, *ubi sup.* Manuscripts in the Hague Archives relating to the tumults at Utrecht, *passim.*

no taint of rebellion, no accusation of unpatriotic motives uttered against the Stadholder.

There was a doubt as to the true maxims by which the Confederacy was to be governed, and at this moment, certainly, the Prince and the Advocate represented opposite ideas. There was a possibility, at a future day, when the religious and political parties might develop themselves on a wider scale and the struggles grow fiercer, that the two great champions in the conflict might exchange swords and inflict mutual and poisoned wounds. At present the party of the Union had triumphed, with Barneveld at its head. At a later but not far distant day, similar scenes might be enacted in the ancient city of Utrecht, but with a strange difference and change in the cast of parts and with far more tragical results.

For the moment the moderate party in the Church, those more inclined to Arminianism and the supremacy of the civil authority in religious matters, had asserted their ascendency in the States-General, and had prevented the threatened rupture.[1]

Meantime it was doubly necessary to hasten the special embassies to France and to England, in both which countries much anxiety as to the political health and strength of the new republic had been excited by these troubles in Utrecht. It was important for the States-General to show that they were not crippled, and would not shrink from the coming conflict, but would justify the reliance placed on them by their allies.

Thus there were reasons enough why Barneveld could not himself leave the country in the eventful spring of 1610. It must be admitted, however, that he was not backward in

---

[1] There is a great mass of manuscripts in the Archives of the Hague relative to these troubles of Utrecht, the greater part of them in the handwriting of Barneveld. As much of their substance as now possesses vital interest has been given in our narrative.

placing his nearest relatives in places of honour, trust, and profit.

His eldest son Reinier, Seignior of Groeneveld, had been knighted by Henry IV.; his youngest, William, afterwards called Seignior of Stoutenburg, but at this moment bearing the not very mellifluous title of Craimgepolder, was a gentleman-in-waiting at that king's court, with a salary of 3000 crowns a year.[1] He was rather a favourite with the easy-going monarch, but he gave infinite trouble to the Dutch ambassador Aerssens, who, feeling himself under immense obligations to the Advocate and professing for him boundless gratitude, did his best to keep the idle, turbulent, extravagant, and pleasure-loving youth up to the strict line of his duties.

" Your son is in debt again," wrote Aerssens, on one occasion, "and troubled for money. He is in danger of going to the usurers. He says he cannot keep himself for less than 200 crowns a month. This is a large allowance, but he has spent much more than that. His life is not irregular nor his dress remarkably extravagant. His difficulty is that he will not dine regularly with me nor at court. He will keep his own table and have company to dinner. That is what is ruining him. He comes sometimes to me, not for the dinner nor the company, but for tennis, which he finds better in my faubourg than in town. His trouble comes from the table, and I tell you frankly that you must regulate his expenses or they will become very onerous to you. I am ashamed of them and have told him so a hundred times, more than if he had been my own brother. It is all for love of you . . . . I have been all to him that could be expected of a man who is under such vast obligations to you ; and I so much esteem the honour of your friendship that I should always neglect my private affairs in order to do everything

_______________
[1] See Vreede, ' Inl. Ned. Dipl.'

for your service and meet your desires. . . . . If M. de Craimgepolder comes back from his visit home, you must restrict him in two things, the table and tennis, and you can do this if you require him to follow the King assiduously as his service requires."[1]

Something at a future day was to be heard of William of Barneveld, as well as of his elder brother Reinier, and it is good, therefore, to have these occasional glimpses of him while in the service of the King and under the supervision of one who was then his father's devoted friend, Francis Aerssens. There were to be extraordinary and tragical changes in the relations of parties and of individuals ere many years should go by.

Besides the sons of the Advocate, his two sons-in-law, Brederode, Seignior of Veenhuizen, and Cornelis van der Myle, were constantly employed in important embassies. Van der Myle had been the first ambassador to the great Venetian republic, and was now placed at the head of the embassy to France, an office which it was impossible at that moment for the Advocate to discharge. At the same critical moment Barneveld's brother Elias, Pensionary of Rotterdam, was appointed one of the special high commissioners to the King of Great Britain.

It is necessary to give an account of this embassy.

They were provided with luminous and minute instructions from the hand of the Advocate.[2]

They were, in the first place, and ostensibly, to thank the King for his services in bringing about the truce, which, truly,

---

[1] Aerssens to Barneveld, 5 March 1609. (MS.) Same to same, 28 March 1609. (MS.)

[2] 'Rapport van den Heeren Gecommitteerden geweest hebbende in Engelandt in der Jaere 1610.' (MS. Hague Archives.) Many citations will be made from this important report, which has never been published.

The members of the embassy were: John van Duivenvoorde, Seignior of Warmond; John Berck, Pensionary of Dordrecht; Albert de Veer, Pensionary of Amsterdam; Elias van Oldenbarneveld, Pensionary of Rotterdam; and Albert Joachimi, deputy from Zealand to the States-General.

had been of the slightest, as was very well known. They were to explain, on the part of the States, their delay in sending this solemn commission, caused by the tardiness of the King of Spain in sending his ratification to the treaty, and by the many disputations caused by the irresolutions of the Archdukes and the obstinacy of their commissioners in regard to their many contraventions of the treaty. After those commissioners had gone, further hindrances had been found in the "extraordinary tempests, high floods, rising of the waters, both of the ocean and the rivers, and the very disastrous inundations throughout nearly all the United Provinces, with the immense and exorbitant damage thus inflicted, both on the public and on many individuals ; in addition to all which were to be mentioned the troubles in the city of Utrecht."

They were, in almost hyperbolical language, directed to express the eternal gratitude of the States for the constant favours received by them from the crown of England, and their readiness to stand forth at any moment with sincere affection and to the utmost of their power, at all times and seasons, in resistance of any attempts against his Majesty's person or crown, or against the Prince of Wales or the royal family. They were to thank him for his " prudent, heroic, and courageous resolve to suffer nothing to be done under colour of justice, authority, or any other pretext, to the hindrance of the Elector of Brandenburg and Palatine of Neuburg, in the maintenance of their lawful rights and possession of the principalities of Jülich, Cleve, and Berg, and other provinces."

By this course his Majesty, so the commissioners were to state, would put an end to the imaginations of those who thought they could give the law to everybody according to their pleasure.

They were to assure the King that the States-General

would exert themselves to the utmost to second his heroic resolution, notwithstanding the enormous burthens of their everlasting war, the very exorbitant damage caused by the inundations, and the sensible diminution in the contributions and other embarrassments then existing in the country.

They were to offer 2000 foot and 500 horse for the general purpose under Prince Henry of Nassau, besides the succours furnished by the King of France and the electors and princes of Germany. Further assistance in men, artillery, and supplies were promised under certain contingencies, and the plan of the campaign on the Meuse in conjunction with the King of France was duly mapped.

They were to request a corresponding promise of men and money from the King of Great Britain, and they were to propose for his approval a closer convention for mutual assistance between his Majesty, the United Netherlands, the King of France, the electors and princes and other powers of Germany ; as such close union would be very beneficial to all Christendom. It would put a stop to all unjust occupations, attempts, and intrigues, and if the King was thereto inclined, he was requested to indicate time and place for making such a convention.

The commissioners were further to point out the various contraventions on the part of the Archdukes of the Treaty of Truce, and were to give an exposition of the manner in which the States-General had quelled the tumults at Utrecht, and reasons why such a course had of necessity been adopted.

They were instructed to state that, "over and above the great expenses of the late war and the necessary maintenance of military forces to protect their frontiers against their suspected new friends or old enemies, the Provinces were burthened with the cost of the succour to the Elector of Brandenburg and Palatine of Neuburg, and would be

therefore incapable of furnishing the payments coming due
to his Majesty. They were accordingly to sound his Majesty
as to whether a good part of the debt might not be remitted
or at least an arrangement made by which the terms should
begin to run only after a certain number of years."

They were also directed to open the subject of the fisheries
on the coasts of Great Britain, and to remonstrate against
the order lately published by the King forbidding all
foreigners from fishing on those coasts. This was to be set
forth as an infringement both of natural law and of ancient
treaties, and as a source of infinite danger to the inhabitants
of the United Provinces.[1]

The Seignior of Warmond, chief of the commission, died
on the 15th April. His colleagues met at Brielle on the
16th, ready to take passage to England in the ship
of war, the *Hound*. They were, however, detained
April 15,
1610.
there six days by head winds and great storms, and it was
not until the 22nd that they were able to put to sea. The
following evening their ship cast anchor in Gravesend. Half
an hour before, the Duke of Würtemberg had arrived from
Flushing in a ship of war brought from France by the
Prince of Anhalt.

Sir Lewis Lewkener, master of ceremonies, had been
waiting for the ambassadors at Gravesend, and informed
them that the royal barges were to come next morning from
London to take them to town. They remained that night
on board the *Hound*, and next morning, the wind blowing up
the river, they proceeded in their ship as far as Blackwall,
where they were formally received and bade welcome in the
name of the King by Sir Thomas Cornwallis and Sir George
Carew, late ambassador in France. Escorted by them and
Sir Lewis, they were brought in the court barges to Tower
Wharf. Here the royal coaches were waiting, in which they

---

[1] Instructions, dated 31 March 1610, in the Report already cited. (MS.)

were taken to lodgings provided for them in the city at the house of a Dutch merchant. Noel de Caron, Seignior of Schonewal, resident ambassador of the States in London, was likewise there to greet them. This was Saturday night. On the following Tuesday they went by appointment to the Palace of Whitehall in royal carriages for their first audience. Manifestations of as entire respect and courtesy had thus been made to the Republican envoys as could be shown to the ambassadors of the greatest sovereigns. They found the King seated on his throne in the audience chamber, accompanied by the Prince of Wales, the Duke of York, the Lord High Treasurer and Lord High Admiral, the Duke of Lenox, the Earls of Arundel and Northampton, and many other great nobles and dignitaries. James rose from his seat, took off his hat, and advanced several paces to meet the ambassadors, and bade them courteously and respectfully welcome. He then expressed his regret at the death of the Seignior of Warmond, and after the exchange of a few commonplaces listened, still with uncovered head, to the opening address.[1]

April 27, 1610.

The spokesman, after thanking the King for his condolences on the death of the chief commissioner, whom, as was stated with whimsical simplicity, "the good God had called to Himself after all his luggage had been put on board ship,"[2] proceeded in the French language to give a somewhat abbreviated paraphrase of Barneveld's instructions.

When this was done and intimation made that they would confer more fully with his Majesty's council on the subjects committed to their charge, the ambassadors were conducted home with the same ceremonies as had accompanied their arrival. They received the same day the first visit from the ambassadors of France and Venice, Boderie and Carrero, and had a long conference a few days afterwards with the High Treasurer, Lord Salisbury.

[1] MS. before cited.        [2] Ibid.

On the 3rd May they were invited to attend the pompous celebration of the festival of St. George in the palace at Westminster, where they were placed together with the French ambassador in the King's oratorium ; the Dukes of Würtemberg and Brunswick being in that of the Queen.

May 3, 1610.

These details are especially to be noted, and were at the moment of considerable importance, for this was the first solemn and extraordinary embassy sent by the rebel Netherlanders, since their independent national existence had been formally vindicated, to Great Britain, a power which a quarter of a century before had refused the proffered sovereignty over them.  Placed now on exactly the same level with the representatives of emperors and kings, the Republican envoys found themselves looked upon by the world with different eyes from those which had regarded their predecessors askance, and almost with derision, only seven years before. At that epoch the States' commissioners, Barneveld himself at the head of them, had gone solemnly to congratulate King James on his accession, had scarcely been admitted to audience by king or minister, and had found themselves on great festivals unsprinkled with the holy water of the court, and of no more account than the crowd of citizens and spectators who thronged the streets, gazing with awe at the distant radiance of the throne.[1]

But although the ambassadors were treated with every external consideration befitting their official rank, they were not likely to find themselves in the most genial atmosphere when they should come to business details.  If there was one thing in the world that James did not intend to do, it was to get himself entangled in war with Spain, the power of all others which he most revered and loved.  His " heroic and courageous resolve " to defend the princes, on which the commissioners by instructions of the Advocate had so highly

<hr>

[1] ' Hist. United Netherlands,' vol. iv. chap. xli.

complimented him, was not strong enough to carry him much beyond a vigorous phraseology. He had not awoke from the delusive dream of the Spanish marriage which had dexterously been made to flit before him, and he was not inclined, for the sake of the Republic which he hated the more because obliged to be one of its sponsors, to risk the animosity of a great power which entertained the most profound contempt for him. He was destined to find himself involved more closely than he liked, and through family ties, with the great Protestant movement in Germany, and the unfortunate " Winter King " might one day find his father-in-law as unstable a reed to lean upon as the States had found their godfather, or the Brandenburgs and Neuburgs at the present juncture their great ally. Meantime, as the Bohemian troubles had not yet reached the period of actual explosion, and as Henry's wide-reaching plan against the House of Austria had been strangely enough kept an inviolable secret by the few statesmen, like Sully and Barneveld, to whom they had been confided, it was necessary for the King and his ministers to deal cautiously and plausibly with the Dutch ambassadors. Their conferences were mere dancing among eggs, and if no actual mischief were done, it was the best result that could be expected.

On the 8th of May, the commissioners met in the council chamber at Westminster, and discussed all the matters May 6, contained in their instructions with the members 1610. of the council ; the Lord Treasurer Salisbury, Earl of Northampton, Privy Seal and Warden of the Cinque Ports, Lord Nottingham, Lord High Admiral, the Lord Chamberlain, Earl of Suffolk, Earls of Shrewsbury, Worcester, and several others being present.

The result was not entirely satisfactory. In regard to the succour demanded for the possessory princes, the commissioners were told that they seemed to come with a long narrative of their great burthens during the war, damage from inundations, and the like, to excuse themselves from doing their share in the succour, and thus the more to overload his Majesty, who was not much interested in the matter, and was likewise greatly encumbered by various expenses. The King had already frankly declared his intention to assist the princes with the payment of 4000 men, and to send proportionate artillery and powder from England. As the States had supplies in their magazines enough to move 12,000 men, he proposed to draw upon those, reimbursing the States for what was thus consumed by his contingent.

With regard to the treaty of close alliance between France, Great Britain, the princes, and the Republic, which the ambassadors had proposed, the Lord Treasurer and his colleagues gave a reply far from gratifying. His Majesty had not yet decided on this point, they said. The King of France had already proposed to treat for such an alliance, but it did not at present seem worth while for all to negotiate together.

This was a not over-courteous hint that the Republic was after all not expected to place herself at the council-board of kings on even terms of intimacy and fraternal alliance

What followed was even less flattering. If his Majesty, it was intimated, should decide to treat with the King of France, he would not shut the door on their High Mightinesses ; but his Majesty was not yet exactly informed whether his Majesty had not certain rights over the provinces *in petitorio.*[1]

This was a scarcely veiled insinuation against the sovereignty of the States, a sufficiently broad hint that they were to be considered in a certain degree as British provinces. To a soldier like Maurice, to a statesman like Barneveld, whose sympathies already were on the side of

[1] MS. Report.

France, such rebuffs and taunts were likely to prove unpalatable. The restiveness of the States at the continual
possession by Great Britain of those important sea-ports the
cautionary towns, a fact which gave colour to these innuendoes,
was sure to be increased by arrogant language on the part
of the English ministers. The determination to be rid of
their debt to so overbearing an ally, and to shake off the
shackles imposed by the costly mortgages, grew in strength
from that hour.

In regard to the fisheries, the Lord Treasurer and his
colleagues expressed amazement that the ambassadors should
consider the subjects of their High Mightinesses to be so
much beloved by his Majesty. Why should they of all
other people be made an exception of, and be exempt from,
the action of a general edict ? The reasons for these orders
in council ought to be closely examined. It would be very
difficult to bring the opinions of the English jurists into
harmony with those of the States. Meantime it would be
well to look up such treaties as might be in existence, and
have a special joint commission to confer together on the
subject. It was very plain, from the course of the conversation, that the Netherland fishermen were not to be allowed,
without paying roundly for a license, to catch herrings on
the British coasts as they had heretofore done.

Not much more of importance was transacted at this first
interview between the ambassadors and the King's ministers.
Certainly they had not yet succeeded in attaining their great
object, the formation of an alliance offensive and defensive
between Great Britain and the Republic in accordance
with the plan concerted between Henry and Barneveld.
They could find but slender encouragement for the warlike
plans to which France and the States were secretly committed ; nor could they obtain satisfactory adjustment of
affairs more pacific and commercial in their tendencies. The

English ministers rather petulantly remarked that, while last year everybody was talking of a general peace, and in the present conjuncture all seemed to think, or at least to speak, of nothing but a general war, they thought best to defer consideration of the various subjects connected with duties on the manufactures and products of the respective countries, the navigation laws, the "*entrecours*," and other matters of ancient agreement and controversy, until a more convenient season.[1]

After the termination of the verbal conference, the ambassadors delivered to the King's government, in writing, to be pondered by the council and recorded in the archives, a summary of the statements which had been thus orally treated. The document was in French, and in the main a paraphrase of the Advocate's instructions, the substance of which has been already indicated. In regard, however, to the far-reaching designs of Spain, and the corresponding attitude which it would seem fitting for Great Britain to assume, and especially the necessity of that alliance the proposal for which had in the conference been received so haughtily, their language was far plainer, bolder, and more vehement than that of the instructions.

"Considering that the effects show," they said, "that those who claim the monarchy of Christendom, and indeed of the whole world, let slip no opportunity which could in any way serve their designs, it is suitable to the grandeur of his Majesty the King, and to the station in which by the grace of the good God he is placed, to oppose himself thereto for the sake of the common liberty of Christendom, to which end, and in order the better to prevent all unjust usurpations, there could be no better means devised than a closer alliance between his Majesty and the Most Christian King, My Lords the States-General, and the electors, princes, and states of

______
[1] "Rapport," &c.

Germany. Their High Mightinesses would therefore be most glad to learn that his Majesty was inclined to such a course, and would be glad to discuss the subject when and wherever his Majesty should appoint, or would readily enter into such an alliance on reasonable conditions."[1]

This language and the position taken up by the ambassadors were highly approved by their government, but it was fated that no very great result was to be achieved by this embassy. Very elaborate documents, exhaustive in legal lore, on the subject of the herring fisheries, and of the right to fish in the ocean and on foreign coasts, fortified by copious citations from the 'Pandects' and 'Institutes' of Justinian, were presented for the consideration of the British government, and were answered as learnedly, exhaustively, and ponderously. The English ministers were also reminded that the curing of herrings had been invented in the fifteenth century by a citizen of Biervliet, the inscription on whose tombstone recording that fact might still be read in the church of that town.

All this did not prevent, however, the Dutch herring fishermen from being excluded from the British waters unless they chose to pay for licenses.

The conferences were however for a season interrupted, and a new aspect was given to affairs by an unforeseen and terrible event.

Meanwhile it is necessary to glance for a moment at the doings of the special embassy to France, the instructions for which were prepared by Barneveld almost at the same moment at which he furnished those for the commission to England.

The ambassadors were Walraven, Seignior of Brederode,

<hr>

[1] "Raisons que les Ambassadeurs de Mess" les Etats-gén' des Provinces-Unies pensent militer pour la conservation et maintenement du droit de la pêcherie."—Art. xxiii. "Rapport," &c. *ubi sup.* (MS.)

Cornelis van der Myle, son-in-law of the Advocate, and Jacob van Maldere. Remembering how impatient the King of France had long been for their coming, and that all the preparations and decisions for a great war were kept in suspense until the final secret conferences could be held with the representatives of the States-General, it seems strange enough to us to observe the extreme deliberation with which great affairs of state were then conducted and the vast amount of time consumed in movements and communications which modern science has either annihilated or abridged from days to hours. While Henry was chafing with anxiety in Paris, the ambassadors, having received Barneveld's instructions dated 31st March, set forth on the 8th April from the Hague, reached Rotterdam at noon, and slept at Dordrecht. Next day they went to Breda, where the Prince of Orange insisted upon their passing a couple of days with him in his castle, Easter-day being 11th April. He then provided them with a couple of coaches and pair in which they set forth on their journey, going by way of Antwerp, Ghent, Courtray, Ryssel, to Arras, making easy stages, stopping in the middle of the day to bait, and sleeping at each of the cities thus mentioned, where they duly received the congratulatory visit and hospitalities of their respective magistracies.[1]

While all this time had been leisurely employed in the Netherlands in preparing, instructing, and despatching the commissioners, affairs were reaching a feverish crisis in France.

The States' ambassador resident thought that it would have been better not to take such public offence at the retreat of

---

[1] "Rapport ofte Verhael van 't gene datin de Legatie aen den allerchristelyksten Koninck by den Welgeboren Heer Walraven, Heer tot Brederode, Vianen etc. eude de Heer Cornelius van der Myle en Jacques van Malderen is geproponeert, gehandelt etc. tot afschrift gegeven." (Archives at the Hague, MS.) Several citations will be made from this important and unpublished document.

the Prince of Condé.  The King had enough of life and vigour in him; he could afford to leave the Dauphin to grow up, and when he should one day be established on the throne, he would be able to maintain his heritage.  "But," said Aerssens, "I fear that our trouble is not where we say it is, and we don't dare to say where it is."[1]  Writing to Carew, former English ambassador in Paris, whom we have just seen in attendance on the States' commissioners in London, he said : "People think that the Princess is wearying herself much under the protection of the Infanta, and very impatient at not obtaining the dissolution of her marriage, which the Duchess of Angoulême is to go to Brussels to facilitate. This is not our business, but I mention it only as the continuation of the Tragedy which you saw begin.  Nevertheless I don't know if the greater part of our deliberations is not founded on this matter."[2]

It had been decided to cause the Queen to be solemnly crowned after Easter.  She had set her heart with singular persistency upon the ceremony, and it was thought that so public a sacrament would annihilate all the wild projects attributed to Spain through the instrumentality of Condé to cast doubts on the validity of her marriage and the legitimacy of the Dauphin.  The King from the first felt and expressed a singular repugnance, a boding apprehension in regard to the coronation, but had almost yielded to the Queen's importunity.  He told her he would give his consent provided she sent Concini to Brussels to invite in her own name the Princess of Condé to be present on the occasion. Otherwise he declared that at least the festival should be postponed till September.[3]

---

[1] Aerssens to Barneveld, 9 March 1610.  (MS.)

[2] Same to Carew, 10 March 1610. (MS.)

[3] ". . . sur les très-exprès désir qu'il soit au mois de Mai, mais à condition que le S<sup>r</sup> Concini en son nom aille quérir la princesse de Condé à Bruxelles pour y assister," &c.—Aerssens to Barneveld, 30 March 1610.  (MS.)

The Marquis de Coeuvres remained in disgrace after the failure of his mission, Henry believing that like all the world he had fallen in love with the Princess, and had only sought to recommend himself, not to further the suit of his sovereign.[1]

Meanwhile Henry had instructed his ambassador in Spain, M. de Vaucelas, to tell the King that his reception of Condé within his dominions would be considered an infraction of the treaty of Vervins and a direct act of hostility. The Duke of Lerma answered with a sneer[2] that the Most Christian King had too greatly obliged his Most Catholic Majesty by sustaining his subjects in their rebellion and by aiding them to make their truce to hope now that Condé would be sent back. France had ever been the receptacle of Spanish traitors and rebels from Antonio Perez down, and the King of Spain would always protect wronged and oppressed princes like Condé. France had just been breaking up the friendly relations between Savoy and Spain and goading the Duke into hostilities.

On the other hand the King had more than one stormy interview with Don Inigo de Cardenas in Paris. That ambassador declared that his master would never abandon his only sister the most serene Infanta, such was the affection he bore her, whose dominions were obviously threatened by these French armies about to move to the frontiers. Henry replied that the friends for whom he was arming had great need of his assistance ; that his Catholic Majesty was quite right to love his sister, whom he also loved ; but that he did not choose that his own relatives should be so much beloved in Spain as they were. " What relatives ? " asked Don Inigo. " The Prince of Condé," replied the King, in a rage, " who has been debauched by the Spaniards just as Marshal Biron was, and the

<hr>

[1] Aerssens to Barneveld, 30 March 1610.  (MS.)
[2] Same to same, 9 March 1610.  (MS.)

Marchioness Verneuil, and so many others. There are none left for them to debauch now but the Dauphin and his brothers." The Ambassador replied that, if the King had consulted him about the affair of Condé, he could have devised a happy issue from it. Henry rejoined that he had sent messages on the subject to his Catholic Majesty, who had not deigned a response, but that the Duke of Lerma had given a very indiscreet one to his ambassador. Don Inigo professed ignorance of any such reply. The King said it was a mockery to affect ignorance of such matters. Thereupon both grew excited and very violent in their discourses ; the more so as Henry knowing but little Spanish and the Envoy less French they could only understand from tone and gesture that each was using exceedingly unpleasant language. At last Don Inigo asked what he should write to his sovereign. "Whatever you like," replied the King, and so the audience terminated, each remaining in a towering passion.[1]

Subsequently Villeroy assured the Archduke's ambassador that the King considered the reception given to the Prince in the Spanish dominions as one of the greatest insults and injuries that could be done to him. Nothing could excuse it, said the Secretary of State, and for this reason it was very difficult for the two kings to remain at peace with each other, and that it would be wiser to prevent at once the evil designs of his Catholic Majesty than to leave leisure for the plans to be put into execution, and the claims of the Dauphin to his father's crown to be disputed at a convenient season.

He added that war would not be made for the Princess, but for the Prince, and that even the war in Germany, although Spain took the Emperor's side and France that of the possessory princes, would not necessarily produce a rupture between the two kings if it were not for this affair of the

_______________
[1] Pecquius to Archduke Albert, 7 April 1610, in Henrard.

Prince—true cause of the disaster now hanging over Christianity.  Pecquius replied by smooth commonplaces in favour of peace with which Villeroy warmly concurred ; both sadly expressing the conviction however that the wrath divine had descended on them all on account of their sins.[1]

A few days later, however, the Secretary changed his tone.

" I will speak to you frankly and clearly," he said to Pecquius, "and tell you as from myself that there is passion, and if one is willing to arrange the affair of the Princess, everything else can be accommodated and appeased. But if the Princess remain where she is, we are on the eve of a rupture which may set fire to the four corners of Christendom."  Pecquius said he liked to talk roundly, and was glad to find that he had not been mistaken in his opinion, that all these commotions were only made for the Princess, and if all the world was going to war, she would be the principal subject of it.  He could not marvel sufficiently, he said, at this vehement passion which brought in its train so great and horrible a conflagration ; adding many arguments to show that it was no fault of the Archdukes, but that he who was the cause of all might one day have reason to repent.

Villeroy replied that " the King believed the Princess to be suffering and miserable for love of him, and that therefore he felt obliged to have her sent back to her father." Pecquius asked whether in his conscience the Secretary of State believed it right or reasonable to make war for such a cause.  Villeroy replied by asking " whether even admitting the negative, the Ambassador thought it were wisely done for such a trifle, for a formality, to plunge into extremities and to turn all Christendom upside down."  Pecquius, not considering honour a trifle or a formality, said that " for nothing in the world would his Highness the Archduke

<hr>

[1] Pecquius to Archduke Albert, 7 April 1610. in Henrard.

descend to a cowardly action or to anything that would sully his honour." Villeroy said that the Prince had compelled his wife, pistol in hand, to follow him to the Netherlands, and that she was no longer bound to obey a husband who forsook country and king. Her father demanded her, and she said "she would rather be strangled than ever to return to the company of her husband." The Archdukes were not justified in keeping her against her will in perpetual banishment. He implored the Ambassador in most pathetic terms to devise some means of sending back the Princess, saying that he who should find such expedient would do the greatest good that was ever done to Christianity, and that otherwise there was no guarantee against a universal war. The first design of the King had been merely to send a moderate succour to the Princes of Brandenburg and Neuburg, which could have given no umbrage to the Archdukes, but now the bitterness growing out of the affairs of the Prince and Princess had caused him to set on foot a powerful army to do worse. He again implored Pecquius to invent some means of sending back the Princess, and the Ambassador besought him ardently to divert the King from his designs. Of this the Secretary of State left little hope and they parted, both very low and dismal in mind. Subsequent conversations with the leading councillors of state convinced Pecquius that these violent menaces were only used to shake the constancy of the Archduke, but that they almost all highly disapproved the policy of the King. "If this war goes on, we are all ruined," said the Duke d'Épernon to the Nuncius.[1]

Thus there had almost ceased to be any grimacing between the two kings, although it was still a profound mystery where or when hostilities would begin, and whether they would break out at all. Henry frequently remarked that the common opinion all over Europe was working in his

[1] Pecquius to Archduke Albert, 19 April 1610. (MS.)

favour. Few people in or out of France believed that he meant a rupture, or that his preparations were serious. Thus should he take his enemies unawares and unprepared.[1] Even Aerssens, who saw him almost daily, was sometimes mystified, in spite of Henry's vehement assertions that he was resolved to make war at all hazards and on all sides, provided My Lords the States would second him as they ought, their own existence being at stake.

"For God's sake," cried the King, "let us take the bit into our mouths. Tell your masters that I am quite resolved, and that I am shrieking loudly at their delays." He asked if he could depend on the States, if Barneveld especially would consent to a league with him. The Ambassador replied that for the affair of Cleve and Jülich he had instructions to promise entire concurrence, that Barneveld was most resolute in the matter, and had always urged the enterprise and wished information as to the levies making in France and other military preparations.[2]

"Tell him," said Henry, "that they are going on exactly as often before stated, but that we are holding everything in suspense until I have talked with your ambassadors, from whom I wish counsel, safety, and encouragement for doing much more than the Jülich business. That alone does not require so great a league and such excessive and unnecessary expense."

The King observed however that the question of the duchies would serve as just cause and excellent pretext to remove those troublesome fellows for ever from his borders and those of the States. Thus the princes would be established safely in their possession and the Republic as well as himself freed from the perpetual suspicions which the Spaniards excited by their vile intrigues, and it was on this

---

[1] Pecquius to Archduke Albert, 26 March 1610.  (MS.)
[2] Aerssens to Barneveld, 9 March 1610.  (MS.)

general subject that he wished to confer with the special commissioners. It would not be possible for him to throw succour into Jülich without passing through Luxemburg in arms. The Archdukes would resist this, and thus a cause of war would arise. His campaign on the Meuse would help the princes more than if he should only aid them by the contingent he had promised. Nor could the jealousy of King James be excited since the war would spring out of the Archdukes' opposition to his passage towards the duchies, as he obviously could not cut himself off from his supplies, leaving a hostile province between himself and his kingdom. Nevertheless he could not stir, he said, without the consent and active support of the States, on whom he relied as his principal buttress and foundation.

The levies for the Milanese expedition were waiting until Marshal de Lesdiguières could confer personally with the Duke of Savoy. The reports as to the fidelity of that potentate were not to be believed. He was trifling with the Spanish ambassadors, so Henry was convinced, who were offering him 300,000 crowns a year besides Piombino, Monaco, and two places in the Milanese, if he would break his treaty with France. But he was thought to be only waiting until they should be gone before making his arrangements with Lesdiguières. " He knows that he can put no trust in Spain, and that he can confide in me," said the King. " I have made a great stroke by thus entangling the King of Spain by the use of a few troops in Italy. But I assure you that there is none but me and My Lords the States that can do anything solid. Whether the Duke breaks or holds fast will make no difference in our first and great designs. For the honour of God I beg them to lose no more time, but to trust in me. I will never deceive them, never abandon them." [1]

<hr>

[1] Aerssens to Barneveld, 26 March 1610.  (MS.)

At last 25,000 infantry and 5000 cavalry were already in marching order, and indeed had begun to move towards the Luxemburg frontier, ready to co-operate with the States' army and that of the possessory princes for the campaign of the Meuse and Rhine.

Twelve thousand more French troops under Lesdiguières were to act with the Duke of Savoy, and an army as large was to assemble in the Pyrenees and to operate on the Spanish frontier, in hope of exciting and fomenting an insurrection caused by the expulsion of the Moors.[1] That gigantic act of madness by which Spain thought good at this juncture to tear herself to pieces, driving hundreds of thousands of the most industrious, most intelligent, and most opulent of her population into hopeless exile, had now been accomplished, and was to stand prominent for ever on the records of human fatuity.[2]

Twenty-five thousand Moorish families had arrived at Bayonne, and the Viceroy of Canada had been consulted as to the possibility and expediency of establishing them in that province,[3] although emigration thither seemed less tempting to them than to Virginia. Certainly it was not unreasonable for Henry to suppose that a kingdom thus torn by internal convulsions might be more open to a well organized attack than capable of carrying out at that moment fresh projects of universal dominion.

As before observed, Sully was by no means in favour of this combined series of movements, although at a later day, when dictating his famous memoirs to his secretaries, he seems to describe himself as enthusiastically applauding and almost originating them. But there is no doubt at all that throughout this eventful spring he did his best to concentrate the whole attack on Luxemburg and the Meuse

---

[1] Van Meteren, b. xxxi. 693, 694.  'Mém. de Bassompierre,' i. 451. 455.
[2] Van Meteren, *ubi sup.*       [3] Aerssens to Carew, 10 March 1610. (MS.)

districts, and wished that the movements in the Milanese and in Provence should be considered merely a slight accessory, as not much more than a diversion to the chief design, while Villeroy and his friends chose to consider the Duke of Savoy as the chief element in the war.[1]   Sully thoroughly distrusted the Duke, whom he deemed to be always put up at auction between Spain and France and incapable of a sincere or generous policy.  He was entirely convinced that Villeroy and Épernon and Jeannin and other earnest Papists in France were secretly inclined to the cause of Spain, that the whole faction of the Queen, in short, were urging this scattering of the very considerable forces now at Henry's command in the hope of bringing him into a false position, in which defeat or an ignominious peace would be the alternative.[2]  To concentrate an immense attack upon the Archdukes in the Spanish Netherlands and the debateable duchies would have for its immediate effect the expulsion of the Spaniards out of all those provinces and the establishment of the Dutch commonwealth on an impregnable basis.  That this would be to strengthen infinitely the Huguenots in France and the cause of Protestantism in Bohemia, Moravia and Austria, was unquestionable.  It was natural, therefore, that the stern and ardent Huguenot should suspect the plans of the Catholics with whom he was in daily council.  One day he asked the King plumply in the presence of Villeroy if his Majesty meant anything serious by all these warlike preparations.  Henry was wroth, and complained bitterly that one who knew him to the bottom of his soul should doubt him.[3]  But Sully could not persuade himself that a great

---

[1] Aerssens to Barneveld, 9 March 1610.  Same to same, 24 March 1610. Same to same, 9 Feb. 1610.  (MSS.)
[2] Same to same, 31 Jan. 1610. Same to same, 25 Dec. 1609.  Same to same, 7 Feb. 1610.  Same to Digart, 3 Feb. 1610.  (MSS.)
[3] Letter of Aerssens, 24 March 1610.

and serious war would be carried on both in the Netherlands and in Italy.

As much as his sovereign he longed for the personal presence of Barneveld, and was constantly urging the States' ambassador to induce his coming to Paris. "You know," said Aerssens, writing to the French ambassador at the Hague, de Russy, "that it is the Advocate alone that has the universal knowledge of the outside and the inside of our commonwealth."[1]

Sully knew his master as well as any man knew him, but it was difficult to fix the chameleon hues of Henry at this momentous epoch. To the Ambassador expressing doubts as to the King's sincerity the Duke asserted that Henry was now seriously piqued with the Spaniard on account of the Condé business. Otherwise Anhalt and the possessory princes and the affair of Cleve might have had as little effect in driving him into war as did the interests of the Netherlands in times past. But the bold demonstration projected would make the "whole Spanish party bleed at the nose;[2] a good result for the public peace."

Therefore Sully sent word to Barneveld, although he wished his name concealed, that he ought to come himself, with full powers to do everything, without referring to any superiors or allowing any secrets to be divulged.[3] The King was too far committed to withdraw, unless coldness on part of the States should give him cause. The Advocate must come prepared to answer all questions; to say how much in men and money the States would contribute, and whether they would go into the war with the King as their only ally. He must come with the bridle on his neck. All

<hr>

[1] Aerssens to de Russy, 10 March 1610. (MS.)
[3] Same to Barneveld, 25 Dec.
1609. (MS.)
[2] Ibid. Also same to same, 24 Jan 1610. (MS.)

that Henry feared was being left in the lurch by the States; otherwise he was not afraid of Rome. Sully was urgent that the Provinces should now go vigorously into the war without stumbling at any consideration. Thus they would confirm their national power for all time, but if the opportunity were now lost, it would be their ruin, and posterity would most justly blame them.[1] The King of Spain was so stripped of troops and resources, so embarrassed by the Moors, that in ten months he would not be able to send one man to the Netherlands.

Meantime the Nuncius in Paris was moving heaven and earth; storming, intriguing, and denouncing the course of the King in protecting heresy, when it would have been so easy to extirpate it, encouraging rebellion and disorder throughout Christendom, and embarking in an action against the Church and against his conscience. A new legate was expected daily with the Pope's signature to the new league, and a demand upon the King to sign it likewise, and to pause in a career of which something was suspected, but very little accurately known. The preachers in Paris and throughout the kingdom delivered most vehement sermons against the King, the government, and the Protestants, and seemed to the King to be such "trumpeters of sedition" that he ordered the seneschals and other officers to put a stop to these turbulent discourses, censure their authors, and compel them to stick to their texts.[2]

But the preparations were now so far advanced and going on so warmly that nothing more was wanting than, in the words of Aerssens, "to uncouple the dogs and let them run."[3] Recruits were pouring steadily to their places of rendezvous; their pay having begun to run from the

---

[1] Letter of Aerssens, 25 Dec. 1609.

[2] Aerssens to Digart, 11 March 1610. Same to Barneveld, 22 Dec. 1609. Same to same, 21 Jan. 1610. (MSS.)

[3] Same to same, 24 March 1610. (MS.)

25th March at the rate of eight sous a day for the private
foot soldier and ten sous for a corporal.  They were moved
in small parties of ten, lodged in the wayside inns, and
ordered, on pain of death, to pay for everything they consumed.[1]

It was growing difficult to wait much longer for the arrival
of the special ambassadors, when at last they were known
to be on their way.  Aerssens obtained for their use the
Hotel Gondy, formerly the residence of Don Pedro de Toledo,
the most splendid private palace in Paris, and recently purchased by the Queen.  It was considered expedient that the
embassy should make as stately an appearance as that of
royal or imperial envoys.  He engaged an upholsterer by
the King's command to furnish, at his Majesty's expense, the
apartments, as the Baron de Gondy, he said, had long since
sold and eaten up all the furniture.  He likewise laid in
six pieces of wine and as many of beer, "tavern drinks"
being in the opinion of the thrifty ambassador "both dear
and bad."

He bought a carriage lined with velvet for the commissioners, and another lined with broadcloth for the principal
persons of their suite, and with his own coach as a third he
proposed to go to Amiens to meet them.  They could not
get on with fewer than these, he said, and the new carriages
would serve their purpose in Paris.  He had paid 500
crowns for the two, and they could be sold, when done with,
at a slight loss.  He bought likewise four dapple-grey
horses, which would be enough, as nobody had more than two
horses to a carriage in town, and for which he paid 312
crowns—a very low price, he thought, at a season when
every one was purchasing.  He engaged good and experienced
coachmen at two crowns a month, and, in short, made all

<hr>

[1] Aerssens to Barneveld, 24 March 1610.  (MS.)
[2] Ibid.

necessary arrangements for their comfort and the honour of the state.[1]

The King had been growing more and more displeased at the tardiness of the commission, petulantly ascribing it to a design on the part of the States to "excuse themselves from sharing in his bold conceptions," but said that "he could resolve on nothing without My Lords the States, who were the only power with which he could contract confidently, as mighty enough and experienced enough to execute the designs to be proposed to them ; so that his army was lying useless on his hands until the commissioners arrived," and lamented more loudly than ever that Barneveld was not coming with them.  He was now rejoiced, however, to hear that they would soon arrive, and went in person to the Hotel Gondy to see that everything was prepared in a manner befitting their dignity and comfort.[2]

His anxiety had moreover been increased, as already stated, by the alarming reports from Utrecht and by his other private accounts from the Netherlands.

De Russy expressed in his despatches grave doubts whether the States would join the king in a war against the King of Spain, because they feared the disapprobation of the King of Great Britain, "who had already manifested but too much jealousy of the power and grandeur of the Republic."  Pecquius asserted that the Archdukes had received assurances from the States that they would do nothing to violate the truce.  The Prince of Anhalt, who, as chief of the army of the confederated princes, was warm in his demonstrations for a general war by taking advantage of the Cleve expedition, was entirely at cross purposes with the States' ambassador in Paris, Aerssens maintaining that

<hr>

[1] Aerssens to Barneveld, 24 March 1610.  Same to same, 30 March 1610. Same to van der Myle, 26 March 1610.  (MSS.)

[2] Same to Barneveld, 26 March 1610.  (MS.)  "Rapport" of the special ambassadors.  (MS. before cited.)

the forty-three years' experience in their war justified the States in placing no dependence on German princes except with express conventions. They had no such conventions now, and if they should be attacked by Spain in consequence of their assistance in the Cleve business, what guarantee of aid had they from those whom Anhalt represented? Anhalt was loud in expressions of sympathy with Henry's designs against Spain, but said that he and the States meant a war of thirty or forty years, while the princes would finish what they meant to do in one.[1]

A more erroneous expression of opinion, when viewed in the light of subsequent events, could hardly have been hazarded. Villeroy made as good use as he could of these conversations to excite jealousy between the princes and the States for the furtherance of his own ends, while affecting warm interest in the success of the King's projects.

Meantime Archduke Albert had replied manfully and distinctly to the menaces of the King and to the pathetic suggestions made by Villeroy to Pecquius as to a device for sending back the Princess. Her stay at Brussels being the chief cause of the impending war, it would be better, he said, to procure a divorce or to induce the Constable to obtain the consent of the Prince to the return of his wife to her father's house. To further either of these expedients, the Archduke would do his best. "But if one expects by bravados and threats," he added, "to force us to do a thing against our promise, and therefore against reason, our reputation, and honour, resolutely we will do nothing of the kind. And if the said Lord King decided on account of this misunderstanding for a rupture and to make war upon us, we will do our best to wage war on him. In such case, however, we shall be obliged to keep the Princess closer in our own house, and probably to send her to such parts as may be

<hr>

[1] Aerssens to Barneveld, 5 April 1610. (MS.)

most convenient in order to remove from us an instrument of the infinite evils which this war will produce." [1]

Meantime the special commissioners whom we left at Arras had now entered the French kingdom.

On the 17th April, Aerssens with his three coaches met them on their entrance into Amiens, having been waiting there for them eight days. As they passed through the gate, they found a guard of soldiers drawn up to receive them with military honours, and an official functionary to apologize for the necessary absence of the governor, who had gone with most of the troops stationed in the town to the rendezvous in Champagne. He expressed regret, therefore, that the King's orders for their solemn reception could not be literally carried out. The whole board of magistrates, however, in their costumes of ceremony, with sergeants bearing silver maces marching before them, came forth to bid the ambassadors welcome. An advocate made a speech in the name of the city authorities, saying that they were expressly charged by the King to receive them as coming from his very best friends, and to do them all honour. He extolled the sage government of their High Mightinesses and the valour of the Republic, which had become known to the whole world by the successful conduct of their long and mighty war.

The commissioners replied in words of compliment, and the magistrates then offered them, according to ancient usage, several bottles of hippocras.

Next day, sending back the carriages of the Prince of Orange, in which they had thus far performed the journey, April 18, they set forth towards Paris, reaching Saint-Denis 1610. at noon of the third day. Here they were met by de Bonoeil, introducer of ambassadors, sent thither

<hr>

[1] Archdukes to Pecqnius, 22 April 1610, in Henrard.
[2] "Rapport ofte Verhael." (MS. before cited.)

by the King to give them welcome, and to say that they would be received on the road by the Duke of Vendôme, eldest of the legitimatized children of the King. Accordingly before reaching the Saint-Denis gate of Paris, a splendid cavalcade of nearly five hundred noblemen met them, the Duke at their head, accompanied by two marshals of France, de Brissac and Boisdaulphin. The three instantly dismounted, and the ambassadors alighted from their coach. The Duke then gave them solemn and cordial welcome, saying that he had been sent by his father the King to receive them as befitted envoys of the best and most faithful friends he possessed in the world.[1]

The ambassadors expressed their thanks for the great and extraordinary honour thus conferred on them, and they were then requested to get into a royal carriage which had been sent out for that purpose. After much ceremonious refusal they at last consented and, together with the Duke of Vendôme, drove through Paris in that vehicle into the Faubourg Saint-Germain. Arriving at the Hotel Gondy, they were, notwithstanding all their protestations, escorted up the staircase into the apartments by the Duke.

"This honour is notable," said the commissioners in their report to the States,[2] "and never shown to anyone before, so that our ill-wishers are filled with spite."

And Peter Pecquius was of the same opinion. "Everyone is grumbling here," about the reception of the States' ambassadors, "because such honours were never paid to any ambassador whatever, whether from Spain, England, or any other country."[3]

And there were many men living and employed in great affairs of State, both in France and in the Republic—the King and Villeroy, Barneveld and Maurice—who could re-

April 20,<br>1610.

---

[1] "Rapport ofte Verhael." (MS. before cited.)   [2] Ibid.
[3] Pecquius to Archduke Albert, 22 April 1610, in Henrard.

member how twenty-six years before a solemn embassy from the States had proceeded from the Hague to France to offer the sovereignty of their country to Henry's predecessor, had been kept ignominiously and almost like prisoners four weeks long in Rouen, and had been thrust back into the Netherlands without being admitted even to one audience by the monarch. Truly time, in the course of less than one generation of mankind, had worked marvellous changes in the fortunes of the Dutch Republic.[1]

President Jeannin came to visit them next day, with friendly proffers of service, and likewise the ambassador of Venice and the chargé d'affaires of Great Britain.

On the 22nd the royal carriages came by appointment to the Hotel Gondy, and took them for their first audience to the Louvre. They were received at the gate by a guard of honour, drums beating and arms presented, and conducted with the greatest ceremony to an apartment in the palace. Soon afterwards they were ushered into a gallery where the King stood, surrounded by a number of princes and distinguished officers of the crown. These withdrew on the approach of the Netherlanders, leaving the King standing alone. They made their reverence, and Henry saluted them all with respectful cordiality. Begging them to put on their hats again, he listened attentively to their address.

April 22, 1610.

The language of the discourse now pronounced was similar in tenour to that almost contemporaneously held by the States' special envoys in London. Both documents, when offered afterwards in writing, bore the unmistakable imprint of the one hand that guided the whole political machine. In various passages the phraseology was identical, and, indeed, the Advocate had prepared and signed the instructions for both embassies on the same day.

[1] See 'History of the United Netherlands,' vol. i. ch. ii.

The commissioners acknowledged in the strongest possible terms the great and constant affection, quite without example, that Henry had manifested to the Netherlands during the whole course of their war. They were at a loss to find language adequately to express their gratitude for that friendship, and the assistance subsequently afforded them in the negotiations for truce. They apologized for the tardiness of the States in sending this solemn embassy of thanksgiving, partly on the ground of the delay in receiving the ratifications from Spain, partly by the protracted contraventions by the Archdukes of certain articles in the treaty, but principally by the terrible disasters occasioned throughout their country by the great inundations, and by the commotions in the city of Utrecht, which had now been "so prudently and happily pacified."[1]

They stated that the chief cause of their embassy was to express their respectful gratitude, and to say that never had prince or state treasured more deeply in memory benefits received than did their republic the favours of his Majesty, or could be more disposed to do their utmost to defend his Majesty's person, crown, or royal family against all attack. They expressed their joy that the King had with prudence and heroic courage undertaken the defence of the just rights of Brandenburg and Neuburg to the duchies of Cleve, Jülich, and the other dependent provinces. Thus had he put an end to the presumption of those who thought they could give the law to all the world. They promised the co-operation of the States in this most important enterprise of their ally, notwithstanding their great losses in the war just concluded, and the diminution of revenue occasioned by the inundations by which they had been afflicted ; for they were willing neither to tolerate so unjust an usurpation as that attempted by the Emperor nor to fail to second his Majesty in his

[1] MS. Report.

generous designs. They observed also that they had been instructed to enquire whether his Majesty would not approve the contracting of a strict league of mutual assistance between France, England, the United Provinces, and the princes of Germany.

The King, having listened with close attention, thanked the envoys in words of earnest and vigorous cordiality for their expressions of affection to himself. He begged them to remember that he had always been their good friend, and that he never would forsake them; that he had always hated the Spaniards, and should ever hate them; and that the affairs of Jülich must be arranged not only for the present but for the future.[1] He requested them to deliver their propositions in writing to him, and to be ready to put themselves into communication with the members of his council, in order that they might treat with each other roundly and without reserve. He should always deal with the Netherlanders as with his own people, keeping no back-door open, but pouring out everything as into the lap of his best and most trusty friends.[2]

After this interview conferences followed daily between the ambassadors and Villeroy, Sully, Jeannin, the Chancellor, and Puysieux.

The King's counsellors, after having read the written paraphrase of Barneveld's instructions, the communication of which followed their oral statements, and which, among other specifications, contained a respectful remonstrance against the projected French East India Company, as likely to benefit the Spaniards only, while seriously injuring the States, complained that "the representations were too general, and that the paper seemed to contain nothing but compliments."

The ambassadors, dilating on the various points and

---

[1] "Rapport," &c. (MS.)　　　　　　[2] Ibid.

articles, maintained warmly that there was much more than compliments in their instructions. The ministers wished to know what the States practically were prepared to do in the affair of Cleve, which they so warmly and encouragingly recommended to the King. They asked whether the States' army would march at once to Düsseldorf to protect the princes at the moment when the King moved from Mezières, and they made many enquiries as to what amount of supplies and munitions they could depend upon from the States' magazines.

The envoys said that they had no specific instructions on these points, and could give therefore no conclusive replies. More than ever did Henry regret the absence of the great Advocate at this juncture. If he could have come, with the bridle on his neck, as Henry had so repeatedly urged upon the resident ambassador, affairs might have marched more rapidly. The despotic king could never remember that Barneveld was not the unlimited sovereign of the United States, but only the seal-keeper of one of the seven provinces and the deputy of Holland to the General Assembly. His indirect power, however vast, was only great because it was so carefully veiled.

It was then proposed by Villeroy and Sully, and agreed to by the commissioners, that M. de Béthune, a relative of the great financier, should be sent forthwith to the Hague, to confer privately with Prince Maurice and Barneveld especially, as to military details of the coming campaign.

It was also arranged that the envoys should delay their departure until de Béthune's return. Meantime Henry and the Nuncius had been exchanging plain and passionate language. Ubaldini reproached the King with disregarding all the admonitions of his Holiness, and being about to plunge Christendom into misery and war for the love of the Princess of Condé. He held up to him the enormity of thus converting the King of Spain and the Archdukes into his deadly enemies, and warned him that he would by such desperate measures make even the States-General and the King of Britain his foes, who certainly would never favour such schemes. The King replied that "he trusted to his own forces, not to those of his neighbours, and even if the Hollanders should not declare for him still he would execute his designs. On the 15th of May most certainly he would put himself at the head of his army, even if he was obliged to put off the Queen's coronation till October, and he could not consider the King of Spain nor the Archdukes his friends unless they at once made him some demonstration of friendship. Being asked by the Nuncius what demonstration he wished, he answered flatly that he wished the Princess to be sent back to the Constable her father, in which case the affair of Jülich could be arranged amicably, and, at all events, if the war continued there, he need not send more than 4000 men." [1]

Thus, in spite of his mighty preparations, vehement demands for Barneveld, and profound combinations revealed to that statesman, to Aerssens, and to the Duke of Sully only, this wonderful monarch was ready to drop his sword on the spot, to leave his friends in the lurch, to embrace his enemies, the Archduke first of all, instead of bombarding Brussels [2] the very next week, as he had been threatening to do, provided the beautiful Margaret could be restored to his arms through those of her venerable father.

He suggested to the Nuncius his hope that the Archduke would yet be willing to wink at her escape, which he was now trying to arrange through de Preaux at Brussels, while Ubaldini, knowing the Archduke incapable of anything so dishonourable, felt that the war was inevitable.

[1] Pecquius to Archduke Albert, 28 April 1610, in Henrard.      [2] Ibid.

At the very same time too, Father Cotton, who was only too ready to betray the secrets of the confessional when there was an object to gain, had a long conversation with the Archduke's ambassador, in which the holy man said that the King had confessed to him that he made the war expressly to cause the Princess to be sent back to France, so that as there could be no more doubt on the subject the father-confessor begged Pecquius, in order to prevent so great an evil, to devise "some prompt and sudden means to induce his Highness the Archduke to order the Princess to retire secretly to her own country." The Jesuit had different notions of honour, reputation, and duty from those which influenced the Archduke. He added that "at Easter the King had been so well disposed to seek his salvation that he could easily have forgotten his affection for the Princess, had she not rekindled the fire by her letters, in which she caressed him with amorous epithets, calling him 'my heart,' 'my chevalier,' and similar terms of endearment." Father Cotton also drew up a paper, which he secretly conveyed to Pecquius, " to prove that the Archduke, in terms of conscience and honour, might decide to permit this escape, but he most urgently implored the Ambassador that for the love of God and the public good he would influence his Serene Highness to prevent this from ever coming to the knowledge of the world, but to keep the secret inviolably." [1]

Thus, while Henry was holding high council with his own most trusted advisers, and with the most profound statesmen of Europe, as to the opening campaign within a fortnight of a vast and general war, he was secretly plotting with his father-confessor to effect what he avowed to be the only pur-

[1] Pecquius to Archduke Albert, 28 April 1610, in Henrard. The Chancellor (Sillery) also urged Pecquius to induce his master "to give up the merchandize which he held in deposit, and so to extinguish the torch about to blaze through Christendom. He who could induce the Archduke to consent would do the most salutary work that had been done for a hundred years."—Pecquius to Archduke Albert, 30 April 1610.

pose of that war, by Jesuitical bird-lime to be applied to the chief of his antagonists.  Certainly Barneveld and his colleagues were justified in their distrust.  To move one step in advance of their potent but slippery ally might be a step off a precipice.

On the 1st of May, Sully made a long visit to the commissioners.  He earnestly urged upon them the necessity of making the most of the present opportunity. May 1, 1610.  There were people in plenty, he said, who would gladly see the King take another course, for many influential persons about him were altogether Spanish in their inclinations.

The King had been scandalized to hear from the Prince of Anhalt, without going into details, that on his recent passage through the Netherlands he had noticed some change of feeling, some coolness in their High Mightinesses.  The Duke advised that they should be very heedful, that they should remember how much more closely these matters regarded them than anyone else, that they should not deceive themselves, but be firmly convinced that unless they were willing to go head foremost into the business the French would likewise not commit themselves.  Sully spoke with much earnestness and feeling, for it was obvious that both he and his master had been disappointed at the cautious and limited nature of the instructions given to the ambassadors.[1]

An opinion had indeed prevailed, and, as we have seen, was to a certain extent shared in by Aerssens, and even by Sully himself, that the King's military preparations were after all but a feint, and that if the Prince of Condé, and with him the Princess, could be restored to France, the whole war cloud would evaporate in smoke.[2]

It was even asserted that Henry had made a secret treaty

<hr>

[1] "Rapport."  (MS. before cited.)          Letters of Aerssens, *passim.*

with the enemy, according to which, while apparently ready to burst upon the House of Austria with overwhelming force, he was in reality about to shake hands cordially with that power, on condition of being allowed to incorporate into his own kingdom the very duchies in dispute, and of receiving the Prince of Condé and his wife from Spain. He was thus suspected of being about to betray his friends and allies in the most ignoble manner and for the vilest of motives. The circulation of these infamous reports no doubt paralysed for a time the energy of the enemy who had made no requisite preparations against the threatened invasion, but it sickened his friends with vague apprehensions, while it cut the King himself to the heart and infuriated him to madness.[1]

He asked the Nuncius one day what people thought in Rome and Italy of the war about to be undertaken. Ubaldini replied that those best informed considered the Princess of Condé as the principal subject of hostilities ; they thought that he meant to have her back. "I do mean to have her back," cried Henry, with a mighty oath, and foaming with rage, "and I shall have her back. No one shall prevent it, not even the Lieutenant of God on earth."[2]

But the imputation of this terrible treason weighed upon his mind and embittered every hour.

The commissioners assured Sully that they had no knowledge of any coolness or change such as Anhalt had reported on the part of their principals, and the Duke took his leave.

It will be remembered that Villeroy had, it was thought, been making mischief between Anhalt and the States by reporting and misreporting private conversations between that Prince and the Dutch ambassador.

---

[1] 'Mémoires de Sully.' vii. liv. xxvii. 399.
[2] Ibid. Notes for 'Mémoires pour servir à l'Hist. de France.'
[3] MS. Report, &c.

As soon as Sully had gone, van der Myle waited upon Villeroy to ask, in name of himself and colleagues, for audience of leave-taking, the object of their mission having been accomplished. The Secretary of State, too, like Sully, urged the importance of making the most of the occasion. The affair of Cleve, he said, did not very much concern the King, but his Majesty had taken it to heart chiefly on account of the States and for their security. They were bound, therefore, to exert themselves to the utmost, but more would not be required of them than it would be possible to fulfil.

Van der Myle replied that nothing would be left undone by their High Mightinesses to support the King faithfully and according to their promise.

On the 5th, Villeroy came to the ambassadors, bringing with him a letter from the King for the States-General, and likewise a written reply to the declarations made orally and in writing by the ambassadors to his Majesty.

May 5, 1610.

The letter of Henry to "his very dear and good friends, allies, and confederates," was chiefly a complimentary acknowledgment of the expressions of gratitude made to him on part of the States-General, and warm approbation of their sage resolve to support the cause of Brandenburg and Neuburg. He referred them for particulars to the confidential conferences held between the commissioners and himself. They would state how important he thought it that this matter should be settled now so thoroughly as to require no second effort at any future time when circumstances might not be so propitious ; and that he intended to risk his person, at the head of his army, to accomplish this result.

To the ambassadors he expressed his high satisfaction at their assurances of affection, devotion, and gratitude on the

<hr>

¹ MS. Report, &c.

part of the States. He approved and commended their resolution to assist the Elector and the Palatine in the affair of the duchies. He considered this a proof of their prudence and good judgment, as showing their conviction that they were more interested and bound to render this assistance than any other potentates or states, as much from the convenience and security to be derived from the neighbourhood of princes who were their friends as from dangers to be apprehended from other princes who were seeking to appropriate those provinces. The King therefore begged the States to move forward as soon as possible the forces which they offered for this enterprise according to his Majesty's suggestion sent through de Béthune. The King on his part would do the same with extreme care and diligence, from the anxiety he felt to prevent My Lords the States from receiving detriment in places so vital to their preservation.

He begged the States likewise to consider that it was meet not only to make a first effort to put the princes into entire possession of the duchies, but to provide also for the durable success of the enterprise; to guard against any invasions that might be made in the future to eject those princes. Otherwise all their present efforts would be useless; and his Majesty therefore consented on this occasion to enter into the new league proposed by the States with all the princes and states mentioned in the memoir of the ambassadors for mutual assistance against all unjust occupations, attempts, and baneful intrigues.

Having no special information as to the infractions by the Archdukes of the recent treaty of truce, the King declined to discuss that subject for the moment, although holding himself bound to all required of him as one of the guarantees of that treaty.

In regard to the remonstrance made by the ambassadors concerning the trade of the East Indies, his Majesty disclaimed any intention of doing injury to the States in permitting his subjects to establish a company in his kingdom for that commerce. He had deferred hitherto taking action in the matter only out of respect to the States, but he could no longer refuse the just claims of his subjects if they should persist in them as urgently as they had thus far been doing. The right and liberty which they demanded was common to all, said the King, and he was certainly bound to have as great care for the interests of his subjects as for those of his friends and allies.[1]

Here, certainly, was an immense difference in tone and in terms towards the Republic adopted respectively by their great and good friends and allies the Kings of France and Great Britain. It was natural enough that Henry, having secretly expressed his most earnest hope that the States would move at his side in his broad and general assault upon the House of Austria, should impress upon them his conviction, which was a just one, that no power in the world was more interested in keeping a Spanish and Catholic prince out of the duchies than they were themselves. But while thus taking a bond of them as it were for the entire fulfilment of the primary enterprise, he accepted with cordiality, and almost with gratitude, their proposition of a close alliance of the Republic with himself and with the Protestant powers which James had so superciliously rejected.

It would have been difficult to inflict a more petty and more studied insult upon the Republic than did the King of Great Britain at that supreme moment by his preposterous claim of sovereign rights over the Netherlands. He would make no treaty with them, he said, but should he find it worth while to treat with his royal brother of France, he should probably not shut the door in their faces.

<hr>

[1] Letter of King, 5 May 1610, in the MS. Report.

Certainly Henry's reply to the remonstrances of the ambassadors in regard to the India trade was as moderate as that of James had been haughty and peremptory in regard to the herring fishery. It is however sufficiently amusing to see those excellent Hollanders nobly claiming that " the sea was as free as air " when the right to take Scotch pilchards was in question, while at the very same moment they were earnest for excluding their best allies and all the world besides from their East India monopoly. But Isaac Le Maire and Jacques Le Roy had not lain so long disguised in Zamet's house in Paris for nothing, nor had Aerssens so completely " broke the 'neck of the French East India Company" as he supposed. A certain Dutch freebooter, however, Simon Danzer by name, a native of Dordrecht, who had been alternately in the service of Spain, France, and the States, but a general marauder upon all powers, was exercising at that moment perhaps more influence on the East India trade than any potentate or commonwealth.

He kept the seas just then with four swift-sailing and well-armed vessels, that potent skimmer of the ocean, and levied tribute upon Protestant and Catholic, Turk or Christian, with great impartiality. The King of Spain had sent him letters of amnesty and safe-conduct, with large pecuniary offers, if he would enter his service. The King of France had outbid his royal brother and enemy, and implored him to sweep the seas under the white flag.

The States' ambassador begged his masters to reflect whether this " puissant and experienced corsair" should be permitted to serve Spaniard or Frenchman, and whether they could devise no expedient for turning him into another track. " He is now with his fine ships at Marseilles," said Aerssens. " He is sought for in all quarters by the Spaniard and by the directors of the new French East India Company, private persons who equip vessels of war. If he is not satisfied with

this king's offers, he is likely to close with the King of
Spain, who offers him 1000 crowns a month.   Avarice tickles
him, but he is neither Spaniard nor Papist, and I fear will
be induced to serve with his ships the East India Company, and so will return to his piracy, the evil of which will
always fall on our heads.   If My Lords the States will send
me letters of abolition for him, in imitation of the French
king, on condition of his returning to his home in Zealand
and quitting the sea altogether, something might be done.
Otherwise he will be off to Marseilles again, and do more
harm to us than ever.   Isaac Le Maire is doing as much evil
as he can, and one holds daily council with him here." [1]

Thus the slippery Simon skimmed the seas from Marseilles
to the Moluccas, from Java to Mexico, never to be held
firmly by Philip, or Henry, or Barneveld.   A dissolute
but very daring ship's captain, born in Zealand, and formerly in the service of the States, out of which he had
been expelled for many evil deeds, Simon Danzer had now
become a professional pirate, having his head-quarters chiefly
at Algiers.   His English colleague Warde stationed himself
mainly at Tunis, and both acted together in connivance with
the pachas of the Turkish government.   They with their
considerable fleet, one vessel of which mounted sixty guns,
were the terror of the Mediterranean, extorted tribute from
the commerce of all nations indifferently, and sold licenses
to the greatest governments of Europe.   After growing
rich with his accumulated booty, Simon was inclined to
become respectable, a recourse which was always open to
him—France, England, Spain, the United Provinces, vieing
with each other to secure him by high rank and pay as an
honoured member of their national marine.   He appears
however to have failed in his plan of retiring upon his

---

[1] "Rapport." (MS.)   Acrssens to Barneveld, 6 Sept. 1609.   Same to same,
1 Nov. 1609.   Same to same, 22 Dec. 1609.   (MSS.)

laurels, having been stabbed in Paris by a man whom he had formerly robbed and ruined.[1]

Villeroy, having delivered the letters with his own hands to the ambassadors, was asked by them when and where it would be convenient for the King to arrange the convention of close alliance.  The Secretary of State—in his secret heart anything but kindly disposed for this loving union with a republic he detested and with heretics whom he would have burned—answered briefly that his Majesty was ready at any time, and that it might take place then if they were provided with the necessary powers.  He said in parting that the States should "have an eye to everything, for occasions like the present were irrecoverable."  He then departed, saying that the King would receive them in final audience on the following day.[2]

Next morning accordingly Marshal de Boisdaulphin and de Bonœil came with royal coaches to the Hotel Gondy and escorted the ambassadors to the Louvre.  On the way they met de Béthune, who had returned [May 6, 1610.] from the Hague bringing despatches for the King and for themselves.  While in the antechamber, they had opportunity to read their letters from the States-General, his Majesty sending word that he was expecting them with impatience, but preferred that they should read the despatches before the audience.

They found the King somewhat out of humour.  He expressed himself as tolerably well satisfied with the general tenour of the despatches brought by de Béthune, but complained loudly of the request now made by the States, that the maintenance and other expenses of 4000 French in the States' service should be paid in the coming campaign out of the royal exchequer.  He declared that this pro-

---

[1] Meteren, 'Ned. Hist.' book xxxi. p. 673.  Ibid. b. xxxii. 584. 630. Wagenaar, x. 51.        [2] "Rapport" of the Ambassadors, before cited.

position was "a small manifestation of ingratitude," that my Lords the States were "little misers," and that such proceedings were "little avaricious tricks" such as he had not expected of them.[1]

So far as England was concerned, he said there was a great difference. The English took away what he was giving. He did cheerfully a great deal for his friends, he said, and was always ready doubly to repay what they did for him. If, however, the States persisted in this course, he should call his troops home again.

The King, as he went on, became more and more excited, and showed decided dissatisfaction in his language and manner. It was not to be wondered at, for we have seen how persistently he had been urging that the Advocate should come in person with "the bridle on his neck," and now he had sent his son-in-law and two colleagues tightly tied up by stringent instructions. And over and above all this, while he was contemplating a general war with intention to draw upon the States for unlimited supplies, behold, they were haggling for the support of a couple of regiments which were virtually their own troops.

There were reasons, however, for this cautiousness besides those unfounded, although not entirely chimerical, suspicions as to the King's good faith, to which we have alluded. It should not be forgotten that, although Henry had conversed secretly with the States' ambassador at full length on his far-reaching plans, with instructions that he should confidentially inform the Advocate and demand his co-operation, not a word of it had been officially propounded to the States-General, nor to the special embassy with whom he was now negotiating. No treaty of alliance offensive or defensive existed between the Kingdom and the Republic

---

[1] "Rapport" of the Ambassadors, before cited: "petit temoignage d'ingratitude"—"petits avaricieux"—"petits avaricos."

or between the Republic and any power whatever.  It would have been culpable carelessness therefore at this moment for the prime minister of the States to have committed his government in writing to a full participation in a general assault upon the House of Austria ; the first step in which would have been a breach of the treaty just concluded and instant hostilities with the Archdukes Albert and Isabella.

That these things were in the immediate future was as plain as that night would follow day, but the hour had not yet struck for the States to throw down the gauntlet.

Hardly two months before, the King, in his treaty with the princes at Hall, had excluded both the King of Great Britain and the States-General from participation in those arrangements, and it was grave matter for consideration, therefore, for the States whether they should allow such succour as they might choose to grant the princes to be included in the French contingent.  The opportunity for treating as a sovereign power with the princes and making friends with them was tempting, but it did not seem reasonable to the States that France should make use of them in this war without a treaty, and should derive great advantage from the alliance, but leave the expense to them.

Henry, on the other hand, forgetting, when it was convenient to him, all about the Princess of Condé, his hatred of Spain, and his resolution to crush the House of Austria, chose to consider the war as made simply for the love of the States-General and to secure them for ever from danger.

The ambassadors replied to the King's invectives with great respect, and endeavoured to appease his anger.  They had sent a special despatch to their government, they said, in regard to all those matters, setting forth all the difficulties that had been raised, but had not wished to trouble his Majesty with premature discussions of them.  They did not

<hr>

<sup>1</sup> Aerssens to Barneveld, 22 Feb. 1610.  (MS.)

doubt, however, that their High Mightinesses would so conduct this great affair as to leave the King no ground of complaint.

Henry then began to talk of the intelligence brought by de Béthune from the Hague, especially in regard to the sending of States' troops to Düsseldorf and the supply of food for the French army.   He did not believe, he said, that the Archdukes would refuse him the passage with his forces through their territory, inasmuch as the States' army would be on the way to meet him.   In case of any resistance, however, he declared his resolution to strike his blow and to cause people to talk of him.   He had sent his quartermaster-general to examine the passes, who had reported that it would be impossible to prevent his Majesty's advance.   He was also distinctly informed that Marquis Spinola, keeping his places garrisoned, could not bring more than 8000 men into the field.   The Duke of Bouillon, however, was sending advices that his communications were liable to be cut off, and that for this purpose Spinola could set on foot about 16,000 infantry and 4000 horse.

If the passage should be allowed by the Archdukes, the King stated his intention of establishing magazines for his troops along the whole line of march through the Spanish Netherlands and neighbouring districts, and to establish and fortify himself everywhere in order to protect his supplies and cover his possible retreat.   He was still in doubt, he said, whether to demand the passage at once or to wait until he had began to move his army.   He was rather inclined to make the request instantly in order to gain time, being persuaded that he should receive no answer either of consent or refusal.

Leaving all these details, the King then frankly observed that the affair of Cleve had a much wider outlook than

---

[1] MS. Report, before cited.

people thought. Therefore the States must consider well what was to be done to secure the whole work as soon as the Cleve business had been successfully accomplished. Upon this subject it was indispensable that he should consult especially with his Excellency (Prince Maurice) and some members of the General Assembly, whom he wished that My Lords the States-General should depute to the army.

"For how much good will it do," said the King, "if we drive off Archduke Leopold without establishing the princes in security for the future? Nothing is easier than to put the princes in possession. Every one will yield or run away before our forces, but two months after we have withdrawn the enemy will return and drive the princes out again. I cannot always be ready to spring out of my kingdom, nor to assemble such great armies. I am getting old, and my army moreover costs me 400,000 crowns a month, which is enough to exhaust all the treasures of France, Spain, Venice, and the States-General together."[1]

He added that, if the present occasion were neglected, the States would afterwards bitterly lament and never recover it. The Pope was very much excited, and was sending out his ambassadors everywhere. Only the previous Saturday the new nuncius destined for France had left Rome. If My Lords the States would send deputies to the camp with full powers, he stood there firm and unchangeable, but if they remained cool in the business, he warned them that they would enrage him.

The States must seize the occasion, he repeated. It was bald behind, and must be grasped by the forelock. It was not enough to have begun well. One must end well. "*Finis coronat opus.*" It was very easy to speak of a league, but a league was not to be made in order to sit with arms tied, but to do good work. The States ought not to suffer that the

<hr>

[1] MS. "Rapport," &c.

Germans should prove themselves more energetic, more courageous, than themselves.

And again the King vehemently urged the necessity of his Excellency and some deputies of the States coming to him " with absolute power" to treat.  He could not doubt in that event of something solid being accomplished.[1]

" There are three things," he continued, " which cause me to speak freely.  I am talking with my friends whom I hold dear—yes, dearer, perhaps, than they hold themselves.  I am a great king, and say what I choose to say.  I am old, and know by experience the ways of this world's affairs.  I tell you, then, that it is most important that you should come to me resolved and firm on all points.[2]

He then requested the ambassadors to make full report of all that he had said to their masters, to make the journey as rapidly as possible, in order to encourage the States to the great enterprise and to meet his wishes.  He required from them, he said, not only activity of the body, but labour of the intellect.

He was silent for a few moments, and then spoke again. " I shall not always be here," he said, " nor will you always have Prince Maurice, and a few others whose knowledge of your commonwealth is perfect.  My Lords the States must be up and doing while they still possess them.  Next Tuesday I shall cause the Queen to be crowned at Saint-Denis ; the following Thursday she will make her entry into Paris. Next day, Friday, I shall take my departure.  At the end of this month I shall cross the Meuse at Mezières or in that neighbourhood."[3]

He added that he should write immediately to Holland, to urge upon his Excellency and the States to be ready to make the junction of their army with his forces without delay.  He charged the ambassadors to assure their High

<hr>

[1] MS. " Rapport," &c.                    [2] Ibid.                    [3] Ibid.

Mightinesses that he was and should remain their truest friend, their dearest neighbour.  He then said a few gracious and cordial words to each of them, warmly embraced each, and bade them all farewell.[1]

The next day was passed by the ambassadors in paying and receiving farewell visits, and on Saturday, the 8th, they departed from Paris, being escorted out of the gate by the Marshal de Boisdaulphin, with a cavalcade of noblemen.  They slept that night at Saint-Denis, and then returned to Holland by the way of Calais and Rotterdam, reaching the Hague on the 16th of May.  May 8, 1610.<br>May 16.

I make no apology for the minute details thus given of the proceedings of this embassy, and especially of the conversations of Henry.

The very words of those conversations were taken down on the spot by the commissioners who heard them, and were carefully embodied in their report made to the States-General on their return, from which I have transcribed them.

It was a memorable occasion.  The great king—for great he was, despite his numerous vices and follies—stood there upon the threshold of a vast undertaking, at which the world, still half incredulous, stood gazing, half sick with anxiety.  He relied on his own genius and valour chiefly, and after these on the brain of Barneveld and the sword of Maurice.  Nor was his confidence misplaced.

But let the reader observe the date of the day when those striking utterances were made, and which have never before been made public.  It was Thursday, the 6th May.  "I shall not always be here," said the King. . . . "I cannot be ready at any moment to spring out of my kingdom." . . . "Friday of next week I take my departure."

How much of heroic pathos in Henry's attitude at this

<hr>

[1] MS. "Rapport," &c.

supreme moment!   How mournfully ring those closing words of his address to the ambassadors!

The die was cast.   A letter drawn up by the Duc de Sully was sent to Archduke Albert by the King.

"My brother," he said; "Not being able to refuse my best allies and confederates the help which they have asked of me against those who wish to trouble them in the succession to the duchies and counties of Cleve, Jülich, Mark, Berg, Ravensberg, and Ravenstein, I am advancing towards them with my army.   As my road leads me through your country, I desire to notify you thereof, and to know whether or not I am to enter as a friend or enemy."

Such was the draft as delivered to the Secretary of State; "and as such it was sent," said Sully, "unless Villeroy changed it, as he had a great desire to do."[1]

Henry was mistaken in supposing that the Archduke would leave the letter without an answer.   A reply was sent in due time, and the permission demanded was not refused. For although France was now full of military movement, and the regiments everywhere were hurrying hourly to the places of rendezvous, though the great storm at last was ready to burst, the Archdukes made no preparations for resistance, and lapped themselves in fatal security that nothing was intended but an empty demonstration.[2]

Six thousand Swiss newly levied, with 20,000 French infantry and 6000 horse, were waiting for Henry to place himself at their head at Mezières.   Twelve thousand foot and 2000 cavalry, including the French and English contingents—a splendid army, led by Prince Maurice—were ready to march from Holland to Düsseldorf.   The army of the princes under Prince Christian of Anhalt numbered 10,000 men.   The last scruples of the usually unscrupulous Charles Emmanuel had been overcome, and the Duke was

---

[1] 'Mémoires de Sully,' vii. 375.                    [2] Ibid. 300, notes.

quite ready to act, 25,000 strong, with Marshal de Lesdiguières, in the Milanese; while Marshal de la Force was already at the head of his forces in the Pyrenees, amounting to 12,000 foot and 2000 horse.

Sully had already despatched his splendid trains of artillery to the frontier. "Never was seen in France, and perhaps never will be seen there again, artillery more complete and better furnished,"[1] said the Duke, thinking probably that artillery had reached the climax of perfect destructiveness in the first decade of the seventeenth century.

His son, the Marquis de Rosny, had received the post of grand master of artillery, and placed himself at its head. His father was to follow as its chief, carrying with him as superintendent of finance a cash-box of eight millions.

The King had appointed his wife, Mary de' Medici, regent, with an eminent council.[2]

The new nuncius had been requested to present himself with his letters of credence in the camp. Henry was unwilling that he should enter Paris, being convinced that he came to do his best, by declamation, persuasion, and intrigue, to paralyse the enterprise. Sully's promises to Ubaldini, the former nuncius, that his Holiness should be made king, however flattering to Paul V., had not prevented his representatives from vigorously denouncing Henry's monstrous scheme to foment heresy and encourage rebellion.[3]

The King's chagrin at the cautious limitations imposed upon the States' special embassy was, so he hoped, to be removed by full conferences in the camp. Certainly he had shown in the most striking manner the respect he felt for the States, and the confidence he reposed in them.

---

[1] 'Mémoires de Sully,' vii. 374.

[2] It consisted of the Cardinals de Joyeuse and du Perron, the Dukes of Mayenne, Montmorency, and Montbaron, the Marshals de Brissac and de Ferraques, with Châteauneuf, Harlay, Nicolay, Châteauvieux, de Liancourt, de Pontcarré, de Gèvres, de Villemontée, and de Maupéon.

[3] Ibid. 357.

" In the reception of your embassy," wrote Aerssens to the Advocate, " certainly the King has so loosened the strap of his affection that he has reserved nothing by which he could put the greatest king in the world above your level." [1]

He warned the States, however, that Henry had not found as much in their propositions as the common interest had caused him to promise himself. " Nevertheless he informs me in confidence," said Aerssens, " that he will engage himself in nothing without you ; nay, more, he has expressly told me that he could hardly accomplish his task without your assistance, and it was for our sakes alone that he has put himself into this position and incurred this great expense." [2]

Some days later he informed Barneveld that he would leave to van der Myle and his colleagues the task of describing the great dissatisfaction of the King at the letters brought by de Béthune. He told him in confidence that the States must equip the French regiments and put them in marching order if they wished to preserve Henry's friendship. He added that since the departure of the special embassy the King had been vehemently and seriously urging that Prince Maurice, Count Lewis William, Barneveld, and three or four of the most qualified deputies of the States-General, entirely authorized to treat for the common safety, should meet with him in the territory of Jülich on a fixed day. [3]

The crisis was reached. The King stood fully armed, thoroughly prepared, with trustworthy allies at his side, disposing of overwhelming forces ready to sweep down with irresistible strength upon the House of Austria, which, as he said and the States said, aspired to give the law to the whole world. Nothing was left to do save, as the Ambassador said, to " uncouple the dogs of war and let them run."

<hr>

[1] Aerssens to Barneveld. 26 April 1610.  (MS.)      [2] Ibid.
[3] Same to same, 11 May 1610.  (MS.)

What preparations had Spain and the Empire, the Pope and the League, set on foot to beat back even for a moment the overwhelming onset ?  None whatever.  Spinola in the Netherlands, Fuentes in Milan, Bucquoy and Lobkowitz and Lichtenstein in Prague, had hardly the forces of a moderate peace establishment at their disposal, and all the powers save France and the States were on the verge of bankruptcy.

Even James of Great Britain—shuddering at the vast thundercloud which had stretched itself over Christendom growing blacker and blacker, precisely at this moment, in which he had proved to his own satisfaction that the peace just made would perpetually endure—even James did not dare to traverse the designs of the king whom he feared, and the republic which he hated, in favour of his dearly loved Spain.  Sweden, Denmark, the Hanse Towns, were in harmony with France, Holland, Savoy, and the whole Protestant force of Germany—a majority both in population and resources of the whole empire.  What army, what combination, what device, what talisman, could save the House of Austria, the cause of Papacy, from the impending ruin ?

A sudden, rapid, conclusive victory for the allies seemed as predestined a result as anything could be in the future of human affairs.

On the 14th or 15th day of May, as he had just been informing the States' ambassadors, Henry meant to place himself at the head of his army. That was the moment fixed by himself for " taking his departure."

May 14, 1610.

And now the ides of May had come—but not gone.

In the midst of all the military preparations with which Paris had been resounding, the arrangements for the Queen's coronation had been simultaneously going forward.  Partly to give check in advance to the intrigues which would probably at a later date be made by Condé, supported by the power of Spain, to invalidate the legitimacy of the Dauphin, but more especially perhaps to further and to conceal what the faithful Sully called the "damnable artifices" of the Queen's intimate councillors—sinister designs too dark to be even whispered[1] at that epoch, and of which history, during the lapse of more than two centuries and a half, has scarcely dared to speak above its breath—it was deemed all important that the coronation should take place.

A certain astrologer, Thomassin by name, was said to have bidden the King to beware the middle of the next month of May. Henry had tweaked the soothsayer by the beard and made him dance twice or thrice about the room.[2] To the Duc de Vendôme expressing great anxiety in regard to Thomassin, Henry replied, "The astrologer is an old fool, and you are a young fool." A certain prophetess called Pasithea had informed the Queen that the King could not survive his fifty-seventh year. She was much in the confidence of Mary de' Medici, who had insisted this year on her returning to Paris.[3] Henry, who was ever chafing and struggling to escape the invisible and dangerous net which he felt closing about him, and who connected the sorceress with all whom he most loathed among the intimate associates of the Queen, swore a mighty oath that she should not show her face again at court. "My heart presages that some signal disaster will befall me on this coronation. Concini and his wife are urging the Queen obstinately to send for this fanatic. If she should come, there is no doubt that my wife and I shall squabble well about her. If I discover more about these private plots of hers with Spain, I shall be in a mighty passion." And the King then assured the faithful minister of his conviction that all the jealousy affected by the Queen in regard to the Princess of Condé was but a veil to cover

---

[1] 'Mémoires de Sully,' vii. 175.
[2] L'Estoile, iii. 433.  Sully, 'Mém.' vii. 381.  [3] Ibid. 175.

dark designs.  It was necessary in the opinion of those who governed her, the vile Concini and his wife, that there should be some apparent and flagrant cause of quarrel.  The public were to receive payment in these pretexts for want of better coin.  Henry complained that even Sully and all the world besides attributed to jealousy that which was really the effect of a most refined malice.[1]

And the minister sometimes pauses in the midst of these revelations made in his old age, and with self-imposed and shuddering silence intimates that there are things he could tell which are too odious and dreadful to be breathed.

Henry had an invincible repugnance to that coronation on which the Queen had set her heart.  Nothing could be more pathetic than the isolated position in which he found himself, standing thus as he did on the threshold of a mighty undertaking in which he was the central figure, an object for the world to gaze upon with palpitating interest.  At his hearth in the Louvre were no household gods.  Danger lurked behind every tapestry in that magnificent old palace.  A nameless dread dogged his footsteps through those resounding corridors.

And by an exquisite refinement in torture the possible father of several of his children not only dictated to the Queen perpetual outbreaks of frantic jealousy against her husband, but moved her to refuse with suspicion any food and drink offered her by his hands.  The Concini's would even with unparalleled and ingenious effrontery induce her to make use of the kitchen arrangements in their apartments for the preparation of her daily meals.[2]

Driven from house and home, Henry almost lived at the Arsenal.  There he would walk for hours in the long alleys of the garden, discussing with the great financier and soldier his vast, dreamy, impracticable plans.  Strange combina-

---

[1] Sully. vii. 175.                    [2] Ibid. 177, 178.

tion of the hero, the warrior, the voluptuary, the sage, and the schoolboy—it would be difficult to find in the whole range of history a more human, a more attractive, a more provoking, a less venerable character.

Haunted by omens, dire presentiments, dark suspicions with and without cause, he was especially averse from the coronation to which in a moment of weakness he had given his consent.

Sitting in Sully's cabinet, in a low chair which the Duke had expressly provided for his use, tapping and drumming on his spectacle case, or starting up and smiting himself on the thigh, he would pour out his soul hours long to his one confidential minister. "Ah, my friend, how this sacrament displeases me," he said;[1] "I know not why it is, but my heart tells me that some misfortune is to befall me. By God ! I shall die in this city, I shall never go out of it ; I see very well that they are finding their last resource in my death. Ah, accursed coronation ! thou wilt be the cause of my death."

So many times did he give utterance to these sinister forebodings that Sully implored him at last for leave to countermand the whole ceremony notwithstanding the great preparations which had been made for the splendid festival. "Yes, yes," replied the King, "break up this coronation at once. Let me hear no more of it. Then I shall have my mind cured of all these impressions. I shall leave the town and fear nothing."

He then informed his friend that he had received intimations that he should lose his life at the first magnificent festival he should give, and that he should die in a carriage. Sully admitted that he had often, when in a carriage with him, been amazed at his starting and crying out at the slightest shock, having so often seen him intrepid among guns and cannon, pikes and naked swords.[2]

[1] Sully, vii. 383.      [2] Ibid.

The Duke went to the Queen three days in succession, and with passionate solicitations and arguments and almost upon his knees implored her to yield to the King's earnest desire, and renounce for the time at least the coronation. In vain. Mary de' Medici was obdurate as marble to his prayers.[1]

The coronation was fixed for Thursday, the 13th May, two days later than the time originally appointed when the King conversed with the States' ambassadors. On the following Sunday was to be the splendid and solemn entrance of the crowned Queen. On the Monday, Henry, postponing likewise for two days his original plan of departure, would leave for the army.

Meantime there were petty annoyances connected with the details of the coronation. Henry had set his heart on having his legitimatized children, the offspring of the fair Gabrielle, take their part in the ceremony on an equal footing with the princes of the blood. They were not entitled to wear the lilies of France upon their garments, and the King was solicitous that " the Count "—as Soissons, brother of Prince Conti and uncle of Condé, was always called—should dispense with those ensigns for his wife upon this solemn occasion, and that the other princesses of the blood should do the same. Thus there would be no appearance of inferiority on the part of the Duchess of Vendôme.[2]

The Count protested that he would have his eyes torn out of his head rather than submit to an arrangement which would do him so much shame. He went to the Queen and urged upon her that to do this would likewise be an injury to her children, the Dukes of Orleans and of Anjou. He refused flatly to appear or allow his wife to appear except in the costume befitting their station. The King on his part was determined not to abandon his purpose. He tried to

---

[1] Sully, vii. 383.     [2] Aerssens to Barneveld, 11 May 1610. (MS.)

gain over the Count by the most splendid proposals, offering him the command of the advance-guard of the army, or the lieutenancy-general of France in the absence of the King, 30,000 crowns for his equipment and an increase of his pension if he would cause his wife to give up the fleurs-de-lys on this occasion. The alternative was to be that, if she insisted upon wearing them, his Majesty would never look upon him again with favourable eyes.

The Count never hesitated, but left Paris, refusing to appear at the ceremony. The King was in a towering passion, for to lose the presence of this great prince of the blood at a solemnity expressly intended as a demonstration against the designs hatching by the first of all the princes of the blood under patronage of Spain was a severe blow to his pride and a check to his policy.[1]

Yet it was inconceivable that he could at such a moment commit so superfluous and unmeaning a blunder. He had forced Condé into exile, intrigue with the enemy, and rebellion, by open and audacious efforts to destroy his domestic peace, and now he was willing to alienate one of his most powerful subjects in order to place his bastards on a level with royalty. While it is sufficiently amusing to contemplate this proposed barter of a chief command in a great army or the lieutenancy-general of a mighty kingdom at the outbreak of a general European war against a bit of embroidery on the court dress of a lady, yet it is impossible not to recognize something ideal and chivalrous from his own point of view in the refusal of Soissons to renounce those emblems of pure and high descent, those haughty lilies of St. Louis, against any bribes of place and pelf however dazzling.

The coronation took place on Thursday, 13th May, with the pomp and glitter becoming great court festivals ; the more

<hr>

[1] Aerssens to Barneveld, 11 May 1610. (MS.)

pompous and glittering the more the monarch's heart was wrapped in gloom.  The representatives of the great powers were conspicuous in the procession ; Aerssens, the Dutch ambassador, holding a foremost place.  The ambassadors of Spain and Venice as usual squabbled about precedence and many other things, and actually came to fisticuffs, the fight lasting a long time and ending somewhat to the advantage of the Venetian.[1]  But the sacrament was over, and Mary de' Medici was crowned Queen of France and Regent of the Kingdom during the absence of the sovereign with his army.

Meantime there had been mysterious warnings darker and more distinct than the babble of the soothsayer Thomassin or the ravings of the lunatic Pasithea.  Count Schomberg, dining at the Arsenal with Sully, had been called out to converse with Mademoiselle de Gournay, who implored that a certain Madame d'Escomans might be admitted to audience of the King.[2]  That person, once in direct relations with the Marchioness of Verneuil, the one of Henry's mistresses who most hated him, affirmed that a man from the Duke of Épernon's country was in Paris, agent of a conspiracy seeking the King's life.

The woman not enjoying a very reputable character found it impossible to obtain a hearing, although almost frantic with her desire to save her sovereign's life.  The Queen observed that it was a wicked woman, who was accusing all the world, and perhaps would accuse her too.[3]

The fatal Friday came.  Henry drove out in his carriage to see the preparations making for the triumphal entrance of the Queen into Paris on the following Sunday.  What need to repeat the tragic, familiar tale ?  The

May 14, 1610.

---

[1] Aerssens to Barneveld. 15 May 1610. (MS.) " . . . le Jeudi so battirent longuement à coups de poings les ambassadeurs d'Espagne et Venice pour l'excellence et illustrissime.  Le Vénitien eut l'avantage. Ce seroit une belle comédie sans cette sanglante tragédie que ne cesserai oncques de pleurer," &c.

[2] Sully, vii. 387, sqq.

[3] 'Mém. pour servir à l'hist. de France,' 257.  Sully, vii. 3–9, note.

coach was stopped by apparent accident in the narrow street de la Féronnière, and Francis Ravaillac, standing on the wheel, drove his knife through the monarch's heart. The Duke of Épernon, sitting at his side, threw his cloak over the body and ordered the carriage back to the Louvre.

"They have killed him, *è ammazato*," cried Concini (so says tradition), thrusting his head into the Queen's bed-chamber.[1]

That blow had accomplished more than a great army could have done, and Spain now reigned in Paris. The House of Austria, without making any military preparations, had conquered, and the great war of religion and politics was postponed for half a dozen years.

This history has no immediate concern with solving the mysteries of that stupendous crime. The woman who had sought to save the King's life now denounced Épernon as the chief murderer, and was arrested, examined, accused of lunacy, proved to be perfectly sane, and, persisting in her statements with perfect coherency, was imprisoned for life for her pains; the Duke furiously demanding her instant execution.

The documents connected with the process were carefully suppressed. The assassin, tortured and torn by four horses, was supposed to have revealed nothing and to have denied the existence of accomplices.

The great accused were too omnipotent to be dealt with by humble accusers or by convinced but powerless tribunals. The trial was all mystery, hugger-mugger, horror. Yet the

---

[1] Michelet, 197. It is not probable that the documents concerning the trial, having been so carefully suppressed from the beginning, especially the confession dictated to Voisin— who wrote it kneeling on the ground, and was perhaps so appalled at its purport that he was afraid to write it legibly—will ever see the light. I add in the Appendix some contemporary letters of persons, as likely as any one to know what could be known, which show how dreadful were the suspicions which men entertained, and which they hardly ventured to whisper to each other.

murderer is known to have dictated to the Greffier Voisin, just before expiring on the Grève, a declaration which that functionary took down in a handwriting perhaps purposely illegible.

Two centuries and a half have passed away, yet the illegible original record is said to exist, to have been plainly read, and to contain the names of the Queen and the Duke of Épernon.[1]

Twenty-six years before, the pistol of Balthasar Gérard had destroyed the foremost man in Europe and the chief of a commonwealth just struggling into existence. Yet Spain and Rome, the instigators and perpetrators of the crime, had not reaped the victory which they had the right to expect. The young republic, guided by Barneveld and loyal to the son of the murdered stadholder, was equal to the burthen suddenly descending upon its shoulders. Instead of despair there had been constancy. Instead of distracted counsels there had been heroic union of heart and hand. Rather than bend to Rome and grovel to Philip, it had taken its sovereignty in its hands, offered it successively, without a thought of self-aggrandizement on the part of its children, to the crowns of France and Great Britain, and, having been repulsed by both, had learned after fiery trials and incredible exertions to assert its own high and foremost place among the independent powers of the world.

And now the knife of another priest-led fanatic, the wretched but unflinching instrument of a great conspiracy, had at a blow decapitated France. No political revolution could be much more thorough than that which had been accomplished in a moment of time by Francis Ravaillac.

On the 14th of May, France, while in spiritual matters

---

[1] See 'Mémoires de Sully,' t. vii. (ed. cit. 1747), 357, 386–446, and the notes. See also le Père Daniel,' Hist. de la France' (ed. cit.), t. xii. 644–650, *qq.*; t. xiii. 51–53. See especially the remarkable volume of the great historian Michelet, 'Henry IV et Richelieu,' chs. xii. and xiii. *passim,* pp. 209 and 225.

obedient to the Pope, stood at the head of the forces of Protestantism throughout Europe, banded together to effect the downfall of the proud house of Austria, whose fortunes and fate were synonymous with Catholicism. The Baltic powers, the majority of the Teutonic races, the Kingdom of Britain, the great Republic of the Netherlands, the northernmost and most warlike governments of Italy, all stood at the disposition of the warrior-king. Venice, who had hitherto, in the words of a veteran diplomatist, "shunned to look a league or a confederation in the face, if there was any Protestant element in it, as if it had been the head of Medusa,"[1] had formally forbidden the passage of troops northwards to the relief of the assailed power. Savoy, after direful hesitations, had committed herself body and soul to the great enterprise. Even the Pope,[2] who feared the overshadowing personality of Henry, and was beginning to believe his house's private interests more likely to flourish under the protection of the French than the Spanish king, was wavering in his fidelity to Spain and tempted by French promises. If he should prove himself incapable of effecting a pause in the great crusade, it was doubtful on which side he would ultimately range himself; for it was at least certain that the new Catholic League, under the chieftainship of Maximilian of Bavaria, was resolved not to entangle its fortunes inextricably with those of the Austrian house.

The great enterprise, first unfolding itself with the episode of Cleve and Berg and whimsically surrounding itself with the fantastic idyl of the Princess of Condé, had attained vast

---

[1] 'Letters from and to Sir Dudley Carleton' (London, 1757), p. 384.

[2] "'Dominus exercituum fecit hoc,' thus moralized his Holiness on hearing of the murder, 'et quia erat datus in reprobum sensum,' through the blindness of love and the instigations of the Duke of Savoy, both being resolved to disturb the repose of Italy. Now, therefore, his Holiness was represented as 'hoping a change for the better in public affairs.'"—Ortemberg, ambassador at Rome, to the Archdukes. 29 May 1610, in Henrard.

and misty proportions in the brain of its originator.  Few
political visions are better known in history than the
"grand design" of Henry for rearranging the map of the
world at the moment when, in the middle of May, he was
about to draw his sword.  Spain reduced to the Mediterranean and the Pyrenees, but presented with both the
Indies, with all America and the whole Orient in fee ; the
Empire taken from Austria and given to Bavaria ; a constellation of States in Italy, with the Pope for president-
king ; throughout the rest of Christendom a certain number
of republics, of kingdoms, of religions—a great confederation
of the world, in short—with the most Christian king for its
dictator and protector, and a great Amphictyonic council
to regulate all disputes by solemn arbitration, and to make
war in the future impossible, such in little was his great
design.

Nothing could be more humane, more majestic, more
elaborate, more utterly preposterous.  And all this gigantic
fabric had passed away in an instant—at one stroke of a
broken table knife sharpened on a carriage wheel.

Most pitiful was the condition of France on the day after,
and for years after, the murder of the King.  Not only was
the kingdom for the time being effaced from the roll of
nations, so far as external relations were concerned, but it
almost ceased to be a kingdom.  The ancient monarchy of
Hugh Capet, of Saint-Louis, of Henry of France and Navarre,
was transformed into a turbulent, self-seeking, quarrelsome,
pillaging, pilfering democracy of grandees.  The Queen-
Regent was tossed hither and thither at the sport of the
winds and waves which shifted every hour in that tem-
pestuous court.

No man pretended to think of the State.  Every man
thought only of himself.  The royal exchequer was plun-
dered with a celerity and cynical recklessness such as have

been rarely seen in any age or country. The millions so carefully hoarded by Sully, and exhibited so dramatically by that great minister to the enraptured eyes of his sovereign ; that treasure in the Bastille on which Henry relied for payment of the armies with which he was to transform the world, all disappeared in a few weeks to feed the voracious maw of courtiers, paramours, and partisans.[1]

The Queen showered gold like water upon her beloved Concini that he might purchase his Marquisate of Ancre, and the charge of first gentleman of the court from Bouillon ; that he might fit himself for the government of Picardy ; that he might elevate his marquisate into a dukedom. Condé, having no further reason to remain in exile, received as a gift from the trembling Mary de' Medici the magnificent Hotel Gondy, where the Dutch ambassadors had so recently been lodged, for which she paid 65,000 crowns, together with 25,000 crowns to furnish it, 50,000 crowns to pay his debts, 50,000 more as yearly pension.[2]

He claimed double, and was soon at sword's point with the Queen in spite of her lavish bounty.

Épernon, the true murderer of Henry, trampled on courts of justice [3] and councils of ministers, frightened the court by threatening to convert his possession of Metz into an independent sovereignty, as Balagny had formerly seized upon Cambray, smothered for ever the process of Ravaillac, caused those to be put to death or immured for life in dungeons who dared to testify to his complicity in the great crime, and strode triumphantly over friends and enemies throughout France, although so crippled by the gout that he could scarcely walk up stairs.

---

[1] Aerssens to Barneveld, 29 July 1610 (MS.). *et passim*.

[2] Aerssens. *ubi sup.* J. Simons to Prats, 6 Aug. 1610, in Henrard.

[3] P. Pecquius to Archduke Albert, 28 Jan. 1611. Same to same, 2 Feb. 1611. (Archives of Belgium, at Brussels. MSS.) Aerssens to Barneveld, Jan., Feb., and March 1611. (Hague Archives MS.)

There was an end to the triumvirate. Sully's influence was gone for ever. The other two dropped the mask. The Chancellor and Villeroy revealed themselves to be what they secretly had always been—humble servants and stipendiaries of Spain.[1] The formal meetings of the council were of little importance, and were solemn, tearful, and stately; draped in woe for the great national loss. In the private cabinet meetings in the entresol of the Louvre, where the Nuncius and the Spanish ambassador held counsel with Épernon and Villeroy and Jeannin and Sillery, the tone was merry and loud ; the double Spanish marriage and confusion to the Dutch being the chief topics of consultation.

But the anarchy grew day by day into almost hopeless chaos. There was no satisfying the princes of the blood nor the other grandees. Condé, whose reconciliation with the Princess followed not long after the death of Henry and his own return to France, was insatiable in his demands for money, power, and citadels of security. Soissons, who might formerly have received the lieutenancy-general of the kingdom by sacrificing the lilies on his wife's gown, now disputed for that office with his elder brother Conti, the Prince claiming it by right of seniority, the Count denouncing Conti as deaf, dumb, and imbecile, till they drew poniards on each other in the very presence of the Queen ;[2] while Condé on one occasion, having been refused the citadels which he claimed, Blaye and Château Trompette, threw his cloak over his nose and put on his hat while the Queen was speaking, and left the council in a fury, declaring that

---

[1] Aerssens to Barneveld, 16 Nov. 1610. (MS.): "Étant plus que notoire que Messrs. le chancelier et de Villeroy sont de tous points Espagnols et le long temps pensionnaires d'Espagne." Same to same, 6 Dec. 1610: "la faiblesse de la Reine lui permet (Villeroy) à lever le masque," &c. "Villeroy, qui seul, possède toutes les affaires du royaume avec une jalousie incroyable de tous les grands et petits....Rome gouverne tout et l'Espagne grande part aux affaires." —Same to same, 8 Sept. 1610. (H. Archives MS.)

[2] Same to Jacques v. Maldere, 8 Aug. 1610. (MS.)

Villeroy and the Chancellor were traitors, and that he would have them both soundly cudgelled.[1]  Guise, Lorraine, Épernon, Bouillon, and other great lords always appeared in the streets of Paris at the head of three, four, or five hundred mounted and armed retainers; while the Queen in her distraction gave orders to arm the Paris mob to the number of fifty thousand, and to throw chains across the streets to protect herself and her son against the turbulent nobles.[2]

Sully, hardly knowing to what saint to burn his candle, being forced to resign his great posts, was found for a time in strange political combination with the most ancient foes of his party and himself.  The kaleidoscope whirling with exasperating quickness showed ancient Leaguers and Lorrainers banded with and protecting Huguenots against the Crown, while princes of the blood, hereditary patrons and chiefs of the Huguenots, became partisans and stipendiaries of Spain.

It is easy to see that circumstances like these rendered the position of the Dutch commonwealth delicate and perilous.

Sully informed Aerssens and van der Myle, who had been sent back to Paris on special mission very soon after the death of the King, that it took a hundred hours now to accomplish a single affair, whereas under Henry a hundred affairs were transacted in a single hour.  But Sully's sun had set, and he had few business conferences now with the ambassadors.[3]

Villeroy and the Chancellor had fed fat their ancient grudge to the once omnipotent minister, and had sworn his political ruin.  The old secretary of state had held now com-

---

[1] Aerssens to Jacques v. Maldere, 14 Dec. 1610.  (MS.)
[3] Ibid.

[2] Same to Barneveld, 14 June 1610.  (MS.)  Van der Myle. Report of the Special Embassy.  (MS.)

plete control of the foreign alliances and combinations of France, and the Dutch ambassadors could be under no delusion as to the completeness of the revolution.

"You will find a passion among the advisers of the Queen," said Villeroy to Aerssens and van der Myle, " to move in diametrical opposition to the plans of the late king."[1]  And well might the ancient Leaguer and present pensionary of Spain reveal this foremost fact in a policy of which he was in secret the soul.  He wept profusely when he first received Francis Aerssens, but after these " useless tears," as the Envoy called them, he soon made it manifest that there was no more to be expected of France, in the great project which its government had so elaborately set on foot.[2]

Villeroy was now sixty-six years of age, and had been secretary of state during forty-two years and under four kings.  A man of delicate health, frail body, methodical habits, capacity for routine, experience in political intrigue, he was not personally as greedy of money as many of his contemporaries, and was not without generosity; but he loved power, the Pope, and the House of Austria.  He was singularly reserved in public, practised successfully the talent of silence, and had at last arrived at the position he most coveted, the virtual presidency of the council, and saw the men he most hated beneath his feet.

At the first interview of Aerssens with the Queen-Regent she was drowned in tears, and could scarcely articulate an intelligible sentence.  So far as could be understood she expressed her intention of carrying out the King's plans, of maintaining the old alliances, of protecting both religions.  Nothing, however, could be more preposterous than such phrases.  Villeroy, who now entirely directed the foreign affairs of the kingdom, assured the Ambassador that

<hr>

[1] Aerssens' letter last cited.                [2] Ibid.

France was much more likely to apply to the States for assistance than render them aid in any enterprise whatever. "There is no doubt," said Aerssens, "that the Queen is entirely in the hands of Spain and the priests." Villeroy, whom Henry was wont to call the pedagogue of the council, went about sighing dismally, wishing himself dead, and perpetually ejaculating, "Ho! poor France, how much hast thou still to suffer!" In public he spoke of nothing but of union, and of the necessity of carrying out the designs of the King, instructing the docile Queen to hold the same language. In private he was quite determined to crush those designs for ever, and calmly advised the Dutch government to make an amicable agreement with the Emperor in regard to the Cleve affair as soon as possible; a treaty which would have been shameful for France and the possessory princes, and dangerous, if not disastrous, for the States-General. "Nothing but feverish and sick counsels," he said, "could be expected from France, which had now lost its vigour and could do nothing but groan." [1]

Not only did the French council distinctly repudiate the idea of doing anything more for the princes than had been stipulated by the treaty of Hall—that is to say, a contingent of 8000 foot and 2000 horse—but many of them vehemently maintained that the treaty, being a personal one of the late king, was dead with him. [2] The duty of France was now in their opinion to withdraw from these mad schemes as soon as possible, to make peace with the House of Austria without delay, and to cement the friendship by the double marriages. [3]

[1] Aerssens to Barneveld, 26 May 1610. Same to same, 5 June 1610. Same to same, 19 May 1610. Same to van Maldere, 25 May 1610. (MSS.)

[2] Van der Myle, MS. Report. Villeroy took this ground, saying, "dat hare M<sup>t</sup> hierinne niet gehouden en waeren de beloften vand' overleden Coninck personeel zynde." &c.

[3] Aerssens to Prince Maurice, 14 June 1610. (MS.) Van der Myle, MS. Report.

Bouillon, who at that moment hated Sully as much as the most vehement Catholic could do, assured the Dutch envoy that the government was, under specious appearances, attempting to deceive the States ; a proposition which it needed not the evidence of that most intriguing duke to make manifest to so astute a politician ; particularly as there was none more bent on playing the most deceptive game than Bouillon.[1]  There would be no troops to send, he said, and even if there were, there would be no possibility of agreeing on a chief.  The question of religion would at once arise.  As for himself, the Duke protested that he would not accept the command if offered him.  He would not agree to serve under the Prince of Anhalt, nor would he for any consideration in the world leave the court at that moment. At the same time Aerssens was well aware that Bouillon, in his quality of first marshal of France, a Protestant and a prince having great possessions on the frontier, and the brother-in-law of Prince Maurice, considered himself entitled to the command of the troops should they really be sent, and was very indignant at the idea of its being offered to any one else.[2]

He advised earnestly therefore that the States should make a firm demand for money instead of men, specifying the amount that might be considered the equivalent of the number of troops originally stipulated.

It is one of the most singular spectacles in history ; France sinking into the background of total obscurity in an instant of time, at one blow of a knife, while the Republic, which

---

[1] Aerssens worked assiduously, two hours long on one occasion, to effect a reconciliation between the two great Protestant chiefs, but found Bouillon's demands " so shameful and unreasonable " that he felt obliged to renounce all further attempts.  In losing Sully from the royal councils, the States' envoy acknowledged that the Republic had lost everything that could be depended on at the French court.  "All the others are timeserving friends," he said, " or saints without miracles." — Aerssens to Barneveld, 11 June, 1610.  Same to same, 29 May 1610.  (MSS.)

[2] Same to same, 31 March 1610. (MS.)

she had been patronizing, protecting, but keeping always in a subordinate position while relying implicitly upon its potent aid, now came to the front, and held up on its strong shoulders an almost desperate cause. Henry had been wont to call the States-General "his courage and his right arm," [1] but he had always strictly forbidden them to move an inch in advance of him, but ever to follow his lead, and to take their directions from himself. They were a part, and an essential one, in his vast designs ; but France, or he who embodied France, was the great providence, the destiny, the all-directing, all-absorbing spirit, that was to remodel and control the whole world. He was dead, and France and her policy were already in a state of rapid decomposition.

Barneveld wrote to encourage and sustain the sinking state. "Our courage is rising in spite and in consequence of the great misfortune," he said. He exhorted the Queen to keep her kingdom united, and assured her that My Lords the States would maintain themselves against all who dared to assail them. He offered in their name the whole force of the Republic to take vengeance on those who had procured the assassination, and to defend the young king and the Queen-Mother against all who might make any attempt against their authority. He further declared, in language not to be mistaken, that the States would never abandon the princes and their cause.[2]

This was the earliest indication on the part of the Advocate of the intention of the Republic—so long as it should be directed by his counsels—to support the cause of the young king, helpless and incapable as he was, and directed for the time being by a weak and wicked mother, against the reckless and depraved grandees, who were doing their best to destroy the unity and the independence of France,

[1] Aerssens to Prince Maurice, 14 June 1610.  (MS.)
[2] Same to Duplessis-Mornay, 27 May 1610.  (MS.)

and to convert it into a group of outlying provinces of Spain.

Cornelis van der Myle was sent back to Paris on special mission of condolence and comfort from the States-General to the sorely afflicted kingdom.

On the 7th of June, accompanied by Aerssens, he had a long interview with Villeroy.[1]  That minister, as usual, wept profusely, and said that in regard to Cleve it was impossible for France to carry out the designs of the late king. He then listened to what the ambassadors had to urge, and continued to express his melancholy by weeping.[2]  Drying his tears for a time, he sought by a long discourse to prove that France during this tender minority of the King would be incapable of pursuing the policy of his father.  It would be even too burthensome to fulfil the Treaty of Hall.  The friends of the crown, he said, had no occasion to further it, and it would be much better to listen to propositions for a treaty.  Archduke Albert was content not to interfere in the quarrel if the Queen would likewise abstain ; Leopold's forces were altogether too weak to make head against the army of the princes, backed by the power of My Lords the States, and Jülich was neither strong nor well garrisoned. He concluded by calmly proposing that the States should take the matter in hand by themselves alone, in order to lighten the burthen of France, whose vigour had been cut in two by that accursed knife.[3]

A more sneaking and shameful policy was never announced by the minister of a great kingdom.  Surely it might seem that Ravaillac had cut in twain not the vigour only but the honour and the conscience of France.  But the

[1] " Rapport ofte Verhaal van het besoigneerde in de legatie die ik van wege de H. M. H. Staaten General der V. N. gedaan hebbe aan de Coninck ende Coninckin Regentin 1610."  (MS. Hague Archives.)

[2] Ibid.  Aerssens to Barneveld, 7 June 1610.  (MS.)

[3] Ibid.  Ibid.

envoys, knowing in their hearts that they were talking not with a French but a Spanish secretary of state, were not disposed to be the dupes of his tears or his blandishments.

They reminded him that the Queen-Regent and her ministers since the murder of the King had assured the States-General and the princes of their firm intention to carry out the Treaty of Hall, and they observed that they had no authority to talk of any negotiation. The affair of the duchies was not especially the business of the States, and the Secretary was well aware that they had promised their succour on the express condition that his Majesty and his army should lead the way, and that they should follow. This was very far from the plan now suggested, that they should do it all, which would be quite out of the question. France had a strong army, they said, and it would be better to use it than to efface herself so pitiably. The proposition of abstention on the part of the Archduke was a delusion intended only to keep France out of the field.

Villeroy replied by referring to English affairs. King James, he said, was treating them perfidiously. His first letters after the murder had been good, but by the following ones England seemed to wish to put her foot on France's throat, in order to compel her to sue for an alliance. The British ministers had declared their resolve not to carry out that convention of alliance, although it had been nearly concluded in the lifetime of the late king, unless the Queen would bind herself to make good to the King of Great Britain that third part of the subsidies advanced by France to the States which had been furnished on English account.[1]

This was the first announcement of a grievance devised by the politicians now governing France to make trouble for the States with that kingdom and with Great Britain likewise. According to a treaty made at Hampton Court

---

[1] Van der Myle, "Rapport," *ubi sup.* Aerssens, *ubi sup.*

by Sully during his mission to England at the accession of James, it had been agreed that one-third of the moneys advanced by France in aid of the United Provinces should be credited to the account of Great Britain, in diminution of the debt for similar assistance rendered by Elizabeth to Henry. In regard to this treaty the States had not been at all consulted, nor did they acknowledge the slightest obligation in regard to it. The subsidies in men and in money provided for them both by France and by England in their struggle for national existence had always been most gratefully acknowledged by the Republic, but it had always been perfectly understood that these expenses had been incurred by each kingdom out of an intelligent and thrifty regard for its own interest. Nothing could be more ridiculous than to suppose France and England actuated by disinterested sympathy and benevolence when assisting the Netherland people in its life-and-death struggle against the dire and deadly enemy of both crowns.[1] Henry protested that, while adhering to Rome in spiritual matters, his true alliances and strength had been found in the United Provinces, in Germany, and in Great Britain. As for the States, he had spent sixteen millions of livres, he said, in acquiring a perfect benevolence on the part of the States to his person. It was the best bargain he had ever made, and he should take care to preserve it at any cost whatever, for he considered himself able, when closely united with them, to bid defiance to all the kings in Europe together.[2]

Yet it was now the settled policy of the Queen-Regent's council, so far as the knot of politicians guided by the Nuncius and the Spanish ambassador in the entresols of the Louvre could be called a council, to force the States to refund that third, estimated at something between three

---

[1] Aerssens to Barneveld, 25 Dec. 1610. (MS.)
[2] Ibid.

and four million livres, which France had advanced them on account of Great Britain.

Villeroy told the two ambassadors at this interview that, if Great Britain continued to treat the Queen-Regent in such fashion, she would be obliged to look about for other allies. There could hardly be doubt as to the quarter in which Mary de' Medici was likely to look. Meantime, the Secretary of State urged the envoys "to intervene at once to mediate the difference." There could be as little doubt that to mediate the difference was simply to settle an account which they did not owe.

The whole object of the Minister at this first interview was to induce the States to take the whole Cleve enterprise upon their own shoulders, and to let France off altogether. The Queen-Regent as then advised meant to wash her hands of the possessory princes once and for ever. The envoys cut the matter short by assuring Villeroy that they would do nothing of the kind. He begged them piteously not to leave the princes in the lurch, and at the same time not to add to the burthens of France at so disastrous a moment.[1]

So they parted. Next day, however, they visited the Secretary again, and found him more dismal and flaccid than ever.

He spoke feebly and drearily about the succour for the great enterprise, recounted all the difficulties in the way, and, having thrown down everything that the day before had been left standing, he tried to excuse an entire change of policy by the one miserable crime.[2]

He painted a forlorn picture of the council and of France. "I can myself do nothing as I wish," added the undisputed controller of that government's policy, and then

---

[1] Aerssens to Barneveld, 7 June 1610. (MS.)
[2] "Rapport" of van der Myle.

with a few more tears he concluded by requesting the envoys
to address their demands to the Queen in writing.

This was done with the customary formalities and fine
speeches on both sides ; a dull comedy by which no one
was amused.

Then Bouillon came again, and assured them that there
had been a chance that the engagements of Henry, followed
up by the promise of the Queen-Regent, would be carried
out, but now the fact was not to be concealed that the
continued battery of the Nuncius, of the ambassadors
of Spain and of the Archdukes, had been so effective that
nothing sure or solid was thenceforth to be expected ; the
council being resolved to accept the overtures of the Archduke for mutual engagement to abstain from the Jülich
enterprise.[2]

Nothing in truth could be more pitiable than the helpless
drifting of the once mighty kingdom, whenever the men
who governed it withdrew their attention for an instant from
their private schemes of advancement and plunder to cast
a glance at affairs of State.  In their secret heart they
could not doubt that France was rushing on its ruin, and
that in the alliance of the Dutch commonwealth, Britain,
and the German Protestants, was its only safety.  But they
trembled before the Pope, grown bold and formidable since
the death of the dreaded Henry.  To offend his Holiness,
the King of Spain, the Emperor, and the great Catholics
of France, was to make a crusade against the Church.
Garnier, the Jesuit, preached from his pulpit that " to strike
a blow in the Cleve enterprise was no less a sin than to
inflict a stab in the body of our Lord." [3]  The Parliament
of Paris having ordered the famous treatise of the Jesuit

---

[1] Aerssens to Barneveld, 7 June 1610.  (MS.)
[2] Same to same, 11 June 1610.  (MS.)
[3] Ibid.

Mariana—justifying the killing of excommunicated kings by their subjects—to be publicly burned before Notre Dame, the Bishop opposed the execution of the decree. The Parliament of Paris, although crushed by Épernon in its attempts to fix the murder of the King upon himself as the true culprit, was at least strong enough to carry out this sentence upon a printed volume recommending the deed, and the Queen's council could only do its best to mitigate the awakened wrath of the Jesuits at this exercise of legal authority.[1] At the same time it found on the whole so many more difficulties in a cynical and shameless withdrawal from the Treaty of Hall than in a nominal and tardy fulfilment of its conditions that it resolved at last to furnish the 8000 foot and 2000 horse promised to the possessory princes. The next best thing to abandoning entirely even this little shred, this pitiful remnant, of the splendid designs of Henry was to so arrange matters that the contingent should be feebly commanded, and set on foot in so dilatory a manner that the petty enterprise should on the part of France be purely perfunctory. The grandees of the kingdom had something more important to do than to go crusading in Germany, with the help of a heretic republic, to set up the possessory princes. They were fighting over the prostrate dying form of their common mother for their share of the spoils, stripping France before she was dead, and casting lots for her vesture.

Soissons was on the whole in favour of the Cleve expedition. Épernon was desperately opposed to it, and maltreated Villeroy in full council when he affected to say a word, insincere as the Duke knew it to be, in favour of executing agreements signed by the monarch, and sealed with the great seal of France.[2] The Duke of Guise, finding

---

[1] Aerssens to Barneveld, 11 June 1610. (MS.)
[2] Same to same, 8 Aug. 1610. (MS.)

himself abandoned by the Queen, and bitterly opposed and hated by Soissons, took sides with his deaf and dumb and imbecile brother, and for a brief interval the Duke of Sully joined this strange combination of the House of Lorraine and chiefs of ancient Leaguers, who welcomed him with transport, and promised him security.

Then Bouillon, potent by his rank, his possessions, and his authority among the Protestants, publicly swore that he would ruin Sully and change the whole order of the government. What more lamentable spectacle, what more desolate future for the cause of religious equality, which for a moment had been achieved in France, than this furious alienation of the trusted leaders of the Huguenots, while their adversaries were carrying everything before them ?  At the council board Bouillon quarrelled ostentatiously with Sully, shook his fist in his face, and but for the Queen's presence would have struck him.[1]  Next day he found that the Queen was intriguing against himself as well as against Sully, was making a cat's-paw of him, and was holding secret councils daily from which he as well as Sully was excluded.  At once he made overtures of friendship to Sully, and went about proclaiming to the world that all Huguenots were to be removed from participation in affairs of state.[2]  His vows of vengeance were for a moment hushed by the unanimous resolution of the council that, as first marshal of France, having his principality on the frontier, and being of the Reformed religion, he was the fittest of all to command the expedition.  Surely it might be said that the winds and tides were not more changeful than the politics of the Queen's government.[3]  The Dutch ambassador was secretly requested by Villeroy to negotiate with Bouillon and offer him the command of the Jülich expedition.  The Duke

<hr>

[1] Aerssens to Barneveld, 8 Aug. 1610.  (MS.)
[2] Ibid.                         [3] Ibid.

affected to make difficulties, although burning to obtain the post, but at last consented. All was settled. Aerssens communicated at once with Villeroy, and notice of Bouillon's acceptance was given to the Queen, when, behold, the very next day Marshal de la Châtre was appointed to the command expressly because he was a Catholic. Of course the Duke of Bouillon, furious with Soissons and Épernon and the rest of the government, was more enraged than ever against the Queen. His only hope was now in Condé, but Condé at the outset, on arriving at the Louvre, offered his heart to the Queen as a sheet of white paper. Épernon and Soissons received him with delight, and exchanged vows of an eternal friendship of several weeks' duration. And thus all the princes of the blood, all the cousins of Henry of Navarre, except the imbecile Conti, were ranged on the side of Spain, Rome, Mary de' Medici, and Concino Concini, while the son of the Balafré, the Duke of Mayenne, and all their adherents were making common cause with the Huguenots. What better example had been seen before, even in that country of pantomimic changes, of the effrontery with which Religion was made the strumpet of Political Ambition ?

All that day and the next Paris was rife with rumours that there was to be a general massacre of the Huguenots to seal the new-born friendship of a Condé with a Medici.[1] France was to renounce all her old alliances and publicly to enter into treaties offensive and defensive with Spain. A league like that of Bayonne made by the former Medicean Queen-Regent of France was now, at Villeroy's instigation, to be signed by Mary de' Medici. Meantime, Marshal de la Châtre, an honest soldier and fervent Papist, seventy-three years of age, ignorant of the language, the geography, the politics of the country to which he was sent, and knowing the road thither about as well, according to Aerssens, who was

---

[1] Aerssens, *ubi sup.* Aerssens to Barneveld, 8 Sept. 1610.

requested to give him a little preliminary instruction, as he did the road to India, was to co-operate with Barneveld and Maurice of Nassau in the enterprise against the duchies.[1]

These were the cheerful circumstances amid which the first step in the dead Henry's grand design against the House of Austria and in support of Protestantism in half Europe and of religious equality throughout Christendom, was now to be ventured.

Cornelis van der Myle took leave of the Queen on terminating his brief special embassy, and was fain to content himself with languid assurances from that corpulent Tuscan dame of her cordial friendship for the United Provinces. Villeroy repeated that the contingent to be sent was furnished out of pure love to the Netherlands, the present government being in no wise bound by the late king's promises.[2]  He evaded the proposition of the States for renewing the treaty of close alliance by saying that he was then negotiating with the British government on the subject, who insisted as a preliminary step on the repayment of the third part of the sums advanced to the States by the late king.

He exchanged affectionate farewell greetings and good wishes with Jeannin and with the dropsical Duke of Mayenne, who was brought in his chair to his old fellow Leaguer's apartments at the moment of the Ambassador's parting interview.[3]

There was abundant supply of smooth words, in the plentiful lack of any substantial nutriment, from the representatives of each busy faction into which the Mediccan court was divided.  Even Épernon tried to say a gracious word to the retiring envoy, assuring him that he would do

---

[1] Aerssens to Prince Maurice, 14 June 1610.  Same to same, 23 July 1610.  Same to Barneveld, 1 July 1610.  (MSS.)

[2] Van der Myle, "Rapport." (MS already cited.)
[3] Ibid.

as much for the cause as a good Frenchman and lover of his fatherland could do. He added, in rather a surly way, that he knew very well how foully he had been described to the States, but that the devil was not as black as he was painted. It was necessary, he said, to take care of one's own house first of all, and he knew very well that the States and all prudent persons would do the same thing.[1]

[1] Van der Myle, "Rapport." (MS. already cited.)

# CHAPTER V.

Interviews between the Dutch Commissioners and King James — Prince Maurice takes command of the Troops — Surrender of Jülich — Matthias crowned King of Bohemia — Death of Rudolph — James's Dream of a Spanish Marriage — Appointment of Vorstius in place of Arminius at Leyden — Interview between Maurice and Winwood — Increased Bitterness between Barneveld and Maurice — Projects of Spanish Marriages in France.

It is refreshing to escape from the atmosphere of self-seeking faction, feverish intrigue, and murderous stratagem in which unhappy France was stifling into the colder and calmer regions of Netherland policy.

No sooner had the tidings of Henry's murder reached the States than they felt that an immense responsibility had fallen on their shoulders. It is to the eternal honour of the Republic, of Barneveld, who directed her councils, and of Prince Maurice, who wielded her sword, that she was equal to the task imposed upon her.

There were open bets on the Exchange in Antwerp, after the death of Henry, that Maurice would likewise be killed within the month. Nothing seemed more probable, and the States implored the Stadholder to take special heed to himself. But this was a kind of caution which the Prince was not wont to regard. Nor was there faltering, distraction, cowardice, or parsimony in Republican councils.[1]

We have heard the strong words of encouragement and sympathy addressed by the Advocate's instructions to the

---

[1] Van Rees and Brill's Continuation of Arend, i. 111 ; ii. 406.

Queen-Regent and the leading statesmen of France. We have seen their effects in that lingering sentiment of shame which prevented the Spanish stipendiaries who governed the kingdom from throwing down the mask as cynically as they were at first inclined to do.

Not less manful and statesmanlike was the language held to the King of Great Britain and his ministers by the Advocate's directions. The news of the assassination reached the special ambassadors in London at three o'clock of Monday, the 17th May. James returned to Whitehall from a hunting expedition on the 21st, and immediately signified his intention of celebrating the occasion by inviting the high commissioners of the States to a banquet and festival at the palace.[1]

Meantime they were instructed by Barneveld to communicate the results of the special embassy of the States to the late king according to the report just delivered to the Assembly. Thus James was to be informed of the common resolution and engagement then taken to support the cause of the princes. He was now seriously and explicitly to be summoned to assist the princes not only with the stipulated 4000 men, but with a much greater force, proportionate to the demands for the security and welfare of Christendom, endangered by this extraordinary event. He was assured that the States would exert themselves to the full measure of their ability to fortify and maintain the high interests of France, of the possessory princes, and of Christendom, so that the hopes of the perpetrators of the foul deed would be confounded.[2]

"They hold this to be the occasion," said the envoys, "to show to all the world that it is within your power to rescue the affairs of France, Germany, and of the United Provinces

---

[1] Report of the Special Ambassadors to England. (MS. before cited.)
[2] Ibid.

from the claws of those who imagine for themselves universal monarchy."[1]

They concluded by requesting the King to come to "a resolution on this affair royally, liberally, and promptly, in order to take advantage of the time, and not to allow the adversary to fortify himself in his position"; and they pledged the States-General to stand by and second him with all their power.

The commissioners, having read this letter to Lord Salisbury before communicating it to the King, did not find the Lord Treasurer very prompt or sympathetic in his reply There had evidently been much jealousy at the English court of the confidential and intimate relations recently established with Henry, to which allusions were made in the documents read at the present conference. Cecil, while expressing satisfaction in formal terms at the friendly language of the States, and confidence in the sincerity of their friendship for his sovereign, intimated very plainly that more had passed between the late king and the authorities of the Republic than had been revealed by either party to the King of Great Britain, or than could be understood from the letters and papers now communicated. He desired further information from the commissioners, especially in regard to those articles of their instructions which referred to a general rupture. They professed inability to give more explanations than were contained in the documents themselves. If suspicion was felt, they said, that the French King had been proposing anything in regard to a general rupture, either on account of the retreat of Condé, the affair of Savoy, or anything else, they would reply that the ambassadors in France had been instructed to decline committing the States until after full communication and advice and

[1] Report of the Special Ambassadors to England. (MS. before cited.)
[2] Letter of 24 May 1610, in Report. (MS.)

ripe deliberation with his British Majesty and council, as well as the Assembly of the States-General ; and it had been the intention of the late king to have conferred once more and very confidentially with Prince Maurice and Count Lewis William before coming to a decisive resolution.

It was very obvious however to the commissioners that their statement gave no thorough satisfaction, and that grave suspicions remained of something important kept back by them. Cecil's manner was constrained and cold, and certainly there were no evidences of profound sorrow at the English court for the death of Henry.

"The King of France," said the High Treasurer, "meant to make a master-stroke—a *coup de maistre*—but he who would have all may easily lose all. Such projects as these should not have been formed or taken in hand without previous communication with his Majesty of Great Britain." [1]

All arguments on the part of the ambassadors to induce the Lord Treasurer or other members of the government to enlarge the succour intended for the Cleve affair were fruitless. The English troops regularly employed in the States' service might be made use of with the forces sent by the Republic itself. More assistance than this it was idle to expect, unless after a satisfactory arrangement with the present regency of France. The proposition, too, of the States for a close and general alliance was coldly repulsed. "No resolution can be taken as to that," said Cecil ; "the death of the French king has very much altered such matters." [2]

At a little later hour on the same day the commissioners, according to previous invitation, dined with the King. May 24, No one sat at the table but his Majesty and them-1610. selves, and they all kept their hats on their heads.[3] The King was hospitable, gracious, discursive, loquacious, very theological.

<hr>

[1] MS. Report.            [2] Ibid.            [3] Ibid.

He expressed regret for the death of the King of France, and said that the pernicious doctrine out of which such vile crimes grew must be uprooted. He asked many questions in regard to the United Netherlands, enquiring especially as to the late commotions at Utrecht, and the conduct of Prince Maurice on that occasion. He praised the resolute conduct of the States-General in suppressing those tumults with force, adding, however, that they should have proceeded with greater rigour against the ringleaders of the riot. He warmly recommended the Union of the Provinces.[1]

He then led the conversation to the religious controversies in the Netherlands, and in reply to his enquiries was informed that the points in dispute related to predestination and its consequences.

"I have studied that subject," said James, "as well as anybody, and have come to the conclusion that nothing certain can be laid down in regard to it. I have myself not always been of one mind about it, but I will bet that my opinion is the best of any, although I would not hang my salvation upon it. My Lords the States would do well to order their doctors and teachers to be silent on this topic. I have hardly ventured, moreover, to touch upon the matter of justification in my own writings, because that also seemed to hang upon predestination."[2]

Thus having spoken with the air of a man who had left nothing further to be said on predestination or justification,

[1] MS. Report.

[2] ". . . verstaende datter verschil was int poinct vande predestinatie ende t' geene daervan dependeerde verclaerde Z. M. dat hy dat stuck soewel als jemant anders hadde geexamineert ende bevonden hadde dat men daerinne nyet seeckers conde statueren dat hy selffs darinne nyet altyt van een gevoelen hadde geweest dat hy wel wilde wedden dat zyn opinie de beste was maer nyet dier dat hy zyn salicheit daeran wilde hangen, dat d'heeren staten wel souden doen ende de doctoren en Leeraers gebieden van die materie te swygen, dat Syne Mat. selffs het stuck van de Justificatie in zyne geschriften qualyck hadde derven roeren om dat t' selve oock scheen aen predestinatie te hangen."—MS. "Rapport" of the Ambassadors.

the King rose, took off his hat, and drank a bumper to the health of the States-General and his Excellency Prince Maurice, and success to the affair of Cleve.

After dinner there was a parting interview in the gallery. The King, attended by many privy councillors and high functionaries of state, bade the commissioners a cordial farewell, and, in order to show his consideration for their government, performed the ceremony of knighthood upon them, as was his custom in regard to the ambassadors of Venice. The sword being presented to him by the Lord Chamberlain, James touched each of the envoys on the shoulder as he dismissed him. "Out of respect to My Lords the States," said they in their report, "we felt compelled to allow ourselves to be burthened with this honour." [1]

Thus it became obvious to the States-General that there was but little to hope for from Great Britain or France. France, governed by Concini and by Spain, was sure to do her best to traverse the designs of the Republic, and, while perfunctorily and grudgingly complying with the letter of the Hall treaty, was secretly neutralizing by intrigue the slender military aid which de la Châtre was to bring to Prince Maurice.[2] The close alliance of France and Protestantism had melted into air. On the other hand the new Catholic League sprang into full luxuriance out of the grave of Henry, and both Spain and the Pope gave their hearty adhesion to the combinations of Maximilian of Bavaria, now that the mighty designs of the French king were buried with him. The Duke of Savoy, caught in the trap of his own devising, was fain to send his son to sue to Spain for pardon for the family upon his knees,[3] and expiated

---

[1] " . . . genoodsaeckt geweest ten respecte van de Ho. Mo. Heeren Staten ons met dese Eere te laten beswaeren."—"Rapport," &c.

[2] "Pendant que vous battez Juliers on combat secrètement vos desseins en cette cour."—Aerssens to Prince Maurice, 22 Aug. 1610.   (MS.)

[3] 'Mémoires de Sully,' viii. notes. 'Mém. de Nevers,' tom. ii. p. 880.

by draining a deep cup of humiliation his ambitious designs upon the Milanese and the matrimonial alliance with France. Venice recoiled in horror from the position she found herself in as soon as the glamour of Henry's seductive policy was dispelled, while James of Great Britain, rubbing his hands with great delight at the disappearance from the world of the man he so admired, bewailed, and hated, had no comfort to impart to the States-General thus left in virtual isolation. The barren burthen of knighthood and a sermon on predestination were all he could bestow upon the high commissioners in place of the alliance which he eluded, and the military assistance which he point-blank refused. The possessory princes, in whose cause the sword was drawn, were too quarrelsome and too fainthearted to serve for much else than an incumbrance either in the cabinet or the field.

And the States-General were equal to the immense responsibility. Steadily, promptly, and sagaciously they confronted the wrath, the policy, and the power of the Empire, of Spain, and of the Pope. Had the Republic not existed, nothing could have prevented that debateable and most important territory from becoming provinces of Spain, whose power thus dilated to gigantic proportions in the very face of England would have been more menacing than in the days of the Armada. Had the Republic faltered, she would have soon ceased to exist. But the Republic did not falter.

On the 13th July, Prince Maurice took command of the States' forces, 13,000 foot and 3000 horse, with thirty pieces of cannon, assembled at Schenkenschans. The English and French regiments in the regular service of the United Provinces were included in these armies, but there were no additions to them. "The States did seven times as much," Barneveld justly averred, "as they had

July 13, 1610.

stipulated to do." Maurice, moving with the precision and promptness which always marked his military operations, marched straight upon Jülich, and laid siege to that important fortress. The Archdukes at Brussels, determined to keep out of the fray as long as possible, offered no opposition to the passage of his supplies up the Rhine, which might have been seriously impeded by them at Rheinberg. The details of the siege, as of all the Prince's sieges, possess no more interest to the general reader than the working out of a geometrical problem. He was incapable of a flaw in his calculations, but it was impossible for him quite to complete the demonstration before the arrival of de la Châtre. Maurice received with courtesy the Marshal, who arrived on the 18th August, at the head of his contingent of 8000 foot and a few squadrons of cavalry, and there was great show of harmony between them. For any practical purposes, de la Châtre might as well have remained in France. For political ends his absence would have been preferable to his presence.

Maurice would have rejoiced, had the Marshal blundered longer along the road to the debateable land than he had done. He had almost brought Jülich to reduction. A fortnight later the place surrendered. The terms granted by the conqueror were equitable. No change was to be made in the liberty of Roman Catholic worship, nor in the city magistracy. The citadel and its contents were to be handed over to the Princes of Brandenburg and Neuburg. Archduke Leopold and his adherents departed to Prague, to carry out as he best could his farther designs upon the crown of Bohemia, this first portion of them having so lamentably failed, and Sergeant-Major Frederick Pithan, of the regiment of Count Ernest Casimir of Nassau, was appointed governor of Jülich in the interest of the possessory princes.[1]

---

[1] Van Rees and Brill's Continuation of Arend, iii. ii. p. 410, *sqq.*

Thus without the loss of a single life, the Republic, guided by her consummate statesman and unrivalled general, had gained an immense victory, had installed the Protestant princes in the full possession of those splendid and important provinces, and had dictated her decrees on German soil to the Emperor of Germany, and had towed, as it were, Great Britain and France along in her wake, instead of humbly following those powers, and had accomplished all that she had ever proposed to do, even in alliance with them both.

The King of England considered that quite enough had been done, and was in great haste to patch up a reconciliation. He thought his ambassador would soon " have as good occasion to employ his tongue and his pen as General Cecil and his soldiers have done their swords and their mattocks."

He had no sympathy with the cause of Protestantism, and steadily refused to comprehend the meaning of the great movements in the duchies. " I only wish that I may handsomely wind myself out of this quarrel, where the principal parties do so little for themselves," he said.[1]

De la Châtre returned with his troops to France within a fortnight after his arrival on the scene. A mild proposition made by the French government through the Marshal, that the provinces should be held in sequestration by France until a decision as to the true sovereignty could be reached, was promptly declined.[2] Maurice of Nassau had hardly gained so signal a triumph for the Republic and for the Protestant cause only to hand it over to Concini and Villeroy for the benefit of Spain. Jülich was thought safer in the keeping of Sergeant Pithan.

By the end of September the States' troops had returned to their own country.

Sept. 8,<br>1610.

---

[1] King to Earl of Salisbury, 1610. (Hatfield Archives MS.) See Appendix.
[2] Aerssens to Barneveld, 8 Sept. 1610. (MS.)

Thus the Republic, with eminent success, had accomplished a brief and brilliant campaign, but no statesman could suppose that the result was more than a temporary one. These coveted provinces, most valuable in themselves and from their important position, would probably not be suffered peacefully to remain very long under the protection of the heretic States-General and in the *Condominium* of two Protestant princes. There was fear among the Imperialists, Catholics, and Spaniards, lest the baleful constellation of the Seven Provinces might be increased by an eighth star. And this was a project not to be tolerated. It was much already that the upstart confederacy had defied Pope, Emperor, and King, as it were, on their own domains, had dictated arrangements in Germany directly in the teeth of its emperor, using France as her subordinate, and compelling the British king to acquiesce in what he most hated.

But it was not merely to surprise Jülich, and to get a foothold in the duchies, that Leopold had gone forth on his adventure. His campaign, as already intimated, was part of a wide scheme in which he had persuaded his emperor-cousin to acquiesce. Poor Rudolph had been at last goaded into a feeble attempt at revolt against his three brothers and his cousin Ferdinand. Peace-loving, inert, fond of his dinner, fonder of his magnificent collections of gems and intagli, liking to look out of window at his splendid collection of horses, he was willing to pass a quiet life, afar from the din of battles and the turmoil of affairs. As he happened to be emperor of half Europe, these harmless tastes could not well be indulged. Moon-faced and fat, silent and slow, he was not imperial of aspect on canvas or coin, even when his brows were decorated with the conventional laurel wreath. He had been stripped of his authority and all but discrowned by his more bustling brothers Matthias and Max, while the sombre figure of Styrian Ferdinand, pupil of the Jesuits, and passionate admirer of Philip II., stood ever in the background, casting a prophetic shadow over the throne and over Germany.

The brothers were endeavouring to persuade Rudolph that he would find more comfort in Innsbruck than in Prague; that he required repose after the strenuous labours of government. They told him, too, that it would be wise to confer the royal crown of Bohemia upon Matthias, lest, being elective and also an electorate, the crown and vote of that country might pass out of the family, and so both Bohemia and the Empire be lost to the Habsburgs. The kingdom being thus secured to Matthias and his heirs, the next step, of course, was to proclaim him King of the Romans. Otherwise there would be great danger and detriment to Hungary, and other hereditary states of that conglomerate and anonymous monarchy which owned the sway of the great Habsburg family.

The unhappy emperor was much piqued. He had been deprived by his brother of Hungary, Moravia, and Austria, while Matthias was now at Prague with an army, ostensibly to obtain ratification of the peace with Turkey, but in reality to force the solemn transfer of those realms and extort the promise of Bohemia. Could there be a better illustration of the absurdities of such a system of Imperialism?

And now poor Rudolph was to be turned out of the Hradschin, and sent packing with or without his collections to the Tyrol.[1]

The bellicose bishop of Strassburg and Passau, brother of Ferdinand, had little difficulty in persuading the down-trodden man to rise to vengeance. It had been secretly agreed between the two that Leopold, at the head of a considerable army of mercenaries which he had contrived to levy, should dart into Jülich as the Emperor's representative,

---

[1] Van Meteren, b. **xxx.** and **xxxii.** fo. 645, *sqq.*

seize the debateable duchies, and hold them in sequestration until the Emperor should decide to whom they belonged, and, then, rushing back to Bohemia, should annihilate Matthias, seize Prague, and deliver Rudolph from bondage. It was further agreed that Leopold, in requital of these services, should receive the crown of Bohemia, be elected King of the Romans, and declared heir to the Emperor, so far as Rudolph could make him his heir.[1]

The first point in the program he had only in part accomplished. He had taken Jülich, proclaimed the intentions of the Emperor, and then been driven out of his strong position by the wise policy of the States under the guidance of Barneveld and by the consummate strategy of Maurice. It will be seen therefore that the Republic was playing a world's game at this moment, and doing it with skill and courage. On the issue of the conflict which had been begun and was to be long protracted in the duchies, and to spread over nearly all Christendom besides, would depend the existence of the United Netherlands and the fate of Protestantism.

The discomfited Leopold swept back at the head of his mercenaries, 9000 foot and 3000 horse, through Alsace and along the Danube to Linz and so to Prague, marauding, harrying, and black-mailing the country as he went. He entered the city on the 15th of February 1611, fighting his way through crowds of exasperated burghers. Sitting in full harness on horseback in the great square before the cathedral, the warlike bishop compelled the population to make oath to him as the Emperor's commissary.[2] The street fighting went on however day by day, poor Rudolph meantime cowering in the Hradschin. On the

---

[1] Teynagel's Confession. His statements were confirmed by those of other prisoners, especially Hagenmül-ler, Welser, and Count von Zollern Van Meteren, xxxii. 655.

[2] Van Meteren, *ubi sup.*

third day, Leopold, driven out of the town, took up a position on the heights, from which he commanded it with his artillery.  Then came a feeble voice from the Hradschin, telling all men that these Passau marauders and their episcopal chief were there by the Emperor's orders.  The triune city—the old, the new, and the Jew—was bidden to send deputies to the palace and accept the Imperial decrees.  No deputies came at the bidding.  The Bohemians, especially the Praguers, being in great majority Protestants knew very well that Leopold was fighting the cause of the Papacy and Spain in Bohemia as well as in the duchies.[1]

And now Matthias appeared upon the scene.  The Estates had already been in communication with him, better hopes, for the time at least, being entertained from him than from the flaccid Rudolph.  Moreover a kind of compromise had been made in the autumn between Matthias and the Emperor after the defeat of Leopold in the duchies.  The real king had fallen at the feet of the nominal one by proxy of his brother Maximilian.  Seven thousand men of the army of Matthias now came before Prague under command of Colonitz.  The Passauers, receiving three months' pay from the Emperor, marched quietly off.  Leopold disappeared for the time.  His chancellor and counsellor in the duchies, Francis Teynagel, a Geldrian noble, taken prisoner and put to the torture, revealed the little plot of the Emperor in favour of the Bishop, and it was believed that the Pope, the King of Spain, and Maximilian of Bavaria were friendly to the scheme.  This was probable, for Leopold at least made no mystery of his resolve to fight Protestantism to the death, and to hold the duchies, if he could, for the cause of Rome and Austria.

Both Rudolph and Matthias had committed themselves to the toleration of the Reformed religion.  The famous

Oct. 9,<br>1610.

---

[1] Van Meteren, 645–655.

"Majesty-Letter," freshly granted by the Emperor (1609), and the Compromise between the Catholic and Protestant Estates had become the law of the land. Those of the Bohemian confession, a creed commingled of Hussism, Lutheranism, and Calvinism,[1] had obtained toleration. In a country where nine-tenths of the population were Protestants it was permitted to Protestants to build churches and to worship God in them unmolested. But these privileges had been extorted by force, and there was a sullen, dogged determination which might be easily guessed at to revoke them should it ever become possible. The House of Austria, reigning in Spain, Italy, and Germany, was bound by the very law of their being to the Roman religion. Toleration of other worship signified in their eyes both a defeat and a crime.

Thus the great conflict, to be afterwards known as the Thirty Years' War, had in reality begun already, and the Netherlands, in spite of the truce, were half unconsciously taking a leading part in it. The odds at that moment in Germany seemed desperately against the House of Austria, so deep and wide was the abyss between throne and subjects which religious difference had created. But the reserved power in Spain, Italy, and Southern Germany was sure enough to make itself felt sooner or later on the Catholic side.

Meantime the Estates of Bohemia knew well enough that the Imperial house was bent on destroying the elective principle of the Empire, and on keeping the crown of Bohemia in perpetuity. They had also discovered that Bishop-Archduke Leopold had been selected by Rudolph as chief of the reactionary movement against Protestantism. They could not know at that moment whether his plans were likely to prove fantastic or dangerous.

[1] Gindely, ' Gesch. des dreissigjähr. Kriegs ' (Prag. 1869), b. i. 60–62.

So Matthias came to Prague[1] at the invitation of the Estates, entering the city with all the airs of a conqueror. Rudolph received his brother with enforced polite- March 23, 1611. ness, and invited him to reside in the Hradschin. This proposal was declined by Matthias, who sent a colonel however, with six pieces of artillery, to guard and occupy that palace. The Passau prisoners were pardoned and released, and there was a general reconciliation. May 23, 1611. A month later,[2] Matthias went in pomp to the chapel of the holy Wenceslaus, that beautiful and barbarous piece of mediæval, Sclavonic architecture, with its sombre arches, and its walls encrusted with huge precious stones. The Estates of Bohemia, arrayed in splendid Zchech costume, and kneeling on the pavement, were asked whether they accepted Matthias, King of Hungary, as their lawful king. Thrice they answered Aye. Cardinal Dietrichstein then put the historic crown of St. Wenceslaus on the King's head, and Matthias swore to maintain the laws and privileges of Bohemia, including the recent charters granting liberty of religion to Protestants. Thus there was temporary, if hollow, truce between the religious parties, and a sham reconciliation between the Emperor and his brethren. The forlorn Rudolph moped away the few months Jan. 20, 1612. of life left to him in the Hradschin, and died soon after the new year.[3] The House of Austria had not been divided, Matthias succeeded his brother, Leopold's visions melted into air, and it was for the future to reveal whether the Majesty-Letter and the Compromise had been written on very durable material.

And while such was the condition of affairs in Germany immediately following the Cleve and Jülich campaign, the relations of the Republic both to England and France were

---

[1] Van Meteren, 655–659.　　　　[2] Ibid.
[3] Ibid. 673.

become rapidly more dangerous than they ever had been. It was a severe task for Barneveld, and enough to overtax the energies of any statesman, to maintain his hold on two such slippery governments as both had become since the death of their great monarchs. It had been an easier task for William the Silent to steer his course, notwithstanding all the perversities, short-comings, brow-beatings, and inconsistencies that he had been obliged to endure from Elizabeth and Henry. Genius, however capricious and erratic at times, has at least vision, and it needed no elaborate arguments to prove to both those sovereigns that the severance of their policy from that of the Netherlands was impossible without ruin to the Republic and incalculable danger to themselves.

But now France and England were both tending towards Spain through a stupidity on the part of their rulers such as the gods are said to contend against in vain. Barneveld was not a god nor a hero, but a courageous and wide-seeing statesman, and he did his best. Obliged by his position to affect admiration, or at least respect, where no emotion but contempt was possible, his daily bread was bitter enough. It was absolutely necessary to humour those whom he knew to be traversing his policy and desiring his ruin, for there was no other way to serve his country and save it from impending danger. So long as he was faithfully served by his subordinates, and not betrayed by those to whom he gave his heart, he could confront external enemies and mould the policy of wavering allies.

Few things in history are more pitiable than the position of James in regard to Spain. For seven long years he was as one entranced, the slave to one idea, a Spanish marriage for his son. It was in vain that his counsellors argued, Parliament protested, allies implored. Parliament was told that a royal family matter regarded himself alone, and that interference on their part was an impertinence.  Parliament's duty was a simple one, to give him advice if he asked it, and money when he required it, without asking for reasons.  It was already a great concession that he should ask for it in person.  They had nothing to do with his affairs nor with general politics.  The mystery of government was a science beyond their reach, and with which they were not to meddle. " *Ne sutor ultra crepidam*," said the pedant.[1]

Upon that one point his policy was made to turn.  Spain held him in the hollow of her hand.  The Infanta, with two million crowns in dowry, was promised, withheld, brought forward again like a puppet to please or irritate a froward child.  Gondemar, the Spanish ambassador, held him spell-bound.  Did he falter in his opposition to the States—did he cease to goad them for their policy in the duchies—did he express sympathy with Bohemian Protestantism, or, as time went on, did he dare to lift a finger or touch his pocket in behalf of his daughter and the unlucky Elector-Palatine ; did he, in short, move a step in the road which England had ever trod and was bound to tread—the road of determined resistance to Spanish ambition—instantaneously the Infanta was withheld, and James was on his knees again.  A few years later, when the great Raleigh returned from his trans-Atlantic expedition, Gondemar fiercely denounced him to the King as the worst enemy of Spain.  The usual threat was made, the wand was waved, and the noblest head in England fell upon the block, in pursuance of an obsolete sentence fourteen years old.[2]

It is necessary to hold fast this single clue to the crooked and amazing entanglements of the policy of James.  The insolence, the meanness, and the prevarications of this royal toad-eater are only thus explained.

Yet Philip III. declared on his death-bed that he had

<hr>

[1] Rapin, iii. 186. 187.    [2] Ibid. 122.

never had a serious intention of bestowing his daughter on the Prince.

The vanity and the hatreds of theology furnished the chief additional material in the policy of James towards the Provinces. The diplomacy of his reign so far as the Republic was concerned is often a mere mass of controversial divinity, and gloomy enough of its kind. Exactly at this moment Conrad Vorstius had been called by the University of Leyden to the professorship vacant by the death of Arminius, and the wrath of Peter Plancius and the whole orthodox party knew no bounds. Born in Cologne, Vorstius had been a lecturer in Geneva, and beloved by Beza. He had written a book against the Jesuit Belarmino, which he had dedicated to the States-General. But he was now accused of Arminianism, Socianism, Pelagianism, Atheism—one knew not what. He defended himself in writing against these various charges, and declared himself a believer in the Trinity, in the Divinity of Christ, in the Atonement.[2] But he had written a book on the Nature of God, and the wrath of Gomarus and Plancius and Bogerman was as nothing to the ire of James when that treatise was one day handed to him on returning from hunting. He had scarcely looked into it before he was horror-struck, and instantly wrote to Sir Ralph Winwood, his ambassador at the Hague, ordering him to insist that this blasphemous monster should at once be removed from the country.[3] Who but James knew anything of the Nature of God, for had he not written a work in Latin explaining it all, so that humbler beings might read and be instructed.

Sir Ralph accordingly delivered a long sermon to the States on the brief supplied by his Majesty, told them that to have Vorstius as successor to Arminius was to fall out of

<hr>

[1] Rapin, vii. 201.    [2] Van Rees and Brill, iii. 470, *sqq.*
[3] Ibid.

the frying-pan into the fire,[1] and handed them a " catalogue " prepared by the King of the blasphemies, heresies, and atheisms of the Professor. " Notwithstanding that the man in full assembly of the States of Holland," said the Ambassador with headlong and confused rhetoric, " had found the means to palliate and plaster the dung of his heresies, and thus to dazzle the eyes of good people," yet it was necessary to protest most vigorously against such an appointment, and to advise that " his works should be publicly burned in the open places of all the cities."

The Professor never was admitted to perform his functions of theology, but he remained at Leyden, so Winwood complained, " honoured, recognized as a singularity and ornament to the Academy in place of the late Joseph Scaliger." " The friendship of the King and the heresy of Vorstius are quite incompatible," said the Envoy.[2]

Meantime the Advocate, much distressed at the animosity of England bursting forth so violently on occasion of the appointment of a divinity professor at Leyden, and at the very instant too when all the acuteness of his intellect was taxed to keep on good or even safe terms with France, did his best to stem these opposing currents. His private letters to his old and confidential friend, Noel de Caron, States' ambassador in London, reveal the perplexities of his soul and the upright patriotism by which he was guided in these gathering storms. And this correspondence, as well as that maintained by him at a little later period with the successor of Aerssens at Paris, will be seen subsequently to have had a direct and most important bearing upon the policy of the Republic and upon his own fate. It is necessary therefore that the reader, interested in these complicated affairs which were soon to bring on a sanguinary war on a scale even

---

[1] " . . . tomber de fièvre en chaud mal."—Winwood's ' Memorials,' iii. 291.
[2] Ibid. 301, 309, 317.

vaster than the one which had been temporarily suspended, should give close attention to papers never before exhumed from the musty sepulchre of national archives, although constantly alluded to in the records of important state trials. It is strange enough to observe the apparent triviality of the circumstances out of which gravest events seem to follow. But the circumstances were in reality threads of iron which led down to the very foundations of the earth.

" I wish to know," wrote the Advocate to Caron,[1] " from whom the Archbishop of Canterbury received the advices concerning Vorstius in order to find out what is meant by all this."

It will be remembered that Whitgift was of opinion that James was directly inspired by the Holy Ghost, and that as he affected to deem him the anointed High-priest of England, it was natural that he should encourage the King in his claims to be *Pontifex maximus* for the Netherlands likewise.

" We are busy here," continued Barneveld, " in examining all things for the best interests of the country and the churches.  I find the nobles and cities here well resolved in this regard, although there be some disagreements *in modo*. Vorstius, having been for many years professor and minister of theology at Steinfurt, having manifested his learning in many books written against the Jesuits, and proved himself pure and moderate in doctrine, has been called to the vacant professorship at Leyden.  This appointment is now countermined by various means.  We are doing our best to arrange everything for the highest good of the Provinces and the churches.  Believe this and believe nothing else.  Pay heed to no other information.  Remember what took place in Flanders, events so well known to you.  It is not for me to pass judgment in these matters.  Do you, too, suspend your judgment."

---

[1] Barneveld to Caron, 12 Sept. 1611.  (Hague Archives MS.)

The Advocate's allusion was to the memorable course of affairs in Flanders at an epoch when many of the most inflammatory preachers and politicians of the Reformed religion, men who refused to employ a footman or a house-maid not certified to be thoroughly orthodox, subsequently after much sedition and disturbance went over to Spain and the Catholic religion.

A few weeks later [1] Barneveld sent copies to Caron of the latest harangues of Winwood in the Assembly and the reply of My Lords on the Vorstian business ; that is to say, the freshest dialogue-on predestination between the King and the Advocate. For as James always dictated word for word the orations of his envoy, so had their Mightinesses at this period no head and no mouthpiece save Barneveld alone. Nothing could be drearier than these controversies, and the reader shall be spared as much as possible the infliction of reading them. It will be necessary, however, for the proper understanding of subsequent events that he should be familiar with portions of the Advocate's confidential letters.

" Sound well the gentleman you wot of," said Barneveld, " and other personages as to the conclusive opinions over there. The course of the propositions does not harmonize with what I have myself heard out of the King's mouth at other times, nor with the reports of former ambassadors. I cannot well understand that the King should, with such pre-ciseness, condemn all other opinions save those of Calvin and Beza. It is important to the service of this country that one should know the final intention of his Majesty."

And this was the misery of the position. For it was soon to appear that the King's definite and final intentions varied from day to day. It was almost humorous to find him at that moment condemning all opinions but those of Calvin

[1] Barneveld to Caron, 3 Oct. 1611. (Hague Archives MS.)

and Beza in Holland, while his course to the strictest confessors of that creed in England was so ferocious.

But Vorstius was a rival author to his Majesty on subjects treated of by both, so that literary spite of the most venomous kind, stirred into theological hatred, was making a dangerous mixture. Had a man with the soul and sense of the Advocate sat on the throne which James was regarding at that moment as a professor's chair, the world's history would have been changed.

"I fear," continued Barneveld, "that some of our own precisians have been spinning this coil for us over there,[1] and if the civil authority can be thus countermined, things will go as in Flanders in your time. Pray continue to be observant, discreet, and moderate."

The Advocate continued to use his best efforts to smooth the rising waves. He humoured and even flattered the King, although perpetually denounced by Winwood in his letters to his sovereign as tyrannical, over-bearing, malignant, and treacherous.[2] He did his best to counsel moderation and mutual toleration, for he felt that these needless theological disputes about an abstract and insoluble problem of casuistry were digging an abyss in which the Republic might be swallowed up for ever. If ever man worked steadily with the best lights of experience and inborn sagacity for the good of his country and in defence of a constitutional government, horribly defective certainly, but the only legal one, and on the whole a more liberal polity than any then existing, it was Barneveld. Courageously, steadily, but most patiently, he stood upon that position so vital and daily so madly assailed ; the defence of the civil authority against the priesthood. He felt instinctively and keenly that where any portion of the subjects or citizens of

<hr>

[1] "Ick dachte dat eenige van onse preeyste ons dit spel aldaer berokkenden." (MS. just cited.)    [2] Winwood's 'Memorials,' vol. iii. *passim.*

a country can escape from the control of government and obey other head than the lawful sovereignty, whether monarchical or republican, social disorder and anarchy must be ever impending.

"We are still tortured by ecclesiastical disputes," he wrote[1] a few weeks later to Caron. "Besides many libels which have appeared in print, the letters of his Majesty and the harangues of Winwood have been published ; to what end you who know these things by experience can judge. The truth of the matter of Vorstius is that he was legally called in July 1610, that he was heard last May before My Lords the States with six preachers to oppose him, and in the same month duly accepted and placed in office.  He has given no public lectures as yet.  You will cause this to be known on fitting opportunity.  Believe and cause to be believed that his Majesty's letters and Sir R. Winwood's propositions have been and shall be well considered, and that I am working with all my strength to that end.  You know the constitution of our country, and can explain every-thing for the best.  Many pious and intelligent people in this State hold themselves assured that his Majesty accord-ing to his royal exceeding great wisdom, foresight, and affection for the welfare of this land will not approve that his letters and Winwood's propositions should be scattered by the press among the common people.  Believe and cause to be believed, to your best ability, that My Lords the States of Holland desire to maintain the true Christian, Reformed religion as well in the University of Leyden as in all their cities and villages.  The only dispute is on the high points of predestination and its adjuncts, concerning which moderation and a more temperate teaching is furthered by some amongst us.  Many think that such is the edifying practice in England.  Pray have the kindness to send me

[1] Barneveld to Caron, 17 Nov 1611. (Hague Archives MS )

the English Confession of the year 1572, with the corrections and alterations up to this year."

But the fires were growing hotter, fanned especially by Flemish ministers, a brotherhood of whom Barneveld had an especial distrust, and who certainly felt great animosity to him. His moderate counsels were but oil to the flames. He was already depicted by zealots and calumniators as false to the Reformed creed.

" Be assured and assure others," he wrote again to Caron,[1] " that in the matter of religion I am, and by God's grace shall remain, what I ever have been. Make the same assurances as to my son-in-law and brother. We are not a little amazed that a few extraordinary Puritans, mostly Flemings and Frisians, who but a short time ago had neither property nor kindred in the country, and have now very little of either, and who have given but slender proofs of constancy or service to the fatherland, could through pretended zeal gain credit over there against men well proved in all respects. We wonder the more because they are endeavouring, in ecclesiastical matters at least, to usurp an extraordinary authority, against which his Majesty, with very weighty reasons, has so many times declared his opinion founded upon God's Word and upon all laws and principles of justice."

It was Barneveld's practice on this as on subsequent occasions very courteously to confute the King out of his own writings and speeches, and by so doing to be unconsciously accumulating an undying hatred against himself in the royal breast. Certainly nothing could be easier than to show that James, while encouraging in so reckless a manner the emancipation of the ministers of an advanced sect in the Reformed Church from control of government, and their usurpation of supreme authority which had been destroyed

<hr>

[1] Barneveld to Caron, 21 Jan. 1612.   (Hague Archives MS.)

in England, was outdoing himself in dogmatism and inconsistency. A king-highpriest, who dictated his supreme will to bishops and ministers as well as to courts and parliaments, was ludicrously employed in a foreign country in enforcing the superiority of the Church to the State.

" You will give good assurances," said the Advocate, " upon my word, that the conservation of the true Reformed religion is as warmly cherished here, especially by me, as at any time during the war."

He next alluded to the charges then considered very grave against certain writings of Vorstius, and with equal fairness to his accusers as he had been to the Professor gave a pledge that the subject should be examined.

" If the man in question," he said, " be the author, as perhaps falsely imputed, of the work *De Filiatione Christi* or things of that sort, you may be sure that he shall have no furtherance here." He complained, however, that before proof the cause was much prejudiced by the circulation through the press of letters on the subject from important personages in England. His own efforts to do justice in the matter were traversed by such machinations. If the Professor proved to be guilty of publications fairly to be deemed atheistical and blasphemous, he should be debarred from his functions, but the outcry from England was doing more harm than good.

" The published extract from the letter of the Archbishop," he wrote,[1] " to the effect that the King will declare My Lords the States to be his enemies if they are not willing to send the man away is doing much harm."

Truly, if it had come to this—that a King of England was to go to war with a neighbouring and friendly republic because an obnoxious professor of theology was not instantly hurled from a university of which his Majesty was not one

[1] MS. last cited.

of the overseers—it was time to look a little closely into the functions of governments and the nature of public and international law.  Not that the sword of James was in reality very likely to be unsheathed, but his shriekings and his scribblings, pacific as he was himself, were likely to arouse passions which torrents of blood alone could satiate.

"The publishing and spreading among the community," continued Barneveld, "of M. Winwood's protestations and of many indecent libels are also doing much mischief, for the nature of this people does not tolerate such things. I hope, however, to obtain the removal according to his Majesty's desire.  Keep me well informed, and send me word what is thought in England by the tour divines of the book of Vorstius, *De Deo*, and of his declarations on the points sent here by his Majesty.  Let me know, too, if there has been any later confession published in England than that of the year 1562, and whether the nine points pressed in the year 1595 were accepted and published in 1603.  If so, pray send them, as they may be made use of in settling our differences here."

Thus it will be seen that the spirit of conciliation, of a calm but earnest desire to obtain a firm grasp of the most reasonable relations between Church and State through patient study of the phenomena exhibited in other countries, were the leading motives of the man.  Yet he was perpetually denounced in private as an unbeliever, an atheist, a tyrant, because he resisted dictation from the clergy within the Provinces and from kings outside them.

"It was always held here to be one of the chief infractions of the laws and privileges of this country," he said,[1] "that former princes had placed themselves in matter of religion in the tutelage of the Pope and the Spanish Inquisition, and that they therefore on complaint of their good subjects

---

[1] Barneveld to Caron, 21 Jan. 1612.  (Hague Archives MS.)

could take no orders on that subject.  Therefore it cannot
be considered strange that we are not willing here to fall
into the same obloquy.  That one should now choose to turn
the magistrates, who were once so seriously summoned on
their conscience and their office to adopt the Reformation
and to take the matter of religion to heart, into ignorants,
to deprive them of knowledge, and to cause them to see with
other eyes than their own, cannot by many be considered
right and reasonable.  *Intelligenti pauca.*" [1]

Meantime M. de Refuge, as before stated, was on his way
to the Hague, to communicate the news of the double marriage.  He had fallen sick at Rotterdam,[2] and the nature of
his instructions and of the message he brought remained unknown, save from the previous despatches of Aerssens.  But
reports were rife that he was about to propose new terms of
alliance to the States, founded on large concessions to the
Roman Catholic religion.  Of course intense jealousy was
excited at the English court, and calumny plumed her
wings for a fresh attack upon the Advocate.  Of course he
was sold to Spain, the Reformed religion was to be trampled
out in the Provinces, and the Papacy and Holy Inquisition
established on its ruins.  Nothing could be more diametri-
cally the reverse of the fact than such hysterical suspicions
as to the instructions of the ambassador extraordinary from
France, and this has already appeared.  The Vorstian affair
too was still in the same phase, the Advocate professing a
willingness that justice should be done in the matter, while
courteously but firmly resisting the arrogant pretensions of
James to take the matter out of the jurisdiction of the
States.

[1] The interesting letter from which
I have given these copious extracts
was ordered by its writer to be
burned.  "*Lecta vulcano*" was noted
at the end of it, as was not unfre-
quently the case with the Advocate.

It never was burned; but, innocent
and reasonable as it seems, was made
use of by Barneveld's enemies with
deadly effect.

[2] Barneveld to Caron, 28 Jan.
1612. (Hague Archives MS.)

"I stand amazed," he said,[1] "at the partisanship and the calumnious representations which you tell me of, and cannot imagine what is thought nor what is proposed. Should M. de Refuge make any such propositions as are feared, believe, and cause his Majesty and his counsellors to believe, that they would be of no effect. Make assurances upon my word, notwithstanding all advices to the contrary, that such things would be flatly refused. If anything is published or proven to the discredit of Vorstius, send it to me. Believe that we shall not defend heretics nor schismatics against the pure Evangelical doctrine, but one cannot conceive here that the knowledge and judicature of the matter belongs anywhere else than to My Lords the States of Holland, in whose service he has legally been during four months before his Majesty made the least difficulty about it. Called hither legally a year before, with the knowledge and by the order of his Excellency and the councillors of state of Holland, he has been countermined by five or six Flemings and Frisians, who, without recognizing the lawful authority of the magistrates, have sought assistance in foreign countries —in Germany and afterwards in England. Yes, they have been so presumptuous as to designate one of their own men for the place. If such a proceeding should be attempted in England, I leave it to those whose business it would be to deal with it to say what would be done. I hope therefore that one will leave the examination and judgment of this matter freely to us, without attempting to make us—against the principles of the Reformation and the liberties and laws of the land—executors of the decrees of others, as the man here [2] wishes to obtrude it upon us."

He alluded to the difficulty in raising the ways and means; saying that the quota of Holland, as usual, which

---

[1] Barneveld to Caron, 28 Jan. 1612.   (Hague Archives MS.)
[2] To wit, Winwood.

was more than half the whole, was ready, while other provinces were in arrears. Yet they were protected, while Holland was attacked.

"Methinks I am living in a strange world," he said, "when those who have received great honour from Holland, and who in their conscience know that they alone have conserved the Commonwealth, are now traduced with such great calumnies. But God the Lord Almighty is just, and will in His own time do chastisement." [1]

The affair of Vorstius dragged its slow length along, and few things are more astounding at this epoch than to see such a matter, interesting enough certainly to theologians, to the University, and to the rising generation of students, made the topic of unceasing and embittered diplomatic controversy between two great nations, who had most pressing and momentous business on their hands. But it was necessary to humour the King, while going to the verge of imprudence in protecting the Professor. In March he was heard, three or four hours long, before the Assembly of Holland, in answer to various charges made against him,[2] being warned that " he stood before the Lord God and before the sovereign authority of the States." Although thought by many to have made a powerful defence, he was ordered to set it forth in writing, both in Latin and in the vernacular. Furthermore it was ordained that he should make a complete refutation of all the charges already made or that might be made during the ensuing three months against him in speech, book, or letter in England, Germany, the Netherlands, or anywhere else. He was allowed one year and a half to accomplish this work, and meantime was to reside not in Leyden, nor the Hague, but in some other town of Holland, not delivering lectures or practising his

<hr>

[1] MS. last cited.
[2] Barneveld to Caron, 28 March 1612. (Hague Archives MS.)

profession in any way.[1]  It might be supposed that sufficient work had been thus laid out for the unfortunate doctor of divinity without lecturing or preaching.  The question of jurisdiction was saved.  The independence of the civil authority over the extreme pretensions of the clergy had been vindicated by the firmness of the Advocate.  James had been treated with overflowing demonstrations of respect, but his claim to expel a Dutch professor from his chair and country by a royal fiat had been signally rebuked.  Certainly if the Provinces were dependent upon the British king in regard to such a matter, it was the merest imbecility for them to affect independence.  Barneveld had carried his point and served his country strenuously and well in this apparently small matter which human folly had dilated into a great one.  But deep was the wrath treasured against him in consequence in clerical and royal minds.

Returning from Wesel after the negotiations, Sir Ralph Winwood had an important interview at Arnheim with April 7, 1612.  Prince Maurice, in which they confidentially exchanged their opinions in regard to the Advocate, and mutually confirmed their suspicions and their jealousies in regard to that statesman.

The Ambassador earnestly thanked the Prince in the King's name for his "careful and industrious endeavours for the maintenance of the truth of religion, lively expressed in prosecuting the cause against Vorstius and his adherents."

He then said:

"I am expressly commanded that his Majesty conferring the present condition of affairs of this quarter of the world with those advertisements he daily receives from his ministers abroad, together with the nature and disposition of those men who have in their hands the managing of all business in these foreign parts, can make no other judgment than this.

---

[1]  Barneveld to Caron, 28 March 1612.  (Hague Archives MS.)

"There is a general ligue and confederation complotted for the subversion and ruin of religion upon the subsistence whereof his Majesty doth judge the main welfare of your realms and of these Provinces solely to consist.

"Therefore his Majesty has given me charge out of the knowledge he has of your great worth and sufficiency," continued Winwood, "and the confidence he reposes in your faith and affection, freely to treat with you on these points, and withal to pray you to deliver your opinion what way would be the most compendious and the most assured to contrequarr these complots, and to frustrate the malice of these mischievous designs."

The Prince replied by acknowledging the honour the King had vouchsafed to do him in holding so gracious an opinion of him, wherein his Majesty should never be deceived.

"I concur in judgment with his Majesty," continued the Prince, "that the main scope at which these plots and practices do aim, for instance, the alliance between France and Spain, is this, to root out religion, and by consequence to bring under their yoke all those countries in which religion is professed.

"The first attempt," continued the Prince, "is doubtless intended against these Provinces. The means to counter-mine and defeat these projected designs I take to be these : the continuance of his Majesty's constant resolution for the protection of religion, and then that the King would be pleased to procure a general confederation between the kings, princes, and commonwealths professing religion, namely, Denmark, Sweden, the German princes, the Protestant cantons of Switzerland, and our United Provinces.

"Of this confederation, his Majesty must be not only the director, but the head and protector.

"Lastly, the Protestants of France should be, if not supported, at least relieved from that oppression which the alliance of Spain doth threaten upon them.  This, I insist," repeated Maurice with great fervour, "is the only coupe-gorge of all plots whatever between France and Spain."

He enlarged at great length on these points, which he considered so vital.

"And what appearance can there be," asked Winwood insidiously and maliciously, "of this general confederation now that these Provinces, which heretofore have been accounted a principal member of the Reformed Church, begin to falter in the truth of religion ?

"He who solely governs the metropolitan province of Holland," continued the Ambassador, with a direct stab in the back at Barneveld, "is reputed generally, as your Excellency best knows, to be the only patron of Vorstius, and the protector of the schisms of Arminius.  And like-wise, what possibility is there that the Protestants of France can expect favour from these Provinces when the same man is known to depend at the devotion of France ? "

The international, theological, and personal jealousy of the King against Holland's Advocate having been thus plainly developed, the Ambassador proceeded to pour into the Prince's ear the venom of suspicion, and to inflame his jealousy against his great rival.  The secret conversation showed how deeply laid was the foundation of the political hatred, both of James and of Maurice, against the Advocate, and certainly nothing could be more preposterous than to imagine the King as the director and head of the great Protestant League.  We have but lately seen him confiden-tially assuring his minister that his only aim was "to wind himself handsomely out of the whole business."  Maurice must have found it difficult to preserve his gravity when assigning such a part to "Master Jacques."

"Although Monsieur Barneveld has cast off all care of re-ligion," said Maurice, "and although some towns in Holland, wherein his power doth reign, are infected with the like neglect, yet so long as so many good towns in Holland stand sound, and all the other provinces of this confederacy, the proposition would at the first motion be cheerfully accepted.

"I confess I find difficulty in satisfying your second question," continued the Prince, "for I acknowledge that Barneveld is wholly devoted to the service of France. During the truce negotiations, when some difference arose between him and myself, President Jeannin came to me, requiring me in the French king's name to treat Monsieur Barneveld well, whom the King had received into his protection. The letters which the States' ambassador in France wrote to Barneveld (and to him all ambassadors address their despatches of importance), the very autographs themselves, he sent back into the hands of Villéroy."

Here the Prince did not scruple to accuse the Advocate of doing the base and treacherous trick against Aerssens which he had expressly denied doing, and which had been done during his illness, as he solemnly avowed, by a subordinate probably for the sake of making mischief.

Maurice then discoursed largely and vehemently of the suspicious proceedings of Barneveld, and denounced him as dangerous to the State. "When one man who has the conduct of all affairs in his sole power," he said, "shall hold underhand intelligence with the ministers of Spain and the Archduke, and that without warrant, thereby he may have the means so to carry the course of affairs that, do what they will, these Provinces must fall or stand at the mercy and discretion of Spain. Therefore some good resolutions must be taken in time to hold up this State from a sudden downfall, but in this much moderation and discretion must be used."

The Prince added that he had invited his cousin Lewis

William to appear at the Hague at May day, in order to consult as to the proper means to preserve the Provinces from confusion under his Majesty's safeguard, and with the aid of the Englishmen in the States' service whom Maurice pronounced to be " the strength and flower of his army."

Thus the Prince developed his ideas at great length, and accused the Advocate behind his back, and without the faintest shadow of proof, of base treachery to his friends and of high-treason.  Surely Barneveld was in danger, and was walking among pitfalls.  Most powerful and deadly enemies were silently banding themselves together against him. Could he long maintain his hold on the slippery heights of power, where he was so consciously serving his country, but where he became day by day a mere shining mark for calumny and hatred ?

The Ambassador then signified to the Prince that he had been instructed to carry to him the King's purpose to confer on him the Order of the Garter.

" If his Majesty holds me worthy of so great honour," said the Prince, " I and my family shall ever remain bound to his service and that of his royal posterity.

" That the States should be offended I see no cause, but holding the charge I do in their service, I could not accept the honour without first acquainting them and receiving their approbation."

Winwood replied that, as the King knew the terms on which the Prince lived with the States, he doubted not his Majesty would first notify them and say that he honoured the mutual amity between his realms and these Provinces by honouring the virtues of their general, whose services, as they had been most faithful and affectionate, so had they been accompanied with the blessings of happiness and prosperous success.

Thus said Winwood to the King: " Your Majesty may

plaster two walls with one trowel (*una fidelia duos dealbare parietes*), reverse the designs of them who to facilitate their own practices do endeavour to alienate your affections from the good of these Provinces, and oblige to your service the well-affected people, who know that there is no surety for themselves, their wives and children, but under the protection of your Majesty's favour. Perhaps, however, the favourers of Vorstius and Arminius will buzz into the ears of their associates that your Majesty would make a party in these Provinces by maintaining the truth of religion and also by gaining unto you the affections of their chief commander. But your Majesty will be pleased to pass forth whose worthy ends will take their place, which is to honour virtue where you find it, and the suspicious surmises of malice and envy in one instant will vanish into smoke."[1]

Winwood made no scruple in directly stating to the English government that Barneveld's purpose was to "cause a divorce between the King's realms and the Provinces, the more easily to precipitate them into the arms of Spain."[2] He added that the negotiation with Count Maurice then on foot was to be followed, but with much secrecy, on account of the place he held in the State.

Soon after the Ambassador's secret conversation with Maurice he had an interview with Barneveld. He assured the Advocate that no contentment could be given to his Majesty but by the banishment of Vorstius. "If the town of Leyden should understand so much," replied Barneveld, "I fear the magistrates would retain him still in their town."

"If the town of Leyden should retain Vorstius," answered Winwood, "to brave or despight his Majesty, the King has the means, if it pleases him to use them, and that without

---

[1] Winwood to the King, 7 April (o. s.) 1612. (Cecil Papers, Hatfield Archives MS.) See Appendix.

[2] Same to Viscount Rochester, 7 April 1612. (Hatfield Archives MS.) See Appendix.

drawing sword, to range them to reason, and to make the magistrates on their knees demand his pardon, and I say as much of Rotterdam."

Such insolence on the part of an ambassador to the first minister of a great republic was hard to bear. Barneveld was not the man to brook it. He replied with great indignation. "I was born in liberty," he said with rising choler, " I cannot digest this kind of language. The King of Spain himself never dared to speak in so high a style." [1]

" I well understand that logie," returned the Ambassador with continued insolence. " You hold your argument to be drawn *à majori ad minus;* but I pray you to believe that the King of Great Britain is peer and companion to the King of Spain, and that his motto is, '*Nemo me impune lacessit.*' "

And so they parted in a mutual rage ; Winwood adding on going out of the room, " Whatsoever I propose to you in his Majesty's name can find with you neither goust nor grace."

He then informed Lord Rochester that " the man was extremely distempered and extremely distasted with his Majesty.

" Some say," he added, " that on being in England when his Majesty first came to the throne he conceived some offence, which ever since hath rankled in his heart, and now doth burst forth with more violent malice."

Nor was the matter so small as it superficially appeared. Dependence of one nation upon the dictation of another can never be considered otherwise than grave. The subjection of all citizens, clerical or lay, to the laws of the land, the supremacy of the State over the Church, were equally grave subjects. And the question of sovereignty now raised for the first time, not academically merely, but practically,

_______
[1] MS. last cited.

was the gravest one of all.  It was soon to be mooted
vigorously and passionately whether the United Provinces
were a confederacy or a union ; a league of sovereign and independent states bound together by treaty for certain specified
purposes or an incorporated whole.  The Advocate and all
the principal lawyers in the country had scarcely a doubt
on the subject.  Whether it were a reasonable system or an
absurd one, a vigorous or an imbecile form of government,
they were confident that the Union of Utrecht, made about a
generation of mankind before, and the only tie by which
the Provinces were bound together at all, was a compact
between sovereigns.

Barneveld styled himself always the servant and officer
of the States of Holland.  To them was his allegiance, for
them he spoke, wrought, and thought, by them his meagre
salary was paid.  At the congress of the States-General, the
scene of his most important functions, he was the ambassador of Holland, acting nominally according to their
instructions, and exercising the powers of minister of foreign
affairs and, as it were, prime minister for the other confederates by their common consent.  The system would
have been intolerable, the great affairs of war and peace
could never have been carried on so triumphantly, had not
the preponderance of the one province Holland, richer, more
powerful, more important in every way than the other six
provinces combined, given to the confederacy illegally, but
virtually, many of the attributes of union.  Rather by usu-
caption than usurpation Holland had in many regards come
to consider herself and be considered as the Republic
itself.  And Barneveld, acting always in the name of
Holland and with the most modest of titles and appointments, was for a long time in all civil matters the chief of
the whole country.  This had been convenient during the
war, still more convenient during negotiations for peace, but

it was inevitable that there should be murmurs now that the cessation from military operations on a large scale had given men time to look more deeply into the nature of a constitution partly inherited and partly improvised, and having many of the defects usually incident to both sources of government.

The military interest, the ecclesiastical power, and the influence of foreign nations exerted through diplomatic intrigue, were rapidly arraying themselves in determined hostility to Barneveld and to what was deemed his tyrannous usurpation. A little later the national spirit, as opposed to provincial and municipal patriotism, was to be aroused against him, and was likely to prove the most formidable of all the elements of antagonism.

It is not necessary to anticipate here what must be developed on a subsequent page. This much, however, it is well to indicate for the correct understanding of passing events. Barneveld did not consider himself the officer or servant of their *High* Mightinesses the States-General, while in reality often acting as their master, but the vassal and obedient functionary of their *Great* Mightinesses the States of Holland, whom he almost absolutely controlled.

His present most pressing business was to resist the encroachments of the sacerdotal power and to defend the magistracy. The casuistical questions which were fast maddening the public mind seemed of importance to him only as enclosing within them a more vital and practical question of civil government.

But the anger of his opponents, secret and open, was rapidly increasing. Envy, jealousy, political and clerical hate, above all, that deadliest and basest of malignant spirits which in partisan warfare is bred out of subserviency to rising and rival power, were swarming about him and stinging him at every step. No parasite of Maurice could more effectively pay his court and more confidently hope for promotion or reward than by vilipending Barneveld. It would be difficult to comprehend the infinite extent and power of slander without a study of the career of the Advocate of Holland.

"I thank you for your advices," he wrote to Caron,[1] "and I wish from my heart that his Majesty, according to his royal wisdom and clemency towards the condition of this country, would listen only to My Lords the States or their ministers, and not to his own or other passionate persons who, through misunderstanding or malice, furnish him with information and so frequently flatter him. I have tried these twenty years to deserve his Majesty's confidence, and have many letters from him reaching through twelve or fifteen years, in which he does me honour and promises his royal favour. I am the more chagrined that through false and passionate reports and information—because I am resolved to remain good and true to My Lords the States, to the fatherland, and to the true Christian religion—I and mine should now be so traduced. I hope that God Almighty will second my upright conscience, and cause his Majesty soon to see the injustice done to me and mine. To defend the resolutions of My Lords the States of Holland is my office, duty, and oath, and I assure you that those resolutions are taken with wider vision and scope than his Majesty can believe. Let this serve for My Lords' defence and my own against indecent calumny, for my duty allows me to pursue no other course."

He again alluded to the dreary affair of Vorstius, and told the Envoy that the vexation caused by it was incredible. "That men unjustly defame our cities and their regents is nothing new," he said; "but I assure you that it is far more damaging to the common weal than the defamers imagine."

[1] Barneveld to Caron, 21 May 1612. (Hague Archives MS.)

Some of the private admirers of Arminius who were deeply grieved at so often hearing him "publicly decried as the enemy of God"[1] had been defending the great heretic to James, and by so doing had excited the royal wrath not only against the deceased doctor and themselves, but against the States of Holland who had given them no commission.

On the other hand the advanced orthodox party, most bitter haters of Barneveld, and whom in his correspondence with England he uniformly and perhaps designedly called the Puritans, knowing that the very word was a scarlet rag to James, were growing louder and louder in their demands. "Some thirty of these Puritans," said he, "of whom at least twenty are Flemings or other foreigners equally violent, proclaim that they and the like of them mean alone to govern the Church.  Let his Majesty compare this proposal with his *Royal Present*, with his salutary declaration at London in the year 1603 to Doctor Reynolds and his associates, and with his admonition delivered to the Emperor, kings, sovereigns, and republics, and he will best understand the mischievous principles of these people, who are now gaining credit with him to the detriment of the freedom and laws of these Provinces."[2]

A less enlightened statesman than Barneveld would have found it easy enough to demonstrate the inconsistency of the King in thus preaching subserviency of government to church and favouring the rule of Puritans over both.  It needed but slender logic to reduce such a policy on his part to absurdity, but neither kings nor governments are apt to value themselves on their logic.  So long as James could play the pedagogue to emperors, kings, and republics, it mattered little to him that the doctrines which he preached in one place he had pronounced flat blasphemy in another.

---

[1] Barneveld to Caron, 21 May 1612.   (Hague Archives MS.)
[2] Ibid.

That he would cheerfully hang in England the man whom he would elevate to power in Holland might be inconsistency in lesser mortals ; but what was the use of his infallibility if he was expected to be consistent ?

But one thing was certain. The Advocate saw through him as if he had been made of glass, and James knew that he did. This fatal fact outweighed all the decorous and respectful phraseology under which Barneveld veiled his remorseless refutations. It was a dangerous thing to incur the wrath of this despot-theologian.

Prince Maurice, who had originally joined in the invitation given by the overseers of Leyden to Vorstius, and had directed one of the deputies and his own "court trumpeter," Uytenbogaert, to press him earnestly to grant his services to the University,[1] now finding the coldness of Barneveld to the fiery remonstrances of the King, withdrew his protection of the Professor.

"The Count Maurice, who is a wise and understanding prince," said Winwood, "and withal most affectionate to his Majesty's service, doth foresee the miseries into which these countries are likely to fall, and with grief doth pine away."

It is probable that the great stadholder had never been more robust, or indeed inclining to obesity, than precisely at this epoch ; but Sir Ralph was of an imaginative turn. He had discovered, too, that the Advocate's design was " of no other nature than so to stem the course of the State that insensibly the Provinces shall fall by relapse into the hands of Spain."[2]

A more despicable idea never entered a human brain. Every action, word, and thought, of Barneveld's life was a refutation of it. But he was unwilling, at the bidding of a king, to treat a professor with contumely who had just been

---

[1] Bayle, *in voce*. Winwood's 'Mem.' iii. 294, note.
[2] Winwood, iii. 343.

solemnly and unanimously invited by the great university, by the States of Holland, and by the Stadholder to an important chair, and that was enough for the diplomatist and courtier. "He, and only he," said Winwood passionately, "hath opposed his Majesty's purposes with might and main."[1] Formerly the Ambassador had been full of complaints of "the craving humour of Count Maurice,"[2] and had censured him bitterly in his correspondence for having almost by his inordinate pretensions for money and other property brought the Treaty of Truce to a standstill. And in these charges he was as unjust and as reckless as he was now in regard to Barneveld.

The course of James and his agents seemed cunningly devised to sow discord in the Provinces, to inflame the growing animosity of the Stadholder to the Advocate, and to paralyse the action of the Republic in the duchies. If the King had received direct instructions from the Spanish cabinet how to play the Spanish game, he could hardly have done it with more docility. But was not Gondemar ever at his elbow, and the Infanta always in the perspective?

And it is strange enough that, at the same moment, Spanish marriages were in France as well as England the turning-point of policy.

Henry had been willing enough that the Dauphin should espouse a Spanish infanta, and that one of the Spanish princes should be affianced to one of his daughters. But the proposition from Spain had been coupled with a condition that the friendship between France and the Netherlands should be at once broken off, and the rebellious heretics left to their fate. And this condition had been placed before him with such arrogance that he had rejected the whole scheme. Henry was not the man to do anything dishonourable at the dictation of another sovereign. He was

---

[1] Winwood, iii. 343.        [2] Ibid. 1, 2.

also not the man to be ignorant that the friendship of the Provinces was necessary to him, that cordial friendship between France and Spain was impossible, and that to allow Spain to reoccupy that splendid possession between his own realms and Germany, from which she had been driven by the Hollanders in close alliance with himself, would be unworthy of the veriest schoolboy in politics. But Henry was dead, and a Medici reigned in his place, whose whole thought was to make herself agreeable to Spain.

Aerssens, adroit, prying, experienced, unscrupulous, knew very well that these double Spanish marriages were resolved upon, and that the inevitable condition refused by the King would be imposed upon his widow. He so informed the States-General, and it was known to the French government that he had informed them. His position soon became almost untenable, not because he had given this information, but because the information and the inference made from it were correct.

It will be observed that the policy of the Advocate was to preserve friendly relations between France and England, and between both and the United Provinces. It was for this reason that he submitted to the exhortations and denunciations of the English ambassadors. It was for this that he kept steadily in view the necessity of dealing with and supporting corporate France, the French government, when there were many reasons for feeling sympathy with the internal rebellion against that government. Maurice felt differently. He was connected by blood or alliance with more than one of the princes now perpetually in revolt. Bouillon was his brother-in-law, the sister of Condé was his brother's wife. Another cousin, the Elector-Palatine, was already encouraging distant and extravagant hopes of the Imperial crown. It was not unnatural that he should feel promptings of ambition and sympathy difficult to avow even to himself, and that he should feel resentment against the man by whom this secret policy was traversed in the well-considered interest of the Republican government.

Aerssens, who, with the keen instinct of self-advancement was already attaching himself to Maurice as to the wheels of the chariot going steadily up the hill, was not indisposed to loosen his hold upon the man through whose friendship he had first risen, and whose power was now perhaps on the decline. Moreover, events had now caused him to hate the French government with much fervour. With Henry IV. he had been all-powerful. His position had been altogether exceptional, and he had wielded an influence at Paris more than that exerted by any foreign ambassador. The change naturally did not please him, although he well knew the reasons. It was impossible for the Dutch ambassador to be popular at a court where Spain ruled supreme. Had he been willing to eat humiliation as with a spoon, it would not have sufficed. They knew him, they feared him, and they could not doubt that his sympathies would ever be with the malcontent princes. At the same time he did not like to lose his hold upon the place, nor to have it known, as yet, to the world that his power was diminished.

" The Queen commands me to tell you," said the French ambassador de Russy to the States-General,[1] " that the language of the Sieur Aerssens has not only astonished her, but scandalized her to that degree that she could not refrain from demanding if it came from My Lords the States or from himself. He having, however, affirmed to her Majesty that he had express charge to justify it by reasons so remote from the hope and the belief that she had conceived of your gratitude to the Most Christian King and herself, she is constrained to complain of it, and with great frankness."

[1] Speech of de Russy, 19 April 1611. (Hague Archives MS.)

Some months later than this Aerssens communicated to the States-General the project of the Spanish marriage, "which," said he, "they have declared to me with so many oaths to be false."[1]   He informed them that M. de Refuge was to go on special mission to the Hague, "having been designated to that duty before Aerssens' discovery of the marriage project."   He was to persuade their Mightinesses that the marriages were by no means concluded, and that, even if they were, their Mightinesses were not interested therein, their Majesties intending to remain by the old maxims and alliances of the late king.   Marriages, he would be instructed to say, were mere personal conventions, which remained of no consideration when the interests of the crown were touched.   "Nevertheless, I know very well," said Aerssens, "that in England these negotiations are otherwise understood, and that the King has uttered great complaints about them, saying that such a negotiation as this ought not to have been concealed from him.   He is pressing more than ever for reimbursement of the debt to him, and especially for the moneys pretended to have been furnished to your Mightinesses in his Majesty's name."[2]

Thus it will be seen how closely the Spanish marriages were connected with the immediate financial arrangements of France, England, and the States, without reference to the wider political consequences anticipated.

"The princes and most gentlemen," here continued the Ambassador, "believe that these reciprocal and double marriages will bring about great changes in Christendom if they take the course which the authors of them intend, however much they may affect to believe that no novelties are impending.   The marriages were proposed to the late king, and approved by him, during the negotiations for the

<hr>

[1] Aerssens to the States-General, 8 Nov. 1611. (Hague Archives MS.)
[2] MS. last cited.

truce, and had Don Pedro de Toledo been able to govern himself, as Jeannin has just been telling me, the United Provinces would have drawn from it their assured security. What he means by that, I certainly cannot conceive, for Don Pedro proposed the marriage of the Dauphin (now Louis XIII.) with the Infanta on the condition that Henry should renounce all friendship .with your Mightinesses, and neither openly nor secretly give you any assistance.  You were to be entirely abandoned, as an example for all who throw off the authority of their lawful prince.  But his Majesty answered very generously that he would take no conditions ; that he considered your Mightinesses as his best friends, whom he could not and would not forsake.  Upon this Don Pedro broke off the negotiation.  What should now induce the King of Spain to resume the marriage negotiations but to give up the conditions, I am sure I don't know, unless, through the truce, his designs and his ambition have grown flaccid.[1]  This I don't dare to hope, but fear, on the contrary, that he will so manage the irresolution, weakness, and faintheartedness of this kingdom as through the aid of his pensioned friends here to arrive at all his former aims."[2]

Certainly the Ambassador painted the condition of France in striking and veracious colours, and he was quite right in sending the information which he was first to discover, and which it was so important for the States to know.  It was none the less certain in Barneveld's mind that the best, not the worst, must be made of the state of affairs, and that France should not be assisted in throwing herself irrecoverably into the arms of Spain.

" Refuge will tell you," said Aerssens, a little later,[3] " that these marriages will not interfere with the friendship of

<hr>

[1] " Vermurwt."                         [2] MS. just cited.
[3] Aerssens to the States-General, 11 Jan. 1612.  (Hague Archives MS.)

France for you nor with her subsidies, and that no advantage will be given to Spain in the treaty to your detriment or that of her other allies. But whatever fine declarations they may make, it is sure to be detrimental. And all the princes, gentlemen, and officers here have the same conviction. Those of the Reformed religion believe that the transaction is directed solely against the religion which your Mightinesses profess, and that the next step will be to effect a total separation between the two religions and the two countries."

Refuge arrived soon afterwards, and made the communication [1] to the States-General of the approaching nuptials between the King of France and the Infanta of Spain, and of the Prince of Spain with Madame, eldest daughter of France, exactly as Aerssens had predicted four months before. There was a great flourish of compliments, much friendly phrase-making, and their Mightinesses were informed that the communication of the marriages was made to them before any other power had been notified, in proof of the extraordinary affection entertained for them by France. "You are so much interested in the happiness of France," said Refuge, "that this treaty by which it is secured will be for your happiness also." He did not indicate, however, the precise nature of the bliss beyond the indulgence of a sentimental sympathy, not very refreshing in the circumstances, which was to result to the Confederacy from this close alliance between their firmest friend and their ancient and deadly enemy. He would have found it difficult to do so.

"Don Rodrigo de Calderon, secretary of state, is daily expected from Spain," wrote Aerssens once more.[2] "He brings probably the articles of the marriages, which have hitherto been kept secret, so they say. 'Tis a shrewd negotiator; and in this alliance the King's chief design is to injure your Mightinesses, as M. de Villeroy now confesses, although he says that this will not be consented to on this side. It behoves your Mightinesses to use all your ears and eyes. It is certain these are much more than private conventions. Yes, there is nothing private about them, save the conjunction of the persons whom they concern. In short, all the conditions regard directly the state, and directly likewise, or by necessary consequence, the state of your Mightinesses' Provinces. I reserve explanations until it shall please your Mightinesses to hear me by word of mouth."

For it was now taken into consideration by the States' government whether Aerssens was to remain at his post or to return. Whether it was his wish to be relieved of his embassy or not was a question. But there was no question that the States at this juncture, and in spite of the dangers impending from the Spanish marriages, must have an ambassador ready to do his best to keep France from prematurely sliding into positive hostility to them. Aerssens was enigmatical in his language, and Barneveld was somewhat puzzled.

"I have according to your reiterated requests," wrote the Advocate to the Ambassador, "sounded the assembly of My Lords the States as to your recall; but I find among some gentlemen the opinion that if earnestly pressed to continue you would be willing to listen to the proposal. This I cannot make out from your letters. Please to advise me frankly as to your wishes, and assure yourself in everything of my friendship."[1]

Nothing could be more straightforward than this language, but the Envoy was less frank than Barneveld, as will subsequently appear. The subject was a most important one, not only in its relation to the great affairs of state,

<hr>

[1] Barneveld to Aerssens, 2 April 1611.  (Hague Archives MS.)

but to momentous events touching the fate of illustrious personages.

Meantime a resolution was passed by the States of Holland[1] "in regard to the question whether Ambassador Aerssens should retain his office, yes or no?"  And it was decided by a majority of votes "to leave it to his candid opinion if in his free conscience he thinks he can serve the public cause there any longer.  If yes, he may keep his office one year more.  If no, he may take leave and come home.  In no case is his salary to be increased." *May 11, 1611.*

Surely the States, under the guidance of the Advocate, had thus acted with consummate courtesy towards a diplomatist whose position from no apparent fault of his own but by the force of circumstances—and rather to his credit than otherwise—was gravely compromised.

[1] Van Rees and Brill, 512, *sqq.*

# CHAPTER VI.

Establishment of the *Condominium* in the Duchies — Dissensions between the Neuburgers and Brandenburgers — Occupation of Jülich by the Brandenburgers assisted by the States-General — Indignation in Spain and at the Court of the Archdukes — Subsidy despatched to Brussels — Spinola descends upon Aix-la-Chapelle and takes possession of Orsoy and other places — Surrender of Wesel — Conference at Xanten — Treaty permanently dividing the Territory between Brandenburg and Neuburg — Prohibition from Spain — Delays and Disagreements.

Thus the *Condominium* had been peaceably established.

Three or four years passed away in the course of which the evils of a joint and undivided sovereignty of two rival houses over the same territory could not fail to manifest themselves. Brandenburg, Calvinist in religion, and for other reasons more intimately connected with and more favoured by the States' government than his rival, gained ground in the duchies. The Palatine of Neuburg, originally of Lutheran faith like his father, soon manifested Catholic tendencies, which excited suspicion in the Netherlands. These suspicions grew into certainties at the moment when he espoused the sister of Maximilian of Bavaria and of the Elector of Cologne. That this close connection with the very heads of the Catholic League could bode no good to the cause of which the States-General were the great promoters was self-evident. Very soon afterwards the Palatine, a man of mature age and of considerable talents, openly announced his conversion to the ancient church. Obviously the sympathies of the States could not thenceforth fail to be on the side of Brandenburg. The Elector's brother died,

and was succeeded in the governorship of the *Condominium*
by the Elector's brother, a youth of eighteen. He took up
his abode in Cleve, leaving Düsseldorf to be the sole residence of his co-stadholder.

Rivalry growing warmer, on account of this difference of
religion, between the respective partisans of Neuburg and
Brandenburg, an attempt was made in Düsseldorf by a
sudden entirely unsuspected rising of the Brandenburgers
to drive their antagonist colleagues and their portion of the
garrison out of the city. It failed, but excited great anger.
A more successful effort was soon afterwards made in Jülich ;
the Neuburgers were driven out, and the Brandenburgers
remained in sole possession of the town and citadel, far the
most important stronghold in the whole territory. This
was partly avenged by the Neuburgers, who gained absolute
control of Düsseldorf.[1] Here were however no important
fortifications, the place being merely an agreeable palatial
residence and a thriving mart. The States-General, not
concealing their predilection for Brandenburg, but under
pretext of guarding the peace which they had done so much
to establish, placed a garrison of 1000 infantry and a troop
or two of horse in the citadel of Jülich.

Dire was the anger not unjustly excited in Spain when
the news of this violation of neutrality reached that government. Jülich, placed midway between Liège and Cologne,
and commanding those fertile plains which make up the
opulent duchy, seemed virtually converted into a province
of the detested heretical republic. The German gate of the
Spanish Netherlands was literally in the hands of its most
formidable foe.

The Spaniards about the court of the Archduke did not

---

[1] Bentivoglio. 'Relazione della
Mossa d' arme che segui in Fiandra
d' anno 1614 per haver le Provincie
Unite occupato la Terra e Castello
di Giuliers,' &c. ('Opere,' ed. Parigi.
1747.)

dissemble their rage. The seizure of Jülich was a stain upon his reputation, they cried. Was it not enough, they asked, for the United Provinces to have made a truce to the manifest detriment and discredit of Spain, and to have treated her during all the negotiation with such insolence? Were they now to be permitted to invade neutral territory, to violate public faith, to act under no responsibility save to their own will? What was left for them to do except to set up a tribunal in Holland for giving laws to the whole of Northern Europe? Arrogating to themselves absolute power over the controverted states of Cleve, Jülich, and the dependencies, they now pretended to dispose of them at their pleasure in order at the end insolently to take possession of them for themselves.

These were the egregious fruits of the truce, they said tauntingly to the discomfited Archduke. It had caused a loss of reputation, the very soul of empires, to the crown of Spain. And now, to conclude her abasement, the troops in Flanders had been shaven down with such parsimony as to make the monarch seem a shopkeeper, not a king. One would suppose the obedient Netherlands to be in the heart of Spain rather than outlying provinces surrounded by their deadliest enemies. The heretics had gained possession of the government at Aix-la-Chapelle; they had converted the insignificant town of Mülheim into a thriving and fortified town in defiance of Cologne and to its manifest detriment, and in various other ways they had insulted the Catholics throughout those regions. And who could wonder at such insolence, seeing that the army in Flanders, formerly the terror of heretics, had become since the truce so weak as to be the laughing-stock of the United Provinces?[1] If it was expensive to maintain these armies in the obedient Netherlands, let there be economy elsewhere, they urged.

---

[1] Bentivoglio, 'Relazione,' &c.

From India came gold and jewels.  From other kingdoms came ostentation and a long series of vain titles for the crown of Spain.  Flanders was its place of arms, its nursery of soldiers, its bulwark in Europe, and so it should be preserved.[1]

There was ground for these complaints.  The army at the disposition of the Archduke had been reduced to 8000 infantry and a handful of cavalry.  The peace establishment of the Republic amounted to 20,000 foot, 3000 horse, besides the French and English regiments.[2]

So soon as the news of the occupation of Jülich was officially communicated to the Spanish cabinet, a subsidy of 400,000 crowns was at once despatched to Brussels.  Levies of Walloons and Germans were made without delay by order of Archduke Albert and under guidance of Spinola, so that by midsummer the army was swollen to 18,000 foot and 3000 horse.  With these the great Genoese captain took the field in the middle of August.  On the 22nd of that month the army was encamped on some plains mid-  Aug. 22, 1614.
way between Maestricht and Aachen.  There was profound mystery both at Brussels and at the Hague as to the objective point of these military movements.  Anticipating an attack upon Jülich, the States had meantime strengthened the garrison of that important place with 3000 infantry and a regiment of horse.  It seemed scarcely probable therefore that Spinola would venture a foolhardy blow at a citadel so well fortified and defended.  Moreover, there was not only no declaration of war, but strict orders had been given by each of the apparent belligerents to their military commanders to abstain from all offensive movements against the adversary.  And now began one of the strangest series of warlike evolutions that were ever recorded.  Maurice at the head of an army of 14,000 foot and 3000 horse manœuvred in the

[1] Bentivoglio, 'Relazione,' &c.[2] Ibid.

neighbourhood of his great antagonist and professional rival without exchanging a blow.  It was a phantom campaign, the prophetic rehearsal of dreadful marches and tragic histories yet to be, and which were to be enacted on that very stage and on still wider ones during a whole generation of mankind.  That cynical commerce in human lives which was to become one of the chief branches of human industry in the century had already begun.

Spinola, after hovering for a few days in the neighbourhood, descended upon the Imperial city of Aachen (Aix-la-Chapelle).  This had been one of the earliest towns in Germany to embrace the Reformed religion, and up to the close of the sixteenth century the control of the magistracy had been in the hands of the votaries of that creed.  Subsequently the Catholics had contrived to acquire and keep the municipal ascendency, secretly supported by Archduke Albert, and much oppressing the Protestants with imprisonments, fines, and banishment, until a new revolution which had occurred in the year 1610, and which aroused the wrath of Spinola.[1]  Certainly, according to the ideas of that day, it did not seem unnatural in a city where a very large majority of the population were Protestants that Protestants should have a majority in the town council.[2]  It seemed, however, to those who surrounded the Archduke an outrage which could no longer be tolerated, especially as a garrison of 600 Germans, supposed to have formed part of the States' army, had recently been introduced into the town.  Aachen, lying mostly on an extended plain, had but very slight fortifications, and it was commanded by a neighbouring range of hills.  It had no garrison but the 600 Germans.  Spinola placed a battery or two on the hills, and within three days the town surrendered.  The

<hr>

[1] Grotii 'Hist.' lxvii. p. 472.  Wagenaar, x. 74, 75.
[2] Bentivoglio, 'Relazione,' &c.

inhabitants expected a scene of carnage and pillage, but not a life was lost.  No injury whatever was inflicted on person or property, according to the strict injunctions of the Archduke.  The 600 Germans were driven out, and 1200 other Germans then serving under Catholic banners were put in their places to protect the Catholic minority, to whose keeping the municipal government was now confided.[1]

Spinola, then entering the territory of Cleve, took possession of Orsoy, an important place on the Rhine, besides Düren, Duisburg, Kaster, Greevenbroek, and Berchem.  Leaving garrisons in these places, he razed the fortifications of Mülheim, much to the joy of the Archbishop and his faithful subjects of Cologne, then crossed the Rhine at Rheinberg, and swooped down upon Wesel.  This flourishing and prosperous city had formerly belonged to the <sub>Sept. 7, 1614.</sub> Duchy of Cleve.  Placed at the junction of the Rhine and Lippe and commanding both rivers, it had become both powerful and Protestant, and had set itself up as a free Imperial city, recognising its dukes no longer as sovereigns, but only as protectors.  So fervent was it in the practice of the Reformed religion that it was called the Rhenish Geneva, the very cradle of German Calvinism.  So important was its preservation considered to the cause of Protestantism that the States-General had urged its authorities to accept from them a garrison.  They refused.  Had they complied, the city would have been saved, because it was the rule in this extraordinary campaign that the belligerents made war not upon each other, nor in each other's territory, but against neutrals and upon neutral soil.  The Catholic forces under Spinola or his lieutenants, meeting occasionally and accidentally with the Protestants under Maurice or his generals, exchanged no cannon shots or buffets, but only acts of courtesy ; falling away each before the other, and each ceding to the other

---

[1] Bentivoglio, ' Relazione,' &c.  Wagenaar, x. 76.

with extreme politeness the possession of towns which one had preceded the other in besieging.[1]

The citizens of Wesel were amazed at being attacked, considering themselves as Imperial burghers. They regretted too late that they had refused a garrison from Maurice, which would have prevented Spinola from assailing them. They had now nothing for it but to surrender, which they did within three days. The principal condition of the capitulation was that when Jülich should be given up by the States Wesel should be restored to its former position. Spinola then took and garrisoned the city of Xanten, but went no further. Having weakened his army sufficiently by the garrisons taken from it for the cities captured by him, he declined to make any demonstration upon the neighbouring and important towns of Emmerich and Rees. The Catholic commander falling back, the Protestant moved forward. Maurice seized both Emmerich and Rees, and placed garrisons within them, besides occupying Goch, Kranenburg, Gennip, and various places in the County of Mark. This closed the amicable campaign.[2]

Spinola established himself and his forces near Wesel. The Prince encamped near Rees. The two armies were within two hours' march of each other. The Duke of Neuburg—for the Palatine had now succeeded on his father's death to the ancestral dukedom and to his share of the *Condominium* of the debateable provinces—now joined Spinola with an army of 4000 foot and 400 horse. The young Prince of Brandenburg came to Maurice with 800 cavalry and an infantry regiment of the Elector-Palatine.

Negotiations destined to be as spectral and fleeting as the campaign had been illusory now began. The whole Protestant world was aflame with indignation at the loss of Wesel. The States' government had already proposed to

---

[1] Wagenaar, x. 76.  Bentivoglio.
[2] Baudartius, vi. 42, 43.  Wagenaar, x. 76, 77.  Bentivoglio.

deposit Jülich in the hands of a neutral power if the Archduke would abstain from military movements.  But Albert,
proud of his achievements in Aachen, refused to pause in
his career.  Let them make the deposit first, he said.

Both belligerents, being now satiated with such military
glory as could flow from the capture of defenceless cities
belonging to neutrals, agreed to hold conferences at Xanten.
To this town, in the Duchy of Cleve, and midway between
the rival camps, came Sir Henry Wotton and Sir Dudley
Carleton, ambassadors of Great Britain ; de Refuge and de
Russy, the special and the resident ambassador of France at
the Hague ; Chancellor Peter Pecquius and Counsellor Visser,
to represent the Archdukes ; seven deputies from the United
Provinces, three from the Elector of Cologne, three from
Brandenburg, three from Neuburg, and two from the Elector-
Palatine, as representative of the Protestant League.[1]

In the earlier conferences the envoys of the Archduke
and of the Elector of Cologne were left out, but they were
informed daily of each step in the negotiation.  The most
important point at starting was thought to be to get rid of
the *Condominium*.  There could be no harmony nor peace
in joint possession.  The whole territory should be cut
provisionally in halves, and each possessory prince rule
exclusively within the portion assigned to him.  There
might also be an exchange of domain between the two every
six months.  As for Wesel and Jülich, they could remain
respectively in the hands then holding them, or the fortifications of Jülich might be dismantled and Wesel restored
to the *status quo*.[2]  The latter alternative would have best
suited the States, who were growing daily more irritated at
seeing Wesel, that Protestant stronghold, with an exclusively
Calvinistic population, in the hands of Catholics.

The Spanish ambassador at Brussels remonstrated, how-

<hr>

[1] Wagenaar, x. 78–80.          [2] Ibid. Bentivoglio.

ever, at the thought of restoring his precious conquest, obtained without loss of time, money, or blood, into the hands of heretics, at least before consultation with the government at Madrid and without full consent of the King.

"How important to your Majesty's affairs in Flanders," wrote Guadaleste to Philip, "is the acquisition of Wesel may be seen by the manifest grief of your enemies. They see with immense displeasure your royal ensigns planted on the most important place on the Rhine, and one which would become the chief military station for all the armies of Flanders to assemble in at any moment.

"As no acquisition could therefore be greater, so your Majesty should never be deprived of it without thorough consideration of the case. The Archduke fears, and so do his ministers, that if we refuse to restore Wesel, the United Provinces would break the truce. For my part I believe, and there are many who agree with me, that they would on the contrary be more inclined to stand by the truce, hoping to obtain by negotiation that which it must be obvious to them they cannot hope to capture by force. But let Wesel be at once restored. Let that be done which is so much desired by the United Provinces and other great enemies and rivals of your Majesty, and what security will there be that the same Provinces will not again attempt the same invasion ? Is not the example of Jülich fresh ? And how much more important is Wesel ! Jülich was after all not situate on their frontiers, while Wesel lies at their principal gates. Your Majesty now sees the good and upright intentions of those Provinces and their friends. They have made a settlement between Brandenburg and Neuburg, not in order to breed concord but confusion between those two, not tranquillity for the country, but greater turbulence than ever before. Nor have they done this with any other thought than that the United Provinces might find new opportunities to derive the same profit from fresh tumults as they have already done so shamelessly from those which are past. After all I don't say that Wesel should never be restored, if circumstances require it, and if your Majesty, approving the Treaty of Xanten, should sanction the measure. But such a result should be reached only after full consultation with your Majesty, to whose glorious military exploits these splendid results are chiefly owing." [1]

The treaty finally decided upon rejected the principle of alternate possession, and established a permanent division of the territory in dispute between Brandenburg and Neuburg.

The two portions were to be made as equal as possible, and lots were to be thrown or drawn by the two princes for the first choice. To the one side were assigned the Duchy of Cleve, the County of Mark, and the Seigniories of Ravensberg and Ravenstein, with some other baronies and feuds in Brabant and Flanders ; to the other the Duchies of Jülich and Berg with their dependencies. Each prince was to reside exclusively within the territory assigned to him by lot. The troops introduced by either party were to be withdrawn, fortifications made since the preceding month of May to be razed, and all persons who had been expelled, or who had emigrated, to be restored to their offices, property, or benefices. It was also stipulated that no place within the whole debateable territory should be put in the hands of a third power. [2]

These articles were signed by the ambassadors of France and England, by the deputies of the Elector-Palatine and of the United Provinces, all binding their superiors to the execution of the treaty. The arrangement was supposed to refer to the previous conventions between those two crowns,

Dec.<br>1614.

---

[1] Bentivoglio, ' Relazione,' &c.
[2] Ibid. Wagenaar, x. 78, 79.

with the Republic, and the Protestant princes and powers. Count Zollern, whom we have seen bearing himself so arrogantly as envoy from the Emperor Rudolph to Henry IV., was now despatched by Matthias on as fruitless a mission to the congress at Xanten, and did his best to prevent the signature of the treaty, except with full concurrence of the Imperial government. He likewise renewed the frivolous proposition that the Emperor should hold all the provinces in sequestration until the question of rightful sovereignty should be decided. The "proud and haggard" ambassador was not more successful in this than in the diplomatic task previously entrusted to him, and he then went to Brussels, there to renew his remonstrances, menaces, and intrigues.

For the treaty thus elaborately constructed, and in appearance a triumphant settlement of questions so complicated and so burning as to threaten to set Christendom at any moment in a blaze, was destined to an impotent and most unsatisfactory conclusion.

The signatures were more easily obtained than the ratifications. Execution was surrounded with insurmountable difficulties which in negotiation had been lightly skipped over at the stroke of a pen. At the very first step, that of military evacuation, there was a stumble. Maurice and Spinola were expected to withdraw their forces, and to undertake to bring in no troops in the future, and to make no invasion of the disputed territory.

But Spinola construed this undertaking as absolute; the Prince as only binding in consequence of, with reference to, and for the duration of, the Treaty of Xanten. The ambassadors and other commissioners, disgusted with the long controversy which ensued, were making up their minds to depart when a courier arrived from Spain, bringing not a ratification but strict prohibition of the treaty. The articles were not to be executed, no change whatever was to be made, and, above all, Wesel was not to be restored without fresh negotiations with Philip, followed by his explicit concurrence.[1]

Thus the whole great negotiation began to dissolve into a shadowy, unsatisfactory pageant. The solid barriers which were to imprison the vast threatening elements of religious animosity and dynastic hatreds, and to secure a peaceful future for Christendom, melted into films of gossamer, and the great war of demons/ no longer to be quelled by the commonplaces of diplomatic exorcism, revealed its close approach. The prospects of Europe grew blacker than ever.

The ambassadors, thoroughly disheartened and disgusted, all took their departure from Xanten, and the treaty remained rather a by-word than a solution or even a suggestion

"The accord could not be prevented," wrote Archduke Albert to Philip, "because it depended alone on the will of the signers. Nor can the promise to restore Wesel be violated, should Jülich be restored. Who can doubt that such contravention would arouse great jealousies in France, England, the United Provinces, and all the members of the heretic League of Germany? Who can dispute that those interested ought to procure the execution of the treaty? Suspicions will not remain suspicions, but they light up the flames of public evil and disturbance. Either your Majesty wishes to maintain the truce, in which case Wesel must be restored, or to break the truce, a result which is certain if Wesel be retained. But the reasons which induced your Majesty to lay down your arms remain the same as ever. Our affairs are not looking better, nor is the requisition of Wesel of so great importance as to justify our involving Flanders in a new and more atrocious war than that which

[1] Wagenaar, Bentivoglio, Baudartius, *ubi sup.*

has so lately been suspended. The restitution is due to the tribunal of public faith. It is a great advantage when actions done for the sole end of justice are united to that of utility. Consider the great successes we have had. How well the affairs of Aachen and Mülheim have been arranged ; those of the Duke of Neuburg how completely re-established. The Catholic cause, always identical with that of the House of Austria, remains in great superiority to the cause of the heretics. We should use these advantages well, and to do so we should not immaturely pursue greater ones. Fortune changes, flies when we most depend on her, and delights in making her chief sport of the highest quality of mortals." [1]

Thus wrote the Archduke sensibly, honourably from his point of view, and with an intelligent regard to the interests of Spain and the Catholic cause. After months of delay came conditional consent from Madrid to the conventions, but with express condition that there should be absolute undertaking on the part of the United Provinces never to send or maintain troops in the duchies. Tedious and futile correspondence followed between Brussels, the Hague, London, Paris. But the difficulties grew every moment. It was a Penelope's web of negotiation, said one of the envoys. Amid pertinacious and wire-drawn subtleties, every trace of practical business vanished. Neuburg departed to look after his patrimonial estates, leaving his interests in the duchies to be watched over by the Archduke. Even Count Zollern, after six months of wrangling in Brussels, took his departure. Prince Maurice distributed his army in various places within the debateable land, and Spinola did the same, leaving a garrison of 3000 foot and 300 horse in the important city of Wesel. The town and citadel of Jülich were as firmly held by Maurice for the

<hr>

[1] Bentivoglio, 'Relazione.'

Protestant cause. Thus the duchies were jointly occupied by the forces of Catholicism and Protestantism, while nominally possessed and administered by the princes of Brandenburg and Neuburg. And so they were destined to remain until that Thirty Years' War, now so near its outbreak, should sweep over the earth, and bring its fiery solution at last to all these great debates.

# CHAPTER VII.



THUS the Republic had placed itself in as proud a position as it was possible for commonwealth or kingdom to
occupy.   It had dictated the policy and directed the
combined military movements of Protestantism.   It had
gathered into a solid mass the various elements out of
which the great Germanic mutiny against Rome, Spain, and
Austria had been compounded.   A breathing space of un-
certain duration had come to interrupt and postpone the
general and inevitable conflict.   Meantime the Republic
was encamped upon the enemy's soil.

France, which had hitherto commanded, now obeyed.
England, vacillating and discontented, now threatening and
now cajoling, saw for the time at least its influence over the
councils of the Netherlands neutralized by the genius of
the great statesman who still governed the Provinces,
supreme in all but name.   The hatred of the British
government towards the Republic, while in reality more
malignant than at any previous period, could now only
find vent in tremendous, theological pamphlets, composed
by the King in the form of diplomatic instructions, and
hurled almost weekly at the heads of the States-General,
by his ambassador, Dudley Carleton.

Few men hated Barneveld more bitterly than did Carleton.

I wish to describe as rapidly, but as faithfully, as I can the outline at least of the events by which one of the saddest and most superfluous catastrophes in modern history was brought about. The web was a complex one, wrought apparently of many materials ; but the more completely it is unravelled the more clearly we shall detect the presence of the few simple but elemental fibres which make up the tissue of most human destinies, whether illustrious or obscure, and out of which the most moving pictures of human history are composed.

The religious element, which seems at first view to be the all pervading and controlling one, is in reality rather the atmosphere which surrounds and colours than the essence which constitutes the tragedy to be delineated.

Personal, sometimes even paltry, jealousy ; love of power, of money, of place ; rivalry between civil and military ambition for predominance in a free state ; struggles between Church and State to control and oppress each other ; conflict between the cautious and healthy, but provincial and centrifugal, spirit on the one side, and the ardent centralizing, imperial, but dangerous, instinct on the other, for ascendency in a federation ; mortal combat between aristocracy disguised in the plebeian form of trading and political corporations and democracy sheltering itself under a famous sword and an ancient and illustrious name ;—all these principles and passions will be found hotly at work in the melancholy five years with which we are now to be occupied, as they have entered, and will always enter, into every political combination in the great tragi-comedy which we call human history. As a study, a lesson, and a warning, perhaps the fate of Barneveld is as deserving of serious attention as most political tragedies of the last few centuries.

Francis Aerssens, as we have seen, continued to be the Dutch ambassador after the murder of Henry IV. Many of the preceding pages of this volume have been occupied with his opinions, his pictures, his conversations, and his political intrigues during a memorable epoch in the history of the Netherlands and of France. He was beyond all doubt one of the ablest diplomatists in Europe. Versed in many languages, a classical student, familiar with history and international law, a man of the world and familiar with its usages, accustomed to associate with dignity and tact on friendliest terms with sovereigns, eminent statesmen, and men of letters ; endowed with a facile tongue, a fluent pen, and an eye and ear of singular acuteness and delicacy ; distinguished for unflagging industry and singular aptitude for secret and intricate affairs ;—he had by the exercise of these various qualities during a period of nearly twenty years at the court of Henry the Great been able to render inestimable services to the Republic which he represented. Of respectable but not distinguished lineage, not a Hollander, but a Belgian by birth, son of Cornelis Aerssens, Greffier of the States-General, long employed in that important post, he had been brought forward from a youth by Barneveld and early placed by him in the diplomatic career, of which through his favour and his own eminent talents he had now achieved the highest honours.

He had enjoyed the intimacy and even the confidence of Henry IV., so far as any man could be said to possess that monarch's confidence, and his friendly relations and familiar access to the King gave him political advantages superior to those of any of his colleagues at the same court.[1]

Acting entirely and faithfully according to the instruc-

[1] I pass over with disdain one of the causes which scandalous chronicles once assigned to the influence of the Dutch ambassador, being satisfied that the rumour was as malignant and false as political rumours often are.

tions of the Advocate of Holland, he always gratefully and copiously acknowledged the privilege of being guided and sustained in the difficult paths he had to traverse by so powerful and active an intellect.  I have seldom alluded in terms to the instructions and despatches of the chief, but every position, negotiation, and opinion of the envoy—and the reader has seen many of them—is pervaded by their spirit.  Certainly the correspondence of Aerssens is full to overflowing of gratitude, respect, fervent attachment to the person and exalted appreciation of the intellect and high character of the Advocate.[1]

There can be no question of Aerssen's consummate abilities.  Whether his heart were as sound as his head, whether his protestations of devotion had the ring of true gold or not, time would show.  Hitherto Barneveld had not doubted him, nor had he found cause to murmur at Barneveld.

But the France of Henry IV., where the Dutch envoy was so all-powerful, had ceased to exist.  A duller eye than that of Aerssens could have seen at a glance that the potent kingdom and firm ally of the Republic had been converted, for a long time to come at least, into a Spanish province.  The double Spanish marriages (that of the young Louis XIII. with the Infanta Anna, and of his sister with the Infante, one day to be Philip IV.), were now certain, for it was to make them certain that the knife of Ravaillac had been employed.  The condition precedent to those marriages had long been known.  It was the renunciation of the alliance between France and Holland.  It was the condemnation to death, so far as France had the power to condemn her to death, of the young Republic.  Had not Don Pedro de Toledo pompously announced this condition a year and a

<hr>

[1]  Correspondence of Aerssens with Barneveld.  (Royal Archives, Hague, MSS. *passim.*)

half before ?    Had not Henry spurned the bribe with scorn ?
And now had not Francis Aerssens been the first to communicate to his masters the fruit which had already ripened
upon Henry's grave ?    As we have seen, he had revealed
these intrigues long before they were known to the world,
and the French court knew that he had revealed them.
His position had become untenable.    His friendship for
Henry could not be of use to him with the delicate-featured,
double-chinned, smooth and sluggish Florentine, who had
passively authorized and actively profited by her husband's
murder.

It was time for the Envoy to be gone.    The Queen-Regent
and Concini thought so.    And so did Villeroy and Sillery
and the rest of the old servants of the King, now become
pensionaries of Spain.    But Aerssens did not think so.    He
liked his position, changed as it was.    He was deep in the
plottings of Bouillon and Condé and the other malcontents
against the Queen-Regent.    These schemes, being entirely
personal, the rank growth of the corruption and apparent
disintegration of France, were perpetually changing, and
could be reduced to no principle.    It was a mere struggle
of the great lords of France to wrest places, money, governments, military commands from the Queen-Regent, and
frantic attempts on her part to save as much as possible of
the general wreck for her lord and master Concini.

It was ridiculous to ascribe any intense desire on the
part of the Duc de Bouillon to aid the Protestant cause
against Spain at that moment, acting as he was in combination with Condé, whom we have just seen employed by
Spain as the chief instrument to effect the destruction of
France and the bastardy of the Queen's children.    Nor did
the sincere and devout Protestants who had clung to the
cause through good and bad report, men like Duplessis-
Mornay, for example, and those who usually acted with him,

believe in any of these schemes for partitioning France on pretence of saving Protestantism. But Bouillon, greatest of all French fishermen in troubled waters, was brother-in-law of Prince Maurice of Nassau, and Aerssens instinctively felt that the time had come when he should anchor himself to firm holding ground at home.

The Ambassador had also a personal grievance. Many of his most secret despatches to the States-General in which he expressed himself very freely, forcibly, and accurately on the general situation in France, especially in regard to the Spanish marriages and the Treaty of Hampton Court, had been transcribed at the Hague and copies of them sent to the French government. No baser act of treachery to an envoy could be imagined. It was not surprising that Aerssens complained bitterly of the deed. He secretly suspected Barneveld, but with injustice, of having played him this evil turn, and the incident first planted the seeds of the deadly hatred which was to bear such fatal fruit.

" A notable treason has been played upon me," he wrote to Jacques de Maldere, " which has outraged my heart. All the despatches which I have been sending for several months to M. de Barneveld have been communicated by copy in whole or in extracts to this court. Villeroy quoted from them at our interview to-day, and I was left as it were without power of reply. The despatches were long, solid, omitting no particularity for giving means to form the best judgment of the designs and intrigues of this court. No greater damage could be done to me and my usefulness. All those from whom I have hitherto derived information, princes and great personages, will shut themselves up from me. . . . What can be more ticklish than to pass judgment on the tricks of those who are governing this state ? This single blow has knocked me down completely. For I was moving about among all of them, making my profit of all, without any reserve. M. de Barneveld knew by this means the condition of this kingdom as well as I do. Certainly in a well-ordered republic it would cost the life of a man who had thus trifled with the reputation of an ambassador. I believe M. de Barneveld will be sorry, but this will never restore to me the confidence which I have lost. If one was jealous of my position at this court, certainly I deserved rather pity from those who should contemplate it closely. If one wished to procure my downfall in order to raise oneself above me, there was no need of these tricks. I have been offering to resign my embassy this long time, which will now produce nothing but thorns for me. How can I negotiate after my private despatches have been read? L'Hoste, the clerk of Villeroy, was not so great a criminal as the man who revealed my despatches; and L'Hoste was torn by four horses after his death. Four months long I have been complaining of this to M. de Barneveld. . . . Patience! I am groaning without being able to hope for justice. I console myself, for my term of office will soon arrive. Would that my embassy could have finished under the agreeable and friendly circumstances with which it began. The man who may succeed me will not find that this vile trick will help him much. . . . Pray find out whence and from whom this intrigue has come." [1]

Certainly an envoy's position could hardly be more utterly compromised. Most unquestionably Aerssens had reason to be indignant, believing as he did that his conscientious efforts in the service of his government had been made use of by his chief to undermine his credit and blast his character. There was an intrigue between the newly appointed French minister, de Russy, at the Hague and the enemies of Aerssens to represent him to his own government as mischievous, passionate, unreasonably vehement in sup-

---

[1] Aerssens to Maldere, 26 Feb. 1611. (Hague Archives MS.)

porting the claims and dignity of his own country at the court to which he was accredited. Not often in diplomatic history has an ambassador of a free state been censured or removed for believing and maintaining in controversy that his own government is in the right. It was natural that the French government should be disturbed by the vivid light which he had flashed upon their pernicious intrigues with Spain to the detriment of the Republic, and at the pertinacity with which he resisted their preposterous claim to be reimbursed for one-third of the money which the late king had advanced as a free subsidy towards the war of the Netherlands for independence. But no injustice could be more outrageous than for the Envoy's own government to unite with the foreign State in damaging the character of its own agent for the crime of fidelity to itself.

Of such cruel perfidy Aerssens had been the victim, and he most wrongfully suspected his chief as its real perpetrator.

The claim for what was called the "Third" had been invented after the death of Henry. As already explained, the "Third" was not a gift from England to the Netherlands. It was a loan from England to France, or more properly a consent to abstain from pressing for payment for this proportion of an old debt. James, who was always needy, had often desired, but never obtained, the payment of this sum from Henry. Now that the King was dead, he applied to the Regent's government, and the Regent's government called upon the Netherlands, to pay the money.

Aerssens, as the agent of the Republic, protested firmly against such claim. The money had been advanced by the King as a free gift, as his contribution to a war in which he was deeply interested, although he was nominally at peace with Spain. As to the private arrangements between France and England, the Republic, said the Dutch envoy, was in no sense bound by them.  He was no party to the Treaty of Hampton Court, and knew nothing of its stipulations.[1]

Courtiers and politicians in plenty at the French court, now that Henry was dead, were quite sure that they had heard him say over and over again that the Netherlands had bound themselves to pay the Third.  They persuaded Mary de' Medici that she likewise had often heard him say so, and induced her to take high ground on the subject in her interviews with Aerssens.  The luckless queen, who was always in want of money to satisfy the insatiable greed of her favourites, and to buy off the enmity of the great princes, was very vehement—although she knew as much of those transactions as of the finances of Prester John or the Lama of Thibet—in maintaining this claim of her government upon the States.

"After talking with the ministers," said Aerssens, "I had an interview with the Queen.  I knew that she had been

---

[1] " Ils me disent . . . qu'ils ont tous la mémoire assez fraiche pour se souvenir que le feu Roy avait parlé souvent et étoit résol u d'obliger Messieurs les États à reconnaître ce qui a été fourny au nom du Roi de Grande Bretagne, se contentant de ne nous rien demander des deux tiers payés pour sa part.  S'il vivait il s'abahiroit de cette excuse. . . . Ma repartye étoit que nous avons reçu ce secours pour pur don employé par nos voisins en notre guerre par raison d'état, pour notre défense et occupation de leur ennemy, que en l'envoyant on ne nous a point parlé ni d'obligation ni de restitution."—Aerssens to Maldere, 26 Feb. 1611. (Hague Arch. MS.)

" . . . je n'ay pas jugé cette demande moins esloignée de la volonté du feu Roy que de la raison.  Ce tiers n'a jamais été distingué des autres deux, on ne nous a point dit qu'il a été fourny au nom du Roy de la G. Bretagne.  Nos acquits desquels on s'est contenté n'en font nulle mention, et nous avons employé cette somme comme les autres qui ont fait accroitre (?) la dépense de nos préparatifs sans que ayons jamais fait estat d'en rien rendre ni eux de le prétendre.  Le traité fait en Angleterre a été negocié entre le Roy et M. de Sully.  Vous, Monsieur, qui lors y étiez présent n'y intervinstes jamais pour ouyr la distinction de ces payements quand la protestation a été faicte contre la continuation de ce traité.  Elle ne vous a point été insinuée, et d'ici on ne s'est pas départ y d'en continuer le payement de manière que nous devons, et de faict pouvons ignorer ce qu'il ait rien traité entre ces deux couronnes que nous ait peu concerner.  On me reproche là dessus notre ingratitude de ne vouloir pas seulement avouer par écrit qu'avons reçu ce Tiers au nom des Anglois.  Je les renvoye à l'inspection de nos acquits."—Same to same, 28 Aug. 1610.

taught her lesson, to insist on the payment of the Third.  So I did not speak at all of the matter, but talked exclusively and at length of the French regiments in the States' service. She was embarrassed, and did not know exactly what to say. At last, without replying a single word to what I had been saying, she became very red in the face, and asked me if I were not instructed to speak of the money due to England. Whereupon I spoke in the sense already indicated.  She interrupted me by saying she had a perfect recollection that the late king intended and understood that we were to pay the Third to England, and had talked with her very seriously on the subject.  If he were living, he would think it very strange, she said, that we refused ; and so on.

"Soissons, too, pretends to remember perfectly that such were the King's intentions.  'Tis a very strange thing, Sir. Every one knows now the secrets of the late king, if you are willing to listen.  Yet he was not in the habit of taking all the world into his confidence.  The Queen takes her opinions as they give them to her.  'Tis a very good princess, but I am sorry she is so ignorant of affairs.  As she says she remembers, one is obliged to say one believes her.  But I, who knew the King so intimately, and saw him so constantly, know that he could only have said that the Third was paid in acquittal of his debts to and for account of the King of England, and not that we were to make restitution thereof.  The Chancellor tells me my refusal has been taken as an affront by the Queen, and Puysieux says t is a contempt which she can't swallow." [1]

Aerssens on his part remained firm ; his pertinacity being the greater as he thoroughly understood the subject which he was talking about, an advantage which was rarely shared in by those with whom he conversed.  The Queen, highly scandalized by his demeanour, became from that time forth

<hr>

[1] Aerssens to Barneveld, 13 April 1611.  (Hague Arch. MS.)

his bitter enemy, and, as already stated, was resolved to be rid of him.

Nor was the Envoy at first desirous of remaining. He had felt after Henry's death and Sully's disgrace, and the complete transformation of the France which he had known, that his power of usefulness was gone. "Our enemies," he said, "have got the advantage which I used to have in times past, and I recognize a great coldness towards us, which is increasing every day."[1] Nevertheless, he yielded reluctantly to Barneveld's request that he should for the time at least remain at his post. Later on, as the intrigues against him began to unfold themselves, and his faithful services were made use of at home to blacken his character and procure his removal, he refused to resign, as to do so would be to play into the hands of his enemies, and by inference at least to accuse himself of infidelity to his trust.

But his concealed rage and his rancor grew more deadly every day. He was fully aware of the plots against him, although he found it difficult to trace them to their source.

"I doubt not," he wrote to Jacques de Maldere, the distinguished diplomatist and senator, who had recently returned from his embassy to England, "that this beautiful proposition of de Russy has been sent to your Province of Zealand. Does it not seem to you a plot well woven as well in Holland as at this court to remove me from my post with disreputation? What have I done that should cause the Queen to disapprove my proceedings? Since the death of the late king I have always opposed the Third, which they have been trying to fix upon the treasury, on the ground that Henry never spoke to me of restitution, that the receipts given were simple ones, and that the money given was spent for the common benefit of France and the States under direction of the King's government. But I am

---

[1] Aerssens to Barneveld, 31 Aug. 1610. (Hague Archives MS.)

expected here to obey M. de Villeroy, who says that it was the intention of the late king to oblige us to make the payment. I am not accustomed to obey authority if it be not supported by reason. It is for my masters to reply and to defend me. The Queen has no reason to complain. I have maintained the interests of my superiors. But this is not the cause of the complaints. My misfortune is that all my despatches have been sent from Holland in copy to this court. Most of them contained free pictures of the condition and dealings of those who govern here. M. de Villeroy has found himself depicted often, and now under pretext of a public negotiation he has found an opportunity of revenging himself. . . . Besides this cause which Villeroy has found for combing my head, Russy has given notice here that I have kept my masters in the hopes of being honourably exempted from the claims of this government. The long letter which I wrote to M. de Barneveld justifies my proceedings." [1]

It is no wonder that the Ambassador was galled to the quick by the outrage which those concerned in the government were seeking to put upon him. How could an honest man fail to be overwhelmed with rage and anguish at being dishonoured before the world by his masters for scrupulously doing his duty, and for maintaining the rights and dignity of his own country? He knew that the charges were but pretexts, that the motives of his enemies were as base as the intrigues themselves, but he also knew that the world usually sides with the government against the individual, and that a man's reputation is rarely strong enough to maintain itself unsullied in a foreign land when his own government stretches forth its hand not to shield, but to stab, him.

"I know," he said, "that this plot has been woven partly

---

[1] Aerssens to Jacques de Maldere, 20 April 1611. (MS.)

in Holland and partly here by good correspondence, in order to drive me from my post with disreputation. To this has tended the communication of my despatches to make me lose my best friends. This too was the object of the particular imparting to de Russy of all my propositions, in order to draw a complaint against me from this court.

" But as I have discovered this accurately, I have resolved to offer to my masters the continuance of my very humble service for such time and under such conditions as they may think good to prescribe. I prefer forcing my natural and private inclinations to giving an opportunity for the ministers of this kingdom to discredit us, and to my enemies to succeed in injuring me, and by fraud and malice to force me from my post. . . . I am truly sorry, being ready to retire, wishing to have an honourable testimony in recompense of my labours, that one is in such hurry to take advantage of my fall. I cannot believe that my masters wish to suffer this. They are too prudent, and cannot be ignorant of the treachery which has been practised on me. I have maintained their cause. If they have chosen to throw down the fruits of my industry, the blame should be imputed to those who consider their own ambition more than the interests of the public. . . . What envoy will ever dare to speak with vigour if he is not sustained by the government at home ? . . . My enemies have misrepresented my actions, and my language as passionate, exaggerated, mischievous, but I have no passion except for the service of my superiors. They say that I have a dark and distrustful disposition, but I have been alarmed at the alliance now forming here with the King of Spain, through the policy of M. de Villeroy. I was the first to discover this intrigue, which they thought buried in the bosom of the Triumvirate. I gave notice of it to My Lords the States as in duty bound. It all came back to the government in the copies furnished

of my secret despatches.  This is the real source of the
complaints against me.  The rest of the charges, relating to
the Third and other matters, are but pretexts.  To parry
the blow, they pretend that all that is said and done with
the Spaniard is but feigning.  Who is going to believe that ?
Has not the Pope intervened in the affair ? . . . I tell
you they are furious here because I have my eyes open.  I
see too far into their affairs to suit their purposes.  A new
man would suit them better." [1]

His position was hopelessly compromised.  He remained
in Paris, however, month after month, and even year after
year, defying his enemies both at the Queen's court and in
Holland, feeding fat the grudge he bore to Barneveld as the
supposed author of the intrigue against him, and drawing
closer the personal bonds which united him to Bouillon and
through him to Prince Maurice.

The wrath of the Ambassador flamed forth without disguise against Barneveld and all his adherents when his
removal, as will be related on a subsequent page, was at
last effected.  And his hatred was likely to be deadly.
A man with a shrewd, vivid face, cleanly cut features and
a restless eye ; wearing a close-fitting skull cap, which gave
him something the look of a monk, but with the thorough-
bred and facile demeanour of one familiar with the world ;
stealthy, smooth, and cruel, a man coldly intellectual, who
feared no one, loved but few, and never forgot or forgave ;
Francis d'Aerssens, devoured by ambition and burning with
revenge, was a dangerous enemy.

Time was soon to show whether it was safe to injure
him.  Barneveld, from well-considered motives of public
policy, was favouring his honourable recall.  But he allowed
a decorous interval of more than three years to elapse

<hr>

[1] Aerssens to Jacques de Maldere, 3 May 1611.  (MS.)

in which to terminate his affairs, and to take a deliberate departure from that French embassy to which the Advocate had originally promoted him, and in which there had been so many years of mutual benefit and confidence between the two statesmen.  He used no underhand means. He did not abuse the power of the States-General which he wielded to cast him suddenly and brutally from the distinguished post which he occupied, and so to attempt to dishonour him before the world.  Nothing could be more respectful and conciliatory than the attitude of the government from first to last towards this distinguished functionary. The Republic respected itself too much to deal with honourable agents whose services it felt obliged to dispense with as with vulgar malefactors who had been detected in crime. But Aerssens believed that it was the Advocate who had caused copies of his despatches to be sent to the French court, and that he had deliberately and for a fixed purpose been undermining his influence at home and abroad and blackening his character.  All his ancient feelings of devotion, if they had ever genuinely existed towards his former friend and patron, turned to gall.  He was almost ready to deny that he had ever respected Barneveld, appreciated his public services, admired his intellect, or felt gratitude for his guidance.

A fierce controversy—to which at a later period it will be necessary to call the reader's attention, because it is intimately connected with dark scenes afterwards to be enacted —took place between the late ambassador and Cornelis van der Myle.  Meantime Barneveld pursued the policy which he had marked out for the States-General in regard to France.

Certainly it was a difficult problem.  There could be no doubt that metamorphosed France could only be a dangerous ally for the Republic.  It was in reality impossible that she should be her ally at all.  And this Barneveld knew.

Still it was better, so he thought, for the Netherlands that France should exist than that it should fall into utter decomposition. France, though under the influence of Spain, and doubly allied by marriage contracts to Spain, was better than Spain itself in the place of France. This seemed to be the only choice between two evils. Should the whole weight of the States-General be thrown into the scale of the malcontent and mutinous princes against the established but tottering government of France, it was difficult to say how soon Spain might literally, as well as inferentially, reign in Paris.

Between the rebellion and the legitimate government, therefore, Barneveld did not hesitate. France, corporate France, with which the Republic had been so long in close and mutually advantageous alliance, and from whose late monarch she had received such constant and valuable benefits, was in the Advocate's opinion the only power to be recognised, Papal and Spanish though it was. The advantage of an alliance with the fickle, self-seeking, and ever changing mutiny, that was seeking to make use of Protestantism to effect its own ends, was in his eyes rather specious than real.

By this policy, while making the breach irreparable with Aerssens and as many leading politicians as Aerssens could influence, he first brought on himself the stupid accusation of swerving towards Spain. Dull murmurs like these, which were now but faintly making themselves heard against the reputation of the Advocate, were destined ere long to swell into a mighty roar; but he hardly listened now to insinuations which seemed infinitely below his contempt. He still effectually ruled the nation through his influence in the States of Holland, where he reigned supreme. Thus far Barneveld and My Lords the States-General were one personage.

But there was another great man in the State who had at last grown impatient of the Advocate's power, and was secretly resolved to brook it no longer. Maurice of Nassau had felt himself too long rebuked by the genius of the Advocate. The Prince had perhaps never forgiven him for the political guardianship which he had exercised over him ever since the death of William the Silent. He resented the leading strings by which his youthful footstep had been sustained, and which he seemed always to feel about his limbs so long as Barneveld existed. He had never forgotten the unpalatable advice given to him by the Advocate through the Princess-Dowager.

The brief campaign in Cleve and Jülich was the last great political operation in which the two were likely to act in even apparent harmony. But the rivalry between the two had already pronounced itself emphatically during the negotiations for the truce. The Advocate had felt it absolutely necessary for the Republic to suspend the war at the first moment when she could treat with her ancient sovereign on a footing of equality. Spain, exhausted with the conflict, had at last consented to what she considered the humiliation of treating with her rebellious provinces as with free states over which she claimed no authority. The peace party, led by Barneveld, had triumphed, notwithstanding the steady opposition of Prince Maurice and his adherents.

Why had Maurice opposed the treaty? Because his vocation was over, because he was the greatest captain of the age, because his emoluments, his consideration, his dignity before the world, his personal power, were all vastly greater in war than in his opinion they could possibly be in peace. It was easy for him to persuade himself that what was manifestly for his individual interest was likewise essential to the prosperity of the country.

The diminution in his revenues consequent on the return to peace was made good to him, his brother, and his cousin, by most munificent endowments and pensions.  And it was owing to the strenuous exertions of the Advocate that these large sums were voted.  A hollow friendship was kept up between the two during the first few years of the truce, but resentment and jealousy lay deep in Maurice's heart.

At about the period of the return of Aerssens from his French embassy, the suppressed fire was ready to flame forth at the first fanning by that artful hand.  It was impossible, so Aerssens thought and whispered, that two heads could remain on one body politic.  There was no room in the Netherlands for both the Advocate and the Prince. Barneveld was in all civil affairs dictator, chief magistrate, supreme judge ; but he occupied this high station by the force of intellect, will, and experience, not through any constitutional provision.  In time of war the Prince was generalissimo, commander-in-chief of all the armies of the Republic.  Yet constitutionally he was not captain-general at all.  He was only stadholder of five out of seven provinces.

Barneveld suspected him of still wishing to make himself sovereign of the country.  Perhaps his suspicions were incorrect.  Yet there was every reason why Maurice should be ambitious of that position.  It would have been in accordance with the openly expressed desire of Henry IV. and other powerful allies of the Netherlands.  His father's assassination had alone prevented his elevation to the rank of sovereign Count of Holland.  The federal policy of the Provinces had drifted into a republican form after their renunciation of their Spanish sovereign, not because the people, or the States as representing the people, had deliberately chosen a republican system, but because they could get no powerful monarch to accept the sovereignty. They had offered to become subjects of Protestant England

and of Catholic France.  Both powers had refused the offer,
and refused it with something like contumely.  However
deep the subsequent regret on the part of both, there was no
doubt of the fact.  But the internal policy in all the provinces, and in all the towns, was republican.  Local self-
government existed everywhere.  Each city magistracy was
a little republic in itself.  The death of William the Silent,
before he had been invested with the sovereign power of all
seven provinces, again left that sovereignty in abeyance.
Was the supreme power of the Union, created at Utrecht
in 1579, vested in the States-General ?

They were beginning theoretically to claim it, but Barneveld denied the existence of any such power either in law
or fact.  It was a league of sovereignties, he maintained ;
a confederacy of seven independent states, united for certain
purposes by a treaty made some thirty years before.  Nothing could be more imbecile, judging by the light of
subsequent events and the experience of centuries, than such
an organization.  The independent and sovereign republic
of Zealand or of Groningen, for example, would have made
a poor figure campaigning, or negotiating, or exhibiting
itself on its own account before the world.  Yet it was
difficult to show any charter, precedent, or prescription for
the sovereignty of the States-General.  Necessary as such
an incorporation was for the very existence of the Union, no
constitutional union had ever been enacted.  Practically
the Province of Holland, representing more than half the
population, wealth, strength, and intellect of the whole
confederation, had achieved an irregular supremacy in the
States-General.  But its undeniable superiority was now
causing a rank growth of envy, hatred, and jealousy throughout the country, and the great Advocate of Holland, who
was identified with the province, and had so long wielded its
power, was beginning to reap the full harvest of that malice.

Thus while there was so much of vagueness in theory and practice as to the sovereignty, there was nothing criminal on the part of Maurice if he was ambitious of obtaining the sovereignty himself.  He was not seeking to compass it by base artifice or by intrigue of any kind.  It was very natural that he should be restive under the dictatorship of the Advocate.  If a single burgher and lawyer could make himself despot of the Netherlands, how much more reasonable that he—with the noblest blood of Europe in his veins, whose direct ancestor three centuries before had been emperor not only of those provinces, but of all Germany and half Christendom besides, whose immortal father had under God been the creator and saviour of the new commonwealth, had made sacrifices such as man never made for a people, and had at last laid down his life in its defence ; who had himself fought daily from boyhood upwards in the great cause, who had led national armies from victory to victory till he had placed his country as a military school and a belligerent power foremost among the nations, and had at last so exhausted and humbled the great adversary and former tyrant that he had been glad of a truce while the rebel chief would have preferred to continue the war—should aspire to rule by hereditary right a land with which his name and his race were indelibly associated by countless sacrifices and heroic achievements.

It was no crime in Maurice to desire the sovereignty. It was still less a crime in Barneveld to believe that he desired it.  There was no special reason why the Prince should love the republican form of government provided that an hereditary one could be legally substituted for it. He had sworn allegiance to the statutes, customs, and privileges of each of the provinces of which he had been elected stadholder, but there would have been no treason on his part if the name and dignity of stadholder should be changed by the States themselves for those of King or sovereign Prince.

Yet it was a chief grievance against the Advocate on the part of the Prince that Barneveld believed him capable of this ambition.

The Republic existed as a fact, but it had not long existed, nor had it ever received a formal baptism. So undefined was its constitution, and so conflicting were the various opinions in regard to it of eminent men, that it would be difficult to say how high-treason could be committed against it. Great lawyers of highest intellect and learning believed the sovereign power to reside in the separate states, others found that sovereignty in the city magistracies, while during a feverish period of war and tumult the supreme function had without any written constitution, any organic law, practically devolved upon the States-General, who had now begun to claim it as a right. The Republic was neither venerable by age nor impregnable in law. It was an improvised aristocracy of lawyers, manufacturers, bankers, and corporations which had done immense work and exhibited astonishing sagacity and courage, but which might never have achieved the independence of the Provinces unaided by the sword of Orange-Nassau and the magic spell which belonged to that name.

Thus a bitter conflict was rapidly developing itself in the heart of the Commonwealth. There was the civil element struggling with the military for predominance; sword against gown; states' rights against central authority; peace against war; above all the rivalry of one prominent personage against another, whose mutual hatred was now artfully inflamed by partisans.

And now another element of discord had come, more potent than all the rest : the terrible, never ending, struggle of Church against State. Theological hatred which forty years long had found vent in the exchange of acrimony between the ancient and the Reformed churches was now assuming other shapes. Religion in that age and country was more than has often been the case in history the atmosphere of men's daily lives. But during the great war for independence, although the hostility between the two religious forces was always intense, it was modified especially towards the close of the struggle by other controlling influences. The love of independence and the passion for nationality, the devotion to ancient political privileges, was often as fervid and genuine in Catholic bosoms as in those of Protestants, and sincere adherents of the ancient church had fought to the death against Spain in defence of chartered rights.

At that very moment it is probable that half the population of the United Provinces was Catholic. Yet it would be ridiculous to deny that the aggressive, uncompromising, self-sacrificing, intensely believing, perfectly fearless spirit of Calvinism had been the animating soul, the motive power of the great revolt. For the Provinces to have encountered Spain and Rome without Calvinism, and relying upon municipal enthusiasm only, would have been to throw away the sword and fight with the scabbard.

But it is equally certain that those hot gospellers who had suffered so much martyrdom and achieved so many miracles were fully aware of their power and despotic in its exercise. Against the oligarchy of commercial and juridical corporations they stood there the most terrible aristocracy of all: the aristocracy of God's elect, predestined from all time and to all eternity to take precedence of and to look down upon their inferior and lost fellow creatures. It was inevitable that this aristocracy, which had done so much, which had breathed into a new-born commonwealth the breath of its life, should be intolerant, haughty, dogmatic.

The Church of Rome, which had been dethroned after inflicting such exquisite tortures during its period of power, was not to raise its head. Although so large a proportion of the inhabitants of the country were secretly or openly attached to that faith, it was a penal offence to participate openly in its rites and ceremonies. Religious equality, except in the minds of a few individuals, was an unimaginable idea. There was still one Church which arrogated to itself the sole possession of truth, the Church of Geneva. Those who admitted the possibility of other forms and creeds were either Atheists or, what was deemed worse than Atheists, Papists, because Papists were assumed to be traitors also, and desirous of selling the country to Spain. An undevout man in that land and at that epoch was an almost unknown phenomenon. Religion was as much a recognized necessity of existence as food or drink. It were as easy to find people going about without clothes as without religious convictions. The Advocate, who had always adhered to the humble spirit of his ancestral device, *"Nil scire tutissima fides,"* and almost alone among his fellow citizens (save those immediate apostles and pupils of his who became involved in his fate) in favour of religious toleration, began to be suspected of treason and Papacy because, had he been able to give the law, it was thought he would have permitted such horrors as the public exercise of the Roman Catholic religion.

The hissings and screamings of the vulgar against him as he moved forward on his stedfast course he heeded less than those of geese on a common. But there was coming a time when this proud and scornful statesman, conscious of the superiority conferred by great talents and unparalleled experience, would find it less easy to treat the voice of slanderers, whether idiots or powerful and intellectual enemies, with contempt.

# CHAPTER VIII.

Schism in the Church a Public Fact — Struggle for Power between the Sacerdotal and Political Orders — Dispute between Arminius and Gomarus — Rage of James I. at the Appointment of Vorstius — Arminians called Remonstrants — Hague Conference — Contra Remonstrance by Gomarites of Seven Points to the Remonstrants' Five — Fierce Theological Disputes throughout the Country — Ryswyk Secession — Maurice wishes to remain neutral, but finds himself the Chieftain of the Contra-Remonstrant Party — The States of Holland Remonstrant by a large Majority — The States-General Contra-Remonstrant — Sir Ralph Winwood leaves the Hague — Three Armies to take the Field against Protestantism.

SCHISM in the Church had become a public fact, and theological hatred was in full blaze throughout the country.

The great practical question in the Church had been as to the appointment of preachers, wardens, schoolmasters, and other officers. By the ecclesiastical arrangements of 1591 great power was conceded to the civil authority in church matters, especially in regard to such appointments, which were made by a commission consisting of four members named by the churches and four by the magistrates in each district.[1]

Barneveld, who above all things desired peace in the Church, had wished to revive this ordinance, and in 1612 it had been resolved by the States of Holland that each city or village should, if the magistracy approved, provisionally conform to it. The States of Utrecht made at the same time a similar arrangement.

[1] Wagenaar. x. 59. 'Groot Plak-katboek,' iii. deel, bl. 459. 'Groot Utrechtsch Plakkat-boek,' i. d. 259. Van Rees and Brill, Continuation of Arend, iii. d. ii. stuk, pp. 499. seq.

It was the controversy which has been going on since the beginning of history and is likely to be prolonged to the end of time—the struggle for power between the sacerdotal and political orders ; the controversy whether priests shall control the state or the state govern the priests.

This was the practical question involved in the fierce dispute as to dogma.  The famous duel between Arminius and Gomarus ; the splendid theological tournaments which succeeded ; six champions on a side armed in full theological panoply and swinging the sharpest curtal axes which learning, passion, and acute intellect could devise, had as yet produced no beneficent result.  Nobody had been convinced by the shock of argument, by the exchange of those

1608.    desperate blows.  The High Council of the Hague had declared that no difference of opinion in the Church existed sufficient to prevent fraternal harmony and happiness.  But Gomarus loudly declared that, if there were no means of putting down the heresy of Arminius, there would before long be a struggle such as would set province against province, village against village, family against family, throughout the land.[1]  He should be afraid to die in such doctrine.  He shuddered that any one should dare to come before God's tribunal with such blasphemies.  Meantime his great adversary, the learned and eloquent, the musical, frolicsome, hospitable heresiarch was no more.  Worn out with controversy, but peaceful and happy in the convictions which were so bitterly denounced by Gomarus and a large proportion of both preachers and laymen in the Netherlands, and convinced that the schism which in his

Aug.    view had been created by those who called them-
1609.    selves the orthodox would weaken the cause of Protestantism throughout Europe, Arminius died at the age of forty-nine.

[1] Van Rees and Brill, ' Vad. Gesch.' iii. 419, 422, seq.

The magistrates throughout Holland, with the exception of a few cities, were Arminian, the preachers Gomarian; for Arminius ascribed to the civil authority the right to decide upon church matters, while Gomarus maintained that ecclesiastical affairs should be regulated in ecclesiastical assemblies. The overseers of Leyden University appointed Conrad Vorstius to be professor of theology in place of Arminius. The selection filled to the brim the cup of bitterness, for no man was more audaciously latitudinarian than he. He was even suspected of Socinianism. There came a shriek from King James, fierce and shrill enough to rouse Arminius from his grave. James foamed to the mouth at the insolence of the overseers in appointing such a monster of infidelity to the professorship. He ordered his books to be publicly burned in St. Paul's Churchyard and at both Universities,[1] and would have burned the Professor himself with as much delight as Torquemada or Peter Titelman ever felt in roasting their victims, had not the day for such festivities gone by. He ordered the States of Holland on pain of for ever forfeiting his friendship to exclude Vorstius at once from the theological chair and to forbid him from " nestling anywhere in the country."

He declared his amazement that they should tolerate such a pest as Conrad Vorstius. Had they not had enough of the seed sown by that foe of God, Arminius ? He ordered the States-General to chase the blasphemous monster from the land, or else he would cut off all connection with their false and heretic churches and make the other Reformed churches of Europe do the same, nor should the youth of England ever be allowed to frequent the University of Leyden.[2]

In point of fact the Professor was never allowed to qualify, to preach, or to teach ; so tremendous was the outcry of

<hr>

[1] Van Rees and Brill, 'Vad. Gesch.' iii. 495.   [2] Ibid. 'Carleton Letters.'

Peter Plancius and many orthodox preachers, echoing the wrath of the King.  He lived at Gouda in a private capacity for several years, until the Synod of Dordrecht at last publicly condemned his opinions and deprived him of his professorship.

Meantime, the preachers who were disciples of Arminius had in a private assembly drawn up what was called a Remonstrance, addressed to the States of Holland, and defending themselves from the reproach that they were seeking change in the Divine service and desirous of creating tumult and schism.[1]

This Remonstrance, set forth by the pen of the famous Uytenbogaert, whom Gomarus called the Court Trumpeter, because for a long time he had been Prince Maurice's favourite preacher, was placed in the hands of Barneveld, for delivery to the States of Holland. Thenceforth the Arminians were called Remonstrants.

The Hague Conference followed, six preachers on a side, and the States of Holland exhorted to fraternal compromise. Until further notice, they decreed that no man should be required to believe more than had been laid down in the Five Points.

Before the conference, however, the Gomarite preachers

---

[1] Wagenaar, x. 36, 37. 'Haagsche Conferentie,' i. 425. Brandt, 'Hist. der Ref.' ii. 128. Uytenbogaert, 524, 525.

They formulated their position in the famous Five Points:—

I. God has from eternity resolved to choose to eternal life those who through his grace believe in Jesus Christ, and in faith and obedience so continue to the end, and to condemn the unbelieving and unconverted to eternal damnation.

II. Jesus Christ died for all; so, nevertheless, that no one actually except believers is redeemed by His death.

III. Man has not the saving belief from himself, nor out of his free will, but he needs thereto God's grace in Christ.

IV. This grace is the beginning, continuation, and completion of man's salvation; all good deeds must be ascribed to it, but it does not work irresistibly.

V. God's grace gives sufficient strength to the true believers to overcome evil; but whether they cannot lose grace should be more closely examined before it should be taught in full security.

Afterwards they expressed themselves more distinctly on this point, and declared that a true believer, through his own fault, can fall away from God and lose faith.

had drawn up a Contra-Remonstrance of Seven Points in opposition to the Remonstrants' five.[1]

They demanded the holding of a National Synod to settle the difference between these Five and Seven Points, or the sending of them to foreign universities for arbitration, a mutual promise being given by the contending parties to abide by the decision.

Thus much it has been necessary to state concerning what in the seventeenth century was called the platform of the two great parties : a term which has been perpetuated in our own country, and is familiar to all the world in the nineteenth.

There shall be no more setting forth of these subtle and finely wrought abstractions in our pages. We aspire not to the lofty heights of theological and supernatural contemplation, where the atmosphere becomes too rarefied for

---

[1] Authorities last cited.

These were the Seven Points :—

I. God has chosen from eternity certain persons out of the human race, which in and with Adam fell into sin and has no more power to believe and convert itself than a dead man to restore himself to life, in order to make them blessed through Christ ; while He passes by the rest through His righteous judgment, and leaves them lying in their sins.

II. Children of believing parents, as well as full-grown believers, are to be considered as elect so long as they with action do not prove the contrary.

III. God in His election has not looked at the belief and the repentance of the elect ; but, on the contrary, in His eternal and unchangeable design, has resolved to give to the elect faith and stedfastness, and thus to make them blessed.

IV. He, to this end, in the first place, presented to them His only begotten Son, whose sufferings, although sufficient for the expiation of all men's sins, nevertheless, according to God's decree, serves alone to the reconcilia-

tion of the elect.

V. God causest he Gospel to be preached to them, making the same, through the Holy Ghost, of strength upon their minds ; so that they not merely obtain power to repent and to believe, but also actually and voluntarily do repent and believe.

VI. Such elect, through the same power of the Holy Ghost through which they have once become repentant and believing, are kept in such wise that they indeed through weakness fall into heavy sins ; but can never wholly and for always lose the true faith.

VII. True believers from this, however, draw no reason for fleshly quiet, it being impossible that they who through a true faith were planted in Christ should bring forth no fruits of thankfulness; the promises of God's help and the warnings of Scripture tending to make their salvation work in them in fear and trembling, and to cause them more earnestly to desire help from that spirit without which they can do nothing.

ordinary constitutions. Rather we attempt an objective and level survey of remarkable phenomena manifesting themselves on the earth; direct or secondary emanations from those distant spheres.

For in those days, and in that land especially, theology and politics were one. It may be questioned at least whether this practical fusion of elements, which may with more safety to the Commonwealth be kept separate, did not tend quite as much to lower and contaminate the religious sentiments as to elevate the political idea. To mix habitually the solemn phraseology which men love to reserve for their highest and most sacred needs with the familiar slang of politics and trade seems to our generation not a very desirable proceeding.

The aroma of doubly distilled and highly sublimated dogma is more difficult to catch than to comprehend the broader and more practical distinctions of every-day party strife.

King James was furious at the thought that common men —the vulgar, the people in short—should dare to discuss deep problems of divinity which, as he confessed, had puzzled even his royal mind. Barneveld modestly disclaimed the power of seeing with absolute clearness into things beyond the reach of the human intellect. But the honest Netherlanders were not abashed by thunder from the royal pulpit, nor perplexed by hesitations which darkened the soul of the great Advocate.

In burghers' mansions, peasants' cottages, mechanics' back-parlours, on board herring smacks, canal boats, and East Indiamen; in shops, counting-rooms, farmyards, guard-rooms, ale-houses; on the exchange, in the tennis-court, on the mall; at banquets, at burials, christenings, or bridals; wherever and whenever human creatures met each other, there was ever to be found the fierce wrangle of Remon strant and Contra-Remonstrant, the hissing of red-hot theological rhetoric, the pelting of hostile texts. The blacksmith's iron cooled on the anvil, the tinker dropped a kettle half mended, the broker left a bargain unclinched, the Scheveningen fisherman in his wooden shoes forgot the cracks in his pinkie, while each paused to hold high converse with friend or foe on fate, free will, or absolute foreknowledge; losing himself in wandering mazes whence there was no issue. Province against province, city against city, family against family; it was one vast scene of bickering, denunciation, heartburnings, mutual excommunication and hatred.

Alas! a generation of mankind before, men had stood banded together to resist, with all the might that comes from union, the fell spirit of the Holy Inquisition, which was dooming all who had wandered from the ancient fold or resisted foreign tyranny to the axe, the faggot, the living grave. There had been small leisure then for men who fought for Fatherland, and for comparative liberty of conscience, to tear each others' characters in pieces, and to indulge in mutual hatreds and loathing on the question of predestination.

As a rule the population, especially of the humbler classes, and a great majority of the preachers were Contra-Remonstrant; the magistrates, the burgher patricians, were Remonstrant. In Holland the controlling influence was Remonstrant; but Amsterdam and four or five other cities of that province held to the opposite doctrine. These cities formed therefore a small minority in the States Assembly of Holland sustained by a large majority in the States-General. The Province of Utrecht was almost unanimously Remonstrant. The five other provinces were decidedly Contra-Remonstrant.

It is obvious therefore that the influence of Barneveld,

hitherto so all-controlling in the States-General, and which rested on the complete submission of the States of Holland to his will, was tottering. The battle-line between Church and State was now drawn up ; and it was at the same time a battle between the union and the principles of state sovereignty.

It had long since been declared through the mouth of the Advocate, but in a solemn state manifesto, that My Lords the States-General were the foster-fathers and the natural protectors of the Church, to whom supreme authority in church matters belonged.[1]

The Contra-Remonstrants, on the other hand, maintained that all the various churches made up one indivisible church, seated above the States, whether Provincial or General, and governed by the Holy Ghost acting directly upon the congregations.

As the schism grew deeper and the States-General receded from the position which they had taken up under the lead of the Advocate, the scene was changed. A majority of the Provinces being Contra-Remonstrant, and therefore in favour of a National Synod, the States-General as a body were of necessity for the Synod.

It was felt by the clergy that, if many churches existed, they would all remain subject to the civil authority. The power of the priesthood would thus sink before that of the burgher aristocracy. There must be one church—the Church of Geneva and Heidelberg—if that theocracy which the Gomarites meant to establish was not to vanish as a dream. It was founded on Divine Right, and knew no chief magistrate but the Holy Ghost. A few years before the States-General had agreed to a National Synod, but with a condition that there should be revision of the Netherland Confession and the Heidelberg Catechism.

<hr>

[1] Van Rees and Brill, iii. 422.   Baudart. i. 9, 10.

Against this the orthodox infallibilists had protested and thundered, because it was an admission that the vile Arminian heresy might perhaps be declared correct. 'It was now however a matter of certainty that the States-General would cease to oppose the unconditional Synod, because the majority sided with the priesthood.'

The magistrates of Leyden had not long before opposed the demand for a Synod on the ground that the war against Spain was not undertaken to maintain one sect ; that men of various sects and creeds had fought with equal valour against the common foe ; that religious compulsion was hateful, and that no synod had a right to claim Netherlanders as slaves.[1]

'To thoughtful politicians like Barneveld, Hugo Grotius, and men who acted with them, that seemed a doctrine fraught with danger to the state, by which mankind were not regarded as saved or doomed according to belief or deeds, but as individuals divided from all eternity into two classes which could never be united, but must ever mutually regard each other as enemies.'

And like enemies Netherlanders were indeed beginning to regard each other. The men who, banded like brothers, had so heroically fought for two generations long for liberty against an almost superhuman despotism, now howling and jeering against each other like demons, seemed determined to bring the very name of liberty into contempt.'

Where the Remonstrants were in the ascendant, they excited the hatred and disgust of the orthodox by their overbearing determination to carry their Five Points. A broker in Rotterdam of the Contra-Remonstrant persuasion, being about to take a wife, swore he had rather be married by a pig than a parson. For this sparkling epigram he was punished by the Remonstrant magistracy with loss of his citizenship for a year and the right to practise his trade

[1] Van Rees and Brill, 'Vad. Gesch.' iii. 499 *seq.*

for life.[1]  A casuistical tinker, expressing himself violently in the same city against the Five Points, and disrespectfully towards the magistrates for tolerating them, was banished from the town.[2]  A printer in the neighbourhood, disgusted with these and similar efforts of tyranny on the part of the dominant party, thrust a couple of lines of doggrel into the lottery :

"In name of the Prince of Orange, I ask once and again,
  What difference between the Inquisition of Rotterdam and Spain ?"

For this poetical effort the printer was sentenced to forfeit the prize that he had drawn in the lottery, and to be kept in prison on bread and water for a fortnight.[3]

Certainly such punishments were hardly as severe as being beheaded or burned or buried alive, as would have been the lot of tinkers and printers and brokers who opposed the established church in the days of Alva, but the demon of intolerance, although its fangs were drawn, still survived, and had taken possession of both parties in the Reformed Church.  For it was the Remonstrants who had possession of the churches at Rotterdam, and the printer's distich is valuable as pointing out that the name of Orange was beginning to identify itself with the Contra-Remonstrant faction.  At this time, on the other hand, the gabble that Barneveld had been bought by Spanish gold, and was about to sell his country to Spain, became louder than a whisper.  Men were not ashamed, from theological hatred, to utter such senseless calumnies against a venerable statesman whose long life had been devoted to the cause of his country's independence and to the death struggle with Spain.

· As if because a man admitted the possibility of all his fellow-creatures being saved from damnation through re-

[1] Wagenaar, x. 82, 83.              [2] Ibid.              [3] Ibid.

Æ. 17
HORA

pentance and the grace of God, he must inevitably be a
traitor to his country and a pensionary of her deadliest
foe.

And where the Contra-Remonstrants held possession of
the churches and the city governments, acts of tyranny
which did not then seem ridiculous were of everyday occurrence.  Clergymen, suspected of the Five Points, were driven
out of the pulpits with bludgeons or assailed with brickbats
at the church door.  At Amsterdam, Simon Goulart, for
preaching the doctrine of universal salvation and for disputing the eternal damnation of young children, was forbidden thenceforth to preach at all.[1]

But it was at the Hague that the schism in religion and
politics first fatally widened itself.  Henry Rosaeus, an
eloquent divine, disgusted with his colleague Uytenbogaert,
refused all communion with him, and was in consequence
suspended.  Excluded from the Great Church, where he had
formerly ministered, he preached every Sunday at Ryswyk,
two or three miles distant.[2]  Seven hundred Contra-Remonstrants of the Hague followed their beloved   Feb. 12,
pastor, and, as the roads to Ryswyk were muddy      1616.
and sloppy in winter, acquired the unsavoury nickname of
the "Mud Beggars."  The vulgarity of heart which suggested the appellation does not inspire to-day great sympathy with the Remonstrant party, even if one were
inclined to admit, what is not the fact, that they represented the cause of religious equality.  For even the
illustrious Grotius was at that very moment repudiating
the notion that there could be two religions in one state.
"Difference in public worship," he said, "was in kingdoms pernicious, but in free commonwealths in the highest
degree destructive."[3]

[1] Wagenaar, x. 86, 87.  Brandt, 'Hist. Ref.' ii. 261, seq.
[2] Van der Kemp, iv. 2.          [3] Wagenaar, x. 137.

It was the struggle between Church and State for supremacy over the whole body politic. "The Reformation," said Grotius, "was not brought about by synods, but by kings, princes, and magistrates." It was the same eternal story, the same terrible two-edged weapon, "*Cujus regio ejus religio,*" found in the arsenal of the first Reformers, and in every politico-religious arsenal of history.

"By an eternal decree of God," said Gomarus in accordance with Calvin, "it has been fixed who are to be saved and who damned. By His decree some are drawn to faith and godliness, and, being drawn, can never fall away. God leaves all the rest in the general corruption of human nature and their own misdeeds." [1]

"God has from eternity made this distinction in the fallen human race," said Arminius, "that He pardons those who desist from their sins and put their faith in Christ, and will give them eternal life, but will punish those who remain impenitent. Moreover, it is pleasanter to God that all men should repent, and, coming to knowledge of truth, remain therein, but He compels none." [2]

This was the vital difference of dogma. And it was because they could hold no communion with those who believed in the efficacy of repentance that Rosaeus and his followers had seceded to Ryswyk, and the Reformed Church had been torn into two very unequal parts. But it is difficult to believe that out of this arid field of controversy so plentiful a harvest of hatred and civil convulsion could have ripened. More practical than the insoluble problems, whether repentance could effect salvation, and whether dead infants were hopelessly damned, was the question who should rule both Church and State.

There could be but one church. On that Remonstrants

<hr>

[1] Wagenaar, x. 15, 16.  Gomari 'Op.' p. i. 428; p. ii. 27, 277, 280.
[2] Arminii 'Opera,' pp. 283, 288, 389, 943.  Wag. *ubi sup.*

and Contra-Remonstrants were agreed.   But should the Five Points or the Seven Points obtain the mastery ?   Should that framework of hammered iron, the Confession and Catechism, be maintained in all its rigidity around the sheepfold, or should the disciples of the arch-heretic Arminius, the salvation-mongers, be permitted to prowl within it ?

Was Barneveld, who hated the Reformed religion[1] (so men told each other), and who believed in nothing, to continue dictator of the whole Republic through his influence over one province, prescribing its religious dogmas and laying down its laws ; or had not the time come for the States-General to vindicate the rights of the Church, and to crush for ever the pernicious principle of State sovereignty and burgher oligarchy ?

The abyss was wide and deep, and the wild waves were raging more madly every hour.   The Advocate, anxious and troubled, but undismayed, did his best in the terrible emergency.   He conferred with Prince Maurice on the subject of the Ryswyk secession, and men said that he sought to impress upon him, as chief of the military forces, the necessity of putting down religious schism with the armed hand.

The Prince had not yet taken a decided position.   He was still under the influence of John Uytenbogaert, who with Arminius and the Advocate made up the fateful three from whom deadly disasters were deemed to have come upon the Commonwealth.   He wished to remain neutral.   But no man can be neutral in civil contentions threatening the life of the body politic any more than the heart can be indifferent if the human frame is sawn in two.

"I am a soldier," said Maurice, "not a divine.  These are matters of theology which I don't understand, and about which I don't trouble myself."[2]

<hr>

[1] Van der Kemp, iv. 5.       [2] Brandt, ii. 558.  Van der Kemp, iv. 20.

On another occasion he is reported to have said, "I know nothing of predestination, whether it is green or whether it is blue ; but I do know that the Advocate's pipe and mine will never play the same tune."[1]

It was not long before he fully comprehended the part which he must necessarily play.  To say that he was indifferent to religious matters was as ridiculous as to make a like charge against Barneveld.  Both were religious men.  It would have been almost impossible to find an irreligious character in that country, certainly not among its highest-placed and leading minds.  Maurice had strong intellectual powers.  He was a regular attendant on divine worship, and was accustomed to hear daily religious discussions.  To avoid them indeed, he would have been obliged not only to fly his country, but to leave Europe. He had a profound reverence for the memory of his father, Calbo y Calbanista, as William the Silent had called himself.  But the great prince had died before these fierce disputes had torn the bosom of the Reformed Church, and while Reformers still were brethren.  But if Maurice were a religious man, he was also a keen politician ; a less capable politician, however, than a soldier, for he was confessedly the first captain of his age.  He was not rapid in his conceptions, but he was sure in the end to comprehend his opportunity.

The Church, the people, the Union—the sacerdotal, the democratic, and the national element—united under a name so potent to conjure with as the name of Orange-Nassau, was stronger than any other possible combination.  Instinctively and logically therefore the Stadholder found himself the chieftain of the Contra-Remonstrant party, and without the necessity of an apostasy such as had been required of his great contemporary to make himself master of France.

<hr>

[1] Van Kampen, vol. ii.

The power of Barneveld and his partisans was now put
to a severe strain. His efforts to bring back the Hague
seceders were powerless. The influence of Uytenbogaert
over the Stadholder steadily diminished. He prayed to be
relieved from his post in the Great Church of the Hague,
especially objecting to serve with a Contra-Remonstrant
preacher whom Maurice wished to officiate there in place of
the seceding Rosaeus. But the Stadholder refused to let
him go, fearing his influence in other places. "There is
stuff in him," said Maurice, "to outweigh half a dozen
Contra-Remonstrant preachers."[1] Everywhere in Holland
the opponents of the Five Points refused to go to the
churches, and set up tabernacles for themselves in barns,
outhouses, canal-boats. And the authorities in town and
village nailed up the barn-doors, and dispersed the canal-
boat congregations, while the populace pelted them with
stones. The seceders appealed to the Stadholder, pleading
that at least they ought to be allowed to hear the word of
God as they understood it without being forced into churches
where they were obliged to hear Arminian blasphemy. At
least their barns might be left them. "Barns," said
Maurice, "barns and outhouses! Are we to preach in barns?
The churches belong to us, and we mean to have them too."[2]

Not long afterwards the Stadholder, clapping his hand on
his sword hilt, observed that these differences could only be
settled by force of arms.[3] An ominous remark and a dreary
comment on the forty years' war against the Inquisition.

And the same scenes that were enacting in Holland were
going on in Overyssel and Friesland and Groningen ; but
with a difference. Here it was the Five Points men who were
driven into secession, whose barns were nailed up, and whose
preachers were mobbed. A lugubrious spectacle, but less

[1] Van der Kemp. iv. 21.   [2] Ibid. 22.
[3] Wagenaar, x. 201. 'Uytenb. Leven,' c. ix. 122.

painful certainly than the hangings and drownings and burnings alive in the previous century to prevent secession from the indivisible church.

It is certain that stadholders and all other magistrates ever since the establishment of independence were sworn to maintain the Reformed religion and to prevent a public divine worship under any other form. It is equally certain that by the 13th Article of the Act of Union—the organic law of the confederation made at Utrecht in 1579—each province reserved for itself full control of religious questions. It would indeed seem almost unimaginable in a country where not only every province, but every city, every municipal board, was so jealous of its local privileges and traditional rights that the absolute disposition over the highest, gravest, and most difficult questions that can inspire and perplex humanity should be left to a general government, and one moreover which had scarcely come into existence.

Yet into this entirely illogical position the Commonwealth was steadily drifting. The cause was simple enough. The States of Holland, as already observed, were Remonstrant by a large majority. The States-General were Contra-Remonstrant by a still greater majority. The Church, rigidly attached to the Confession and Catechism, and refusing all change except through decree of a synod to be called by the general government which it controlled, represented the national idea. It thus identified itself with the Republic, and was in sympathy with a large majority of the population.

Logic, law, historical tradition were on the side of the Advocate and the States' right party. The instinct of national self-preservation, repudiating the narrow and destructive doctrine of provincial sovereignty, were on the side of the States-General and the Church.

Meantime James of Great Britain had written letters both to the States of Holland and the States-General expressing his satisfaction with the Five Points, and deciding that there was nothing objectionable in the doctrine of predestination therein set forth. He had recommended unity and peace in Church and Assembly, and urged especially that these controverted points should not be discussed in the pulpit to the irritation and perplexity of the common people.

The King's letters had produced much satisfaction in the moderate party. Barneveld and his followers were then still in the ascendant, and it seemed possible that the Commonwealth might enjoy a few moments of tranquillity. That James had given a new exhibition of his astounding inconsistency was a matter very indifferent to all but himself, and he was the last man to trouble himself for that reproach.

It might happen, when he should come to realize how absolutely he had obeyed the tuition of the Advocate and favoured the party which he had been so vehemently opposing, that he might regret and prove willing to retract. But for the time being the course of politics had seemed running smoother. The acrimony of the relations between the English government and dominant party at the Hague was sensibly diminished. The King seemed for an instant to have obtained a true insight into the nature of the struggle in the States. That it was after all less a theological than a political question which divided parties had at last dawned upon him.

"If you have occasion to write on the subject," said Barneveld,[1] "*it is above all necessary to make it clear that ecclesiastical persons and their affairs must stand under the direction of the sovereign authority,* for our preachers understand that the disposal of ecclesiastical persons and affairs belongs

<hr>

[1] Barneveld to Caron, 11 Feb. 1613. (Hague Archives MS.)

[2] These lines are underlined in the original despatch: "dat die kercke-

lycke personen ende hare zaecken moeten staan onder die directie van de souveraine Overicheyt," &c.

to them, so that they alone are to appoint preachers, elders, deacons, and other clerical persons, and to regulate the whole ecclesiastical administration according to their pleasure or by a popular government which they call the community."

"The Counts of Holland from all ancient times were never willing under the Papacy to surrender their right of presentation to the churches and control of all spiritual and ecclesiastical benefices. The Emperor Charles and King Philip even, as Counts of Holland, kept these rights to themselves, save that they in enfeoffing more than a hundred gentlemen, of noble and ancient families with seigniorial manors, enfeoffed them also with the right of presentation to churches and benefices on their respective estates. Our preachers pretend to have won this right against the Countship, the gentlemen, nobles, and others, and that it belongs to them."[1]

It is easy to see that this was a grave, constitutional, legal, and historical problem not to be solved offhand by vehement citations from Scripture, nor by pragmatical dissertations from the lips of foreign ambassadors.

"I believe this point," continued Barneveld, "to be the most difficult question of all, importing far more than subtle searchings and conflicting sentiments as to passages of Holy Writ, or disputations concerning God's eternal predestination and other points thereupon depending. Of these doctrines the Archbishop of Canterbury well observed in the Conference of 1604 that one ought to teach them *ascendendo* and not *descendendo*."

The letters of the King had been very favourably received both in the States-General and in the Assembly of Holland. "You will present the replies," wrote Barneveld to the ambassador in London, "at the best opportunity and with

---

[1] Barneveld to Caron, 3 April 1613.  (Hague Archives MS.)

becoming compliments. You may be assured and assure his Majesty that they have been very agreeable to both assemblies. Our commissioners over there on the East Indian matter ought to know nothing of these letters."[1]

This statement is worthy of notice, as Grotius was one of those commissioners, and, as will subsequently appear, was accused of being the author of the letters.

" I understand from others," continued the Advocate, " that the gentleman well known to you[2] is not well pleased that through other agency than his these letters have been written and presented. I think too that the other business is much against his grain, but on the whole since your departure he has accommodated himself to the situation."

But if Aerssens for the moment seemed quiet, the orthodox clergy were restive.

" I know," said Barneveld,[3] " that some of our ministers are so audacious that of themselves, or through others, they mean to work by direct or indirect means against these letters. They mean to show likewise that there are other and greater differences of doctrine than those already discussed. You will keep a sharp eye on the sails and provide against the effect of counter-currents. To maintain the authority of their Great Mightinesses over ecclesiastical matters is more than necessary for the conservation of the country's welfare and of the true Christian religion. As his Majesty would not allow this principle to be controverted in his own realms, as his books clearly prove, so we trust that he will not find it good that it should be controverted in our state as sure to lead to a very disastrous and inequitable sequel."

And a few weeks later the Advocate and the whole party of toleration found themselves, as is so apt to be the case,

---

[1] Barneveld to Caron, 3 April 1613.   (Hague Archives MS.)
[2] Obviously Francis Aerssens.                    [3] MS. just cited

between two fires. The Catholics became as turbulent as the extreme Calvinists, and already hopes were entertained by Spanish emissaries and spies that this rapidly growing schism in the Reformed Church might be dexterously made use of to bring the Provinces, when they should become fairly distracted, back to the dominion of Spain.

"Our precise zealots in the Reformed religion, on the one side," wrote Barneveld,[1] "and the Jesuits on the other, are vigorously kindling the fire of discord. Keep a good look-out for the countermine which is now working against the good advice of his Majesty for mutual toleration. The publication of the letters was done without order, but I believe with good intent, in the hope that the vehemence and exorbitance of some precise Puritans in our State should thereby be checked. That which is now doing against us in printed libels is the work of the aforesaid Puritans and a few Jesuits. The pretence in those libels, that there are other differences in the matter of doctrine, is mere fiction designed to make trouble and confusion."

In the course of the autumn, Sir Ralph Winwood departed from the Hague, to assume soon afterwards in England the position of secretary of state for foreign affairs. He did not take personal farewell of Barneveld, the Advocate being absent in North Holland at the moment, and detained there by indisposition. The leave-taking was therefore by letter.[2] He had done much to injure the cause which the Dutch statesman held vital to the Republic, and in so doing he had faithfully carried out the instructions of his master. Now that James had written these conciliatory letters to the States, recommending toleration, letters destined to be famous, Barneveld was anxious that the retiring ambassador should foster the spirit of moderation, which for a

---

[1] Barneveld to Caron, 3 May 1613.  (Hague Archives MS.)
[2] Same to same, 10 Sept. 1613.  (Hague Archives MS.)

moment prevailed at the British court.  But he was not very hopeful in the matter.

"Mr. Winwood is doubtless over there now," he wrote to Caron.  "He has promised in public and private to do all good offices.  The States-General made him a present on his departure of the value of £4000.  I fear nevertheless that he, especially in religious matters, will not do the best offices.  For besides that he is himself very hard and precise, those who in this country are hard and precise have made a dead set at him,[1] and tried to make him devoted to their cause, through many fictitious and untruthful means."[2]

The Advocate, as so often before, sent assurances to the King that "the States-General, and especially the States of Holland, were resolved to maintain the genuine Reformed religion, and oppose all novelties and impurities conflicting with it," and the Ambassador was instructed to see that the countermine, worked so industriously against his Majesty's service and the honour and reputation of the Provinces, did not prove successful.

"To let the good mob play the master," he said, "and to permit hypocrites and traitors in the Flemish manner to get possession of the government of the provinces and cities, and to cause upright patriots whose faith and truth has so long been proved, to be abandoned, by the blessing of God, shall never be accomplished.  Be of good heart, and cause these Flemish tricks to be understood on every occasion, and let men know that we mean to maintain, with unchanging constancy, the authority of the government, the privileges and laws of the country, as well as the true Reformed religion."

---

[1] ". . . hem zeer aengeloopen."—Barneveld to Caron, 10 Sept. 1613. (Hague Archives MS.)
[2] Ibid.

The statesman was more than ever anxious for moderate counsels in the religious questions, for it was now more important than ever that there should be concord in the Provinces, for the cause of Protestantism, and with it the existence of the Republic, seemed in greater danger than at any moment since the truce. It appeared certain that the alliance between France and Spain had been arranged, and that the Pope, Spain, the Grand-duke of Tuscany, and their various adherents had organized a strong combination, and were enrolling large armies to take the field in the spring, against the Protestant League of the princes and electors in Germany. The great king was dead. The Queen-Regent was in the hand of Spain, or dreamed at least of an impossible neutrality, while the priest who was one day to resume the part of Henry, and to hang upon the sword of France the scales in which the opposing weights of Protestantism and Catholicism in Europe were through so many awful years to be balanced, was still an obscure bishop.

The premonitory signs of the great religious war in Germany were not to be mistaken. In truth, the great conflict had already opened in the duchies, although few men as yet comprehended the full extent of that movement. The superficial imagined that questions of hereditary succession, like those involved in the dispute, were easily to be settled by statutes of descent, expounded by doctors of law, and sustained, if needful, by a couple of comparatively bloodless campaigns. Those who looked more deeply into causes felt that the limitations of Imperial authority, the ambition of a great republic, suddenly starting into existence out of nothing, and the great issues of the religious reformation, were matters not so easily arranged. When the scene shifted, as it was so soon to do, to the heart of Bohemia, when Protestantism had taken the Holy Roman Empire by the beard in its ancient palace, and thrown Imperial stadholders out of window, it would be evident to the blindest that something serious was taking place.

Meantime Barneveld, ever watchful of passing events, knew that great forces of Catholicism were marshalling in the south. Three armies were to take the field against Protestantism at the orders of Spain and the Pope. One at the door of the Republic, and directed especially against the Netherlands, was to resume the campaign in the duchies, and to prevent any aid going to Protestant Germany from Great Britain or from Holland. Another in the Upper Palatinate was to make the chief movement against the Evangelical hosts. A third in Austria was to keep down the Protestant party in Bohemia, Hungary, Austria, Moravia, and Silesia. To sustain this movement, it was understood that all the troops then in Italy were to be kept all the winter on a war footing.[1]

Was this a time for the great Protestant party in the Netherlands to tear itself in pieces for a theological subtlety, about which good Christians might differ without taking each other by the throat?

"I do not lightly believe or fear," said the Advocate, in communicating a survey of European affairs at that moment to Caron, "but present advices from abroad make me apprehend dangers."[2]

---

[1] Barneveld to Caron, 29 Oct. 1613.   (Hague Archives MS.)
[2] Ibid.

# CHAPTER IX.

Aerssens remains Two Years longer in France—Derives many Personal Advantages from his Post—He visits the States-General—Aubéry du Maurier appointed French Ambassador—He demands the Recall of Aerssens—Peace of Sainte-Ménehould—Asperen de Langerac appointed in Aerssens' Place.

FRANCIS AERSSENS had remained longer at his post than had been intended by the resolution of the States of Holland, passed in May 1611.

It is an exemplification of the very loose constitutional framework of the United Provinces that the nomination of the ambassador to France belonged to the States of Holland, by whom his salary was paid, although, of course, he was the servant of the States-General, to whom his public and official correspondence was addressed. His most important despatches were however written directly to Barneveld so long as he remained in power, who had also the charge of the whole correspondence, public or private, with all the envoys of the States.

Aerssens had, it will be remembered, been authorized to stay one year longer in France if he thought he could be useful there. He stayed two years, and on the whole was not useful. He had too many eyes and too many ears. He had become mischievous by the very activity of his intelligence. He was too zealous. There were occasions in France at that moment in which it was as well to be blind and deaf. It was impossible for the Republic, unless driven to it by dire necessity, to quarrel with its great ally.   It had been calculated by Duplessis-Mornay that France had paid subsidies to the Provinces amounting from first to last to 200 millions of livres.[1]   This was an enormous exaggeration.   It was Barneveld's estimate that before the truce the States had received from France eleven millions of florins in cash, and during the truce up to the year 1613 3,600,000 in addition, besides a million still due, making a total of about fifteen millions.   During the truce France kept two regiments of foot amounting to 4200 soldiers and two companies of cavalry in Holland at the service of the States, for which she was bound to pay yearly 600,000 livres, And the Queen-Regent had continued all the treaties by which these arrangements were secured, and professed sincere and continuous friendship for the States.   While the French-Spanish marriages gave cause for suspicion, uneasiness, and constant watchfulness in the States, still the neutrality of France was possible in the coming storm.   So long as that existed, particularly when the relations of England with Holland through the unfortunate character of King James were perpetually strained to a point of imminent rupture, it was necessary to hold as long as it was possible to the slippery embrace of France.

But Aerssens was almost aggressive in his attitude.   He rebuked the vacillations, the shortcomings, the imbecility, of the Queen's government in offensive terms.   He consorted openly with the princes who were on the point of making war upon the Queen-Regent.   He made a boast to the Secretary of State Villeroy that he had unravelled all his secret plots against the Netherlands.   He declared it to be understood in France, since the King's death, by the dominant and Jesuitical party that the crown depended temporally as well as spiritually on the good pleasure of the Pope.

<hr>

[1] Dup.-Mornay, 'Vie et Corresp.' viii. 514 ; x. 227.   Ouvré's 'Aubéry du Maurier' (Paris, 1853), p. 172.

Barneveld to States of Holland, 31 March 1613. (Hague Archives MS.)

No doubt he was perfectly right in many of his opinions. No ruler or statesman in France worthy of the name would hesitate, in the impending religious conflict throughout Europe and especially in Germany, to maintain for the kingdom that all controlling position which was its splendid privilege. But to preach this to Mary de' Medici was waste of breath. She was governed by the Concini's, and the Concini's were governed by Spain. The woman who was believed to have known beforehand of the plot to murder her great husband, who had driven the one powerful statesman on whom the King relied, Maximilian de Béthune, into retirement, and whose foreign affairs were now completely in the hands of the ancient Leaguer Villeroy—who had served every government in the kingdom for forty years—was not likely to be accessible to high views of public policy.

Two years had now elapsed since the first private complaints against the Ambassador, and the French government were becoming impatient at his presence. Aerssens had been supported by Prince Maurice, to whom he had long paid his court. He was likewise loyally protected by Barneveld, whom he publicly flattered and secretly maligned. But it was now necessary that he should be gone if peaceful relations with France were to be preserved.

After all, the Ambassador had not made a bad business of his embassy from his own point of view. A stranger in the Republic, for his father the Greffier was a refugee from Brabant, he had achieved through his own industry and remarkable talents, sustained by the favour of Barneveld—to whom he owed all his diplomatic appointments—an eminent position in Europe. Secretary to the legation to France in 1594, he had been successively advanced to the post of resident agent, and when the Republic had been acknowledged by the great powers, to that of ambassador. The highest possible functions that representatives of emperors and kings could enjoy had been formally recognized in the person of the minister of a new-born republic. And this was at a moment when, with exception of the brave but insignificant cantons of Switzerland, the Republic had long been an obsolete idea.

In a pecuniary point of view, too, he had not fared badly during his twenty years of diplomatic office. He had made much money in various ways. The King not long before his death sent him one day 20,000 florins as a present, with a promise soon to do much more for him.[1]

Having been placed in so eminent a post, he considered it as due to himself to derive all possible advantage from it. "Those who serve at the altar," he said a little while after his return, "must learn to live by it. I served their High Mightinesses at the court of a great king, and his Majesty's liberal and gracious favours were showered upon me. My upright conscience and steady obsequiousness greatly aided me. I did not look upon opportunity with folded arms, but seized it and made my profit by it. Had I not met with such fortunate accidents, my office would not have given me dry bread."[2]

Nothing could exceed the frankness and indeed the cynicism with which the Ambassador avowed his practice of converting his high and sacred office into merchandise. And these statements of his should be scanned closely, because at this very moment a cry was distantly rising, which at a later day was to swell into a roar, that the great Advocate had been bribed and pensioned. Nothing had occurred to justify such charges, save that at the period of the truce he had accepted from the King of France a fee of 20,000 florins for extra official and legal services rendered

---

[1] From Aerssens' own statements: "Stukken rakende den Twist tusschen Aerssens ende van der Myle, anno 1618." (Hague Archives MS.)
[2] MS. just cited.

him a dozen years before, and had permitted his younger son to hold the office of gentleman-in-waiting at the French court with the usual salary attached to it. The post, certainly not dishonourable in itself, had been intended by the King as a kindly compliment to the leading statesman of his great and good ally the Republic. It would be difficult to say why such a favour conferred on the young man should be held more discreditable to the receiver than the Order of the Garter recently bestowed upon the great soldier of the Republic by another friendly sovereign. It is instructive however to note the language in which Francis Aerssens spoke of favours and money bestowed by a foreign monarch upon himself, for Aerssens had come back from his embassy full of gall and bitterness against Barneveld. Thenceforth he was to be his evil demon.

"I didn't inherit property,"[1] said this diplomatist. "My father and mother, thank God, are yet living. I have enjoyed the King's liberality. It was from an ally, not an enemy, of our country. Were every man obliged to give a reckoning of everything he possesses over and above his hereditary estates, who in the government would pass muster? Those who declare that they have served their country in her greatest trouble, and lived in splendid houses and in service of princes and great companies and the like on a yearly salary of 4000 florins, may not approve these maxims."

It should be remembered that Barneveld, if this was a fling at the Advocate, had acquired a large fortune by marriage, and, although certainly not averse from gathering gear, had, as will be seen on a subsequent page, easily explained the manner in which his property had increased. No proof was ever offered or attempted of the anonymous calumnies levelled at him in this regard.

"I never had the management of finances," continued

<hr>

[1] "Stukken rakende den Twist," &c.

Aerssens.  "My profits I have gained in foreign parts.  My condition of life is without excess, and in my opinion every means are good so long as they are honourable and legal. They say my post was given me by the Advocate.  *Ergo,* all my fortune comes from the Advocate.  Strenuously to have striven to make myself agreeable to the King and his counsellors, while fulfilling my office with fidelity and honour, these are the arts by which I have prospered, so that my splendour dazzles the eyes of the envious.  The greediness of those who believe that the sun should shine for them alone was excited, and so I was obliged to resign the embassy." [1]

So long as Henry lived, the Dutch ambassador saw him daily, and at all hours, privately, publicly, when he would. Rarely has a foreign envoy at any court, at any period of history, enjoyed such privileges of being useful to his government.  And there is no doubt that the services of Aerssens had been most valuable to his country, notwithstanding his constant care to increase his private fortune through his public opportunities.  He was always ready to be useful to Henry likewise.  When that monarch some time before the truce, and occasionally during the preliminary negotiations for it, had formed a design to make himself sovereign of the Provinces, it was Aerssens who charged himself with the scheme, and would have furthered it with all his might, had the project not met with opposition both from the Advocate and the Stadholder.  Subsequently it appeared probable that Maurice would not object to the sovereignty himself, and the Ambassador in Paris, with the King's consent, was not likely to prove himself hostile to the Prince's ambition.

[1] These passages are from an address to the States-General, 18 June 1618, five years later than the date of his return from France, with which we are at this moment occupied.  As they paint the character of the man, and refer precisely to his feelings at the instant of his recall, it is necessary to give them here.  From the collection of MSS. in the Archives at the Hague already cited.  "Stukken rakende," &c.

" There is but this means alone," wrote Jeannin[1] to Villeroy, " that can content him, although hitherto he has done like the rowers, who never look toward the place whither they wish to go."[2]  The attempt of the Prince to sound Barneveld on this subject through the Princess-Dowager has already been mentioned, and has much intrinsic probability. Thenceforward, the republican form of government, the municipal oligarchies, began to consolidate their power. Yet although the people as such were not sovereigns, but subjects, and rarely spoken of by the aristocratic magistrates save with a gentle and patronizing disdain, they enjoyed a larger liberty than was known anywhere else in the world. Buzenval was astonished at the "infinite and almost unbridled freedom" which he witnessed there during his embassy, and which seemed to him however "without peril to the state."[3]

The extraordinary means possessed by Aerssens to be important and useful vanished with the King's death. His secret despatches, painting in sombre and sarcastic colours the actual condition of affairs at the French court, were sent back in copy to the French court itself. It was not known who had played the Ambassador this vilest of tricks, but it was done during an illness of Barneveld, and without his knowledge. Early in the year 1613 Aerssens resolved, not to take his final departure, but to go home on leave of absence. His private intention was to look for some substantial office of honour and profit at home. Failing of this, he meant to return to Paris. But with an eye to the main chance as usual, he ingeniously caused it to be understood at court, without making positive statements to that effect, that his departure was final. On his leavetaking, accordingly, he

<hr>

[1] Jeannin, 'Négociations,' t. ii. 13a, 150, 201 ; t. iii. 4.  Ouvré, 170.
[2] See also Jeannin, iv. 212, 310, 321 ; v. 33.  Ouvré, 184.
[3] Ibid. 199.

received larger presents from the crown than had been often given to a retiring ambassador. At least 20,000 florins were thus added to the frugal store of profits on which he prided himself. Had he merely gone away on leave of absence, he would have received no presents whatever. But he never went back. The Queen-Regent and her ministers were so glad to get rid of him, and so little disposed, in the straits in which they found themselves, to quarrel with the powerful republic, as to be willing to write very complimentary public letters to the States, concerning the character and conduct of the man whom they so much detested.

Pluming himself upon these, Aerssens made his appearance[1] in the Assembly of the States-General, to give account by word of mouth of the condition of affairs, speaking as if he had only come by permission of their Mightinesses for temporary purposes. Two months later he was summoned before the Assembly, and ordered to return to his post.

Meantime a new French ambassador had arrived at the Hague, in the spring of 1613. Aubéry du Maurier, a son of an obscure country squire, a Protestant, of moderate opinions, of a sincere but rather obsequious character, painstaking, diligent, and honest, had been at an earlier day in the service of the turbulent and intriguing Duc de Bouillon. He had also been employed by Sully as an agent in financial affairs between Holland and France, and had long been known to Villeroy. He was living on his estate, in great retirement from all public business, when Secretary Villeroy suddenly proposed him the embassy to the Hague. There was no more important diplomatic post at that time in Europe. Other countries were virtually at peace, but in Holland, notwithstanding the truce, there was really not much more than an armistice, and great armies

May 20,<br>1613.

---

[1] 30 July 1613. (Register in the Hague Archives MS.) 2 Oct. 1613.
(Ouvré, 199.)

lay in the Netherlands, as after a battle, sleeping face to face with arms in their hands. The politics of Christendom were at issue in the open, elegant, and picturesque village which was the social capital of the United Provinces. The gentry from Spain, Italy, the south of Europe, Catholic Germany, had clustered about Spinola at Brussels, to learn the art of war in his constant campaigning against Maurice. English and Scotch officers, Frenchmen, Bohemians, Austrians, youths from the Palatinate and all Protestant countries in Germany, swarmed to the banners of the prince who had taught the world how Alexander Farnese could be baffled, and the great Spinola outmanœuvred. Especially there was a great number of Frenchmen of figure and quality who thronged to the Hague, besides the officers of the two French regiments which formed a regular portion of the States' army. That army was the best appointed and most conspicuous standing force in Europe. Besides the French contingent there were always nearly 30,000 infantry and 3000 cavalry on a war footing, splendidly disciplined, experienced, and admirably armed. The navy, consisting of thirty war ships, perfectly equipped and manned, was a match for the combined marine forces of all Europe, and almost as numerous.[1]

When the Ambassador went to solemn audience of the States-General, he was attended by a brilliant group of gentlemen and officers, often to the number of three hundred, who volunteered to march after him on foot to honour their sovereign in the person of his ambassador; the Envoy's carriage following empty behind. Such were the splendid diplomatic processions often received by the stately Advocate in his plain civic garb, when grave international questions were to be publicly discussed.[2]

---

[1] See Dup.-Mornay, xii. 524.   Ouvré, 201.
[2] Du Maurier, 'Mémoires,' pp. 191–193.

There was much murmuring in France when the appointment of a personage comparatively so humble to a position so important was known.  It was considered as a blow aimed directly at the malcontent princes of the blood, who were at that moment plotting their first levy of arms against the Queen.  Du Maurier had been ill-treated by the Duc de Bouillon, who naturally therefore now denounced the man whom he had injured to the government to which he was accredited.[1]  Being the agent of Mary de' Medici, he was, of course, described as a tool of the court and a secret pensioner of Spain.  He was to plot with the arch traitor Barneveld as to the best means for distracting the Provinces and bringing them back into Spanish subjection.  Du Maurier, being especially but secretly charged to prevent the return of Francis Aerssens to Paris, incurred of course the enmity of that personage and of the French grandees who ostentatiously protected him.  It was even pretended by Jeannin[2] that the appointment of a man so slightly known to the world, so inexperienced in diplomacy, and of a parentage so little distinguished, would be considered an affront by the States-General.

But on the whole, Villeroy had made an excellent choice.  No safer man could perhaps have been found in France for a post of such eminence, in circumstances so delicate, and at a crisis so grave.  The man who had been able to make himself agreeable and useful, while preserving his integrity, to characters so dissimilar as the refining, self-torturing, intellectual Duplessis-Mornay, the rude, aggressive, and straightforward Sully, the deep-revolving, restlessly plotting Bouillon, and the smooth, silent, and tortuous Villeroy—men between whom there was no friendship, but, on the contrary, constant rancour—had material in him to render valuable services at this particular epoch.  Everything depended on

Ouvr., 203.                              [1] Ibid.

patience, tact, watchfulness in threading the distracting, almost inextricable, maze which had been created by personal rivalries, ambitions, and jealousies in the state he represented and the one to which he was accredited. "I ascribe it all to God," he said,[1] in his testament to his children, "the impenetrable workman who in His goodness has enabled me to make myself all my life obsequious, respectful, and serviceable to all, avoiding as much as possible, in contenting some, not to discontent others." He recommended his children accordingly to endeavour "to succeed in life by making themselves as humble, intelligent, and capable as possible."

This is certainly not a very high type of character, but a safer one for business than that of the arch intriguer Francis Aerssens. And he had arrived at the Hague under trying circumstances. Unknown to the foreign world he was now entering, save through the disparaging rumours concerning him, sent thither in advance by the powerful personages arrayed against his government, he might have sunk under such a storm at the outset, but for the incomparable kindness and friendly aid of the Princess-Dowager, Louise de Coligny. "I had need of her protection and recommendation as much as of life," said du Maurier; "and she gave them in such excess as to annihilate an infinity of calumnies which envy had excited against me on every side."[2] He had also a most difficult and delicate matter to arrange at the very moment of his arrival.

For Aerssens had done his best not only to produce a dangerous division in the politics of the Republic, but to force a rupture between the French government and the States. He had carried matters before the assembly with so high a hand as to make it seem impossible to get rid of him without public scandal. He made a parade of the offi-

<hr>

[1] Ouvré, 170.          [2] Ibid. 201.

cial letters from the Queen-Regent and her ministers, in which he was spoken of in terms of conventional compliment. He did not know, and Barneveld wished, if possible, to spare him the annoyance of knowing, that both Queen and ministers, so soon as informed that there was a chance of coming back to them, had written letters breathing great repugnance to him and intimating that he would not be received. Other high personages of state had written to express their resentment at his duplicity, perpetual mischief-making, and machinations against the peace of the kingdom, and stating the impossibility of his resuming the embassy at Paris. And at last the Queen [1] wrote to the States-General to say that, having heard their intention to send him back to a post "from which he had taken leave formally and officially," she wished to prevent such a step. "We should see M. Aerssens less willingly than comports with our friendship for you and good neighbourhood. Any other you could send would be most welcome, as M. du Maurier will explain to you more amply."

And to du Maurier himself she wrote distinctly,[2] "Rather than suffer the return of the said Aerssens, you will declare that for causes which regard the good of our affairs and our particular satisfaction we cannot and will not receive him in the functions which he has exercised here, and we rely too implicitly upon the good friendship of My Lords the States to do anything in this that would so much displease us." [3]

And on the same day Villeroy privately wrote to the Ambassador, "If, in spite of all this, Aerssens should endeavour to return, he will not be received, after the knowledge we have of his factious spirit, most dangerous in a public personage in a state such as ours and in the minority of the King." [4]

[1] 2 Nov. 1613. "Stukken rakende den Twist," &c. (Hague Archives MS.)

[2] MS. just cited.
[3] Ibid. 2 Nov. 1613.
[4] Ibid.

Meantime Aerssens had been going about flaunting letters in everybody's face from the Duc de Bouillon insisting on the necessity of his return.[1]  The fact in itself would have been sufficient to warrant his removal, for the Duke was just taking up arms against his sovereign.  Unless the States meant to interfere officially and directly in the civil war about to break out in France, they could hardly send a minister to the government on recommendation of the leader of the rebellion.

It had, however, become impossible to remove him without an explosion.  Barneveld, who, said du Maurier, "knew the man to his finger nails,"[2] had been reluctant to "break the ice," and wished for official notice in the matter from the Queen.  Maurice protected the troublesome diplomatist. "'Tis incredible," said the French ambassador,[3] "how covertly Prince Maurice is carrying himself, contrary to his wont, in this whole affair.  I don't know whether it is from simple jealousy to Barneveld, or if there is some mystery concealed below the surface."

Du Maurier had accordingly been obliged to ask his government for distinct and official instructions.  " He holds to his place," said he,[4] " by so slight and fragile a root as not to require two hands to pluck him up, the little finger being enough.  There is no doubt that he has been in concert with those who are making use of him to re-establish their credit with the States, and to embark Prince Maurice contrary to his preceding custom in a cabal with them."

Thus a question of removing an obnoxious diplomatist could hardly be graver, for it was believed that he was doing his best to involve the military chief of his own state in a game of treason and rebellion against the government to which he was accredited.  It was not the first

---

[1] Ouvré, 209.
[2] Ibid. 207.

[3] Ibid. 208.
[4] Ibid.

nor likely to be the last of Bouillon's deadly intrigues. But the man who had been privy to Biron's conspiracy against the crown and life of his sovereign was hardly a safe ally for his brother-in-law, the straightforward stadholder.

The instructions desired by du Maurier and by Barneveld had, as we have seen, at last arrived. The French ambassador thus fortified appeared before the Assembly of the States-General,[1] and officially demanded the recall of Aerssens. In a letter addressed privately and confidentially to their Mightinesses, he said, "If in spite of us you throw him at our feet, we shall fling him back at your head."[2]

At last Maurice yielded to the representations of the French envoy, and Aerssens felt obliged to resign his claims to the post. The States-General passed a resolution that it would be proper to employ him in some other capacity in order to show that his services had been agreeable to them, he having now declared that he could no longer be useful in France.[3] Maurice, seeing that it was impossible to save him, admitted to du Maurier his unsteadiness and duplicity, and said that, if possessed of the confidence of a great king, he would be capable of destroying the state in less than a year.[4]

But this had not always been the Prince's opinion, nor was it likely to remain unchanged. As for Villeroy, he denied flatly that the cause of his displeasure had been that Aerssens had penetrated into his most secret affairs. He protested, on the contrary, that his annoyance with him had partly proceeded from the slight acquaintance he had acquired of his policy, and that, while boasting to be better informed than any one, he was in the habit of inventing and imagining things in order to get credit for himself.

---

[1] 13 Nov. 1613. Ouvré, 210.
[2] Ibid. 211.
[3] 13 Dec. 1613, 31 Jan. 1614. Resol. States-Gen. (Hague Arch. MS.)
[4] Ouvré, 213.
[5] 4 Jan. 1614. "Stukken," &c. (Hague Arch. MS.)

It was highly essential that the secret of this affair should be made clear, for its influence on subsequent events was to be deep and wide. For the moment Aerssens remained without employment, and there was no open rupture with Barneveld. The only difference of opinion between the Advocate and himself, he said, was whether he had or had not definitely resigned his post on leaving Paris.[1]

Meantime it was necessary to fix upon a successor for this most important post. The war soon after the new year had broken out in France. Condé, Bouillon, and the other malcontent princes with their followers had taken possession of the fortress of Mezières, and issued a letter in the name of Condé to the Queen-Regent demanding an assembly of the States-General of the kingdom and rupture of the Spanish marriages.[2] Both parties, that of the government and that of the rebellion, sought the sympathy and active succour of the States. Maurice, acting now in perfect accord with the Advocate, sustained the Queen and execrated the rebellion of his relatives with perfect frankness. Condé, he said, had got his head stuffed full of almanacs whose predictions he wished to see realized.[3] He vowed he would have shortened by a head the commander of the garrison who betrayed Mezières, if he had been under his control. He forbade on pain of death the departure of any officer or private of the French regiments from serving the rebels, and placed the whole French force at the disposal of the Queen, with as many Netherland regiments as could be spared. One soldier was hanged and three others branded with the mark of a gibbet on the face for attempting desertion. The legal government was loyally sustained by the authority of the States, notwithstanding all the intrigues of Aerssens with

<hr>

[1] "Stukken," &c. (Hague Archives MS.)

[2] Ouvré, 219.

[3] Ouvré, 215, from du Maurier's MS. despatches.

the agents of the princes to procure them assistance. The
mutiny for the time was brief, and was settled on   May 15,
the 15th of May 1614, by the peace of Sainte-Méne-    1614.
hould, as much a caricature of a treaty as the rising had
been the parody of a war.[1]  Van der Myle, son-in-law of
Barneveld, who had been charged with a special and temporary mission to France, brought back the terms of the
convention to the States-General.  On the other hand,
Condé and his confederates' sent a special agent to the
Netherlands to give their account of the war and the negotiation, who refused to confer either with du Maurier or
Barneveld, but who held much conference with Aerssens.[2]

It was obvious enough that the mutiny of the princes
would become chronic.  In truth, what other condition was
possible with two characters like Mary de' Medici and the
Prince of Condé respectively at the head of the government
and the revolt ?   What had France to hope for but to remain
the bloody playground for mischievous idiots, who threw
about the firebrands and arrows of reckless civil war in
pursuit of the paltriest of personal aims ?

Van der Myle had pretensions to the vacant place of
Aerssens.  He had some experience in diplomacy.  He had
conducted skilfully enough the first mission of the States
to Venice, and had subsequently been employed in matters
of moment.  But he was son-in-law to Barneveld, and
although the Advocate was certainly not free from the
charge of nepotism, he shrank from the reproach of having
apparently removed Aerssens to make a place for one of his
own family.

Van der Myle remained to bear the brunt of the late
ambassador's malice, and to engage at a little later period
in hottest controversy with him, personal and political.
" Why should van der Myle strut about, with his arms

<hr>

[1] Ouvré, 215.        [2] Ibid. 215, 218, 277.

akimbo like a peacock ? " [1] complained Aerssens one day in confused metaphor.  A question not easy to answer satisfactorily.

The minister selected was a certain Baron Asperen de Langerac, wholly unversed in diplomacy or other public affairs, with abilities not above the average.  A series of questions [2] addressed by him to the Advocate, the answers to which, scrawled on the margin of the paper, were to serve for his general instructions, showed an ingenuousness as amusing as the replies of Barneveld were experienced and substantial.

In general he was directed to be friendly and respectful to every one, to the Queen-Regent and her counsellors especially, and, within the limits of becoming reverence for her, to cultivate the good graces of the Prince of Condé and the other great nobles still malcontent and rebellious, but whose present movement, as Barneveld foresaw, was drawing rapidly to a close.  Langerac arrived in Paris on the 5th of April 1614.

Du Maurier thought the new ambassador likely to "fall a prey to the specious language and gentle attractions of the Duc de Bouillon." [3]  He also described him as very dependent upon Prince Maurice.  On the other hand Langerac professed unbounded and almost childlike reverence for Barneveld,[4] was devoted to his person, and breathed as it were only through his inspiration.  Time would show whether those sentiments would outlast every possible storm.

---

[1] " ...ende daerinne met geboechde armen als een Paauw te pronken," &c.—" Stukken rakende," &c.  (MS. before cited.)

[2] MS. Hague Archives.
[3] Ouvré, 213.
[4] MS. before cited.

# CHAPTER X.

Weakness of the Rulers of France and England — The Wisdom of Barneveld inspires Jealousy — Sir Dudley Carleton succeeds Winwood — Young Neuburg under the Guidance of Maximilian — Barneveld strives to have the Treaty of Xanten enforced — Spain and the Emperor wish to make the States abandon their Position with regard to the Duchies — The French Government refuses to aid the States — Spain and the Emperor resolve to hold Wesel—The great Religious War begun—The Protestant Union and Catholic League both wish to secure the Border Provinces — Troubles in Turkey — Spanish Fleet seizes La Roche — Spain places large Armies on a War Footing.

FEW things are stranger in history than the apathy with which the wide designs of the Catholic party were at that moment regarded. The preparations for the immense struggle which posterity learned to call the Thirty Years' War, and to shudder when speaking of it, were going forward on every side. In truth the war had really begun, yet those most deeply menaced by it at the outset looked on with innocent calmness because their own roofs were not quite yet in a blaze. The passage of arms in the duchies, the outlines of which have just been indicated, and which was the natural sequel of the campaign carried out four years earlier on the same territory, had been ended by a mockery. In France, reduced almost to imbecility by the absence of a guiding brain during a long minority, fallen under the distaff of a dowager both weak and wicked, distracted by the intrigues and quarrels of a swarm of self-seeking grandees, and with all its offices, from highest to lowest, of court, state, jurisprudence, and magistracy, sold as openly and as cynically as the commonest wares, there were few to comprehend or to grapple with the danger.[1]   It should have seemed obvious to the meanest capacity in the kingdom that the great house of Austria, reigning supreme in Spain and in Germany, could not be allowed to crush the Duke of Savoy on the one side, and Bohemia, Moravia, and the Netherlands on the other without danger of subjection for France.   Yet the aim of the Queen-Regent was to cultivate an impossible alliance with her inevitable foe.

And in England, ruled as it then was with no master mind to enforce against its sovereign the great lessons of policy, internal and external, on which its welfare and almost its imperial existence depended, the only ambition of those who could make their opinions felt was to pursue the same impossibility, intimate alliance with the universal foe.

Any man with slightest pretensions to statesmanship knew that the liberty for Protestant worship in Imperial Germany, extorted by force, had been given reluctantly, and would be valid only as long as that force could still be exerted or should remain obviously in reserve.   The " Majesty Letter " and the " Convention " of the two religions would prove as flimsy as the parchment on which they were engrossed, the Protestant churches built under that sanction would be shattered like glass, if once the Catholic rulers could feel their hands as clear as their consciences would be for violating their sworn faith to heretics.   Men knew, even if the easy-going and uxorious emperor, into which character the once busy and turbulent Archduke Matthias had subsided, might be willing to keep his pledges, that Ferdinand

---

[1] " Tutti li officii e servigii," says Pietro Contarini, ' Relazione di Francia, 1613–1616.' "della casa del re sino agli ultimi valletti, tutti li carichi militari per ogni magistrati di giustizia si vendono e col pagarsi per questo certa annua imposizione che chiamono la stolletta possono anco disponerne dopo la vita ; ciò causa che non le persone di merito non quelle che travagliano, ma solo chi puo comprare ha posto nelli carichi e nelli primi servigii del regno, dove ben spesso li meno atti ed idonei sono li preferiti e da questo accidente avviene che il rè è mal visto rubato e la giustizia mal aministrata," &c.   Barozzi and Berchet.

of Styria, who would soon succeed him, and Maximilian of Bavaria were men who knew their own minds, and had mentally never resigned one inch of the ground which Protestantism imagined itself to have conquered.

These things seem plain as daylight to all who look back upon them through the long vista of the past; but the sovereign of England did not see them or did not choose to see them.   He saw only the Infanta and her two millions of dowry, and he knew that by calling Parliament together to ask subsidies for an anti-Catholic war he should ruin those golden matrimonial prospects for his son, while encouraging those "shoemakers," his subjects, to go beyond their "last," by consulting the representatives of his people on matters pertaining to the mysteries of government.   He was slowly digging the grave of the monarchy and building the scaffold of his son ; but he did his work with a laborious and pedantic trifling, when really engaged in state affairs, most amazing to contemplate.   He had no penny to give to the cause in which his nearest relatives were so deeply involved and for which his only possible allies were pledged ; but he was ready to give advice to all parties, and with ludicrous gravity imagined himself playing the umpire between great contending hosts, when in reality he was only playing the fool at the beck of masters before whom he quaked.

" You are not to vilipend my counsel," said he one day to a foreign envoy.   "I am neither a camel nor an ass to take up all this work on my shoulders.   Where would you find another king as willing to do it as I am ? "[1]

The King had little time and no money to give to serve his own family and allies and the cause of Protestantism, but he could squander vast sums upon worthless favourites, and consume reams of paper on controverted points of

---

[1] G. W. Vreede, Extract from a MS. Report of F. Aerssens.  (Prov. Utrecht Archives.)

divinity.  The appointment of Vorstius to the chair of theology in Leyden aroused more indignation in his bosom, and
occupied more of his time, than the conquests of Spinola
in the duchies, and the menaces of Spain against Savoy and
Bohemia.  He perpetually preached moderation to the
States in the matter of the debateable territory, although
moderation at that moment meant submission to the House
of Austria.  He chose to affect confidence in the good faith
of those who were playing a comedy by which no statesman
could be deceived, but which had secured the approbation of
the Solomon of the age.

But there was one man who was not deceived.  The
warnings and the lamentations of Barneveld sound to us
out of that far distant time like the voice of an inspired
prophet.  It is possible that a portion of the wrath to come
might have been averted had there been many men in high
places to heed his voice.  I do not wish to exaggerate the
power and wisdom of the man, nor to set him forth as one of
the greatest heroes of history.  But posterity has done far
less than justice to a statesman and sage who wielded a vast
influence at a most critical period in the fate of Christendom,
and uniformly wielded it to promote the cause of temperate
human liberty, both political and religious.  Viewed by the
light of two centuries and a half of additional experience,
he may appear to have made mistakes, but none that were
necessarily disastrous or even mischievous.  Compared with
the prevailing idea of the age in which he lived, his schemes
of polity seem to dilate into large dimensions, his sentiments
of religious freedom, however limited to our modern ideas,
mark an epoch in human progress, and in regard to the
general commonwealth of Christendom, of which he was so
leading a citizen, the part he played was a lofty one.  No
man certainly understood the tendency of his age more
exactly, took a broader and more comprehensive view than

he did of the policy necessary to preserve the largest portion of the results of the past three-quarters of a century, or had pondered the relative value of great conflicting forces more skilfully. Had his counsels been always followed, had illustrious birth placed him virtually upon a throne, as was the case with William the Silent, and thus allowed him occasionally to carry out the designs of a great mind with almost despotic authority, it might have been better for the world. But in that age it was royal blood alone that could command unflinching obedience without exciting personal rivalry. Men quailed before his majestic intellect, but hated him for the power which was its necessary result. They already felt a stupid delight in cavilling at his pedigree. To dispute his claim to a place among the ancient nobility to which he was an honour was to revenge themselves for the rank he unquestionably possessed side by side in all but birth with the kings and rulers of the world. Whether envy and jealousy be vices more incident to the republican form of government than to other political systems may be an open question. But it is no question whatever that Barneveld's every footstep from this period forward was dogged by envy as patient as it was devouring. Jealousy stuck to him like his shadow. We have examined the relations which existed between Winwood and himself; we have seen that ambassador, now secretary of state for James, never weary in denouncing the Advocate's haughtiness and grim resolution to govern the country according to its laws rather than at the dictate of a foreign sovereign, and in flinging forth malicious insinuations in regard to his relations to Spain. The man whose every hour was devoted —in spite of a thousand obstacles strewn by stupidity, treachery, and apathy, as well as by envy, hatred, and bigotry—to the organizing of a grand and universal league of Protestantism against Spain, and to rolling up with strenuous and sometimes despairing arms a dead mountain weight, ever ready to fall back upon and crush him, was accused in dark and mysterious whispers, soon to grow louder and bolder, of a treacherous inclination for Spain.

There is nothing less surprising nor more sickening for those who observe public life, and wish to retain faith in the human species, than the almost infinite power of the meanest of passions.

The Advocate was obliged at the very outset of Langerac's mission to France to give him a warning on this subject.

"Should her Majesty make kindly mention of me," he said, "you will say nothing of it in your despatches as you did in your last, although I am sure with the best intentions. It profits me not, and many take umbrage at it; wherefore it is wise to forbear."

But this was a trifle. By and by there would be many to take umbrage at every whisper in his favour, whether from crowned heads or from the simplest in the social scale. Meantime he instructed the Ambassador, without paying heed to personal compliments to his chief, to do his best to keep the French government out of the hands of Spain, and with that object in view to smooth over the differences between the two great parties in the kingdom, and to gain the confidence, if possible, of Condé and Nevers and Bouillon, while never failing in straightforward respect and loyal friendship to the Queen-Regent and her ministers, as the legitimate heads of the government.

From England a new ambassador was soon to take the place of Winwood. Sir Dudley Carleton was a diplomatist

Jan. 1615.

of respectable abilities, and well trained to business and routine. Perhaps on the whole there was none other, in that epoch of official mediocrity, more competent than he to fill what was then certainly the most important of foreign posts. His course of life had in no wise familiarized him with the intricacies of the Dutch constitution, nor could the diplomatic profession, combined with a long residence at Venice, be deemed especially favourable for deep studies of the mysteries of predestination.  Yet he would be found ready at the bidding of his master to grapple with Grotius and Barneveld on the field of history and law, and thread with Uytenbogaert or Taurinus all the subtleties of Arminianism and Gomarism as if he had been half his life both a regular practitioner at the Supreme Court of the Hague and professor of theology at the University of Leyden. Whether the triumphs achieved in such encounters were substantial and due entirely to his own genius might be doubtful.  At all events he had a sovereign behind him who was incapable of making a mistake on any subject.

"You shall not forget," said James in his instructions to Sir Dudley, "that you are the minister of that master whom God hath made the sole protector of his religion. . . . . and you may let fall how hateful the maintaining of erroneous opinions is to the majesty of God and how displeasing to us." [1]

The warlike operations of 1614 had been ended by the abortive peace of Xanten.  The two rival pretenders to the duchies were to halve the territory, drawing lots for the first choice, all foreign troops were to be withdrawn, and a pledge was to be given that no fortress should be placed in the hands of any power.  But Spain at the last moment had refused to sanction the treaty, and everything was remitted to what might be exactly described as a state of sixes and sevens.  Subsequently it was hoped that the States' troops might be induced to withdraw simultaneously with the Catholic forces on an undertaking by Spinola that there should be no re-occupation of the disputed territory either by the Republic or by Spain.  But Barneveld accurately

<hr>

[1] 'Carleton's Letters' (London, 1780), p. 6.

pointed out that, although the Marquis was a splendid commander and, so long as he was at the head of the armies, a most powerful potentate, he might be superseded at any moment. Count Bucquoy, for example, might suddenly appear in his place and refuse to be bound by any military arrangement of his predecessor. Then the Archduke proposed to give a guarantee that in case of a mutual withdrawal there should be no return of the troops, no recapture of garrisons. But Barneveld, speaking for the States, liked not the security. The Archduke was but the puppet of Spain, and Spain had no part in the guarantee. She held the strings, and might cause him at any moment to play what pranks she chose. It would be the easiest thing in the world for despotic Spain, so the Advocate thought, to reappear suddenly in force again at a moment's notice after the States' troops had been withdrawn and partially disbanded, and it would be difficult for the many-headed and many-tongued republic to act with similar promptness. To withdraw without a guarantee from Spain to the Treaty of Xanten, which had once been signed, sealed, and all but ratified, would be to give up fifty points in the game. Nothing but disaster could ensue. The Advocate as leader in all these negotiations and correspondence was ever actuated by the favourite quotation of William the Silent from Demosthenes, that the safest citadel against an invader and a tyrant is distrust. And he always distrusted in these dealings, for he was sure the Spanish cabinet was trying to make fools of the States, and there were many ready to assist it in the task. Now that one of the pretenders, temporary master of half the duchies, the Prince of Neuburg, had espoused both Catholicism and the sister of the Archbishop of Cologne and the Duke of Bavaria, it would be more safe than ever for Spain to make a temporary withdrawal. Maximilian of Bavaria was beyond all question the ablest

and most determined leader of the Catholic party in
Germany, and the most straightforward and sincere.  No
man before or since his epoch had, like him, been destined
to refuse, and more than once refuse, the Imperial crown.[1]

Through his apostasy the Prince of Neuburg was in
danger of losing his hereditary estates, his brothers endeavouring to dispossess him on the ground of the late duke's
will, disinheriting any one of his heirs who should become a
convert to Catholicism.  He had accordingly implored aid
from the King of Spain.  Archduke Albert had urged Philip
to render such assistance as a matter of justice, and the
Emperor had naturally declared that the whole right as
eldest son belonged, notwithstanding the will, to the Prince.[2]

With the young Neuburg accordingly under the able
guidance of Maximilian, it was not likely that the grasp of
the Spanish party upon these all-important territories would
be really loosened.  The Emperor still claimed the right to
decide among the candidates and to hold the provinces under
sequestration till the decision should be made—that was
to say, until the Greek Kalends.  The original attempt to do
this through Archduke Leopold had been thwarted, as we
have seen, by the prompt movements of Maurice sustained
by the policy of Barneveld.  The Advocate was resolved
that the Emperor's name should not be mentioned either
in the preamble or body of the treaty.  And his course
throughout the simulations, which were never negotiations,
was perpetually baffled as much by the easiness and languor
of his allies as the ingenuity of the enemy.

He was reproached with the loss of Wesel, that Geneva of
the Rhine, which would never be abandoned by Spain if it
was not done forthwith.  Let Spain guarantee the Treaty of
Xanten, he said, and then she cannot come back.  All else

<hr>

[1] *Vide* Gindely, 'Gesch. des dreissigjähr. Kriegs,' vol. i. *passim.*
[2] Archduke Albert to Philip III.  (Archives of Belgium MS.)

is illusion.   Moreover, the Emperor had given positive orders that Wesel should not be given up.[1]   He was assured by Villeroy that France would never put on her harness for Aachen, that cradle of Protestantism.   That was for the States-General to do, whom it so much more nearly concerned.   The whole aim of Barneveld was not to destroy the Treaty of Xanten, but to enforce it in the only way in which it could be enforced, by the guarantee of Spain.   So secured, it would be a barrier in the universal war of religion which he foresaw was soon to break out.   But it was the resolve of Spain, instead of pledging herself to the treaty, to establish the legal control of the territory in the hand of the Emperor.   Neuburg complained that Philip in writing to him did not give him the title of Duke of Jülich and Cleve, although he had been placed in possession of those estates by the arms of Spain.   Philip, referring to Archduke Albert for his opinion on this subject, was advised that, as the Emperor had not given Neuburg the investiture of the duchies, the King was quite right in refusing him the title.   Even should the Treaty of Xanten be executed, neither he nor the Elector of Brandenburg would be anything but administrators until the question of right was decided by the Emperor.[2]

Spain had sent Neuburg the Order of the Golden Fleece [3] as a reward for his conversion, but did not intend him to be anything but a man of straw in the territories which he claimed by sovereign right.   They were to form a permanent bulwark to the Empire, to Spain, and to Catholicism.

Barneveld of course could never see the secret letters passing between Brussels and Madrid, but his insight into

[1] " . . . que no se restituisse Wesel y assi se distrizo la Junta quedando cada una en su posesion." (MS. Archives of Belgium.   A paper entitled " Memoria para informar al M<sup>ro</sup> de Campo D. Inigo de Borsa," &c.)

[2] Philip III. to Archduke Albert, 17 April 1615. (Belg. Arch. MS.) Archduke Albert to Philip III., July 1615.   (Belg. Arch. MS.)

[3] Same to same, 1 Feb. 1615. (Belg. Arch. MS.)

the purposes of the enemy was almost as acute as if the correspondence of Philip and Albert had been in the pigeon-holes of his writing-desk in the Kneuterdyk.

The whole object of Spain and the Emperor, acting through the Archduke, was to force the States to abandon their positions in the duchies simultaneously with the withdrawal of the Spanish troops, and to be satisfied with a bare convention between themselves and Archduke Albert that there should be no renewed occupation by either party. Barneveld, finding it impossible to get Spain upon the treaty, was resolved that at least the two mediating powers, their great allies, the sovereigns of Great Britain and France, should guarantee the convention, and that the promises of the Archduke should be made to them. This was steadily refused by Spain; for the Archduke never moved an inch in the matter except according to the orders of Spain, and besides battling and buffeting with the Archduke, Barneveld was constantly deafened with the clamour of the English king, who always declared Spain to be in the right whatever she did, and forced to endure with what patience he might the goading of that King's envoy. France, on the other hand, supported the States as firmly as could have been reasonably expected.

"We proposed," said the Archduke, instructing an envoy whom he was sending to Madrid with detailed accounts of these negotiations,[1] "that the promise should be made to each other as usual in treaties. But the Hollanders said the promise should be made to the Kings of France and England, at which the Emperor would have been deeply offended,[2] as if in the affair he was of no account at all. At any moment by this arrangement in concert with France and England the Hollanders might walk in and do what they liked."

[1] "Memoria para informar al M<sup>co</sup> de Campo D. Inigo de Borsa de la qu. ha pasado en el neg<sup>o</sup> de Julliers," &c.  (Belg. Arch. MS.)
[2] "offendidissimo."

Certainly there could have been no succincter eulogy of the policy steadily recommended, as we shall have occasion to see, by Barneveld. Had he on this critical occasion been backed by England and France combined, Spain would have been forced to beat a retreat, and Protestantism in the great general war just beginning would have had an enormous advantage in position. But the English Solomon could not see the wisdom of this policy. " The King of England says we are right," continued the Archduke, " and has ordered his ambassador to insist on our view. The French ambassador here says that his colleague at the Hague has similar instructions, but admits that he has not acted up to them. There is not much chance of the Hollanders changing. It would be well that the King should send a written ultimatum that the Hollanders should sign the convention which we propose. If they don't agree, the world at least will see that it is not we who are in fault." [1]

The world would see, and would never have forgiven a statesman in the position of Barneveld, had he accepted a bald agreement from a subordinate like the Archduke, a perfectly insignificant personage in the great drama then enacting, and given up guarantees both from the Archduke's master and from the two great allies of the Republic. He stood out manfully against Spain and England at every hazard, and under a pelting storm of obloquy, and this was the man whose designs the English secretary of state had dared to describe " as of no other nature than to cause the Provinces to relapse into the hands of Spain." [2]

It appeared too a little later that Barneveld's influence with the French government, owing to his judicious support of it so long as it was a government, had been decidedly successful. Drugged as France was by the Spanish marriage

<hr>

[1] " Memoria para informar al Mro de Campo Don Inigo de Borsa." (MS. before cited, Arch. Belg.)                 [2] *Vide antea.*

treaty, she was yet not so sluggish nor spell-bound as the King of Great Britain.

"France will not urge upon the Hollanders to execute the proposal as we made it," wrote the Archduke to the King, " so negotiations are at a standstill.  The Hollanders say it is better that each party should remain with what each possesses.  So that if it does not come to blows, and if these insolences go on as they have done, the Hollanders will be gaining and occupying more territory every day."[1]

Thus once more the ancient enemies and masters of the Republic were making the eulogy of the Dutch statesman. It was impossible at present for the States to regain Wesel, nor that other early stronghold of the Reformation, the old Imperial city of Aachen (Aix-la-Chapelle).  The price to be paid was too exorbitant.

The French government had persistently refused to assist the States and possessory princes in the recovery of this stronghold.  The Queen-Regent was afraid of offending Spain, although her government had induced the citizens of the place to make the treaty now violated by that country. The Dutch ambassador had been instructed categorically to enquire whether their Majesties meant to assist Aachen and the princes if attacked by the Archdukes.  " No," said Villeroy ; " we are not interested in Aachen, 'tis too far off. Let them look for assistance to those who advised their mutiny."

To the Ambassador's remonstrance that France was both interested in and pledged to them, the Secretary of State replied, " We made the treaty through compassion and love, but we shall not put on harness for Aachen.  Don't think it. You, the States and the United Provinces, may assist them if you like."

The Envoy then reminded the Minister that the States-

<hr>

[1] Albert to Philip III. 29 Dec. 1615.  (Arch. Belg. MS.)

General had always agreed to go forward evenly in this business with the Kings of Great Britain and France and the united princes, the matter being of equal importance to all. They had given no further pledge than this to the Union.

It was plain, however, that France was determined not to lift a finger at that moment. The Duke of Bouillon and those acting with him had tried hard to induce their Majesties "to write seriously to the Archduke in order at least to intimidate him by stiff talk,"[1] but it was hopeless. They thought it was not a time then to quarrel with their neighbour and give offence to Spain.

So the stiff talk was omitted, and the Archduke was not intimidated. The man who had so often intimidated him was in his grave, and his widow was occupied in marrying her son to the Infanta. "These are the first-fruits," said Aerssens, "of the new negotiations with Spain."[2]

Both the Spanish king and the Emperor were resolved to hold Wesel to the very last. Until the States should retire from all their positions on the bare word of the Archduke, that the Spanish forces once withdrawn would never return, the Protestants of those two cities must suffer. There was no help for it. To save them would be to abandon all. For no true statesman could be so ingenuous as thus to throw all the cards on the table for the Spanish and Imperial cabinet to shuffle them at pleasure for a new deal. The Duke of Neuburg, now Catholic and especially protected by Spain, had become, instead of a pretender with more or less law on his side, a mere standard-bearer and agent of the Great Catholic League in the debateable land. He was to be supported at all hazard by the Spanish forces, according to the express

---

[1] Aerssens to States-General, 13 Feb. 1612. (Hague Archives MS.) "Serieuselyk aen den Ertshertog te schryven om ten minsten door het styf spreken hem t' intimideren," &c.
[2] Ibid.

command of Philip's government, especially now that his two brothers with the countenance of the States were disputing his right to his hereditary dominions in Germany.[1]

The Archduke was sullen enough at what he called the weakmindedness of France. Notwithstanding that by express orders from Spain he had sent 5000 troops[2] under command of Juan de Rivas to the Queen's assistance just before the peace of Sainte-Ménehould, he could not induce her government to take the firm part which the English king did in browbeating the Hollanders.

"'Tis certain," he complained, "that if, instead of this sluggishness on the part of France, they had done us there the same good services we have had from England, the Hollanders would have accepted the promise just as it was proposed by us."[3] He implored the King, therefore, to use his strongest influence with the French government that it should strenuously intervene with the Hollanders, and compel them to sign the proposal which they rejected. "There is no means of composition if France does not oblige them to sign," said Albert rather piteously.

But it was not without reason that Barneveld had in many of his letters instructed the States' ambassador, Langerac, "to caress the old gentleman" (meaning and never

[1] " . . . y siendo el Niewburg en esto neg⁰ de la calidad q. V. A. pondera justam⁺ obliga mucho a no dexallo caer, pues los herm⁰˙ de N. s⁺ ran favorecidos de los de Olanda y Zel⁺ para sus intentos, y assi deve V. A. poner muy particular cuydado en q. en los conciertos q. se tratan con ocasion de lo de Juliers, quede asegur⁴⁰ todo antes de resolver lo de Wesel; pues de otra manera, si se soltasse de la mano lo q. se tiene sin quedar resguardo, se entreria en nuevos cuydados y trabajos con mucha duda de salir, con lo q. agora se puede teniendo los conciertos de Wesel, en que es bien de creer prevendra V. A. lo que convenga, pues podrian Olandeses con la gente q. han sacado en campaña ya tomando plazas, y assi siendo necessario, ordenara V. A. al marq. Spinola q. traga con esso ex⁺ los mismos movimientos q. hiziera el enemigo," &c. Philip III. to Archduke Albert, 20 Sept. 1615. (Arch. Belg. MS.)

[2] Philip III. to Archduke Albert, 17 April 1615. (Arch. Belg. MS.)

[3] " floxedad con q. se ha procedido de parte de Francia, teniendo por cierto q. si huvieran hecho los oficios q. de la parte d. Inglat⁺, admitieran los Olandeses la promesa propuesta por nos."—"Instrucion por D. Iñigo de Borsa." (Arch. Belg. MS.)

naming Villeroy), for he would prove to be in spite of all obstacles a good friend to the States, as he always had been. And Villeroy did hold firm. Whether the Archduke was right or not in his conviction, that, if France would only unite with England in exerting a strong pressure on the Hollanders, they would evacuate the duchies, and so give up the game, the correspondence of Barneveld shows very accurately. But the Archduke, of course, had not seen that correspondence.

The Advocate knew what was plotting, what was impending, what was actually accomplished, for he was accustomed to sweep the whole horizon with an anxious and comprehensive glance. He knew without requiring to read the secret letters of the enemy that vast preparations for an extensive war against the Reformation were already completed. The movements in the duchies were the first drops of a coming deluge. The great religious war which was to last a generation of mankind had already begun; the immediate and apparent pretext being a little disputed succession to some petty sovereignties, the true cause being the necessity for each great party—the Protestant Union and the Catholic League—to secure these border provinces, the possession of which would be of such inestimable advantage to either. If nothing decisive occurred in the year 1614, the following year would still be more convenient for the League. There had been troubles in Turkey. The Grand Vizier had been murdered. The Sultan was engaged in a war with Persia. There was no eastern bulwark in Europe to the ever menacing power of the Turk and of Mahometanism in Europe save Hungary alone. Supported and ruled as that kingdom was by the House of Austria, the temper of the populations of Germany had become such as to make it doubtful in the present conflict of religious opinions between them and their rulers whether the Turk or the Spaniard would be most odious as an invader.  But for the moment, Spain and the Emperor had their hands free.  They were not in danger of an attack from below the Danube.  Moreover, the Spanish fleet had been achieving considerable successes on the Barbary coast, having seized La Roche, and one or two important citadels, useful both against the corsairs and against sudden attacks by sea from the Turk.  There were at least 100,000 men on a war footing ready to take the field at command of the two branches of the House of Austria, Spanish and German.   In the little war about Mont-serrat, Savoy was on the point of being crushed, and Savoy was by position and policy the only possible ally, in the south, of the Netherlands and of Protestant Germany.

While professing the most pacific sentiments towards the States, and a profound anxiety to withdraw his troops from their borders, the King of Spain, besides daily increasing those forces, had just raised 4,000,000 ducats, a large portion of which was lodged with his bankers in Brussels.  Deeds like those were of more significance than sugared words.

END OF VOL. I.